I Know My Love

I Know My Love is the story of Australia in the frenzied grip of the gold rushes of the 1850's. It is also the story of the years after, when new immigrants turned away from the goldfields to shape new lives in the shanty towns.

Here are the Maguire family—rowdy, rebellious and vital Irish immigrants; and the Langleys—squatter aristocrats born rich and powerful, fighting to hold their own against the newcomers.

But, above all, this is a love story, lived out amidst the people who fought and scrambled to make a place for themselves in a harsh and vigorous country.

CATHERINE GASKIN

I Know My Love

Collins
FONTANA BOOKS

First published 1962
First issued in Fontana Books 1964
Eighteenth Impression July 1976

© Catherine Gaskin Cornberg 1962

Made and printed in Great Britain by
William Collins Sons & Co Ltd Glasgow

BOOK ONE: 1854

Chapter One

The Governor's Lady has left, finishing the polite formula of the afternoon call. The children have behaved well, and I am pleased. She has come, as always, as many like her, to examine my stewardship of these children who bear one of the great names of this country, and who will inherit one of the great colonial fortunes. She thinks it incongruous, as they all do, that I, who came here out of a London draper's shop, should have been given charge of them. But these things still happen in a new country, as they happened to me. And they happened because of that morning, back in 1854, when I met Rose Maguire on the road to Ballarat.

The name I gave myself that morning was Emma Brown. It was not my real name. What that was doesn't matter; it is buried back there, lost.

I was eighteen years old that year. I remember I heard their voices as I lay there in the tumbled bed with the man that I loathed snoring beside me. There was a clear, light quality to those voices as they sounded on the morning air. They were astir early, as most travellers were on the road to the goldfields. They had made their camp beside the hotel last evening, but I had not seen them because the man, Will Gribbon, kept me indoors when there were people about. I had tried before to leave him. He had gone to charge them the usual fee for watering their stock and filling their canteens from the loop of the billabong that flowed through the back of his property, over by the line of she-oaks. No one else would have charged them, but Gribbon did. They had not come into The Digger's Arms, either for food, or for the bad whisky Gribbon sold. Two shepherds on the way to Melbourne to spend six months' wages were the only customers we had had the night before in the bar.

I eased myself from the bed, keeping my eyes on his face, taking care not to disturb him. Even in the half-light that filtered through the dirty curtains, it had no charm. A ten-day growth of beard showed on his fleshy jowl; his mouth had fallen open in his drunken sleep, revealing the stained, pointed teeth. I looked at him, and the fear and disgust rose in me. I had been a virgin when he had taken me to his bed three days ago. I had been used—unwillingly, in fear and in shame. The hatred I had for him was deep and solid. It was nearly like a second self that stood there beside me, and the weight of the feeling seemed almost to menace him. Perhaps he also, in his sleep, sensed that weight, because he stirred and seemed about to wake. I froze into immobility.

But after a time he was quiet, and his snoring again took on its steady rhythm. I moved softly to the window and parted the curtains a trifle.

What I saw was a common sight along this road leading from Melbourne to the goldfields. I had seen it a number of times since I had been here—the canvas-covered dray, the team of oxen, the tents pitched about the fire. This bare ground beside The Digger's Arms was often used this way—encouraged by Will Gribbon because he ran a poor kind of a general store in a shed beside the tavern, and if he could not sell rum, there was a chance he could sell half a sheep or a frying-pan. The dilapidated tavern was not there to accommodate guests, only to sell rum. It stood, surrounded by the great loneliness of the country, at the junction of the Main Road with a twisting dirt road that led from a few farms in the interior. It had changed its name to The Digger's Arms three years ago when it became certain that the discoveries of gold at Ballarat and Mount Alexander and Bendigo were big enough to keep the eager horde of diggers marching past here for some time to come. Three years ago the sign of The Digger's Arms had been bright and crude; now the relentless Australian sun had faded it to softer colours, blending them with the subtle, austere tones of the landscape. The ramshackle building had a defeated, tired look in the midst of a country too big for it.

It was a side window from which I looked, and it gave me a good view of the camp. It was a family down there, instead of the more usual groups of men who travelled this road. A large family—Irish, I thought; I could not distinguish the words, but the rhythm and inflection of their voices was familiar enough, though lacking the roughness of the speech of most of the immigrant Irish. The father was a tall, black-bearded giant of a man, and his three grown sons resembled him in feature and colouring. The youngest was a little boy of perhaps ten or eleven, I guessed, and he had blond straight hair that fell towards his eyes. He kicked stones about, and when that bored him, he threw a stick in the air and ran to catch it. The women were different from most of those I had seen travelling with their men to the diggings. There were two of them—a mother and daughter, the younger still a girl. They both wore bonnets so that I did not see their faces at that time, but I hungrily took in the clothes they wore. The dresses were well-fitted and stylishly cut, and they were far too elaborate for the place in which these women found themselves. The trimming on the bonnets might be suitable for Melbourne, or even London, but certainly not for Ballarat. I knew at once that these were not the general run of immigrant digger families. These people still had some money left—or at least the signs of it. Their oxen were fat and the dray was new. There was not the stamp of poverty about them. They did not shout at each other with the strident, harassed voices of worry and depression. To my eyes, the difference between being poor and not poor was unmistakable on the road the diggers took.

They were merchants or shopkeepers of some kind, I decided then, tired, probably, of the Old Country, and lured by the tales of the richest gold deposits in the world, greater even than California. Since I had come on an immigrant ship too, I knew pretty well their reasons for coming—some came for adventure, some out of desperate need. Whatever the reason, they all found themselves eventually here, crossing this range of hills to the upland gold country. By this stage the journeying and the dreaming was almost finished—for these people down there along with the rest. For me it had finished here, at The Digger's Arms.

The mother dominated the group, and seemed to be accustomed to this. She cooked the breakfast while the men took down the three small tents, and harnessed the oxen. The mother gave most of the directions. I noticed, though, that the girl remained a little aloof from the group. She was desultorily rolling blankets, and taking her own time about it. But no one seemed to be critical of what she did, and when she left that task unfinished and turned to something else, there didn't seem to be a reproof. The tones of their voices as they rose to me at the window were bantering and easy, there was even a moment of laughter. I remember how strange it seemed to hear that laughter. I wasn't used to hearing affection in the voices of those who passed on this road, but I heard it here strongly. It was an astonishing luxury these people still possessed.

And hearing it, I decided that these were the people I would ask to take me to Ballarat. If they had been bound in the opposite direction I still would have asked them. Where I

7

went was of little consequence to me then—nothing mattered so long as I left The Digger's Arms and Gribbon behind.

It was agonizing to have to move with slow deliberate care when the need for speed was so great. They were harnessing the oxen and throwing dirt on the fire to put it out. Soon they would be gone. I dropped my skimpy nightgown and stood for a moment naked beside the pile of clothes that had been tossed on the floor the night before. As I reached for my drawers and worn corset I was desperately afraid that this would be the moment when Gribbon would wake, strong with his sullen kind of passion after his sleep, and command me back to bed. My fingers were clumsy as I pulled on my petticoat and the old faded grey gown. I had a better gown than this, a pretty green plaid from London, but it was in the chest at the foot of the bed and I didn't dare risk the noise of opening it. I wanted it, but it would have to be left. I braided my hair in one long rope but didn't take time to pin it up, though when I wore it this way I looked younger than I wanted to look now. I caught a glimpse of my face in that old cracked mirror—a pallid face, and too thin. It had never been a pretty face—in a moment of kindliness my father had called it interesting. I had greenish eyes that slanted up, but the dim light here in the room had drained the colour from them. Even in this moment of desperate haste I took a second to wish, as I always wished whenever I looked in a mirror, that it was a pretty face.

Finally I threw a shawl over my shoulders and picked up my boots. On the chest at the foot of the bed were Gribbon's clothes, a tobacco pouch, his pipe and the new Webley double action revolver which he liked to wear in the bar to impress his customers. He must have been drunker than usual when he had turned out his pockets the night before because there was also a small pile of coins. He tried always to keep money out of my sight. I looked at it now and, I looked back to his sleeping figure. Then I put down my boots and I began to gather it up with both hands. It came to twenty-seven shillings and four pence, and if I took it it would mean the difference between whether or not I should have to beg my first meal away from The Digger's Arms. It would even buy me a ride, if I had to spend it that way. I put it in the pocket of my gown, going cold with fear at the clinking noise it made. Then I took up my boots again and moved back towards the door.

But a moment later I was at the chest again, and I was carefully, piece by piece, replacing the money. It had been a mistake to take it. Gribbon would value it far more than he valued me; because of it he might come after me. The law could put its hand on me for taking that money. I would not give him that weapon.

All this had taken time, and I knew from the sounds down below that the people were leaving. I went to the window as quickly as I dared, and this time I parted the curtain wider, and pressed my face against the glass. They were ready to go; everyone was in the dray except the girl and one of the boys, who waited to help her climb up. She was over near the creek, and they called to her. She turned back, but reluctantly, taking her time about coming. She seemed to enjoy this small show of independence. Then the mother grew impatient. This time I heard the words distinctly.

"Rose! Come on, Rose!"

The girl quickened her step only a little. Her father held the reins poised in readiness to go. She reached the dray at last, and her brother extended a hand to help her up to a seat at the back where the canvas was open. With her foot on the step she paused and looked around her. I wondered if she was trying to imprint some memory of this dried and dusty halting-place on the way to Ballarat. Why anyone would want to remember it I had no idea. But her eyes swept over The Digger's Arms and came to rest, inevitably, on the window of the upstairs room where I stood. Her face was tilted upwards.

This was the first time that Rose Maguire and I looked at each other fully. In view of all that happened to us later, I like to think sometimes that there was something special in the looks we exchanged, some premonition of the future. But there wasn't, really. She was desperately important to me as a member of the family whom I thought might let me travel with them, might be persuaded to give me work. This moment was memorable for me too because the upturned face of Rose Maguire was one of the most beautiful I had ever seen, a face with the warm loveliness that makes another woman despair. But I don't think there was anything special for Rose—just the face of a woman watching her from a window. No doubt she was used to people watching her, women as well as men. You do not have a face like that and pass by unnoticed. I saw her lips part in a brief smile—was it an acknowledgment, was she already so sure of her powers? This was offered to me as a gay little salute which she didn't even wait to see acknowledged before she accepted her brother's hand and disappeared beneath the canvas hood. It was the sort of smile one gives to a stranger on a journey whom one doesn't ever expect to see again. I had a sudden and unreasonable sense that I was being abandoned.

I pressed closer to the glass, and I found myself mouthing soundlessly: "Wait for me! Please, wait for me!"

There was no answer, of course. There was nothing but the jingle of the harness, and the cloud of dust that rose immediately in their wake.

In the end it was the green plaid dress that was my undoing. There is no woman alive who can look at a beautiful woman and not wish herself beautiful also. And if you're not beautiful, you begin to think of how to adorn yourself in some way, so that the difference between you is not so great. After I had looked at Rose Maguire I thought again about the green plaid dress, remembering that it made my eyes greener, and that it had lace on it, and fitted well to the waist, not like this ugly flapping grey thing I wore now. It was vanity that sent me to that chest to get the dress.

I was almost successful. Carefully I put the pipe, the clothes, the money and the gun on the floor, making no noise; then I lifted the lid of the chest and rummaged until I found the dress. I was conscious of the time passing, but I told myself that the heavily-laden dray would not move too fast, and that I could run to catch up. I rolled the dress and held it under my arm while I closed the lid. Perhaps I grew over-confident then. The lid slipped from my fingers and fell with a crash.

Gribbon woke at once. He seemed to roll over and half-sit up in one quick motion. I had no time to conceal the dress. The open door and the boots waiting beside it must have told him the rest of the story.

"Where are you going? What are you up to?" His voice was a hoarse whisky croak, but he was sober. He woke every morning this way—evil-tempered after drinking the night before, but sober.

I could only stare at him, feeling helpless, feeling the pain of having believed that I could get away and now knowing that he would stop me. My body already carried the bruises from the beating he had given me two days before when I had asked another family to take me with them. I couldn't say anything; I just took one step backwards. It was instinctive, but useless to back away, since I knew what was coming.

"Well . . . ?"

I didn't answer. My refusal seemed to infuriate him; he

liked people to whimper and cower before him, and so far I had managed to do that.

"Are you dumb," he shouted. He lunged across the bed, and then he saw that the top of the chest was bare. The sight of it stopped him for a moment. "My money . . ." he said. "The gun?—what have you done with it?"

I looked down at the floor where I had placed them, and then for the first time I became really aware of the gun. I had always been afraid of firearms, and afraid of the way Gribbon carried this one wherever he went. Now I saw it as something he prized for the fear it put into other people, and I thought that he too must have known this fear.

I bent down and picked it up.

I know nothing about revolvers—or I knew nothing at that time. I didn't know whether it was loaded; I knew nothing of the mechanism of firing. I held it instinctively in the way I had seen Gribbon hold it when he wanted to show off with it in the bar. I curled my finger around the trigger as he had done, and held it in close to me. I don't know what I meant to do with it, I held it because to him it was a symbol of power. But in my hands he didn't seem to fear it. He looked at me for a second, angry, but not afraid, and then lunged towards me, arm drawn back to hit me. He gave me a kind of backhand swipe across the face that snapped my head back sharply. Gribbon was very close to me when my finger squeezed on the trigger.

He tried to support himself against the bedstead for a few seconds. The report of the revolver almost masked his one grunt of pain. Through his spread fingers I could see the black ragged powder burn on his undershirt; there was only the smallest trickle of blood from his chest. He slid to the floor then and, I think, died at once.

All I am certain of is that he was dead when I touched him, but I don't know how long I stood there with the revolver in my hand, numb with the horror of what I had done, before I could make myself touch him.

I sat for a long time on the floor of the landing at the top of the stairs foolishly clutching the plaid dress still, holding the boots by my side, and trying to think what I should do. The choice, really, was very simple. I could stay and wait for the consequences, or run and try to escape them. I knew very quickly that I would not stay. I had not meant to kill Gribbon. I told myself that, and kept denying the underlying thought that said I had hated him enough to want to kill him. I had not meant to do it. And because I had hated him so, I decided

11

that I would not wait quietly here for the law to come and punish me for his death. He was not worth it. But still I sat, in a kind of paralysis. You do not kill a man, not even one like Gribbon, and not suffer.

We had come in off the road more than a month ago, my father, my brother George, and myself. And now my father was buried over there by that line of she-oaks near the creek. He had been dying when he came here, dying really, when we arrived in Melbourne; I remember that persistent, ceaseless cough which he had said the sea voyage would cure, but had not. Like all the rest we had come for gold, leaving England with hardly more money than would pay the passage. My father had insisted on continuing to Ballarat though I doubted even then that he would finish the journey, much less swing a pick when we got there. We had a few pounds left when we reached The Digger's Arms. Gribbon had not wanted to take us in; he had grudgingly given us the lean-to shed beside the kitchen. My father lay there for more than three weeks before he died. By that time our money was gone and we were in debt to Gribbon for our food and lodging, for the money he had given a passing doctor who had attended my father briefly and left him some medication. No clergyman had delivered my father to the grave; there was no church for the district, and the clergyman rode an irregular circuit of his flock. Gribbon was not among them. It had taken George, who had never held a shovel before, more than two days to dig that grave. He had waited only to see my father into it, to carve the rough headboard with his name, and then he had taken off along the road to the goldfields. George knew what he wanted, and it was not the liability of a sister hanging about his neck. He had feared the lonely walk to Ballarat or beyond it and the possibility of bushrangers less than he feared Gribbon. He, like myself, had felt the strength of Gribbon's blows to hurry us on with our work. Gribbon had decreed that we would pay off our debt my working. George had not considered himself responsible for that debt, so he had gone. That was three days ago.

When George had gone, Gribbon had taken me to his bed as naturally as if that too had been a part of the payment of the debt. I did not feel very much of what was done to me that first night. When you have fought and lost you do not fully perceive the first moments of defeat; you cannot believe it. But the next day I had known what had happened to me. and what was happening. It would continue this way as long as I continued to suffer it, so I knew I had to go.

12

Gribbon watched me continually. He used me to cook and clean, to bring water from the creek, even to chop wood, but he did not permit me to serve in the bar. He worked there single-handed since his barman had left after a quarrel two weeks before. I didn't serve in the little store, either. He wanted me in contact with neither people nor money; he knew that I would go if I got the chance, and it was strange, though he had shouted at me that I was an ugly drab, how much he prized me in that place where women were still scarce.

It was true that The Digger's Arms was only a landmark where a dirt track from a few farms in the interior joined the Ballarat road, but traffic passed on that road each day. I knew that one of the drays would take me away from here if only I could seize the moment. I did not care in what direction it went; it made no difference to me. But it had to be a family I went with; from Gribbon I had learned not to trust the groups of men who travelled together to the goldfields. There was no doubt that many of them were good men, and would have helped me; but there were plenty of Gribbon's kind, too. I could see no point in exchanging my present position here for one similar, but even more difficult on the goldfields. For the same reason I could not start the walk alone—to Geelong, or Melbourne, or the goldfields. But after three days of Gribbon's brutality I was almost ready to try it. What held me back was the thought of what had happened when I approached the first family who stopped to water their stock.

They were a Scotch family; the five children were young and their mother shrilled threats of punishment at them to keep them in order. The woman drew back in suspicion when I made the request.

"I'm very strong," I had urged her. "I'm good with children . . . I could help. I don't want any money, just . . ."

"And we've none to give you," the woman answered. "And I need no help." And then, when her husband had drawn near and looked at me curiously, the woman's eyes had hardened. "Awa' wid ye, Jock," she cried, "and tend to yer ain business."

Gribbon discovered what I was about then, and he had come out of the tavern menacingly. He held me tightly by the arm, pinching the skin cruelly, as he explained to the woman that I owed him a debt, and that the law would be on to anyone who tried to take me away.

"We'll no be responsible," the woman said, backing away.

"Please," I said, "this man is . . ."

"We'll no be responsible," she repeated. "I can see what m' ain eyes tell me."

Then she started bundling the children back into the old cart, and she called to her husband to finish watering the ox. Gribbon pulled me back into the kitchen, and he did not even asked them to pay for the water. I could hear the woman's voice rising harshly in explanation to her husband. "We'll no be responsible for picking up stray hussies on the road . . ."

When they were gone, Gribbon beat me. It was done with a kind of ruthless methodicalness. He seemed to take satisfaction in the fact of the beating itself, rather than the reason for which it was given.

Another day passed, and there was no woman in any of the groups that passed on the road, or stopped for water or supplies. I kept my bruised face out of sight, and prayed for some kind of deliverance from Gribbon. I thought it had come when the police constable who rode the district at intervals appeared in the bar. I didn't know at the time, though Gribbon told me later, that Constable Withers had once beaten to death a man who had resisted arrest. He was one of the strange and dubious characters recruited into the police force to cope with the flood of new population which the gold rushes had brought. I remember, though, that an undoubted fear had risen in me when I faced him, at a moment when Gribbon had left the bar, and I tried to tell him my story.

While he drank the whisky Gribbon always supplied to him free, Withers had laughed at me.

"You think I don't know your kind? Trollops, the lot o' you! So yer plannin' to get t' Ballarat where the pickin' is easier for a whore? Goin' where the gold is—is that it?" He waved the glass at me. "Well, let me tell y' something. It does me soul good t' see one o' your kind doin' an honest day's work for a change. The way I see it, Will Gribbon is intitled to all he gets our o' y'. An' if there's another word about this I'll take y' before a magistrate an' charge y' for soliciting. Y' hear me?"

Of course he told Gribbon and there was another beating. I still hurt from the one the day before, but this was less of a shock. It seemed possible that if I stayed here I soon would not notice. And I knew I must go before that kind of apathy should overtake me.

And so when I had heard those voices on the road this morning, when I discovered that there were still people who could smile at each other, who could afford to be uncritical— who could, dear God, even laugh still—the revulsion against

14

Gribbon and my situation here had risen to an unbearable pitch. I wanted so much to be with those people. I wanted it in a desperate degree. And now I wondered, as I sat here on this landing of The Digger's Arms, if it hadn't been that desperation, when Gribbon had threatened to stop me again —if it hadn't been that which had pulled the trigger. I had no answer. I would try never to answer it, but I knew the question would remain with me for the rest of my days.

I had to think now about what I should do. Sooner or later Gribbon would be found dead here—pehaps not for some days, perhaps almost at once. It depended on whether or not the callers at The Digger's Arms were sufficiently disturbed by his absence to investigate ; they would have to be acquaintances or neighbours. Strangers on the road would simply see the closed and deserted tavern and pass on, I hoped. I asked myself who had seen me here, who could identify me. Constable Withers was one. He was a terrible threat, and yet I had to pass over that. Who was to say I had not left yesterday?—or gone with George? Who was to say Gribbon had not been shot by someone bent on robbing him? Besides the stories of the bushrangers, the country was full of tales of shepherds murdered in lonely huts for a few shillings, or the last half of a jug of rum. I told myself these things, because if I hadn't, I would have despaired. I told myself that I could be lost in the anonymous masses of the goldfields, in among the tents that had no numbers, among the people who had no voice in their own governing. On the goldfields people came and went by the day ; no one had ever counted them. If I could reach the shelter of those drifting, wandering people, I felt I had a chance. To stay here was to face imprisonment and trial, if not punishment. There really was no choice.

Once the decision was taken I knew I could no longer afford the luxury of sitting here and waiting for events to take charge of me. I gathered myself up again, the boots and the green plaid dress, and forced myself to return to the bedroom where Gribbon was.

He lay with his face upwards, crumpled between the bed and the chest. I had to step over him to reach the chest, and my skirts brushed his body. I did not look at him. It was no use to pretend sympathy for him dead, when I had so hated him while he lived. I was only sorry that it would have to be a man like Gribbon that I carried on my conscience all my life.

In the chest were the few personal things I had brought with me, a book that bore my name, and my father's clothes. None of them must remain here ; nothing must be left behind to show that I had ever existed, or to those who knew of me, to show that my going had been a flight. I put them all in the canvas bag that had come with me off the ship, closed it, and started to leave. Then once again I went back and collected the money. This time I had no intention of keeping it. But Gribbon's death might look more like the work of a robber if there were no money beside his body to give the lie to it. The revolver I left on the floor where I had dropped it.

I know that I closed the door behind me with great firmness, without once looking back, but I could not have been very calm, because when I sat down again on the landing to put on my boots my hands trembled violently—so much that when I pulled hard on the lace in an effort to steady them, it snapped between my fingers. I did what I could to piece it together, but it would lace only halfway up my foot. The loosely swinging heel clattered noisily on each tread of the stair as I went down, a frighteningly loud sound in the stillness. I had never felt so alone in all my life as in these moments.

Yesterday's cold ashes were in the grate. While I wrapped bread and some cheese to take with me, I resisted the temptation to light a fire and boil water for tea, though I wanted the warmth and comfort of it badly. It would be better to leave those cold ashes to speak for themselves. I didn't even take Gribbon's hip flask for water for the journey because it might be traced back to here. I drank a mug of cold water from the bucket, and then, as the last thing, I went to the loose brick in the fireplace where Gribbon kept his money. He must have thought me more stupid than I was that he didn't realize how early in my stay here I had known where that money was. His drunken fumblings with the brick, the constant straying of his eyes to this spot, were too obvious if you spent as much time in the kitchen as I did. My one thought, during those weeks, had been to keep George from discovering the money. He might have been unable to resist taking it when he left. Now I drew out the grimy wash-leather bag and didn't even bother to count the contents. It was of no interest to me. It would be buried with the rest.

From the lean-to shed where my father had died I took the shovel with which George had dug the grave. I knew that I was going to leave my identity back there at The Digger's Arms; it was going to be another person, called by another name, who set out for the goldfields. This meant I must leave my father's identity as well. I must carry with me none of his clothes, none of the few personal mementoes we had in common. If the newspapers carried items about the police

16

searching for the woman who had been with Gribbon at The Digger's Arms, there must be nothing left to link my new name with the old one. I could only hope that George would have the wit to remain silent if we should meet up on the goldfields, but I somehow thought that he would. He had a very strong sense of self-preservation.

I dug the hole almost directly under the water trough where the stock came to drink. Gribbon filled the trough as many times daily as necessary to keep the billabong itself clear and unmuddied by the animals going down to it. The ground around it, and leading down to the water, was soft and wet, and scored with hundreds of prints left by people and animals who came here. Everybody who stopped at The Digger's Arms left prints around the trough or at this part of the creek bank. The soft, disturbed ground would attract no attention when the police came to search.

I dug the hole almost to the depth of three feet. Once the damp top layer was through it grew hard. I wondered if I should have to bring a pick to break through it, and I knew why George had so complained of the task of digging. It took me a long time, and I kept halting to stare across and through the trees, watching the road for signs of the cloud of dust that would warn me that a dray was approaching. What I feared most of all was the solitary rider, who could be upon me before I knew it. I had marked a place in the scrub on the other side of the creek where I would take cover if there was enough time. I tried not to think about what would happen if that gaping hole were discovered before I could fill it back.

At last I judged it was deep enough, and I went and got my father's clothes, the money, and, reluctantly, the book. I put that in last, not wanting to throw it with the other things. It was not a remarkable book, a dull thing called *The Principles of Book-keeping*. Perhaps it had been Elihu Pearson's little joke to leave it to me as the single memento of the draper shop in London, of the days of learning the lessons from its meticulous pages—a wry reminder, too, that he had warned me I would have to find my way ahead with my brains, because my face was not my fortune. For some reason I had cherished it enough to bring it all the way from London, even whiled away the slow hours of the voyage by reworking its examples. I would have kept it now, but for the fact that below Elihu Pearson's name, written in his crabbed script on the inside of the front cover where it could not be torn out, was also written my name, in the fine legible copperplate of which I was proud. It was a risk to leave it buried this way, but to try

17

to burn it would require a hot fire which still might leave it only half-consumed. So I threw it in, and it was as if I destroyed a part of myself.

The next thing to do was to take the headboard that George had carved bearing my father's name, and consign that also to the hole. With it went the dried sprigs of mimosa I had twisted for a wreath. When this was done I filled it in. I went to the stable then and slipped the bridle on Will Gribbon's horse, and led him to the trough. I walked him back and forth across the place where I had dug the hole, until the soft earth was trampled down and marked with his prints. I would leave him loose to forage, and he had the creek to drink from. Let the police make of the straying horse what they would; I could not leave him to possible starvation.

Will Gribbon had made a habit of closing and locking the lower part of The Digger's Arms every night. I left it that way now. I locked the kitchen door with the key that always stayed on the nail beside it; this I threw into the deepest part of the creek, a good distance from the place where it was normally forded, trusting the silt would cover it up in time.

After that there was nothing to do but take my canvas bag and go. As at the door of the room where Gribbon had died, I did not look back now. I was never going to forget The Digger's Arms. I needed no reminder of what it looked like.

Within the first mile the bootlace broke again. Now the boot almost fell off my foot at each step I took, and slowed me down. I moved at this awkward, stumbling pace though the scrub parallel to the road. I intended to keep out of sight of any traffic on the road until the time when I knew I was within easy distance of the dray that I was following. It was safer this way. Lone women did not walk the roads here; there was simply no reason for them to do so since the farms and dwellings were too far apart to permit walking. But the rutted earth and the undergrowth, along with the flapping boot made the going difficult; in the end I was forced out into the road. I hid on each of the two occasions when drays passed, both of them moving in the direction of Melbourne or Geelong. Nothing passed me going towards Ballarat. I skirted the one farmhouse that was close by the road with great caution; the inevitable barking dogs were there, and I prayed that whatever woman ran that house would not set them loose on the kangaroo or possum or whatever she fancied was out here in the scrub. The laughing jackasses, the birds they called by the weird name of kookaburras, sat in rows on the limbs of the gums, and their insane laughter mocked my loneliness and fear. It was not the gentle, pleasant country-side of England; it was lonely, and great, and oppressive. The wide grassy hills were given over to sheep runs. I saw no cattle except that one cow pastured close to the homestead. It was the brief September springtime of this country, and I knew from what they had told me of this place, that these were the quick-dying greens that would soon give place to the dead browns of summer. It could be cold here, they said, in winter, with a little powdering of snow sometimes in the higher places, and ice on the pails of water in the mornings. But the chill of this September morning was gone quickly as the sun rose higher and burned off the mists. Under the grey gums the mist had been opal-coloured; it broke into shreds, clinging last of all around the very tops of the scraggy trees, intensifying the cast of greyness that their foliage always possessed. The smell of the eucalypts was fresh; it was a smell that had no part of the world of The Digger's Arms. I seemed never to have caught it so strongly before—I fancied that it was the smell of freedom. As the sun rose higher I watched the red of the new uncurling leaves deepen, the tiny, tender shining leaves of the Australian spring that appeared beside the old. I felt the strangeness of this land where all the native trees were evergreen; only the alien and foreign ever thrust bare branches to the winter sky.

I grew thirsty and ate the bread and cheese sitting under a gum far back from the road. I was tired and thirsty, but I had found no water near the road. I wanted to stay and rest here for a while, to idly watch the big ants move about their business on the dry earth. But I picked up the canvas bag and moved on, and soon I lost the smell of the gums as the sun grew hotter and I concentrated only on the dun-coloured road ahead. I took a bonnet out of the bag and put it on, but it didn't relieve the ache in my head. I had the usual companions of the bush. A swarm of flies travelled along with me. I gave up trying to brush them off. It wasted too much energy that I needed to keep myself moving on this road. I strained my eyes for the cloud of dust that would tell me I had almost caught up with the dray. Sometimes I broke into a half-run that set the boot flapping and rubbed my heel into a blister. The shade of the gums grew darker, and as dense as those trees ever provided. The sun reached its noon position, and moved past it.

I caught up with them during the afternoon; the dray had

moved quicker than I had supposed, or else I had spent longer than I remembered sitting on that landing at The Digger's Arms. By the time I saw the dray ahead of me my skin and hair and throat seemed caked with dust ; the sweat forced its way through heavily. I wasn't even conscious of the precise moment when they must have realized that I was following them because I had reached the stage of weariness when my eyes were fixed on the ground. All I knew was that the dray was there ahead of me, moving, and that I tried to break into a run again ; then the next time I looked up it had stopped, and they were waiting.

And now that I was almost upon them I grew doubtful. I was counting so heavily on these people being exactly what they had seemed to be when I had watched them from the window of The Digger's Arms, counting on that light, uncritical laughter they had shared to prove to be what I had thought it was—an indication that they were not narrow people, suspicious and cold with strangers, afraid to be committed or involved, afraid to break the lines of family to admit an outsider. I needed an anchor in Ballarat, and the sheltering protection of their solidarity. I needed to belong to them. But now my quick doubts reminded me that no man is quite what he seems to be, or woman either. This family was human, like the rest of us, with stresses and fears that could not show to the casual observer. And one of them would be stronger than the others ; the nod that I waited for, that would mean I could join them, would come from that one.

By the time I reached the dray the whole family had climbed down into the road—all but the mother, who stayed in her seat up front. I must have looked odd to them, the stumbling walk in that wretched boot, the grey gown that was too loose for me dragging on the ground, my shawl tucked in the handles of the canvas bag. I only grew aware of my bedraggled appearance because of the way they stared at me—enquiringly, surprised, as if I had stepped out of the empty air, or from the cloud of dust that trailed that dray. Quickly I counted them over, remembering what I had noted of them that morning—the father, the mother to whom they all deferred, the three grown sons who looked so much alike, the daughter whose improbable beauty had so moved me, and the youngest child, the boy with his mother's golden hair. They were all looking at me and waiting for me to speak.

At last I found my tongue. "Are you bound for the goldfields?—for Ballarat?"

The father spoke first. "We are. Can we help you?"

I wanted to weep with relief. The first words had been right, and they seemed to take the weariness out of that long walk, almost to remove the horror from what I had left behind. His face, close to, was kindly, gentle—as I had thought it would be—with the quiet eyes you sometimes find in men of great physical strength. I felt already that I leaned on him a little.

"Please . . ." I said, "could I ride with you as far as Ballarat? I've been walking all day, since this morning . . ."

"This morning! That's when I saw you!" the girl broke in. "I remember now. It was at the window . . . back at that place . . ."

"The Digger's Arms," I finished for her. There was no use to deny it; I could only have come from there or that one farmhouse they had passed.

"You lived there?" the older woman asked. She withheld herself a little more than her husband, as women do. It was an alert, lively face. A handsome woman, who knew this fact, and enjoyed it. She even smiled a little, the cracks under her eyes deepened, but her skin was still firm and pink. Her elaborate dress and bonnet, and the fair curls arranged about her ears were too young for her, and yet she was a sight that any man would have been glad to look at—even more so here where it was so wildly inappropriate.

"I worked there," I said. "My father was ill and we had to stop there. We didn't have much money, and after it was gone I worked for the owner to pay for our room and board."

"Where's your father now?" It was one of the sons who spoke—the oldest one, I judged, though he wasn't more than a year or two older than his brothers. He was more detached than either of his parents; the questioning look seemed to ask me to prove what I said.

"He died back there three days ago," I answered him. I decided to say nothing about George.

The father clucked his tongue in sympathy. "Poor child—you're alone then?"

"Now—yes," I said. "I've been waiting for a family to come along who might let me ride with them to Melbourne or Ballarat. It didn't matter really which way I went. You see, I must find some work . . . I don't have any money."

They took this information in silence, and I saw the father glance towards his wife, as if for directions. Suddenly one of the other sons spoke. "You're English?" he said.

I knew at once that he didn't like the English, which wasn't rare among Irishmen. He uttered the word as if it would blister his tongue.

"Oh, hush now, Pat!" his mother cried. "Can't you leave the thing alone for five minutes? Sure what has this poor girl to do with the English at all. As if she can help it."

He wanted to argue. "Well, but . . ."

Then the daughter grew impatient. "Oh, do we have to stand here while you fight the wars again?" she demanded. "We have to take her! We can't leave her here—just here in the road." She had spoken to her father, as if she knew the appeal would not be refused. She had said it in an off-hand fashion, as if she never doubted that he would be willing to take a stranger in among them. I had to remind myself that I had asked only for the ride; nothing more than that had been spoken of.

"You were alone at The Digger's Arms—except for that man?" the mother asked.

I knew I could not really escape this question. It was foolish to expect that any woman would not have asked it. I was helpless before it. I nodded, "After my father died—yes." I made one effort to make them see it as it had been. "That's why I had to leave . . . I thought if you would just take me until . . ."

The woman nodded. "Aye, I know what it is you're sayin'. Your face is all swollen and bruised. I'd make a guess 'twas no bedpost that did *that* t' y'."

I said nothing. I just looked about the circle of faces and saw the change there. She was more worldly than her husband, more experienced than her sons, but she had only brought to their attention what they would eventually have thought of for themselves. And the change was there, according to the character of each of them. The father shook his head a little, perhaps pitying me; the oldest son frowned and stroked his jaw reflectively. The one they had called Pat looked at me more closely, examined me as if he was only now discovering that I was a woman, as well as being English. And beside him, the other son shuffled the ground in shy embarrassment. The girl's lack of impatience was gone. She ran the tip of her tongue across her lips, opening her mouth to speak. Then she caught her mother's eye, and seemed to decide against it. She shrugged.

Only the child didn't know what we were talking about. He fidgeted in the long pause.

Then the mother drew herself together briskly. "Come on, Daniel. Let's be movin'—my sides are stickin' together with the hunger, and if we don't move we'll not be in Ballarat before two weeks from Sunday."

"Aye, Kate," he said. "We'll do that."

"And what about *her*?" the girl demanded.

"We'll take her, of course, you edjit! Weren't you just after tellin' us we couldn't leave her standin' here in the road. Get in, the lot of you."

The little boy reached for the bag to take it from my hand. His smile reminded me of his mother's. "I'm glad you're coming," he said shyly.

They didn't seem to expect me to say anything. They just began to move towards the dray all at once, and the girl waited for her brothers to help her climb aboard. I was bewildered by the swiftness of it, the casualness now that the matter had been settled. "Just a minute . . ." I said. "Well, I mean . . . thank you . . ." I don't think they even heard me. I waited my turn to be helped into the back of the dray as if I were already one of them. The oldest son stretched down to take my hand, and I felt the hands of the one they called Pat close about my waist to help lift me.

"Greeneyes," he said teasingly. "Greeneyes—what do they call you? What's your name?"

It was then I spoke my new name for the first time. It was strange and awkward on my tongue.

"Emma Brown," I said. "I'm called Emmy." That part of it was true.

They named themselves for me as we rode seated on the bedrolls in the back of the dray. Or at least the girl did.

"I'm Rose Maguire," she said. "This is Larry, my oldest brother. And this is Pat . . . and Sean." She spoke the third brother's name almost as an afterthought. I learned that no one separated the two in their thoughts.

"And I'm Con," the child said.

"The baby," Rose added. She said it half in amusement, and to see the flush of annoyance rise in his face, but there was an unconscious edge to her tone which reminded me there was a gap in age between herself and her youngest brother, and that for a long time she had held the position of youngest, as well as the only girl.

"I'm eleven," he almost shouted, and the information was as much for Rose as myself.

23

"A man, almost," I acknowledged. "You have to be a man in this country, don't you? I mean . . . a family needs all the help it can get."

He looked pleased. "They do," he agreed in his oddly grown-up speech. "There's no regular school in Ballarat, so I'll be able to help my father."

Suddenly Larry took the unlit pipe he had been sucking on out of his mouth, and waved it towards Con. "You'll do your lessons the same as always," he said sternly. "We'll have no ignoramuses growing up here. You'll not turn into an Irish Paddy because you happen to get a shovel in your hand once in a while."

"Will you listen to him!" Pat said. "Will you just listen to him? Aye, Larry, you'll make a fine shopkeeper—you will that! I can see you parcelling out the bars of soap, just like a regular Englishman."

Larry did not react in the swift way that Con had done; he looked at his brother rather coldly, as if he had long ago made up his mind that he was a fool. And finally he waved the stem of his pipe towards him also.

"I've come to take the gold out of their pockets," he said. "I've no need to grub for it in the ground. People have to eat, to buy clothes, to buy frying-pans and shovels. I'll sell them what they want, and I'll put their gold in *my* pocket."

"Just as I said—a shopkeeper."

"There's no reason to fear being a shopkeeper," he replied calmly. "This is a new country—you can start any way you want. It's the way you finish up that counts."

They laughed at that, good-natured laughter in which Larry "Rich," was the reply.

They laughed at that, good-natured laugher in which Larry also joined. And yet I sensed very strongly the deadly seriousness behind his statement. He was about twenty-four at the time he spoke those words; he was as sure of what he meant as he was of the solid feel of the pipe in his hand. He was very good-looking, I thought then. They were, all three of these brothers, what I had always supposed people meant when they said "the black Irish." They had black hair and eyes of that dark grey that goes almost to black. Except for their skin tones they could have been Spanish. They took their colouring from their father, as Rose did. And that made the fair-haired Con, with his lighter blue eyes, almost a changeling in their midst. They were remarkably free and unselfconscious before me, a stranger. But then I thought that perhaps they only appeared that way; they thought I was with them only for the duration of the ride, and perhaps—as I had heard of the Irish—they liked to play to every chance audience that came their way. But I felt comfortable among them, hardly a stranger at all. And now that I was shaded from the sun and my feet no longer sensed painfully every stone and rut of the road, I could begin to relax and to let them play their piece, if they had a mind to. What happened after the next few hours would decide itself. As much as I could enjoy anything that day, I would enjoy this precious time of respite.

Pat reached farther into the dray among the luggage and brought out a water canteen. " Sure you've had a long walk," he said. " You'll be needing this."

I took it gratefully and while I drank it the talk went on.

"Well, Sean and I are for the land," Pat said. " I never did see a rich man yet who didn't own land. Sure it'd be no trouble at all if you had the land—just sit and watch the wool grow on the sheep's back. What do you say, Sean?"

The other nodded. " That's for me, Pat." I knew though that if Pat had spoken for any other thing, Sean would have agreed. Pat naturally assumed Sean's compliance and agreement with every decision, every plan. I learned to ask Sean the questions I wanted Pat to answer.

" You've come too late for the land," Larry said. " You know that already. They parcelled that out long ago to those who were here first. The Government gave them a lease in the beginning, and then an option to buy at five shillings an acre. Imagine it, Pat! Five shillings an acre for the richest sheep country in the colony!—and this was after they'd already made a fortune from it! Some of these runs are a couple of hundred thousand acres a piece." He shook his head, frowning—and envying. " Do you think they're going to break up holdings like that to sell to the small farmer? The squatters control the legislature—the diggers don't have a vote —so what can you do about it? That's why it's trade for me. The rich man's got to buy his tea and soap just like the poor . . ."

" To hell with the tea and soap!" Pat shouted. " Isn't it just like those bloody, rotten Englishmen to have all this fixed so that they keep out everyone they don't want. You can be their servants, but not their equals. I've heard it until I'm sick of it." His face darkened. " By rights we shouldn't be here at all, begging for a chance to run a few sheep. If there was any justice in the world we'd still have Great-grandfather Maguire's land in Wicklow, and we'd be living like kings . . ."

Rose gestured with furious impatience. "Pat, don't start that kind of talk again! I don't want to hear again what grand people we used to be. Why, you've never even *seen* the Wicklow land. Our family hasn't owned land for more than a hundred years. What's the use of pretending you're a gentleman when you weren't anything much better than an ordinary stable hand?"

"We used to be gentry, and we would be still if those bloody thieving English hadn't stolen all that we and every other decent Irishman owned. And it'll go on the same way here, if we let it. This is a new country. It's time to make new rules. Everyone's the right to call himself a gentleman if it pleases him. Who's to say the man who rides around on a thoroughbred is any better than me?"

Larry nodded at him. "If it's a gentleman you're hankering to be, Pat, then stay with me. I'm going to make money, and by the time it's made no one will ask me where I came from back in the Old Country—cottage or castle."

Rose giggled. "You'll look handsome in silk waistcoats, Larry, while Pat here is still going about in his flannel shirts talking about 'rights' and 'injustice.'"

"And where will you be, Miss?" Pat retorted. "What use will the piano and singing lessons be to you here? What matters here is how quickly you learn to cook a damper and boil a billy. How are you going to keep your hands white when you have those flannel shirts of mine to wash?"

She laughed at him, a defiant, unbelieving laugh that brushed aside his words. She spread her hands for us all to see—me especially, I thought. They were white and shapely—not small, because she was, for a woman, tall, even at seventeen, which she was then.

"See," she said. "They're not spoiled yet, and I don't mean them to be." She looked at us through the long lashes that fringed eyes which were that impossible colour which is dark blue but seems almost purple. She had very white skin; her lips were pale, but well defined. She had chiselled, rather patrician features which were much more her father's than her mother's. Her mother, at Rose's age, would have been entrancingly pretty. Rose was beautiful, and only a fool would not have known it. Rose knew it.

She was smiling the confident ruthless smile of the very young who are quite sure what is ahead of them. That was Rose when I first knew her, before there had been time for the confidence to be shaken, though the ruthlessness grew.

She said, "I'm going to find the man who digs up the

26

biggest nugget in the whole of Ballarat, and I'm going to marry him. That's how I'll keep my hands white. Or I'll find the man who owns the biggest sheep run in the whole colony and marry his son. And then I'll give you all the land you want, Pat, and you, Larry, will be in charge of selling the wool." She clapped her hands together. " Now, isn't that a grand idea? Isn't that settled nicely?"

Larry smiled back at her. " And what if you fall in love, Rosie girl—what if you fall in love with a poor man?"

" I'd never let it happen! It would be a terrible waste!"

" Let me know when the wedding is," Sean said. " I'll make certain to come and dance. But, sure, I won't shame you before your fine squatter friends, Rosie. I won't wear my flannel shirt."

Suddenly to her it ceased to be a joke. Her face tightened, and the laughter left her eyes; it was an expression as serious as Larry's had been when he had spoken of being rich.

" Laugh!" she said. " Laugh if you want to! But I'll show you who's right. Come to me a year from now and I'll be wearing diamonds on these hands, as Dada always meant me to wear them."

" Dada meant nothing of the kind," Larry said. " He meant you to be a lady—ready to wear rings if they came your way, and ready to do an honest day's work for your husband if that's what he needed of you."

She flushed angrily. " You make me sick with your preaching, Larry. You don't understand women—you don't know anything about them. You think they're all like . . . like cows. Like that meek little Bridie Connelly you admired so much in Dublin. But we're not all like that—some of us are different. I'm different." Her voice grew shrill. " Five years from now I'll buy and sell you all! I won't wash shirts!"

The three older brothers stared at her and there was a kind of dismay in their faces. She had driven a wedge between them; the teasing and the joking had turned into truths.

" Well, don't look at me like that! I was joking—you know that. Whatever I had I'd always share with you . . ."

" Thank you," Pat said sourly. " It'll be a long day before I'd take anything from a woman . . ."

They were going to quarrel in earnest now, their faces sharpened with passion. I turned quickly to the child, Con, beside me.

" And you, Con—you haven't said what you'll do, now that you're a man, almost."

He took a deep breath, as if he had been waiting his chance to say what was on his mind, and yet had been prepared to remain silent. As the youngest of that family, I thought, he had learned that there was hardly ever an audience left for him.

"I'm going to be just like Dada," he said. "When we find all the gold we need in Ballarat we're going back to Melbourne to buy a hotel. Muma told me all about it—she says she has the very place picked out. And we're going to fix it up all just like the place was in Dublin. And I'm going to help Dada. I'm going to be a tavern-keeper like him."

"You had a tavern in Dublin?"

He nodded. "Yes, a big one, and every day I used to help Dada . . ."

"Satan'll tear out your tongue for telling lies, Con Maguire!" Rose cried. "That's not true—you never helped Dada! You were never allowed in the public rooms."

"Nor were you, Miss," said Larry dryly.

"That's as it should be," Rose answered. "Dada always said I'd never marry a gentleman if it got around that I was helping in the public rooms."

"But I was going to help him . . ." Con cut in. "Just as soon as I was finished with schooling. I was going to help him. Like Larry and Pat . . ."

"Greeneyes, did you hear that?" Pat said to me. "That's Ireland for you! That's what happens when the bloody English steal a country. Here's Con now, studying away at his books—Dada hired a young fella from Trinity College to give him lessons because the English won't let the Catholic schools teach you more than enough to write your name—and all there's for him when he finishes is a place in his father's tap room, or the livery stable where the three of us worked. If young Con were another Daniel O'Connor he couldn't even get a job in the Civil Service, much less be a lawyer or go into parliament. We're Catholics, Emmy, and you're as well to be dead as a Catholic in Ireland. That's why we got out. After the Famine, Ireland wasn't worth a tinker's damn. We had to leave it because the tavern didn't make enough to support four sons and a daughter who had to have silk dresses and keep her hands white."

"That isn't why we left," Con cried. "It was because you got into trouble with the English . . ."

Pat looked at me. "He's almost right. That, and other things. You see, Greeneyes, my father made the mistake of educating us above the station the English thought we should

28

keep. So we didn't fit. We had to leave. When an Irishman starts to have ideas about himself he'd better leave Ireland."

"Stupid . . . stupid," Rose said. "It was a stupid thing to leave behind all we had there, to come to . . . this!" Her gesture indicated the dray with the piled household goods, the rutted road, the alien landscape. It was a gesture that revealed the hostility that fear makes. She turned to me, as Pat had, the listener whom they all needed to convince, not because I was important to them then, but because they needed to convince themselves.

"We had everything then," she said. "The tavern was just off College Green and we had the finest clientele . . . gentlemen from the College and the Four Courts. Upstairs in the rooms where we lived we had rose-wood furniture and silk curtains. I had my own piano. There were servants, of course."

"And plenty of debts, of course," Larry observed. "I present to you, Miss Emmy, the picture of the Irishman who spends every penny he earns. His family is large and happy— if they don't look to the future—and he must work every day to make money for the next. We were forced to go—to sell up and settle the debts—because of Pat's trouble. We had some money left—but even if we didn't have a penny left from the sale it would still have been a good thing because you know in the soft air of Dublin a man can go to sleep and wake up when he's fifty and find out that it's all finished for him. No, it was better to go—to risk whatever this country can do to us, than stay and continue with the dreaming."

"The dreaming . . . ?" I said.

"The dream that somehow it would be all right . . . that the English would take their cursed yoke off our country, that we could live as free men able to use whatever talents we had to rise—the dream that next year things would be better."

"And that's why you broke Bridie Connelly's heart," Rose accused him. "You loved her and you wouldn't marry her."

Larry looked at her and his eyes warned her to silence. "I couldn't afford a wife . . . and children " He rapped the cold ashes from his pipe against the back of the dray, and for a moment or two he turned away from us, looking across to the line of hills, seeing them waver and shimmer in the heat haze. Then he turned back.

"But here I'll make it different," he said. "Dada has agreed that I should take whatever money is left and the oxen and dray and go back to Melbourne. Supplies are expensive and scarce on the goldfields, and cartage rates are high. I could make this dray pay for itself, almost in two trips. And after that there's only profits. People must buy food, if they buy nothing else. I can't lose with this—now that Dada has agreed to invest the money this way."

"We'll move more slowly with the digging without your help," Pat said.

Larry shrugged. "Dada sees the sense of not putting all our trust in striking gold."

"You can't make me believe that! Dada knows as well as any of us that you strike gold if you stay at it long enough. The ones who give up miss out. He only agrees to let you have the money because he always does what you say . . . even to coming here instead of America."

"Oh, give over arguing it," Rose said wearily. "Dada listens to Larry—we all know that."

"He listens to good sense . . ."

And so they continued through the remaining miles to Ballarat, bickering, arguing, sometimes laughing together, or at one another, as I had heard them that morning. They were really no different from most other families; there was nothing very special about them as I had wanted to see in them to justify my selecting them above any other. But they had never known the corroding forces of real poverty; they were still untried and so still not possessive of every penny and every pin in the way people are who have gone hungry or ill-clothed. They talked of debts, but debts are only possible for those who have credit. They were well-dressed; their boots were new, their dray was packed with mattresses and food. Even the dray and oxen themselves represented more money than many people I had observed moving towards the goldfields had ever seen in a lifetime. And so their loyalty to one another, their generosity to others had not really been tested yet. They were young—even Larry whose ambition seemed rock-hard, was still young by comparison to what I knew. Life was not yet quite real for them; they were still at the stage of adventuring. Rose's predictions of her own future were naïve and almost childish, Pat's hate for the English, for the forces of authority, was immature by comparison to what it was to become. And Sean waited for life to be unravelled for him by Pat, and he appeared, at times, not much older than Con. I was touched by this—this youth and the sort of innocence they possessed. I was envious of it, and I wanted to be a part of it.

It was Rose, of course, who asked me about myself.

"My father and I are from London," I said. "We lived in a draper's shop in Mount Street."

"Where is that? I mean to go to London some day . . ."

"The fashionable part," I answered, knowing what she meant by the question. "It was owned by an old man called Elihu Pearson. He was a cripple and spent most of his time in a chair, so my father and I had the running of the shop. We'd been there fourteen years. Then Mr. Pearson died and his nephew inherited the shop. It was a big family, and there was no room for us. Father decided on Australia . . ."

"What kind of things did you sell?" she demanded. I could see that the talk of the draper's shop also interested Larry, though it bored the other three.

"Beautiful things—silk, muslin, velvet . . . satin ribbon, lace. It was all very high quality merchandise."

And then I felt her eyes on my terrible grey gown, the bonnet that might have belonged to an old woman, the drab shawl. I wanted to tell her that these were not of my choosing, but I did not begin, because the reason for these things was a part of me that belonged back there, and it was another story.

I hoped she would ask no more questions, and she didn't because from this point on we began to see the first of the tents in the outlying gullies, the first of the stooping figures bent over the task of washing for fine gold in the tin pans, the first of the windlasses that marked a deep sinking, and the canvas wind sleeves that ventilated the shafts. We were coming into the gold country.

Chapter Two

We came to Ballarat just before dusk—the blue hills grew purple with the dusk. It was a wide valley with a small stream winding through it, and the circle of hills about it was low. It was broken by the threads of rough gullies. This was where the gold was, if you could find it. It was scraggily wooded in some places, and it was bare and stark where the people had taken it over. The grassy slopes under the eucalypts gave way to earth that was barren and hard-packed by the passage of feet—or else it was wildly distorted and twisted out of shape by the endless series of mullock heaps, as they called the piles of dirt they dug from the earth before they reached the gold-

31

bearing quartz. Three years after the first gold discoveries there were forty thousand people living in this valley. It was a canvas town, caked with mud; and sinewy streets of tents followed the main leads which flowed westwards, and under that yellow mud stream, the Yarrowee, they called it. To this day the names of those golden gutters are still on my tongue; like anyone else who had ever been there I could never forget Canadian's, the Eureka, the Italian's, where the Gravel Pits flowed into Gum Tree Flat. Tents and workings were jammed on them cheek-by-jowl, and right to the edge of the stream.

But a part of the Main Road, the one we had travelled, was lined on each side by the enterprises of those who came, as Larry did, to take the gold from men's pockets. Here were the theatres, the hotels, and the shops—flimsy weatherboard and canvas structures, ready to disappear as soon as the gold did. There was one stone building, the bank. There were forty thousand people in this valley scrambling every day for the gold in the ground under their feet, and every night a good many of them gambled it away, or passed it over the bars to pay for their whisky. There were stray dogs and barefoot children, and women hauling water in buckets. There were also fine Moroccan leather boots for sale, and silk shirts from Hong Kong. From the hotels came the sound of the pianos tinkling through the day and night, and back along the streets, along the gullies, there were the sound of windlasses creaking, and, when the wind changed, the crack of the canvas sleeves that ventilated the shafts. The Roman Catholics had built their chapel on Bakery Hill; the Presbyterians held services in the Gaelic on Specimen Hill. In this valley they spoke every language, or so it seemed to me when I came here. For the last three years it had been the richest spot on earth.

For that first night, after riding through the town, Dan Maguire pitched the tents a little short of where the big concentration of tents began—as yet he had no claim of his own, and he chose ground that no one else seemed to want. I made myself busy at once, helping with the unloading, unpacking the cooking utensils, starting the fire with wood that Pat brought. I knew at once that the Maguires weren't used to taking care of themselves in these ways. They worked willingly enough, but except for handling the oxen and dray, they seemed to me to fall over themselves a little. Kate Maguire called herself a cook, but it was I who had the sausages going in the pan, and the billy boiling nicely for the tea. I made up most of the bedrolls while Rose muddled about with her own chest, which was stuffed with all kinds of unsuitable clothes.

I was glad they were amiable, but unsure of themselves; it made my own performance look better. I was not at all subtle about what I was doing. I wanted to make myself indispensable to Kate—or to all of them—and I had only this one chance to show that I could. I didn't suggest going. I didn't make any move to pick up my bag and move off and find shelter anywhere else. And to their credit, none of them, even by a look, suggested that I should. When it came time to pass out the tin dishes and the pannikins, one came to me as naturally as if I had always been there. I ate the bread and sausage, and drank the thick, scalding tea, and kept quiet, afraid to open my mouth in case one of them should remember that it wasn't part of the bargain that I should be there. I suppose they were aware of it, just the same. I remember Pat looking over at me and winking, as if I had got away with something, and he was half laughing, half in admiration.

Even that first night they attracted some visitors. It was to be the pattern of all other nights in Ballarat. Con brought another child to the fire we sat around—a boy of about his own age, Eddie O'Donnell. Later his father came from a nearby camp to fetch him back; instead of hurrying the child away, he stayed to talk for a while, and I didn't think it was altogether because of the whisky Dan offered him. People were like that, mostly, on the goldfields—friendly and ready to help if they could. But then I like to think there was something special about the Maguires, after all. Perhaps it was Kate.

The man introduced himself as Tim O'Donnell. "Sure it's grand to meet y', Mr. O'Donnell," she said. And she made a gesture that was half a curtsy and half a nod of welcome, and her whole body seemed to radiate the pleasure of this meeting. I had to look again at Tim O'Donnell to see what about him would have had such an effect. He was a stringy man with a loose moustache, unprepossessing, timid. Kate made him feel like a king—or at least someone vastly wise and experienced as he sat and gave advice to these newcomers. Presently his wife and daughter, Lucy, wandered over. Lucy O'Donnell was a pretty girl, though nothing like as spectacular as Rose. I was interested to see that she had something of the same reaction to Rose as I had had myself—not wanting to like her, but not being able to help doing so. Little Eddie fell asleep against his mother's shoulder as the O'Donnells lingered to listen to Kate's talk of Dublin, and as Dan talked soberly, but not bitterly about politics. They even listened with interest to Pat's rantings about the English, although what he said was nothing new to an Irishman. And Rose, to please her father, sang a verse of his favourite ballad, the one about Robert Emmet and Sarah Curran.

"*She is far from the land where her young lover sleeps . . .*"

It was a strong, warm voice, of great sweetness.

And then I felt Con's weight against me as we sat side by side on a log which Sean had rolled up to the fire. It was the first of the many nights that Con dozed against my shoulder, and the first time that I helped him to bed. I knew that Kate did not mind; she gave me a little nod as we slipped away from the circle of the firelight.

I helped with the bedroll and helped him undress; his fingers were clumsy with sleep. He forgot that he was almost a man. He became a child again, quite easily, especially in the moment when he stretched up to put his arms about me for a kiss.

"I'm glad you've come, Emmy," he said.

He was asleep instantly, but I sat beside him for a little time, my hand close to his cheek; his gentle breathing fanned it. I thought about that kiss he had given me, the feel of his childish body pressed against me. The innocence of this almost seemed to take away the ugliness of what had been with Gribbon. I was wishing that this child belonged to me, instead of Kate. It was the first time that I knew I wanted to have children. It was a cleansing thing that happened to me that night as I sat by Con, a saving grace after the horror at The Digger's Arms. And I felt no longer plain and poor, but suddenly strong after Con's kiss, and for the time unafraid.

When I went back to the group the O'Donnells were preparing to go back to their own camp. There had been no general introduction when they had walked over; they had learned each other's names casually. Mrs. O'Donnell nodded towards me now. "And this is . . . another daughter?" she said doubtfully. I did not look like another daughter.

"No," Kate replied. "This is our friend, Emmy Brown." And so it was, from then on.

They made me up a bedroll on a straw mattress in the little tent which was Rose's. Whatever I thought of Rose afterwards I have to remember that she welcomed me there that night; she was jealous and possessive, but of people, not things. She shared with me without thought, even the luxuries that had come with her, and which must have been precious because they were running low—the scented soap, the cologne, and I even remember that sachet of lavender to put with my things in the canvas bag.

I lay near the flap of the tent and watched the sky over Ballarat as Rose slept quietly beside me. The pink glow left the sky as the ten thousand or so camp-fires died and went grey; the place grew quiet—I heard only the howling of a dingo, a wild dog, in the hills, and a brief noisy song as two diggers stumbled home from the pubs on Main Road. I lay awake and thought of Gribbon and wondered if I would ever have a night free of dreams of him: but when I slept it was peacefully, and well.

I was up before the others the next morning, even before most of our neighbours. Rose slept heavily still, not even stirring as I crouched in that cramped space to dress; she would be a late sleeper always, I thought. I started the fire, and began to heat the water before Larry appeared.

"Some tea?" I said.

"Thank you." He watched me gravely. I knew of all of them he alone had not accepted me. I thought he would not have minded to see me pick up my bag and go. Perhaps it was because only he among the family seemed to realise what were truly the conditions at Ballarat, and how slim the chances of taking more than a bare living from the ground. They were willing, even Dan, to leave their problems and decisions to Larry. Perhaps it was the thought of an extra mouth to feed that troubled him, or perhaps it was the memory of my being alone at The Digger's Arms with Gribbon. Larry was always inclined to make judgments. They were sometimes hard on other people, but they gave him the strength to be sure of what he was himself, and this was a great strength.

I would have to face him directly with my doubts. He knew, perhaps in the end better than Kate, that I was not a shy young girl unable to be spoken to, unable to speak for herself.

The morning was grey still, but the sun was touching the western tips of the hills, and there was the promise of a warm, fair day. About us the town had started to stir, but had not fully come to life yet. We were alone here; more alone for the fact that a few people moved about us than if there had been silence. My respect grew for Larry as I saw how he sat and waited for me to talk, not trying to run away from me, or leave the doubts unspoken. I had thought him young the day before; now he seemed a man beyond his years.

I handed him the pannikin with the hot tea. "You don't trust me, Larry," I said.

He shook his head but he didn't try to avoid my eyes. "What you are is your own business," he said. "I don't want it to become my family's business."

"Your father would let me stay. Your mother . . ."

He gestured, dismissing the suggestion. "My father is a simple man. My mother is a very generous woman. There was a time when they could afford to be those things. They can't now, but they don't know it. I have to protect them."

He was full of arrogance—pompous almost—but he was right.

"Will I pack my bag and go?" I said.

"Where would you go?"

I shrugged. "You know as much about that as I do. If I don't stay with a family, what is there for me? Do I go wandering over the goldfields asking for shelter?" I flung my hands out. "I know what sort of shelter I'd be offered, don't you? Or shall I go down to one of the hotels—they always need help—but that wouldn't be much different from The Digger's Arms. I know I don't look like much, but if they put me in a satin dress I'd do well enough. Do you want me to go to that, Larry?"

"No! I just . . ." He twisted and turned in an anguish of indecision. He was young again now, and it seemed to me that this was the first time he had ever faced a decision about another person, not one of his family, a stranger whose life had suddenly been placed squarely in his hands. He didn't like it. It would have been better for him if he'd been able to make one of those swift and complete judgments which left him no room for doubt. But he couldn't make it. He was human enough for that.

"What are you to that man back there at The Digger's Arms?"

"Whatever I was it was not willingly. It was just three days —till I could get away from him. And before that—never. Never with any man! Never . . ." And I was humiliated to say it, as any woman would have been. ". . . never even to be kissed." And for the first time I took my eyes away from him and fixed them on the ground.

A long time of silence passed between us, and I knew he wasn't going to break it, so I lifted my eyes again. "Could you send me away now, Larry?" I asked. I was begging him, and I didn't care. "If you could forget these three days . . ."

He was terrible in his sternness, so unyielding, seemingly unable to see that anyone might have been driven as I had been. For the first time I was tasting the awful, untempered justice of the innocent. I felt I was losing, and I grew desperate, and angry with him for being so lacking in understanding.

"Oh, to hell with you!" I said. "What do you think I'll do?—seduce your brothers?—corrupt your sister? If I were what you think I am would I bother with such little fish? Would I want to stay here at all? Aren't the hotels easier?—and the pay better?"

I gestured at him angrily with the pannikin, and a little hot tea spilled on my hand; I didn't mind the burn.

"Can't you see that what I'm offering to stay here for is hard work? Do you need someone to see that your mother doesn't give away every sack of flour in the dray?—every extra pound of sugar she won't be needing today. Do you want someone to stop your father keeping the whole of Ballarat in tobacco for the first week, and having none left after that? Do you need a cook who knows how to get three meals out of a pound of beef? Do you need someone to darn the socks? . . . or will we leave them to your mother and Rose to throw away when they get holes? Do you need someone to see that Con gets his lessons?—Oh, yes, Larry, I can read and write better than any of you, and I've been keeping shop since I was ten years old. What else do you want me to be? Just tell me, and I'll be it! Or will I go down to the Palace there on Main Road—you remember that one last night, Larry, with the brightest lights?—will I go there and offer my services?"

He coloured. He was ashamed, and angry with me for having made him so.

"You said you had to protect them, Larry. Who will do it when you're away in Melbourne?"

"Who do you suppose you are to do *that* for them?—why should you?"

"Because I want to stay—because I need you. You wouldn't find me ungrateful. You wouldn't just be buying a servant to help your mother, or someone to keep an eye on Rose. You'd be getting much more than that, Larry—things you can't buy."

"How do I know you'll be what you say? Why should I trust you?"

"Try me! Or tell me to go and then wish you hadn't. It's a long ride back to Melbourne, and there's plenty of time for thinking. . . ."

He tossed the dregs of his tea into the fire, seeming to enjoy the hiss and roar of it. He was still angry, driven back into himself to find the solution. It was not one made in the clear-cut business terms in which he was accustomed to thinking. His black brows were forced together in concentration. It was strange to see that good-looking young face, with the hair still rumpled from sleep, so grim and earnest.

"All right then," he said at last. "You can stay. At least for the first trip—while I'm away on the first trip. After that . . . we'll see."

I smiled. "Then it's a bargain . . . And I'll keep my side of it!" I thrust out my hand towards him.

He hung back, unwilling to take my hand.

I was determined he would take it. "A bargain, Larry," I said. "And you'll pay me the compliment of taking my hand on it."

And finally, with some reluctance, he did. None of the Maguires were astir yet, and the early risers among our neighbours were concerned with their own affairs. I don't think anyone but ourselves ever knew of that handshake.

II

That day the Maguires, and I with them, became one of the mass on the goldfield. Dan Maguire bought a claim on the Eureka from two other men who wanted to move to Bendigo. The fact that the claim had so far yielded nothing was no proof that gold did not lie just a little farther from the surface. The gold in the leads flowed at uneven depths ; the Eureka was one of the richest, but even so it was like buying in a lottery— not far from the Maguire claim three men had taken out two thousand pounds' worth of gold a few weeks before, but farther along the lead a shaft was down to fifty feet and so far not even yielding enough dust to pay daily expenses. But only Larry thought of this. The others—Dan, Pat, Sean—were convinced that there was gold just beyond the eight feet of their claim that had so far been worked. They took out the miner's licence that the law required before they could even start to dig. Since Larry's name was on the claim he also took one though he said the thirty shillings it cost was a swindle. They bought the unfamiliar tools of their trade—the spades, the sharp-edged picks, the barrow for carting the quartz to the creek, the cradle for washing the heavy dirt, the tin dishes for panning the tiny nuggets and the fine dust. They had all the paraphernalia of the digger, but as yet there were no blisters on their hands.

I helped Kate to move the camp again; this time it was to be permanent—or at least until the claim proved itself either fruitful or useless. The Maguire possessions come out of the dray, and out of the boxes and trunks where they had stayed all through the voyage. They were a strange mixture, the practical and sensible thought bought in Melbourne for the rough life on the goldfields mixed incongruously with the relics of the Dublin life. For Kate and Rose and myself there were low cots—Con had insisted on giving me his since it was now a mark of manhood for him to sleep on a bedroll like his brothers—and these were made up with fine linen sheets and lace-trimmed pillow covers. Rose even brought out a satin-quilted coverlet and gave me the patchwork one that had been, she said, her sole effort at needlework as a child.

"You're never going to use them here!" I protested to Kate. "The mud—they'll be ruined!"

She shrugged. "Sure, haven't I always used up what's been under my hand, and hasn't it always come back to be a hundredfold. I never could stand all this saving for to-morrow what could be enjoyed to-day." She looked fondly at her linens, touched them with a pleasured hand. "Sure they're lovely things—'twould be a terrible pity to have them hidden away in old boxes."

It was the same about clothes. I discovered that both Kate and Rose wore their Dublin gowns because they had no others. Even if they had others I doubted that they would have worn them. Kate was more flamboyant in taste than Rose, but both of them liked to make a splash. Their colours were bright—Kate's too young for her—and both of them stood out like peacocks against the sensible browns and greys of the other women. They refused too, to conform to the practice of pulling their hair back neatly into nets. Rose's hair curled naturally, and unless she took trouble with it, which was seldom, it went into an unruly tangle. Kate, however, had to use curling tongs and rags to achieve the ringlets she wore hanging above her ears, and no matter what else was undone, she curled them faithfully every night. She refused to wear a cap. A bonnet kept the sun off her, but a cap she despised. "Too old for me," she said.

It seemed to me that this flamboyance, this disregard for what was accepted on the goldfield among the women who were considered respectable, would have condemned Kate and Rose, but I was wrong. They had no habits of housewifeliness or economy that other women might have approved, but I had not counted on Kate's friendliness, that peculiar warmth in her

39

which seemed to suggest that whatever was hers, whatever she took pleasure in, in some way belonged to everyone. She was not exclusive about her possessions; she behaved as if they were hers today, but tomorrow similar ones might belong to all her neighbours. Women forgave her for what she had because she was generous. Mrs. O'Donnell and Luck were the first callers, and for them Kate actually produced china tea-cups, which scandalised everyone, but pleased them too. They sat in the midst of packing cases and half-empty boxes, and Kate made it seem as if she had invited them into her Dublin parlour.

"Muma," Lucy said, "couldn't I just fetch Mrs. Healy? Sure, her eyes'd pop out to see these things . . ."

Mary Healy came then, trailing two young children, and a third in her arms; she had an older boy who helped his father in the shaft. She was a close neighbour on the Eureka, a worn-down woman fretted by the burden of her family and the fact that her husband worked his claim alone, and made barely enough money to feed them all. He was now down to a depth where he needed someone to wind the windlass for him, to bring up the buckets full of dirt. Mary Healy could only slip away for a cup of tea from the china cups while he was down at the creek panning the last barrowful they had hauled to the surface.

"By right," Hary Healy said, "I should be down there doing it for him, but he knew how I wanted to come . . ." There was a wistfulness in her voice quickly suppressed when she encountered Kate's smile. "Well . . . it'll be grand now to have some new neighbours. . . ."

Her friendliness, and that of all the women on the Eureka, took in Kate, but did not embrace Rose. Women always instinctively sense those of their own sex who are not interested in the doings of women—those, in fact, whose eyes are forever straying past them to the men. She was civil to Rose, but no more, and Rose didn't even notice. I held Mary Healy's child, a big, energetic boy who seemed to thrive on the goldfield's life, but it was not me Mary Healy watched. Her eyes only saw that Rose paid no attention to her children, and mentally, I knew, she had already labelled her as "unwomanly." Any man, looking at Rose, would never have agreed.

Through that day I helped Kate to put the camp in order—more order than she liked in her possessions; but she was good humoured when I insisted on seeing the boxes properly stacked and covered with tarpaulin against the weather. If I lost out on the battle against using the good linen, I managed to prevent her from bringing out some chairs and leaving them to the weather also. They were pretty, delicate chairs, the kind they made a century ago, not the heavier kind that people favour now. I put them under canvas too. The dray had to be emptied completely ; Larry would leave in the morning on the first Melbourne trip. I had Pat roll up three big hardwood logs to form an open square about the fire, and these, I said, for the time being would be our seats. Although she never mentioned it, I had the sense that somehow Kate knew that a decision about me had been reached by Larry. There seemed now to be no question but that I would stay with them.

I had my first talk with Kate that day. It was late in the afternoon, when the camp was at last settled to my liking, and the mutton had gone into the stew-pot that hung over the fire on a tripod. The camp seemed suddenly quiet. All day the activity had been fierce ; the men had made no serious effort to dig—they had wandered about, talked with their neighbours, and watched. They were still plainly new to the business of gold-digging, and a little self-conscious. They were not as driven by the fever for gold as some I had seen—just sure that they would have it in time. It almost seemed that they waited for Larry to go. Now they had gone off in the direction of Main Road—or at least the only part of the Road that counted —where the theatres and shops were. Rose had gone also ; I had thought they took her unwillingly. They were about men's business, and a woman was a nuisance and an encumbrance. Dan had been unable to refuse her, and she had gone, her arm linked in Pat's. It was the first moment of that day I had seen her face awaken with interest.

Kate and I drank tea together—not out of the china cups. I had packed them away. She settled herself on the log at right angles to where I sat, spreading her skirts comfortably, and taking in the whole scene of the crowded pitched tents, the smoke from the supper fires which had started to swirl into the air. It struck me then how much a part of the place she looked already, even in the unsuitable gown, and the pretty blonde curls swinging about her ears. There was an earthiness about Kate that was not evident in any of her children. It was in her speech too.

She looked along the track through the tents where Rose and the men had gone. "Well," she said, "that's Rose. She doesn't have the sense she was born with—always traipsing about with her brothers when she's not wanted. Sure she must be expectin' to meet some young bucko down there. Oh, an' indeed not any ordinary Johnny at that—someone with gold in his pockets who'll fall in love with her the minute he claps eyes on her. And not dirty gold, either, that he dug up, but nice clean gold straight from Melbourne, and him on a white horse!" She sighed and laughed at the same time. "Sure, she's no different from other young girls, I suppose . . . and yet, I wisht she didn't always be turnin' up her nose at every decent young fella that crosses her path. She's lookin' for somethin' she'll not find. Aye, an' maybe break her heart while she's lookin'. 'Twas the same in Dublin. Sure wasn't I after Dan to let her come in an' help manage things about the tavern—not that I needed the kind of mess she would have made, but it might have got some of the nonsense out of her head. But, no, she says, and gives herself airs like she was an earl's daughter. The public rooms were 'common,' she says. 'Dada doesn't mean me to be seen there.' And Dan, poor soft-hearted fool, he listens to her, and he's proud because when she's not actin' like a devil out of hell, she talks like a lady. He ruined her entirely—singing lessons, an' piano lessons, an' the good Lord knows what. And what use will it be to her here? The way I see this place, a man will be lookin' for a pair of useful hands in his wife before he'll ask can she do a little piece for the company. . . ."

She poured herself more tea. Her face was serene enough as she spoke; it was hard to be distressed about someone as favoured as Rose. She continued; "It's the trouble of the grandfather, of course—Dan's father He lived longer than he should have, even though he was on the booze. He could never forget he was a gentleman. He sold the last of the Wicklow lands, he says, to buy the tavern in Dublin. Well, it was a sorry sort of place, I can tell you, when I first went to work there. There I was, as green as grass, straight off a little farm in Meath, but *I* knew the place wasn't properly run. What with the old man boozing in the upstairs rooms, and too proud to come out and talk to his customers, and poor Dan being good for nothing, what with the Latin and that kind o' nonsense the old man tried to stuff into him. The old man didn't like it when Dan wanted t'marry me. But I can tell y' I put that place on its feet. It didn't make a penny until I took it over . . . but the old man never forgave me, because I wasn't up to his ideas of who his son should marry. The old fool couldn't see that his son was only the proprietor of a run-down pub. He still thought he was one o' the Maguires of Wicklow.

"The trouble was, he lived long enough, the damned old

fool, to get some o' that nonsense into the children's heads. A lot o' good may it do them! He made Dan get a tutor for them—the Catholic schools, he says are 'hedgerow' schools. 'An' what difference does it make?' he says. They're no fools, those boys, an' Larry can figure like lightin'. What else will he need, I'm wonderin'? But still an' all . . . they're good boys . . . good sons to me . . ."

She looked down at her tea soberly. "I didn't want to come here—Ireland was all right for me, even after the Famine it was all right. But Dan and me, we're not young and we were satisfied with what we had. But there wasn't enough of it for all the boys. We had t' come where they had a chance . . . where they wouldn't be held back so much because they were Catholic. Then Pat was headin' for trouble. If we didn't want to see him on a gallows—the way Dan's uncle ended because he fought with Wolfe Tone—we had to get him out o' there. So . . . here we are . . ."

She gestured with the pannikin indicating the camp, the piled boxes, the mud tracks between the tents, the whole barren, despoiled landscape that men had made here in Ballarat. "Doesn't look much of an exchange," she said. "But things'll change. My Dan, he was always the lucky young fella . . ." She patted her ringlets into place as she spoke of her husband.

Rose and Con came back a little later when I was showing Kate how to make a damper—the kind of bread that was almost universal here, and which was baked in the ashes of the fire. The barman at The Digger's Arms had taught me the trick before he had his quarrel with Gribbon. Rose was flushed and angry-looking; Con was a little dejected, but he brightened up when I let him rake the ashes up gently about the damper.

"They met one of the shopkeepers—Sampson is his name, an American. Larry started talking business with him, of course, and they've all gone off to one of the pubs." Rose's tone was petulant, and she watched the ceremony of the damper with scant interest.

"Well, that's Larry for y'," Kate said briskly. "He's always on to something. Y' don't find Larry lettin' the grass grow under his feet." She sounded pleased, not about Larry, but about the fact that Rose had been forced to return to the camp. There was the usual jealousy between them, of two handsome women who vie for the attention of the men about them. Kate's was the stronger personality, mature, and its friendliness gave her the advantage of charm. Rose, at seventeen, did not think it was necessary to exert herself to please, except for the times when it was important to her. She was not yet experienced enough to choose these times wisely. That would come later. She relied now a great deal on her beauty to work for her; she was very sure of it.

"As if there'd likely be any grass in a place like this," Rose said contemptuously. "Did you ever see the like of it? Nothing here—nothing at all but a lot of men covered in muck and old as . . . as . . ." She gestured with irritation. "And the shops . . . nothing worth looking at! If it were even Melbourne!"

We all knew what she meant. Melbourne itself was only a little better than a decade older than these gold-rush towns but it had the feeling of a city. True, it had its own Canvas Town, and a poverty of the homeless that was worse than on the goldfields. Immigrants lacking the money even to start the journey to Ballarat or Bendigo slept on the docks where the ships dumped them. It was raw and crude yet, but there were handsome stone buildings and the lines of the planned, wide streets were there. There were pretty suburbs where the élite could retire to escape the chaos of a city in birth. On its streets there was even a fashionable gown or two to be seen, and beautifully matched horses in the harness of the smart carriages. No wonder Rose sighed for Melbourne, even if it were not quite Dublin.

"There are some good shops in Melbourne," she said reflectively. "Perhaps Larry might bring me a shawl . . ." Then she suddenly turned to me. "Did you sell shawls in that shop you were in in London?"

I nodded. "Shawls—and bonnets. Gloves. Everything of that kind. All of it expensive. We had a high-class clientele— none of those ladies would have looked at any but French silk, and the very finest linens."

Rose's eyes opened wide; "Did you select the things yourself?"

"No—Elihu Pearson didn't trust anyone but himself with that. Though I often wonder how he knew what to choose. He was a dry old bachelor, and none too fond of women, it seemed to me. Often he used to tell me his customers were a lot of fools."

"You did most of the selling then?" Kate asked. "If I'd been one of his customers I wouldn't have taken a handkerchief as a gift from an old toad like that."

"He wasn't so bad," I said, and I was surprised because

I meant it. "He taught me a lot of things. My father and I went there when I was young, and right away Elihu saw that I learned. He saw to it that I had some schooling, and even got the books I needed to study. He was patient. He taught me book keeping, and all about how to run the shop."

Kate gave a kind of contemptuous sniff. "And wasn't it to his benefit?" Kate had heard pieces of the story I had told yesterday. She was prepared to dislike Elihu Pearson.

I shrugged. "Why not? Not many would have bothered. My father . . . well, he wasn't very good at business. Elihu could have put him out many times, but he kept us both there, so I was glad to do what I could. He didn't have to keep us. There were plenty others would have taken our place quickly enough. That's the way my father thought about it when Elihu died and we had to leave the shop. He said there were too many people in London. He settled for Australia because he thought there'd be more room here . . . more chance."

I shrugged again, trying to shake off the feeling I had, the memory of my father thinking there would be a place for the weak and unskilled in this big, rough country, thinking that his own timid venturings somehow would wrest for him a slice of fortune. I grew tense and depressed when I thought of how unfitted he had been to pit himself against what he had found here. It had really been on George's insistence that we had come—George, eager for gold, tired of the humble position he would have to occupy all his life if he remained in England and beguiled by the tales of the rapid rise in fortune and society that was possible in this new country. Our father had listened, a meek man who had secret dreams of his own—or was it that he was desperately worn out in the long years of service to men like Elihu Pearson, and George lit a kind of madman's fire in his mind? For whatever reason his small savings had gone into the fares for the three of us. But the fire had gone out for him in that awful little shed at The Digger's Arms, and George, now that my father's usefulness was fully exhausted, had gone. I left the thought there. I wanted to forget about George.

I looked at Kate and Rose, angry, not at them, but against what I had found to be the truth of this place. There were no easy openings here. The strong would win here, as they always did—the entrenched, with money and power. Almost now I understood Rose's ambitions. If I had been beautiful like Rose I would have been tempted to think her way, to take the easier path to have what this country offered.

"I said to them; "But there isn't a chance, really, is there? It's just as Pat says—they have everything settled here the way it was back there. The people who own this country will go on owning it. The rest of us are only outsiders. There isn't the room—the space—my father thought there'd be."

I left them then and went to sort through a pile of Rose's underclothing that needed mending. She had not asked me, but I knew they would never get any attention from her, and I couldn't bear to see them go to pieces in this way. Also I needed something to keep my hands busy, less time to indulge my thoughts.

But since yesterday, since I had tossed that book that bore Elihu Pearson's name into the hole at The Digger's Arms the thought of him had often risen, it seemed, only to mock me. I could see his grey lined face sardonic, taking a kind of malicious pleasure in teasing me. It was he, not my father, who had shaped me as a person. Although he sat in a chair and could not walk far on his cripple legs, he was a dominant and impressive man. He had decreed what I was to be, and he had set about preparing me.

"No man will wed you for your face, Emmy," he said. "Be useful. Learn to make yourself useful, and you'll manage all right. The idle and the stupid get left behind."

We shared a few things together that we enjoyed. The accurate balancing of the books was a triumph. There was also the tiny garden in the damp courtyard behind the shop. Nothing much grew in that soot-laden air in London, but when we together coaxed a sprig of green from that unyielding soil, that too was a triumph. I would read the newspapers to Elihu when his eyes were tired, and sometimes he encouraged me to argue with him—politics, the Prince Consort, how we were running things in India. And in the end he told me I knew too much for a woman, and I'd best learn to hide it.

He gave with one hand, and took away with the other. My clothes, for one thing. He gave me materials from stock, and I learned to make my own gowns. How I hated the hideous grey and browns he chose, without a bit of lace or trimming to help them along. How ugly the bonets were—not ones he would have expected any of his own customers to buy. He got them cheaply from the salesmen—the boots, too. I never forgave him for those dresses, those awful old-woman shawls.

"You're not a lady," he used to say. "Don't try to ape your betters."

Perhaps that was why I so cherished the green plaid gown my father had bought me before we left London—the only present I had ever had from him. Perhaps in those weeks after Elihu had died my father started to see me as a woman for the first time, not as a part of Elihu's property.

In his will Elihu had left me a few books—a savage little joke, I had thought then, a reminder to me of what I was. But still I had kept one of them with me as far as The Digger's Arms. Perhaps a joke from Elihu was better than no recognition at all.

"I thought he'd leave you some money," George had grumbled. He was very good at spending other people's money. I had shrugged and said nothing. I had not expected money from Elihu. To him it was the most precious possession in the world, and not to be lavished on people who were no kin to him. It went to his nephew whom he hadn't seen for years.

So perhaps in the end that had been the old man's best legacy to me—that harsh training, the knowledge that I must do for myself, not relying on anything but energy and quick wits to take me through. In a way he had made me tough; perhaps he had known it was the best he could do for me.

That was probably why I was so attracted to Rose—the opposite of myself. She would make her way with no effort, only dependence on her beauty. She was spoiled and childish, but she had her mother's generosity and I was heavily disposed to admire anyone who was generous. She had shared her tent and her pretty toilet things with me last night without question. And today she seemed quite prepared to accept me as part of the family. I suppose if you are very sure of yourself there is no need for jealousy, for the feeling that someone else may replace you. I knew that soon she would start to demand things of me as she did from her brothers and father. And I knew that when that happened I would do what she asked gladly. It was the beginning of love for me.

Larry was to leave for Melbourne early the next morning. The thought of it seemed to press heavily on all of us that night, even on me, who shouldn't have cared whether he went or stayed. In fact I should have been glad to see him go, glad to have his questioning eye off me. But it was the other way. He was our rock and our anchor here in this unfamiliar world. Tomorrow Dan and his sons would have to do without him, and they looked as lost as I myself felt.

Kate gathered them all to prayers that night. She was drawn to piety in moments of stress. I smiled then to remember how Elihu had scorned and hated "the Papists" and encouraged

47

me to do the same. I wondered now what there had been to fear in these people as I watched them kneel about the fire in obedience to Kate's summons.

"Holy Mother . . . bring Larry back safe."

I forgot then that I was Emmy who had never thought about prayer or expected anything of it. "Bring him back safe," I whispered.

I was already far gone towards loving them all.

Before I went to sleep beside Rose I counted off another day free of Gribbon, and another day when the police had not come riding to catch up with me. I wouldn't let myself think about all the other days facing me. This one had been good.

Chapter Three

We became part of Ballarat in those weeks when Larry was away. We took on its colour; we did not stand out as newcomers any more. The hems of Kate's and Rose's gowns, my own as well, became caked with the inevitable mud, and then with dust when it was dry. The men's flannel shirts and moleskin trousers were no longer new; their cabbage-tree hats were stained with water and sweat. They got blisters on their hands, which festered at first from the minerals in the water, then healed and hardened and became callouses. They learned the rhythm of swinging the pick, and became expert at it. They learned the habit of a few eucalypt leaves thrown into the tea which was the only drink that would cut the noontime thirst. They learned the ways of the goldfields, the expressions, the emotions. What they did not do was to strike gold of any significant value.

The sinking grew deeper and Dan rigged up a canvas wind sleeve to ventilate the shaft. They worked very hard; Dan was a man of unusual strength, and Pat came close to him. All day I watched the loads of dirt come up—I helped to wind the windlass to bring it to the surface. And then I took my turn with Rose at rocking the cradle down at the creek. The banks of the Yarrowee were lined on both sides with the wooden cradles and the valley was alive with the constant tumbling sound they made. One of us turned the handle and broke up the dirt with a stick, while the other kept water pouring on it. The deposit which fell through the wire sieves of the cradle had then to be washed in the tin pan for the dust. Con was deft at this. The quartz rock left in the cradle was picked over for pieces and lumps of gold. We found no lumps of gold. We got just enough from the dust Con panned to pay our daily expenses, and in this we were luckier than some.

We grew accustomed too, to the cry of "Traps! Traps!" which meant that the police were on a licence-hunt. The law required that every miner buy a monthly licence which cost thirty shillings; he was to carry it with him at all times. If it was not produced at the moment the police demanded it, the digger was arrested on the spot, and held until he could pay a fine. Many of them couldn't afford a licence. When the cry went up of "Traps!" or "Joe! Joe!" the men who were without a licence would run for the deep shafts and hope to make it out of sight before the mounted police showed over the lip of the gully. It was a thing we all hated, whether we could afford a licence or not. A lot of men, like Pat, grew bitter about it.

"Taxation without representation," he would shout as loudly as any man on the goldfields. In a way it was true. We were strangers in this country, without property, and therefore without a vote. We were homeless, without a stake in anything but that eight square feet we claimed to dig for gold in . . . We had no one to speak for us in the Legislature. And thousands of men paid this tax without ever taking an ounce of gold out of the ground. It was something to grow bitter about, if you let yourself.

What Pat did, of course Sean followed. They would both of them dive for the nearest shaft when the hunt started. They carried their licences with them, but they made it as difficult as possible for the police to inspect them. Once Pat pretended he couldn't find his, and was handcuffed to the trooper's bridle and rushed back to "the logs," which was what they called the lock-up. If the lock-up was full, the men were chained to a huge trunk of a felled tree until the magistrate could deal with them and levy a fine. That time Pat produced his licence before he was actually chained up. He came back to the camp grinning with his small triumph over authority, but still sore and angry that it should happen at all. It was a perverse, silly thing to do, and gained him nothing.

There were other things to think about. There was no way to be alone there. We were part of everything that happened about us. At a disused, flooded mineshaft on the far edge of the town, a child was drowned. The family belonged on the Eureka. I didn't remember having ever noticed the child before—there were many of them there—but because I was quick with my fingers, I found myself sewing a shroud from a linen shirt that Kate had given me to cut up. I trimmed it with Irish lace that Mary Healy contributed; it was probably the finest garment the child had ever worn. I went to the wake, too, and followed the coffin to the burial ground. This was how involved we all became in the death of a stranger.

There were other kinds of deaths. The police protection was almost non-existent. They were zealous about nothing but the collection of licence fees. So the people of Ballarat protected themselves as best they could, and as brutally. A few nights after we arrived there a man was shot dead on the Eureka as he stumbled back from the pubs on Main Road late at night. There were thieves in the darkness of those unlit streets, and men sometimes opened fire out of sheer nervousness. That death was accidental, of course, like the deaths of the men who were buried alive when their unshored pits caved in. Other deaths were not accidental. The gold escort from Ballarat was ambushed twenty miles from the town, and a policeman was killed, as well as two bush-rangers. The others got away.

It wasn't all death. There were births, too. One woman close to us on the Eureka gave birth to a daughter after a long day in hard labour. We listened to her screams, and Rose cowered against me, her hands over her ears. There was a midwife in attendance, but no doctor. The only doctor we could find was drunk. Doctors, like all the rest of us, were transient on the goldfields.

There was laughter, too. Saturday nights were the gala nights. I put on the green plaid when Rose and Kate dressed in silk, and we went down to the Main Road, like almost everyone else in Ballarat. I paraded with my arm resting in Con's, and it pleased me that he was proud. We looked at the shops, and wished we could buy some of the things we saw there. Some of them were very fine—silk shirts and velvet waistcoats tempted the digger who had struck it rich and couldn't wait to get to Melbourne to spend his money. The tinkle of the pianos from the hotels and theatres beckoned all of us—Con spelled out their names in an awed voice—the Adelphi, the Montezuma, the Charles Napier. They brought their entertainers all the way from Europe. People still talked about the time when Lola Montez had come; it was something for them to think that Ballarat had enough money to attract the one-time mistress of the King of Bavaria. I didn't explain this to Con.

On warm nights the hotels kept their doors open, and we could stand in the road and see the pink shaded lamps, the fringed draperies, the women in the bright satin gowns. Rose would nudge me furiously.

"I wish we could go in," she'd say. "I'd give a lot to go in there and be allowed to drink champagne."

Rose was very restless. She fitted to Ballarat less well than any of us. In those weeks we came as close together as any woman would ever be to Rose, and she would lie awake in the darkness of the tent and whisper her dissatisfaction to me.

"Do you think we'll ever get out of here, Emmy? Do you think we will? It's so awful—this place. There's no one to meet. There's no one even worth talking to."

I knew what she meant. When she said there was no one to meet, she meant there were no men. There were plenty of men, of course, most of them hungry even for the sight of a pretty woman. But the ones she was interested in didn't exist.

"I want him young and handsome, and with money," she would say fiercely. "The only ones here who've found gold are old men—old men I wouldn't look at."

She was aloof and almost haughty with the young men who hung about the Maguire camp. And they hung about in spite of discouragement, because she was, as I began to see, the sort of woman who attracts men without meaning to. She was aware of it, of course, and the knowledge gave her more arrogance. She treated them like fools, and enjoyed the power she held. I had my own admirers—pretty poor sorts, I thought, who didn't even attempt to reach Rose. The ones who wouldn't even try, I thought, weren't worth bothering about. And still Pat continued to call me "Greeneyes," and I was glad about that.

I kept my bargain with Larry in every way I could. I took hours every day to sit with Con and help him with reading and arithmetic—I was a better teacher than Dan, more logical, and I was a great deal more patient than any of the others. I tried to restrain Rose—or at least to give her the sympathy that she demanded, to give her a ready listener so that she could rid herself of some of the frustration that swamped her at times. I did most of the cooking, though Kate was known as the cook; I kept the shirts and breeches patched, and shortened the petticoats so that they wouldn't trail in the dust. I reminded Kate to wear her sun-bonnet, and rubbed grease hopefully on her arms when they were freckled. And I didn't encourage Pat to call me more than "Greeneyes." This wasn't difficult, because Pat had had eyes for perhaps a dozen girls up and down the Eureka.

And so I kept my bargain with Larry, but after a while I

forgot the bargain. I would have done it if there had been no bargain, no Larry. I did it because they had become my people. I knew their faults, and I would have defended those faults against any criticism. It was the first time that I had loved. I wanted to exercise this love in the service I gave them, but there was nothing I could do except the trivial things that came to hand. And I wanted nothing from them that they had not already given me; they gave me the feeling of belonging.

I searched the Ballarat newspaper, *Ballarat Times and Southern Cross,* for any mention of Will Gribbon or The Digger's Arms, but I saw none. Where there is gold there is always violence, and I began to hope that this act would be one of many the police did little about. I began to be less afraid. There came the time when I was able to pass a policeman on Main Road without wanting to shrink behind Rose. I didn't stop searching the faces of the crowds for George, but after the first week I worried less about him. There were many outlying goldfields and he could have gone to any one of them. It would be George's inclination, like my own, to put as much distance as possible between himself and The Digger's Arms.

But the reassurance concerning my own safety did not extend to my feelings about Gribbon. There was really no rest from the eternal re-enactment of that moment when the gun had seemed to explode in my hand. Almost every night in my dreams I saw that slow fall, heard the sound of his body crumpled to the floor. I would wake in a sweat of terror, and sometimes I actually heard my own voice speak his name. I was not free of it. I began to think that I never would be.

I cried sometimes in those nights, quietly against the pillow. And I was thankful that Rose slept so heavily, so that she heard neither the confused mutterings of my dreams, nor the sobs that came after.

By day the thought receded. I was happy there on the Eureka. In those early days we all still had hopes of a big strike that would quickly make us rich, or rich enough. In the meantime we worked hard, ate well, and the weather of that spring was good—warm days, cool nights. Kate held court at her camp fire as she would have back in the Dublin tavern, and Dan still passed out the whisky. I didn't make much effort to restrain them, in spite of the promise to Larry. I began to sense how important Kate's pleasant warm laughter was to all of us—and even to people in the camps about us. It would have been foolish to stop Dan passing his tobacco around. To take these things away would have stripped them, made them vulnerable to passing depression, to a sense of forlornness which could come upon one so easily here on the goldfields. They needed all their vigour, all their sense of enjoyment because the spirits and the hopes of all of us depended on them.

We waited for Larry, of course. We counted off each day. And each evening Kate would make us kneel down. "Holy Mother, bring Larry back safe."

And afterwards in the tent Rose would repeat the thought, but it was not a prayer, but a desperate wish. "How I wish Larry would come back." I don't think she knew what she expected of his return, except a contact with a world that was more familiar, less hated than this one. But in a sense all of us were waiting for something more than his return.

II

Larry was away almost three weeks; it seemed much longer. It was late afternoon when he returned; the men would soon be finishing the day's digging. Con and I were sitting on one of the logs with his lesson books spread before us on packing cases, and Kate was mixing the dough for a fresh batch of damper. Rose had wandered off restlessly—to visit Lucy O'Donnell, she said. Our camp was not far from where the Main Road ran by the Eureka. We heard Larry's shout, and there he was, flourishing a whip at us in greeting, and guiding the oxen on the rough path through the camps.

"Mother of God!" Kate cried. "It's Larry back." She wiped the flour off her arms with her apron, and ran towards the dray. She paused for a second by the sinking. "Dan! —Pat! Come up! It's Larry!"

Con was gone from my side in a flash, and I watched him run and scramble over the wheel to Larry's side on the driver's seat, his almost manhood forgotten as he embraced his brother with a childish ferocity. Before I went to join them I caught one of the children who were always hanging about the camp. It was Tom O'Brien who lived two tents farther along the Eureka. "Quickly," I said, "Go and fetch Rose from the O'Donnells'. Tell her Larry's back!" When the boy seemed disinclined to miss the excitement at hand, I gave him a light box on the ear. I had too often fed him the fudge I made to feel any compunction about this now. "Hurry on," I said. He turned and ran.

By this time the Maguire men were up from the shaft, and gathered about Larry. And our neighbours had started to drift over towards the camp. They were polite; they waited until the first moments of greeting were over before they pressed in, but they were determined just the same. It would have been unthinkable for us not to share Larry's return as they had shared our waiting.

I found myself, along with all the others, hugging Larry, and I even felt his light kiss on my cheek. I imagine I was not the only girl he kissed in those first few minutes. Kate was laughing, and the tears were streaming down her cheeks. She wiped them with the floury apron. Dan was shaking hands all around, as if it were he who had just returned from the journey.

It was Larry who made us aware at last of the second dray. Since we had only been expecting one, we saw only one. After he had hitched his team, he went back to the road, and helped guide the second dray over the unfamiliar ground. It was a big dray, drawn by a pair of well-matched horses. The horses alone would have made us stare. Or perhaps I was staring already at the man who drove them.

Larry mounted the wheel so that he was above the small crowd that had now collected, and he called loudly for their attention. "Everyone—I want you to meet Adam Langley! He's by way of being in business with me. And if you think the dray and these horses are mine, then you're mistaken." Then he laughed, a confident, brash laugh. "But they soon will be."

A roar of approval greeted this remark, and then the men pushed forward to shake hands with the newcomer. He wore a seaman's cap and jacket, and he seemed a few years older than Larry. He responded to the handshakes warmly, and from his accent as he acknowledged the introductions, we knew he was an American.

A voice from the crowd called out jokingly. "You'll have to watch out, Larry-boy. These Yankees'r sharper than a needle. You'd better take care or he'll end up owning *your* outfit."

Adam Langley smiled, and with a gesture deprecated that suggestion. When the team was hitched he climbed down, and we all moved back to the fire. "Leave the teams as they are," Larry called out. "We're only staying a few minutes. This stuff is all going down to Ben Sampson's place."

Adam Langley moved with us, taller than most men, broad

of shoulder, more inclined to nod and listen now than to talk. His teeth were clenched on a pipe. For a second I stood beside him in the crowd, and he towered over me. Even in the midst of it he was somewhat apart from this gathering of excited Irish, and he seemed willing to let Larry do the talking for him. Seamen were common on the goldfields; they jumped ship in Melbourne to come here. But Adam Langley wore the peaked cap of a ship's officer. His deep tan and the intense, sun-strained blue of his eyes spoke of the sea; he did not quite belong here—or at least I sensed that he would have preferred to be elsewhere than in Ballarat. But he took the back-slapping amiably. I thought I saw affection for Larry in his indulgent smiles and nods. Adam Langley was also very handsome—lean and straight, with good firm bones to his face, and an expression of reserve that could not easily be broken in upon. When he took off his cap his hair was brown, though sun-bleached in streaks on the top. He accepted the seat Kate indicated on the log, and waited patiently until the fuss would subside.

I had slipped the kettle back on the fire when I first saw Larry arriving, and soon the tea was made. Kate and I handed around the pannikins, and Dan followed to lace the tea with rum for those who wanted it. There was a party spirit among us. We laughed readily over nothing.

The men were pressing Larry for details of the trip to Melbourne. Kate cut the fruit cake she had baked against Larry's return.

Larry bit into his slice of cake. " Well, I'll tell you. Things seemed bad there for a while until I met up with Adam. It isn't a matter of just going into Melbourne and paying your money for what you want. It depends on the shipping—when things are scarce only the regular merchants can get the goods out of the warehouses. There's been a lot of delays lately—ships overdue. It began to look as if I'd either have to pay the shop prices and take my chance on a profit back here in Ballarat, or I'd come away empty-handed. And then I met Adam and he took me to John Langley . . ."

" Langley . . .?" The name ran through the crowd, and there was recognition, and a touch of respect, too. Someone near him asked Adam " You a Langley then?—one of *those* Langleys? An American . . .?"

Adam shrugged. " Our name's the same. Two branches of the same family. Mine went to New England more than a hundred years ago. My father met John Langley in Van

Diemen's Land when he came out here whaling in the twenties. We're Nantucketers!" he said firmly, as if he expected everyone to know what that meant.

" That's the Langley Stores in Melbourne, is it now?"

" More than that!" a voice called from the back of the crowd. "That's only the Langley of Langley Downs and God knows what else. He owns more sheep than the rest of them put together. And he'd like to see all of our kind—the diggers —run out of the country. He said so in the Legislative Council, a while back."

A little unease fell on the crowd then. They looked at Adam, examining him more closely. You did not associate him with wealth, that water-stained jacket and the battered cap. And you wondered what he was doing here in Ballarat, driving a dray.

Larry gestured to dismiss the talk. " I don't care what he said in the Legislative Council. Like everyone else he'll do business when he can. The diggers are here to stay, and he knows it. So he'll sell them goods the way he sells to anyone else. Adam arranged for me to see him, and after a week I convinced him that I was the man to do business with. So here we are—Langley let me have my pick from his warehouse, the dray and the horses are his, and Adam is here to watch the Langley end of the business."

" Well, they say sailors make good traders—specially Yankee sailors."

Adam's amiability vanished. " Only for the time being," he said quickly. His face was tense. " Only until I get a ship . . ."

" Plenty of ships in Melbourne. The Bay's rotten with 'em."

" And no crews to man them," Larry said. " The captains are sitting there getting fat waiting for their crews to come back from the goldfields. A man has to do something to make a living . . ."

" Aye . . ." There was a general chorus of agreement, and Adam Langley settled back into the commonplace again. The talk of having to earn a living removed him from the aura of wealth that the Langley name conjured. He was just a seaman again. Some of the tension left his face. He knocked out his pipe and refilled it, and managed to refuse Kate's offer of a second piece of cake without offending her.

" Well, you've got yourself a grand thing if its' old man Langley you have behind you, Larry," Mike Healy said.

" Sure there'll be no holdin' y' now yer backed by the Langley money."

Larry disclaimed the notion. " Wait now—it's nothing more than a little credit extended, and he's using me instead of employing someone to do this job. He's content to work through Ben Sampson's shop instead of getting up his own because he says this town hasn't any future. He's waiting for the gold to be finished . . . better let someone else be left holding the real estate when the people move away from here, he says."

" Sure he's mad. The gold'll go on for years . . ."

" He's crafty. That's how he's made so much money. They do tell me he was even in on the whaling, and sealing in the Straits in the early days when it was a big thing . . . What do you say, Langley? Was that how it was?"

Adam Langley shrugged. " I don't know much about his business, and he's not inclined to discuss it with a poor relation. But I remember my father telling me that John Langley set up a whaling station at his first farm here—Hope Bay, it's called. But that's all finished now."

" Yes—they slaughtered the creatures, and now it's been years since they've seen hair or hide of a whale or a seal in the Straits. People choke on their own greed . . ."

" Hush," Kate commanded the speaker. " Is that the kind of talk to make in front of the man's own kin?"

Again Langley shrugged. " It makes no difference to me, Mrs. Maguire. John Langley only employs me. I don't consider myself part of the family. If it weren't for Larry here I don't think I would even have gone to call on him . . ."

" John Langley will change that," Mike Healy commented. He had longer residence here than almost anyone on the Eureka, and he was regarded as an authority on the gossip of the colony. " From what I hear of the man he never lets go once he puts his hand on you. There's his only son now—the boy's right here in Ballarat tryin' t' break loose from the old man, and not succeeding too well. And the Langley daughter —they say she married some English swell—a baronet's heir— and at the end of the year wasn't she back in Melbourne with her father and doesn't look like shifting either."

" You know Tom Langley?" Adam broke in.

" Aye, sure . . . you'll nearly always find him over at Bentley's pub. It's right here on the Eureka. Sure he's always a good touch for a drink, if you know what I mean. He has his pockets full, even if he doesn't do much in the way of diggin'."

Adam nodded in reply to the information. Mike Healy would have liked to talk more about Tom Langley, but Larry gave him no chance. He drained his pannikin and set it down on the ground.

"Well, we'll be getting down to Sampson's. I've got to get these two loads off and checked in before dark. We'll need some help . . ."

"The boys and I will go with you, Larry," Dan said. "We were just finishing up in the shaft. And maybe Mike here would give us a hand . . ."

"I can help," Con said. Everyone started moving off towards the drays. I took the empty pannikin from Adam's hand and he thanked me with a quick smile. He didn't know who I was—we had been introduced in the first wild moments of arrival, but he didn't remember my name.

"I'm Emmy," I said. "Emma Brown."

For a moment he hung back behind the others. "Emma . . . that's a nice name. That was my grandmother's name." He stood looking down at me, a big man whose shoulders strained his jacket. He was still smiling, but it had changed; it was more reflective, even with a trace of wistfulness in it. My name had recalled home to him. I clutched at this small chance.

"You'll be staying here—at the camp?"

He shook his head. "I won't put them to that trouble. I'll get a bed in one of the pubs."

"Kate won't hear of it," I said firmly, knowing it was true. "There's another tent for Larry. You can share it . . . you'll be here a few days, I suppose?"

He nodded, glancing back over his shoulder towards Larry and the drays. He started to turn to go. I followed him with a little stumbling rush—I who was rarely clumsy. I felt like a child at his side, but I wanted him to see me as a woman.

"If you've any washing you want done . . ." I said lamely. "Or mending . . . I'm very good at mending."

He looked at me with some surprise, and I felt foolish. I knew what I was doing, and I wasn't able to stop myself—offering him services this way where another woman would have offered a smile. I had never been so unsure of myself or so eager to do the right thing.

"Thank you, Miss Emma," he said gently. But he didn't accept.

Larry had mounted the seat of the dray. His father, Con and Mike Healy were crowded up there beside him. He held up his hand and motioned the little crowd beside him to silence.

"Everyone! . . . There's a party tonight. You're all invited. Whisky all around and fine big hams from Melbourne."

Someone cheered, and tossed a hat in the air. In the general noise of agreement and pleasure that followed this, Adam slipped away from me to his own dray. Pat and Sean were there, waiting to ride with him down to Sampson's. Matt O'Casey, one of our neighbours, stood ready to guide the team back to the road. The abruptness of the departure made me a little desperate, even though I knew they would be back. I twisted my hands, watching Adam mount the dray, taking the reins from Pat.

"Larry! Larry. Wait . . . wait for me!"

There was a sudden commotion between the tents. Rose came running over the rough ground, scrambling over the mullock heaps, her skirts hitched into her hand, her hair dishevelled and wild. She was trailed by Tom O'Brien, whom I had sent to get her, and farther back was Lucy O'Donnell.

She rushed towards Larry's dray, and climbed up over the wheel to reach him for a kiss. He laughed affectionately, and rumpled her hair even more. "Well—Rosie, what a sight you look."

"Ooh, you're back! I'm so glad you're back, Larry." She was shining-eyed, her cheeks flushed pink from her running.

"Climb down, now, Rosie," he said. "We'll be back soon enough. But I want this stuff in Ben Sampson's before dark."

"Let me come with you," she asked. "I won't get in your way . . ."

He was already shaking his head. "No, Rose. Not this time. We've too much to do. And wherever you are there's sure to be a crowd of men underfoot."

A little laugh went up at this, but for once Rose did not enjoy the acknowledgement of the easy conquests she made. She climbed down slowly, disconsolate, ready to argue if Larry gave her a chance. But she got no chance. Larry waved his whip towards the second dray.

"Rose, this is Adam Langley. He's working with me."

Indifferently she turned, looking at the second dray. Adam raised his cap. "How do you do, Miss Rose," he said.

The change was swift. She was smiling again. Her hand went self-consciously to her hair to try to tidy it; she nervously brushed her skirts. And incredibly, Rose, who had seen ready admiration in so many men's faces, was blushing to see it now. And she seemed to have lost her tongue. She only nodded demurely, and smiled up at him.

And I stood there and saw in Adam's face the look that I had wanted to bring to it, but which had not come for me. It came for Rose, who had only to smile at him.

I couldn't stand it. It was too easy for Rose. Suddenly and rudely I pushed my way through the crowd towards Larry. I didn't care what anyone thought of me.

"Larry," I said. "I'll come with you. If you've a lot to do you'll need someone to make a tally sheet—to check things off. I've done it often before. I'm very quick . . . I don't make mistakes."

He looked doubtful, and seemed inclined to refuse, because Rose had turned away from Adam, and was staring at him with an outraged expression on her face. "Larry . . . !" she protested; it was a warning.

But he was never afraid of Rose's quick anger. He was a practical man; he needed help, and he did not fear that I would be a distraction as she would have been. He nodded briefly. "All right—but hurry!"

I pressed the advantage swiftly. "I'll ride with Pat," I said. "There's more room there." As I went to the other dray I heard the quick intake of Rose's breath, and I sensed the words that were being held back.

Already Pat's hand was down to help me. "Come on, Greeneyes," he said. I found myself squeezed in between him and Adam on the seat. I was glad he had called me Greeneyes, and I was thinking that perhaps Adam would notice that my eyes were green and that my hair was nearer red than brown. But Adam said nothing as the drays started to roll.

I was tired as I walked back from Sampson's. Beside me, Con walked quickly, as if the excitement of the afternoon still propelled him. Although the spring was now well advanced, the nights still grew cold among these hills; I wrapped the shawl closer about me. Darkness had fallen, and with it came a little slackening of activity. The windlasses and derricks no longer creaked, the cradles were silent. On Main Road the lights in the hotels and shops came on, but this was still the hour of comparative quiet before the night got into its pace. But when we moved away from the section, from the pubs and the laughing voices, the glow of the thousands of camp fires took over, dotting the gullies, and lighting our way up the Eureka. A chill wind stirred, and Con instinctively moved closer to me. Around us we could see the camp fires where the children were, fretful sometimes and nodding over their stew in the tin plates. The small sleepy voices seemed to reach out to us as we passed.

"It's pretty, isn't it, Con?" I said. "The little children in the firelight. Look . . . those poor sleepy things that ought to be in bed."

But Con wanted none of it. "I'm staying up—did you know that, Emmy? Dada said I could stay up for the party."

I smiled in the darkness, but answered him seriously. "And why not? What would the party be without you?"

He gave an embarrassed, pleased laugh, and quickened his step, so that I had to lengthen mine to keep up. Although I was tired I didn't mind. It was a good feeling, passing among all these camp fires, to know that there was one of my own to return to; it pleased me. But then I was pleased with myself, and better than that, I knew Larry was pleased. We had worked for three hours at a frantic pace, I standing at the door of Sampson's store and tallying each crate and box as it went by. The men moved quickly, but I had kept up with them, my script legible and orderly, the figures exact. There had been no mistakes, no fumbling. Tomorrow I was returning to Sampson's, at Larry's request, to make a duplicate list, and to help itemise and ticket each article before it went on sale. I had done well, and I and everyone else knew it.

When it was over Larry had gathered up his father and brothers, Adam Langley and Ben Sampson, and they had gone off to a pub. There had been a momentary awkwardness as they had wondered among themselves who would be the one to give up the warm male conviviality of the pub for the task of walking back to the camp-site with me. Then they had remembered Con, who couldn't go with them to the pub, and so the awkwardness had passed. I should have been satisfied with the praise I had won, but I wanted something more. I wanted one of them—no, not one of them—I wanted Adam Langley to walk back with me because he wanted to be with me. I had to remind myself that things like that did not happen gratuitously to me as they did to Rose; I had to work for them—harder even than I had worked that afternoon. I reminded myself, too, of what Elihu Pearson had said about the value of usefulness.

Con broke in upon my thoughts. "Emmy—if there's dancing, will you dance with me? I haven't learned how to yet, but it would be grand if you'd dance with me."

I wanted to hug him, and to cry at the same time. I was

wanting a man, and a child offered himself. And yet I loved the child too.

"I'd be honoured to, Con," I answered. "I'm . . . I'm not much at dancing myself."

"Um . . ." He gave a small grunt that could have been agreement or satisfaction, and then dropped back into silence. We were approaching the Maguire camp.

Larry had sent up a load of provisions which had been unpacked from the drays, and we were greeted by the smell of ham and spices—a welcome smell after the long processions of mutton stew and fried mutton chops. Kate called to us that the hot water was ready. For once Con was eager for washing himself. I took a half jug of it, and moved towards the tent. Inside the lamp was lit, and I could see Rose's shadow. It was only then that I hesitated, remembering what I had done that afternoon, remembering how she had wanted my place in the dray beside Adam. I had pushed past her then, and fought for that place—for all the good it had done me. My pleasure faded as I thought of Rose. I felt tired, and there was no compensating glow of achievement to lighten it. I lifted the tent flap and went in.

She knew I was there, of course. She had heard our voices, must have felt the stirring of air in the tent. But she didn't turn to me, or speak immediately. She was in her bodice and petticoat, and she held a brush in her hand, though she hadn't started yet to subdue the tangle of her hair.

"Where's Adam Langley?" she demanded. "When is he coming back?" She turned towards me as she spoke.

It was as direct as that. She didn't even ask about Larry.

"They're all in one of the hotels . . . a celebration," I said. "I think Adam means to go and look for his cousin, Tom Langley. Cousin—or whatever relationship they are."

"But he's coming back?" she pressed. "You're sure of that?"

I looked away from her, putting down the water jug near the bowl we washed in. "Yes," I said. "I'm sure." There was an edge in my voice, but she didn't hear it. Was it possible, I wondered, that she hadn't noticed how I had pushed forward to get on that dray with Adam? Had she really thought that Larry was responsible for my going down there? I had believed that Rose only saw what she permitted herself to see, but not that she was blind to this extent.

She came close to me, touching my arm and bending

forward to look into my face. "Emmy, do you think he likes me?"

"Who?" I knew well enough.

"Adam, of course."

I smiled at her as gently as I could. "Everyone like you, Rose. You know that. You have only to try the least little bit . . ."

"Oh, *that!*" She shrugged, impatient, suggesting that every other part of her life was all past her now, that the old rules could not measure this situation. "But I mean *Adam*. Does he like me?"

It seemed unbelievable. She had seen him hardly more than a minute, had not even exchanged a word of conversation with him, but already she was totally absorbed. It was not so unbelievable, for it had been the same with me. But Rose didn't know how it was with me. For her all that existed was herself and Adam. She saw no other woman as a threat or a challenge, therefore she could disregard me. It did not occur to her that I could also want what she wanted. She could ask me in complete innocence if Adam liked her, and not know the pain it caused me. There was something terrible and destructive about that kind of innocence.

"I suppose he likes you," I said. "Who could help it?" And I meant that.

She clasped the brush between her hand tightly; I had never seen Rose look really earnest before. "I'll *make* him like me, Emmy! He must! I'll have to make it happen!"

And then, as if that had been settled forever, she became brisk. Manœuvring quickly in that cramped space, she went back to her chest, which was open. The chaos of her possessions was greater than usual, betraying her indecision over what she would wear that evening. Out of the mess she picked one gown and held it towards me.

"Here—you'll still have some stitching to do, but it's almost finished. I've taken up the hem about two inches. You'll have to pull the waist in with this sash, but it'll do until you have time to take some tucks."

The gown was silk, almost of an emerald colour. It was not heavily trimmed; its elegance was just of itself—a beautiful thing.

"You mean . . . I'm to wear it tonight?" I sucked in my breath at the thought of it.

"You're too keep it!"

I shook my head. "It's your best! I couldn't take it."

"Never mind that! It will look well on you. It'll suit your colouring." She tossed it towards me, and I caught it. There wasn't any woman who wouldn't have reached out for a dress like that one.

"You'll have to hurry and finish the hem," she said. "As far as I've done it's a bit rough." She shrugged. "But no one will see it." I held up the hem and inspected the huge, uneven stitches that were Rose's concession to sewing, and then I saw the tiny, brownish smears of dried blood where she had pricked her finger. I touched the silken folds gently, and tried not to think that this was some sort of a consolation prize. And yet when I looked at her I could see no guile in her face; if this was meant to console me, then it was an unconscious gesture. I reminded myself that there was nothing Rose could do about the fact that she was beautiful, and that men came to her easily. She had no guilt about this, so therefore the dress had no meaning other than the simple one of a gift. That was what I told myself.

And meantime it lay in my arms, this beautiful thing—the greenest green to deepen my eyes and darken my hair.

"I . . . I don't know what to say . . . It's so beautiful."

She cut me short. "Oh, Emmy, hush! You don't have time to stand talking. They'll be here soon, and you've got to sew that hem, and help me do my hair before they come."

III

It was something to remember, that night Larry returned from the first trip to Melbourne. There was a sweetness and a gaiety about it that was never there afterwards. This was before the disruptive forces entered all our lives, and tried to drag us apart, to send us—some of us—to destruction of one kind or another.

Our laughter was gay, unconcerned, and the firelight flickered across faces that were full of confidence, full of vitality. It seemed that half the Eureka was there at times, for Kate's sense of hospitality couldn't bear to leave uninvited any one of the people who were drawn to the fringe of the circle, drawn either by the laughter, the voices, or the sound of Jimmy O'Rourke's fiddle. Dan was so proud of his sons; as the whisky took him he boasted, and no one minded the boasting. He was in awe of Larry. His eldest son had moved suddenly into the real leadership of the family, and no one questioned it. Kate was happy because so many people crowded about her fire, and there was ham and cider and whisky for as many as came. She was outlandishly handsome in plum-coloured satin that would have been flamboyant even in the Dublin tavern.

I looked across the fire many times and saw that Adam had lost his seriousness, and he joined in the laughter as if he had belonged with us for a long time. Beside him was his cousin, Tom Langley, whom he had discovered in the bar of the Palace, and who, to honour the occasion had dressed with a silk cravat and waistcoat, and the softest, most elegant pair of boots I had ever seen. They were not alike in feature, Adam and Tom. Too many marriages and new blood lines separated their relationship. Tom, brown haired and brown eyed, had a more conventional handsomeness than Adam. He was only twenty-one, and had the untried look of a boy. But his manners were gentle and gracious; his accent was one I knew from the clientele of the London shop—it had been acquired at a good English public school. He was what some of the diggers called " a swell." For all that he joined in our simple entertainment with an eagerness that was almost pathetic. I noticed that his eyes rarely left Rose for more than a few seconds. And Rose, having inspected Tom Langley and approving what she saw, set out to charm both him and Adam, and succeeded beyond belief. I think she meant only to charm Tom in order to show Adam the extent of her power, but Tom, once caught, was not easily wrenched away.

Then there was the moment when Con, leaning close to me as we sat together at the fire, whispered, " You're pretty, Emmy!" It might have been true. In the green silk, and flushed with excitement, it might almost have been true that I was pretty that night.

There was dancing, after a fashion, on that rough ground. Pat and I danced; we danced well together. You didn't have to be accomplished to dance around the pit-heads on the Eureka. All you needed was to be quick of foot, and I was that. But the couple to watch were Rose and Adam.

There was singing too, the nostalgic songs of exile that immigrants always sing, the ironic ballads that belonged to this new home, and then some songs that had their beginnings here on the Ballarat goldfields.

'We steered our course for Geelong town,
    then north-west for Ballarat,
Where some of us got mighty thin,
And some got sleek and fat.
Some tried their luck at Bendigo . . .'

And then Rose sang alone. She sang the old, beloved songs, the songs of love and rebellion that her audience, mostly Irish, listened to with homesick longing.

'The minstrel boy to the war has gone . . .'

I saw the tears stand out in the eyes of some of the men seated about the fire, and the furtive hands that brushed them away as they begged Rose for another song, and another. That was the night when the families on the Eureka forgave Rose for everything she had been, for the aloofness, the disdain, for not having noticed the existence of many of them before. Her face glowed with a tender beauty that for once had nothing of arrogance or pride in it. She held them rapt and spellbound, and they were ready to adore her. "*There is not in the wide world a valley so sweet . . .*"

That was the night when Tom Langley fell in love with Rose, and I think that Adam, also, began to love Rose that night.

Chapter Four

The Australian spring prepared to give way to summer. The wild flowers had bloomed and faded in the secret, subtle places of the bush where the canvas town had not yet touched and ripped open and torn apart. The scents of mimosa and boronia were sometimes on the wind not often, and only briefly, because the scent of man in the bush was very strong. The new red tips of the eucalypt leaves gave place to the old grey-green. The hills in the distance, though, were always blue. A film of dust began to settle over the town, and even the tree tops were touched with it ; when the dry winds blew they seemed shrunken and wilted. In the deep quiet of the untouched bush, far away from the town and yet aware of it, the passive, solemn kaolas chewed ceaselessly on the leaves of the eucalypts, and found them not so sweet or succulent as a month ago. The great kangaroos ate the spiky grasses on the hill slopes and sometimes they heard the sound of man, his voice, his gun, and the crash of the trees he felled. When they fled for the cover of the sheltering bush their immense hind legs threw up clouds of dust. People who had been in the country for the full twelve month cycle began to say knowingly that it would be a dry summer.

It grew hot and airless down in the pit shafts, and we still panned only enough gold to pay daily expenses. The Maguires were not patient people by nature, and the work was hard; the monotony began to tell. The day by day digging of their claim seemed a pale thing to Pat beside the movement and quick success of Larry's enterprise. He talked of pulling up and going to the Mount Alexander diggings. So far it was only talk.

The rhythm and monotony of our days was punctuated by Larry's comings and goings. Adam was always with him, there was a ready and good market in Ballarat for whatever they brought on those drays. The road between Melbourne and the diggings was bad enough, and the talk of bushrangers persistent enough to make the cartage prices high. They took sometimes a week, sometimes ten days on a round trip of more than a hundred and fifty miles. It depended on how much delay they encountered either here or in Melbourne.

Larry said, "If the gold lasts long enough here in Ballarat we'll be rich."

He also meant—if he and Adam could strain themselves to keep going day in and day out on the seat of the wagon, to work almost without sleep while they were assembling the goods in Melbourne—if they could do these things then they would be rich. So long as the gold lasted.

Some were beginning to doubt that it would. Spectacular strikes were rarer these days; the pits were getting deeper, and small groups of men were no longer able to work them. For some there was poverty on the diggings. And with it came a worsening resentment of the monthly licence fees, and the brutal, humiliating methods of the licence-hunting forays. The hated cry of "Joes! Joes!" rang through the gullies too often, and too often there was violence, and threats of violence. Men began to form themselves into groups to protest the injustice, to talk of sending delegations to the Governor, Sir Charles Hothman, in Melbourne. A few began to emerge as leaders. Pat went to every meeting, taking Sean with him. They began to be absent from the camp until late each evening.

". . . Looking for trouble," Kate said. "Always looking for trouble."

But at last it was trouble that one could speak about, could worry over aloud. I had my own kind of trouble, that was locked up inside me, which only Larry knew about. On the first trip back he had waited until he found me alone, early in the morning, as before, and he had given me a copy of a Melbourne newspaper, the *Argus* dated about two weeks before. Almost lost at the bottom of one of the pages was a small paragraph. The words seemed to hit me. " . . . . *The Digger's Arms . . . the body of the owner, William Gribbon. Police are making enquiries . . .*"

I looked at him mutely, waiting for what he would say. He stretched out his hand and took the paper from me. Then I watched him as he fed it into the newly-lighted fire.

" I'm not going to ask you, Emmy," was all he said.

I shook my head. " It isn't what it seems . . ."

He nodded. " I believe you," he said. And he asked me nothing more. He had been back in Ballarat about three days then, and he knew more of me than when we had sat at this fire that other morning and made our bargain. In the time that had passed since that day my position had changed irrevocably. I was part of them now ; I knew it, and so did he. I had become someone to protect, someone with whom to unite against the world. It was small wonder that I was ready to do anything for any one of the Maguires.

We could hear Kate's voice as she talked to Dan while she dressed. About us the Eureka was coming to life. He said to me in a low voice, " They're looking in Melbourne, not Ballarat. Remember that, and don't worry."

And he never again mentioned The Digger's Arms to me. But occasionally, when there was leisure at night to sit about the fire, I found his eyes on me, and they questioned a little, and wondered. But he never spoke the words.

I worked for a few hours each day in Ben Sampson's shop on Main Road, even after Larry and Adam had gone back to Melbourne. I ticketed the goods, and kept the books, and did some of the selling. And I learned to like Ben Sampson, a wiry-haired, grey-moustached man from Illinois " and every place West of there " as he put it ; that was when I learned that his occasional teasing wasn't reserved for me alone, but for anyone else whom he liked. Ben Sampson was a drinker, an amiable one, and my presence in the shop left him hours free in the day for the Palace.

" Lord love her," he said, when Larry protested my being left alone, " she's a better head for store-keeping than I'll ever have. Leave her be."

I was glad to have it that way, and glad to have the money Ben Sampson paid me to take back to Kate. It wasn't much, my wage, but it made a sweet difference now to each day I woke to. The desire for independence had begun too long ago, with Elihu Pearson, for me to be able to break from it. I ran the shop much as I wanted, also, and ordered what I thought would sell. I started to take special orders for luxuries that some man fancied he wanted, or even simple things that no man had thought a woman would need. People came to me for their peculiar wants; I wrote down the details painstakingly, and either Larry or Adam just as painstakingly searched out the item in Melbourne. It cost time to do this—more than the value of the goods, but Ben Sampson's shop on Main Road started to get the reputation of the place to go when you needed service.

Rose tried helping me for a day, even though she knew Ben Sampson didn't want her there. She grew bored with the slowness of the women who came to spend a few precious shillings; the inarticulate men didn't come near her at all for their purchases. I discovered that there are a few times when it does no good to be beautiful. She muddled the change, and it took me two days to get the stock tidy again. She didn't wait for Ben to ask her not to come back.

"How can you bear it?" she said to me. "All these women fingering half the things on the shelves, and then buying a pound of tea? And the men—stupid big lugs standing there gaping."

I shrugged. "What else do they have for pleasure? Let them come here to look, and when they have money they'll come to buy."

When I could forget about the Melbourne *Argus* and Will Gribbon, they were good hours I spent in Ben Sampson's store.

So I worked the full feasure of the hours of those days, and I liked it. But there were other things in my life beside work —the work was the easier part of it. It is a hard thing to love a man who doesn't seem to see you, or when he sees you, who treats you as a good and trusted friend, but not a lover. This was how it was with Adam and myself. I couldn't help loving him. It is not something that can be stopped once it is begun—not even if you are sensible and prudent, as I told myself I must be. I was finding now, that I was in love for the first time, that there wasn't much sense to it at all. Love is not a sensible thing.

I think he might have noticed me if Rose had not been there —or if she herself had not been in love with him. Rose could be cruel in her indifference to a man she did not care for, but Rose in love was a different creature. All her naïve plans about the kind of man she would marry were swept aside, as they were bound to have been if once she let herself love.

69

Now she concentrated her formidable energy on making Adam notice her, and in noticing her, to see no one else. She had no doubt that he would love her, if not now, then very soon. And why should she doubt? Never before had she failed to gain anything she set her heart on, and her heart was surely set on Adam.

She lived from one visit to the next, as I did—only Rose did not notice that. She was wholly absorbed in her own love; this left her no capacity to see anyone else's. Perhaps it was as well. The pain that came later for us all would have begun that much sooner if she had.

This does not mean that I did not fight for Adam with what weapons I had. But they seemed of small value beside Rose's. I worked hard—I showed off my few skills, but I knew that a man would come around to noticing such things only when he had had his fill of simply looking at what Rose could offer. The earnest and unremarkable virtues don't count much in a situation like this. And although this time in Ballarat with the Maguires had seemed to improve my looks—a better colour to my cheeks, more flesh on my frame—still the face that stared back at me from the little mirror in our tent was not needed to draw attention away from Rose

Tom Langley, Adam's cousin, became part of our lives in these weeks too. He was there because of Rose. We did not even have to ask each other if he was in love with her. It was there quite plain to see. He would come to the camp each night always with a gift of some kind—not for Rose, but for all of us. It was sad to see him come this way, the picture of a man who thought he had to buy our regard, who was so unsure of himself that he had to shelter behind the whisky he brought and the little delicacies from the stores on Main Road —a weak and bewildered man reaching out for something he wanted badly. He could see nothing but Rose; he wanted nothing else.

He was dressed, not in the way we had first seen him, but in the moleskin trousers and flannel shirt of the digger. There were even, I noticed, a few fresh blisters on his hands to prove that sometimes he tried to take a pick and get his money like everyone else here. But it was only a game with him. We all knew that although he had quarrelled with his father and this was the reason for his presence on the goldfields, he still had the money that came from his father each month. It was a small show of independence that convinced no one.

We knew his story by now. We had found out that you didn't have a name like Langley in this colony without anyone who had been here longer than a few months being able to supply most of the details of your life. In bits and pieces we heard it.

All of the colony knew the Langley fortune. " Sheep—he came here with the first merinos in Victoria. Landed them at Hope Bay, and spread out from there. He was a squatter— took a couple of hundred thousand acres and fought the Colonial Secretary for ten years in London to keep them. Got them in the end for a couple of shillings an acre, and a lot of people think he stole more than he ever paid for. He exports more wool than anyone in the country."

And there were those who thought more of the money made in trade. " He was right at the beginning of Melbourne when Hoddle surveyed the first streets and held the first land sale. They say he owns a couple of blocks of Elizabeth and Collins Streets. That's when land was going for five pounds a lot . . . He's got a big shop there, and warehouses. You must have seen the Langley Stores when you came through."

We didn't remember having noticed the Langley Stores, but we didn't interrupt. " What kind of a man is Tom Langley's father?"

Our informer, who could be any one of six anxious to relay gossip about Tom, would shrug. " Sure how would I know? He doesn't mix with the likes o' me." Then there would be a reflective draw on a pipe, and the information would come just the same.

" A gentleman farmer, they say he was, back in England. Came out here with thirty of his own farm hands. He tried to get land in Tasmania, but the good stuff was all taken, so he came over here to these shores before the Government would let anyone settle. He claims he was the first to farm in this colony. He sent his son and his daughter back to England to be schooled. Weren't anything here good enough for them. The daughter married the son of some titled man. She was only married a year, they say, and came running back to her father. Neither of them is a match for the old man. He tells them what to do and they do it. This business of Tom's, now —'twon't last. He's only here because there was some trouble over a girl they had workin' in the father's house. They say Tom wanted to marry her, and the old man sent her away . . . back to England, even. He gets what he wants."

" He hasn't got Tom."

" He will. He's sendin' money, isn't he? It's hard to do without that stuff once you've been used to it."

I puzzled over this. "But why—why does he want him back when they've quarrelled?"

"Blood's thicker than water. He's getting on, old Langley. He married late. There were only two children, and now the girl is finished. She stays close to her papa, and they say she'll never go back to that husband of hers. There's no grandchildren . . . Tom's his heir. A man worries about his heirs when he's got as much to leave as old Langley has."

So it was really John Langley's story we learned, not his son's. Tom stood in his father's shadow and his bid to escape it seemed foolish when we looked at the hands that never hardened on the pick, when we watched the pitiful pretence of doing a day's work.

One other piece of information we had about John Langley. "He brought thoroughbred horses with him from England. His agent still buys them for him. He has the best horses in the colony. Sure every bit of decent horseflesh you lay eyes on here is bound to be bred from a Langley sire."

And that was where Tom belonged, in the world of thoroughbred horses and polite society. He was out of place at our fire, and yet from the way he came to it, his eagerness to be there—and it was not only for Rose's sake—none of us would have had the heart to leave him unwelcome. He fed on the ordinary trivialities of family gossip like a hungry man, as if he had never heard this kind of talk before. The Maguires were not the people to turn him away.

I think they often wanted to. Sometimes when he came to us the smell of whisky was very strong about him. There is a difference between the man who drinks whisky at the end of a long day of hard work, and the one who spends his afternoons in the Palace. Tom might have matched the Maguires in height and the breadth of his shoulders, but he was not their equal in other things. We felt sorry for him, if you could feel sorry for a rich man's son, and we let him stay.

In between Adam's visits Rose encouraged Tom. I don't believe she did it with deliberate heartlessness. She was naïve, and thoughtless; she had forever to have an audience, and Tom with his soft manners and pleasant voice, was the kind of audience she sought. Every evening she would dress up for him, and every evening he came. He was a diversion in the long hot days of waiting for Adam—and he could be used as a means of making Adam jealous. She never thought of what she was doing to Tom himself by this play. She played her foolish woman's game with complete disregard of the consequences.

Of Adam himself it was impossible to know. He kept his own council. He was silent most of the time he was with us, taciturn, almost grim. He had a habit of whittling small pieces of wood, and he would sit by the fire at the time he was with us, and the pile of shavings would grow at his feet. He was very clever with his hands; he fashioned small wooden animals for Con, and a long chain with wooden links. He made a doll for Mary Healy's girl, Helen, and passed it on to me to sew the tiny dress and bonnet. He made some stools for Kate, and on one trip from Melbourne he brought her a table he had been working on in his Melbourne lodgings. But he brought no gifts for Rose.

She hated this habit of whittling. His eyes would be fastened on the wood in his hands for an hour at a time, and he took little part in the conversation. He almost never spoke to Rose, and I thought he did not trust himself. It seemed to me that Adam was like a man tempted by strong drink. Only his eyes betrayed the temptation. Sometimes, when Rose would move about the fire helping Kate, when she was absorbed in something else, he would glance up quickly at her. I saw then something close to desperation in his eyes. I saw all these things because my own gaze hardly ever left him.

I asked him once about the whittling, about the small pieces of furniture he made. " My grandfather was a shipwright," he said. " One of Nantucket's best. He could do anything with a piece of wood. He taught me what I know."

" Have they all been in . . . ships—your family?" I said. This kind of talk was awkward to me, the world of ships was not my place.

He looked up from the little carving he was working on. His face suddenly blazed with pride, though I did not at first understand why. " My mother's father was Farrell Bedlow. He captained the *Julia Jason*—the first one. That ship brought over a million dollars worth of oil back to Nantucket in her time. It made her owners rich."

It was one of the few emotions he permitted to show, this nostalgia for home, for things of the sea. He could not help himself in this. This was why, even after he had completed a number of trips with Larry, when the dust of the road was well worn into his clothes and his body was fashioned to the seat of that dray as if it had been born there, he was still distinguishable from the mass—he still didn't quite belong.

" My father was a whaling captain before I was born," he said. " He was lost rounding the Horn. Lost overboard . . . the ship got back to Nantucket safely."

"And you, Adam . . . ?" I said rashly. "What was your ship?"

He looked at me coldly. "She was the *Julia Jason II*. I wrecked her in the Bass Strait. I was her captain."

I drew back, suddenly chilled by the tone, by the harshness of his face, and the quick glimpse of suffering. He might almost have hated me in that moment.

No one of us had known so much about Adam before. It could have been that Larry also knew this, but Larry was good at keeping information to himself. We had merely followed the unwritten law of this country that a man's past was his own affair. Now I had transgressed this law, and I knew more than perhaps I had wanted to know. A man such as Adam does not forgive you for knowing what kind of hell it is he suffers.

I sat silently beside him, too shamed to move ; he resumed his whittling. Presently Rose came to sit on his other side, and the flow of her easy talk washed over both of us. She didn't seem to know Adam's mood, or at least she paid no attention to it. It was not for Rose to be frozen into silence. She talked on, and presently a smile came to Adam's lips, and quickly, even laughter. Rose could seem so innocent, and yet she was so skilful.

Even so, with all her success, Rose had her hours of doubt. They came generally when Larry and Adam had been away from Ballarat for more than a week, and in his absense Rose had fallen to worrying and questioning—or when she was bored by her too-easy conquest of Tom Langley. I knew the preening before the mirror, the flirtatious hours with Tom that only made her more anxious for Adam's return. I knew her disturbed sleep, and the restless dreams in which she called Adam's name aloud. Everyday she would ask me if I didn't think this as the day Adam would come back. I received her confidences and tried to answer her questions.

"Do you think he likes my hair this way, or pulled up higher . . . ? Do you think he will bring me a present when he comes next time? It would mean something if he brought me a present because he's so proper about things like that? Do you think, Emmy . . . Emmy, do you suppose . . . ?"

And then finally, when the coquetry was dropped in the extreme of her anxiety, she would cry, "Emmy, I love him! What if he doesn't love me? . . . or won't let himself?" She would lie on her pallet, her body shaken with sobbing and fear.

And I could not resist trying to comfort her, because I
74

loved her also. My arm about her shoulder, and holding her like a child I would say,

"It will be all right, love. You'll see. Everything will be all right."

It is not too difficult to be generous with the man you love when you think you have no hope of him yourself.

But there were times when Adam drew a little closer to me —such as the time he and Larry brought back the shawl from Melbourne. I was alone at the camp that day when they returned. I was washing clothes—one of Pat's broad-brimmed hats on my untidy hair, and my hands and arms reddened to the elbows in the hard lye soap. They came walking quietly through the tents each carrying a canvas sack.

"They're all down at the creek," I said. "I'll send Tom O'Brien down to fetch them . . ."

Larry slumped wearily on to one of the logs, waving his hand to dismiss the suggestion. "No, Emmy—no need. Just get us a cup of tea, like a good girl."

Larry no longer took the time to drive the wagons in off the road when he came back. They took them straight down to Sampson's store. The return, like everything else, had become routine. We always kept water just on the boil, and so I made tea at once, conscious of their weariness.

"Was it a good trip?" I said.

Some animation returned to Larry's face. "Great! There was a ship just in from Calcutta—and one from Liverpool. Langley let us have good pickings. These steam ships are making the voyage much faster now . . ." He drew on the hot, strong tea. "That's good, Emmy! Sometimes the dust gets so thick I think I'll choke." He nodded at me approvingly. "I have a message from John Langley for you, Emmy.'

"For me . . .?"

"Yes . . . He complimented me on my bookkeeper, and told me that if he came to Melbourne and needed a position he was to apply at the Langley Stores."

I looked from him to Adam to see if they were joking, but Adam's smile was reassuring.

"And so," Larry continued, "Adam thought we should try to bribe our bookkeeper to stay here with us—pass me the bag, Adam." He laid down the pannikin and started fumbling in one of the canvas bags. He drew out a small bundle carefully wrapped in calico. He handed it to me, and slowly I unfolded the shawl. It was cashmere, embroidered, of silken texture. I sucked in a little breath of delight as I handled it.

"For me? . . . really for me?"

"I wish there were ten more for you, Emmy. You've earned them. Do you like it? Adam did the choosing."

I looked at Adam unbelievingly. It was hard to think of Adam deliberating the choice of something as feminine as this. I told myself again that I did not really know Adam. None of us did. Surprisingly, now, he put out his hand to touch it, as if he also drew pleasure from it.

"It's not good enough for you, Emmy. As Larry said— you've earned ten of them."

Then, as he fingered the shawl, I saw the bandage that roughly wrapped his right hand; it was so begrimed with sweat and dust that it was almost the colour of his sunburned skin.

"Adam—what's this? What happened?"

"A scratch from a harness buckle. It's nothing."

I laid the shawl down on its calico wrapping again. "I'll give you a clean dressing."

Over his protests I bathed and dressed the cut. I applied solution from one of Kate's bottles, and he winced as it bit in. There was a sense of power for me in tending that wound, even in hurting him as I did. I was happy to touch him; I knelt on the ground while I worked, and I took longer than I needed to wind the bandage about his hand.

"Thank you, Emmy." He spoke the words gently, almost submissively. I lifted my eyes to his to revel for a moment longer in this possession of him, when I felt my chin suddenly grasped and tilted sideways. It was Larry who did this.

"You're a good girl, Emma Brown," he said. And he tapped me lightly, affectionately, on the cheek. I flushed with pleasure at his words, and my eyes went immediately back to Adam. He was looking at me, smiling and nodding, an expression on his face that was almost tenderness, was also, in a strange way, almost one of recognition, as if he were searching in his memory for the origin of some resemblance that I bore to someone or something. For an incredible second I thought that he might reach out and touch me as Larry had done. It was one of those rare moments when I not only felt that I was pretty—it actually happened. I know it did.

Rose's voice broke the quiet, and broke that moment.

"Adam! . . . Adam! It's Adam—and Larry!"

I saw the expression change. He looked past me, beyond me, to Rose. For a second that look was one of open, undisguised longing. I decided then, without a doubt, that Adam loved Rose.

I got to my feet and started to fold the shawl back into its calico. My visitation of prettiness was gone, vanished. I felt sour, and hopeless.

II

Time worked on all of us there on the Eureka. We reacted to each other and to the situations about us; the pleasures and irritations of our daily lives both became enlarged. We chafed against the lack of privacy, but yet none of us would have wanted to be entirely alone. The days were hot; the sun plagued us, and the swarming flies. But the nights were of great, healing beauty, balmy, with stars of incredible brilliance in that dark blue sky. We listened to the squalling of children about us, and to the complaints of the low yield of gold in that hard quartz we dug. Under these pressures Dan remained as kindly as ever, but Kate had sometimes to force her cheerfulness, and we all knew it. Rose was pleasant and soft-tempered when Adam was in the camp; when he was away she was moody and snappish, and given to taking out her irritation on Tom Langley. Pat was restless, full of fury about the methods of police administration of Ballarat, and about the licence fee. His feelings infected Sean strongly, as we knew they would, and the two of them were one. It seemed at the time that Larry was the fortunate one; he worked as hard as any of us, or harder, but at least he was not subjected to the killing monotony. Pat envied him his place on the driver's seat of the dray. We seemed to be drifting a long way, in time and in feeling, from that night when Larry first returned from Melbourne.

And I myself?—I ceased dreaming of Will Gribbon so frequently, and to wait for the police to come. And I had to stand by and watch both Adam and Tom Langley become more deeply enmeshed in Rose's charm.

The trouble that was in Pat, the raging against authority and restraint—and the trouble that was growing between himself and Larry—came into the open. That was the night the miners burned Bentley's pub.

A mob had gathered about the pub, Pat and Sean among them, to protest the freeing of Bentley from a charge of murder. He was said to have murdered a miner who had tried to demand service at his hotel, and he had been shielded from justice because of his friendship with the police. The magistrate had heard the case and refused to send Bentley before a jury. The miners now met in furious protest outside the pub. No one was absolutely sure who threw the stone which smashed the window and overturned the lamp. But very soon from the camp we could hear the roar of the flames and the crash of more glass.

Larry sprang to his feet, signalling Adam. "Come on!" he said. Adam followed him at once. So did Dan and Tom Langley, who as usual was with us. So did we all—Kate and Rose and myself. And Con too; he ran beside me.

The building was flaming when we reached it, and the mob howling for Bentley. The men pushed forward, dangerously close to the burning timbers. It was hard to know that these were our peaceful, kindly neighbours, the men who toiled so patiently and endlessly for the gold. For a moment there seemed to be a singing in the blood, a shout of triumph at this defiance hurled at authority.

Inevitably there came the cries. "Bentley—there's Bentley at the back! Get him!"

Pat and Sean were in the midst of the mob that streamed around towards the back of the pub, down the lane between it and a bowling alley. Larry, Adam and Dan pushed in after them. We lost sight of them. The glare of the fire fell on the wide hats and flannel shirts, and everyone looked alike to us. "God in Heaven!" Kate cried.

And then I felt Con leave my side, slip away from me to squirm and thrust his way in among those packed bodies. He was half a man, bent on proving he was more than that. He was a Maguire, and where his brothers had gone, he would go. But to me he was still a child, no matter what I said about him being a man, and I was afraid for him. I began to push my way in too.

I was the wrong height for that crowd. I seemed to be just on the level where the raised elbows, struggling to push, could reach my face and head. The blows almost stunned me. Most men were never aware that they struck a woman, and in any case they would have said I had no business to be there. They were right. I began to be afraid that I would fall and go under those heavy boots. Con had fought his way right to the centre of the mob, where he had seen Larry go. He was still there when I reached him, buffeted and pushed around helplessly. I put my arms about his, but together we hadn't enough power to pull back.

And so we were there, and witnessed the moment when Larry and Adam reached Pat. They were all in the circle that

78

hemmed Bentley, who had escaped the fire and mounted a trooper's horse. The animal was crazed with fright, and four men hauled on its bridle to hold it down; others pulled at Bentley himself to try and drag him from the saddle. He held on, and with one free hand he beat savagely at the heads below him with a trooper's stick. It was Pat who clung to one booted leg, and took the kicks in the face. He was bleeding from a cut on the mouth, and a scalp wound.

Larry tugged at him. "Pat! Get out of this! Are you mad!"

"Hang him!" Pat howled drunkenly. Then he caught another blow from Bentley's stick which seemed to stun him. His eyes glazed. He struggled to keep upright. At that moment Larry heaved back against the crowd to get enough room to swing. He let go a punch which landed straight on Pat's chin. Slowly, unwillingly, Pat gave up his hold on Bentley's leg as he began to sag. Larry caught him, at the same time receiving a kick from Bentley on the side of the head. Between them Larry and Adam made a kind of cradle for Pat, and Dan fought a way clear for them through the crowd. I pushed Con in behind them, and we followed closely. We reached the edge of the mob so dazed that we hardly were aware that Bentley's truncheon, and the thrashing legs of the horse, had finally shaken off the clawing hands, and that he was free.

Pat came back to consciousness at the Maguire camp. He seemed sober. His eyes were alert enough as he gingerly felt his cut lips, and the broken scalp. Kate was sniffing back her tears. She was bathing his forehead and upbraiding him at the same time.

"Trouble and ruin you'll bring on us yet . . ."

He cut her short roughly. He struggled to a sitting position and looked at Larry.

"What did you do it for?" he demanded.

Larry shrugged. He had calmed down; his anger was cold now. "Do I stand by and see you do murder? Do I let you hang yourself? God knows you're a fool, but I wouldn't willingly let even a fool hang."

A sob of rage rose in Pat's throat. "Who do you think you are, Larry? Are you God?"

"Shut up! You're drunk!"

"Yes—I'm drunk! But I don't set myself up to tell other men when they should get drunk. What gives you the right . . . ?"

"I've got the right to keep you out of the hands of the police. If we hadn't dragged you out of that mess they'd have killed you, or you'd be locked up at The Camp with the rest of your no-good friends the police took."

Pat exploded. "God damn you! I'll go to hell if I please, and in good company!"

"No more of that!" his father shouted.

Pat ignored him. "You make me sick, Larry. You come here like some bloody little English shopkeeper, and look down on us because our hands are dirty getting this muck out of the ground—and you only soil yours to handle the money. What do you know about living in this God-forsaken hole?—or care? You sit there like an old maid and tell me when I'll drink, and who'll be my friends . . ."

He sucked in a long, exhausted breath, waving his hand shakily at Larry. "Well, I'll tell you, Larry—I'll tell you this! My trouble is my own. Stay away from me, Larry! Stay out of my affairs!"

Chapter Five

Burning Bentley's pub was only one expression of the growing unrest in Ballarat—a wild and irresponsible expression that had little resemblance to the more moderate men who would have moved by other means to end the injustice of the licence fees, the arbitrary arrests and the corruption in the police force. Half a dozen different groups began to form, some urging forceful resistance to collecting the licence money, others wanting to move by gradual and legal means—by delegations to Governor Sir Charles Hotham, by appeals to the various members of the Legislative Council who might be sympathetic. This way was too slow, too prudent for some in Ballarat. They wanted to see action, and they wanted it soon. They wanted to see Bentley tried and condemned for the murder he had committed, and they wanted the freedom of the men arrested for the firing of Bentley's hotel. It was part and parcel of their perpetual rage against authority. Their voices were always the loudest, drowning out the tones of moderation from their neighbours. Pat's voice was among them. Every night he and Sean would leave the camp and head for the pubs on Main Road. We did not know where they got the money to drink ; we did not know much about Pat's thoughts or doings since the night when he and Larry had quarrelled.

Larry and Adam continued their trips, and the nights they spent in camp on the Eureka were full of tension. We waited and looked for some kind of explosion again between Larry and Pat, something that would break the heavily weighted atmosphere. We sensed that something would happen, and that there would be a change in the routine we had come to know, that one of the group would break away. But in the end the change came from a direction we had not expected.

It happened only a few weeks after Bentley's pub was burned. I remember we were the usual group about the fire—Kate and Dan, Rose, Con, and Tom Langley. Larry was down at Sampson's checking over last-minute additions to the list, for they were to leave again for Melbourne early in the morning. Pat and Sean were somewhere down on Main Road. They would not return until after we were all in bed, waking us, perhaps, because when they were drunk they were often noisy. Sometimes I wondered if the noise were not deliberate; it always seemed loudest when Larry was in the camp.

Adam and I had the stools drawn up to a packing case. By the light of a candle we were copying out lists of goods bought in Melbourne last trip, and entering them and the costs in my books. At the same time I was trying to teach Adam a little about the system I used to enter them. His heart was not in it; he wrote legibly and well, but he scowled constantly at the lists.

"Eighty yards of muslin . . ." he muttered. It did not take much perception to know that he hated the muslin, and every other item. He laboured over them and only will-power kept him on that stool.

I shook my head, and pointed to the page. "No, not there! Over here is where you put it."

He sighed. "I wish I could consign the muslin and the frying-pans and the good value moleskin trousers to the bottom of the sea."

From the other side of the fire Tom spoke. "Surely," he said, "the great game of commerce hasn't begun to pall yet, Adam?" It was said mockingly. Tom was always ill at ease whenever Adam was present. There was a resentment there, which Tom couldn't completely hide, over Adam's association with his father. He needled Adam constantly, and it irritated him when the other wouldn't respond. They were civil to each other, and that about marked the limit of their contact. Tom never mentioned John Langley's name in Adam's presence, nor did Adam ever speak it either. I suppose they tolerated each other but that was all. I think Tom envied Adam's place beside this fire because it was earned; he was jealous of the regard in which we held him. And I think, after weeks of being at Rose's side and studying her moods, that at last he was beginning to understand the reason for the change in her when Adam appeared. Only a fool could not have seen this long ago; but Tom was a fool, and blind, where Rose was concerned.

That night I think he had been drinking heavily before he came to us. He was talkative, quarrelsome, trying to tease Rose, saying anything that came into his head to draw her attention, and seeing it, as he must have done, return again and again to Adam—to Adam who only continued to write in those books and who took little notice of Rose. For once Tom was reckless enough, and hurt enough, to risk Rose's anger.

"Well—what do you say, Cousin Adam?" He only called him cousin when he wanted to stress the difference between them. "Where are your dreams of being a captain of commerce?"

Adam's head jerked up. "The only dreams I have are of ships. I don't mind frying-pans and muslin just so long as they stay in the hold of a ship."

Tom smiled, his glance flickering over towards Rose. "Ah —but I see you have the makings of an excellent clerk . . . under Miss Emma's tutelage."

Rose broke in peevishly. "Oh, Tom, do let them alone! You've done nothing but interrupt all evening, and they'll never be finished with those old books . . ."

"Then sing for me, Rose," Tom replied. "I promise I'll behave if you'll just be nice to me and sing."

"I don't feel like singing." An impatient frown knit her forehead. As always she was irritated by this too-easy conquest of Tom so long as Adam remained uncommitted to her. At times she tried to hide it but Rose wasn't used to restraining her feelings.

"You won't sing . . . then let me sing to you. Let me woo you with a song."

"Tom, you're a fool," she snapped. Be quiet!"

He ignored her command; he wanted only one thing— to make sure she did not forget he was there.

"*Greensleeves is my delight . . . greensleeves is all my joy . . .*" he sang. He had a pleasant, true voice; it would have been good to listen to if he had not been so taut with pain and humiliation.

"Would you be my Greensleeves, Rose?" he said. "Shall

I buy you a gown with green sleeves, and then you'll be my Lady Greensleeves?"

Kate jerked back into wakefulness from her doze. "What's that about a gown?"

"Nothing," Rose said. "Tom talks a lot of foolishness."

"I wouldn't talk foolishness if you'd sing, Rose. You could keep me quiet that way."

"Yes, Rosie darlin' . . . give us a song now," Dan urged. He came to life suddenly, knocking out his cold pipe and reaching for the tobacco.

She shrugged. "Well . . ."

Tom slapped his hand on his thigh. "That's it, lovely Rose. Let us have a song . . ."

She looked at Adam as she sang. For a moment his pen was poised motionless. But at last he bent over the books again, casting away the song she offered.

> "I know where I'm going,
> I know who goes with me,
> I know who I love,
> But the dear knows who I'll marry."

It was a hard moment for me, to see this happen before my eyes. Both these men wanting Rose, and the one who could have her was denying himself. I noticed the fingers that gripped the pen were rigid. He did not write. I don't think he saw the words on the page before him. It was a torture for all of us to listen to the verses.

> "Feather beds are soft,
> Painted rooms are bonny,
> But I'd leave them all,
> To go with my love Johnny . . ."

Abruptly Tom broke into the song. His face was flushed darkly.

"Would you ' leave them all ' Rose? Would you truly leave all those good things to go with a ship-wrecker? With this clerk here?—this shopkeeper?"

Adam sprang to his feet. "You shut your mouth!"

"Why should I? Are you afraid to have Rose know the truth about you? Will you be less of a hero if she knows that you wrecked your ship in the Strait—that you lost it through stupidity, and the only reason you sit here and add up your figures is because no owner will trust you with a vessel again? Your name would be a laughing stock in Melbourne if it weren't for the men you took down with you, the men that were lost on the *Julia Jason*. Does that tarnish the gilt somewhat? That sea-cap doesn't fit any longer, Cousin Adam . . ."

We heard him in silence, and Adam did also. His eyes were very hard as he looked across at Tom; there was the kind of coldness in them, the tightness that tries to shut out agony. It was a casting away of thought, so that the thought cannot hurt. The flesh on his face seemed pinched; I noticed the hollows that were suddenly at his temples. He rose to his feet. His whole body looked as if it were tensed against the assault of pain.

"You've no business to talk about what you don't know . . . you don't know the truth of this."

"I know what I see," Tom replied. He too had risen. "I know a fool and a cheat when I see one."

"Who are you calling a cheat? I'll make you take back those words if I have to kill you . . ." Adam took a step towards Tom, but he checked when Dan suddenly sprang to his feet and stepped between them.

"That'll do now! I'll have no fighting here! You, Tom, mind your tongue . . ."

Tom ignored him, talking on in a tone that rose in pitch with his fury and excitement.

"Well, aren't you a cheat? Didn't you worm your way into my father's graces? Aren't you riding his wagons, and taking his money? And aren't you telling yourself that it's a fine thing that I'm out of the way because it leaves the field free and clear for you. Well, let me tell you I'm not out of the way. Not with my father—not with Rose, either. Any day I want I'll have them both . . ." he snapped his fingers ". . . like that!"

"Shut your mouth!" Dan ordered.

"I'm telling you," Tom went on, "that blood counts with my father. No one will be his heir except his own blood. It doesn't matter how much cheating and sneaking you do you won't have what's mine. Nothing . . . do you hear. Nothing!"

Adam fumbled on the books to find his cap; he clamped it on his head firmly. Then he turned to Tom again.

"And I say that you're a liar."

He brushed past Dan, toppling a stool as he went. All of us watched him go from the camp, out of the circle of our firelight, and then into the circle of the next fire, and then beyond that down the Eureka until we finally lost him in the darkness.

84

Rose let out a wail of despair. She wheeled upon Tom, her face passionate with rage. " *You* did this! "

And standing there staring at him she began to weep, noisily, hysterically.

II

I lay awake and I listened for him. Beside me Rose had tossed, restlessly seeking sleep, for a while; now her breathing was deep and even. I heard Pat and Sean come back, and Larry. It seemed to be very late before Adam came. I told myself I could go to sleep now.

Then the whisper reached me. " Emmy—Emmy! " I was up immediately, but remembering to move carefully so as not to disturb Rose. He was crouched on the ground close to the tent flap.

" Adam! What is it? " It was impossible to see his face. The fire had died to a few embers.

" Can you help me, Emmy? I've hurt my hand."

I reached back for my shawl. " I'm coming . . ."

I asked no questions until I had led him to the fire, and lit a candle, placing it down on the ground near the packing case so that the light would not strike the tents. Then I knelt beside him and he held out his hand.

" It's burned! " I said. I looked up, trying to read his face. " How did this happen . . .? " For answer he gave me only a shrug. " I'll get something to put on it." I took the candle over to the box where Kate kept her stock of medicines. It was supposed to be locked, but Kate never remembered to lock it. Then I came back to him and started to clean the wound. There were ashes and cinders in it—a bad burn across the back of his hand. As I wrapped the bandages about it I grew annoyed with him; I wanted no more of his silence.

" How did it happen? " I demanded in a fierce whisper.

" A fight," he said. " I was knocked down and I rolled back and put my hand in the fire . The other man was on top of me . . ."

" Tom? "

" Yes . . . Tom."

"Did you have to fight? "

" Yes—you know I did. I knocked him out in the end."

I wanted to say what was unhappily in my heart—" Did you have to fight over Rose," but I didn't say that. I went on with the wrapping quite calmly. " Does it make you feel better to have fought?"

" No," he admitted miserably. " It changes nothing."

" It never does." I went on wrapping the bandage carefully, knowing how even the lightest touch must hurt him. " It's a pity . . ." I said. " Just when that cut had begun to heal so well. You must see a doctor in the morning. He'll dress it again, and see that it's cleaned properly . . ."

" In the morning I'm leaving."

" Yes, I know . . . but you must see someone before you go. Don't wait until you get to Melbourne."

" I mean I'm leaving for good. I'm not coming back to Ballarat."

I sat back on my heels. The realization of it struck me at once ; I think I had always been afraid to hear these words, and a foreboding of them had heightened the joy each time Adam had returned with Larry. Now they had come at last ; they were spoken. For a moment my private world was chaos. I suppose it showed on my face.

" Emmy, don't look that way. What else is there for me? Could I stay after what Tom has said?"

" Why should you care what he said? Do you take notice of someone like Tom?—who's jealous of you? It's cowardly to run away from what Tom says. A woman would stay . . ."

" Women are stronger in these things," he said. " I've known that for a long time. A man has to fight—or run."

" And you think by doing both you're more of a man?" I said harshly. " You fail yourself to let Tom drive you out." Then I got to my feet. " Wait here!"

When I came back I handed him a mug half-full of whisky. " It won't ease the pain, but it'll help you forget it a little." I brought a stool to sit near him. " And we can be thankful Dan didn't hear me and bring out the gun."

" You're good, Emmy," he said, and smiled.

" I'm tired of hearing that. No woman wants to be only good—we all want to be something else as well." Did he know what was in my heart, the wild need to beg and plead with him to stay, which must be subdued. Did he know how painful it was to talk of him going, so painful that I must be curt with him to hide it. And although he had come to me with his burned hand, and I knew what the gesture meant, I still did not want him to think me merely " good " or " kind." I wanted him to regret leaving me for other reasons. But he would only regret Rose. In my savage ill-humour I was prepared to think then that men never know what is best and right for them.

" You remind me . . ." he began.

I gestured impatiently. "I don't want to know. I don't care what I remind you of." If he told me his mother or his sister I would begin to cry, I thought.

"Why do you have to go?" I said. "It's foolishness."

"Do you think I could stay here and have another man accuse me of stealing his inheritance? It's not true, Emmy. None of it. Even if I wanted to, John Langley would never permit it. It was right what Tom said . . . his father wants an heir but an heir of his own blood. He's a possessive old man. I am nothing more to him than a man who drives his wagon. I have never been to his house. When I talk to him I stand before his desk at the Stores. Like a clerk. I don't want to be any man's clerk, Emmy."

"You have his name."

He shrugged. "What's a name? Nothing! It's what you make it mean for yourself that counts. That's why I must go. I must make my own way . . ."

"Where will you go?" I asked miserably. "What will you do?"

"Back to sea. It's the only thing I'm fit for. I can't live any other way. I'll wait in Melbourne until someone signs me on. It won't be too hard . . . crews are jumping ships all the time and they're always short of hands."

"A hand?" I said. "Are you mad? You have a master's ticket!"

"What use is it to me? They know the story in Melbourne. They know about the *Julia Jason*. Once a man loses a ship owners aren't very eager to give him the chance to do it again. If I'm lucky I'll get a third mate's berth. If I can't get that I'll go as a hand."

"Where will you go?—home, back to Nantucket?"

He shook his head. "I'll go where the ship takes me—but not back to Nantucket." He bent over the mug. "I lost a ship that was out of Nantucket. You understand, Emmy—I can't go back."

"But that's happened a thousand times before. Men go back . . . they have families, and they go back. Nothing is so bad as staying away."

"I'll never go back," he repeated. It was the worst thing in Adam—this absurd pride. It made him blind to certain things, arrogant, too. He did not take advice easily, he thrust away help that might have been offered to him. He would hurl himself a hundred times against the impossible, and would hurt himself. He would never acknowledge that there was hurt or bewilderment or loneliness. And now he was bent on

87

walking away from Larry and the rest of us; throwing aside every bit of good that might have come from the partnership, everything that John Langley might do for him. And all because of his pride that could not shrug off Tom's sneer. I sighed, feeling helpless before it.

"You're making a mistake, Adam. There's too much for you here . . ."

"Not what I want," he answered curtly. "Don't you understand? It isn't what I want."

"What is it you want, then?"

He looked confused, shaking his head over the whisky. "I don't know." His voice was gentler. "I want to be able to forget it—or to have another chance. To make up, some way."

"For what?"

"The wreck. It was a bad thing, the wreck," he said slowly. "It was in the Bass Strait. You've heard of wreckers, Emmy?"

"Yes."

"The islands in the Strait were once used as whaling stations. The stations were abandoned when the whales left these waters, but the islands were still used as hiding places for anyone who wanted away from the law. Over the years they've attracted a fine crew of escaped convicts from Van Diemen's Land—the men even kidnap black women and bring them with them. They live off wrecking—whatever they can draw to their shores. The *Julia Jason* was bound for Melbourne—not whaling, just a trading voyage in the Pacific —out of Nantucket. We were in a storm. The storms come bad in the Strait. We hadn't seen the sun for more than four days, and we weren't sure of our position. We mistook their lights for some on the mainland. The *Julia Jason* went on the rocks and broke up. Twenty-six men were lost in the surf, and all the cargo. But four of us beat our way into the beach, and we found that the wreckers were only seven men—They were half starved, out of ammunition, and they had nothing to fight us with. I killed one of them with my bare hands, Emmy. Even after the surf I was stronger than he, and I held him by the neck until he died."

"The others . . . ?" I whispered.

"Too weak to fight. They're probably dead now. We built a raft from the broken timbers from the *Julia Jason*, and we put out to sea again. We were picked up by the *Thistle* and landed in Melbourne. The convicts were too weak to stop us getting off the island. They kept walking the beach and picking the pockets of the bodies that came ashore. The wreck was too far out for them to reach, so they got poor pickings. I tell you, Emmy, they were like carrion. The *Julia Jason* wasn't the kind of ship they were hoping for—the ship supplies went down with her, and there weren't any women passengers with rings on their fingers and watches and bracelets—for any good those kind of things would do those men where they were. They only got the poor common seamen who were half a world away from home! Maybe a sailor expects to drown— but to drown honestly, when the sea gets the better of you, not done to death by other men. They deserved better than that, and it was my fault they got what they did."

"It wasn't your fault—don't torment yourself, Adam!"

"A captain is always responsible. There's no other way to look at it. I wrote to the owners when I landed in Melbourne and I accepted the responsibility. Tom wasn't lying about that."

"Forget it, Adam. You'll have to forget it."

"I want to. I want to forget it, but I never will—not as long as I live. I tell you, Emmy, it's as if I lived it again every night. I see it still."

His voice went on and on, a little slurred with the drink, passionate, full of the suffering he never let himself tell before. I heard of the wreck again, and yet again, of the drowned white faces of his crew, their names . . . Jeremiah . . . Luke . . . names of men he had grown up with on the Nantucket waterfront. I heard his whispered guilt and shame, the misery that he carried inside him. I knew he had never spoken these words to any one by myself. I put my hand on the back of his neck, and drew his face against my breast. For a short time he was mine. I whispered back to him the comforting words he needed to hear.

Then finally he drew apart from me a little, seeming to search my face. Then I felt his kiss on my lips; I tried to hold him to me, but it was finished almost before I could know it had begun.

"I'll sleep down at Sampson's." He got to his feet unsteadily. "Good-bye, Emmy. Tell Rose . . ."

I didn't hear what he meant me to tell Rose. I think I hated him for that moment because his last thoughts and words were for her.

"Take care of Rose, Emmy. She's not as wise as you."

Chapter Six

Things did not go well for us after Adam left.

Perhaps Rose's happiness was at the core of it. She was never one to be silent in her grief. We heard her tears and her reproaches; we endured her ill-humours because there was no escape from them.

"Will you hush now," Kate would cry in desperation. "It isn't decent to go on this way about a man that didn't belong to you!"

"What do I care about being decent? What's the use of that if I can't have Adam."

"Then what of those fancy dreams of yours about a rich man who'd keep you in silk and let you play the piano all day? Adam is poor . . ."

"Being poor didn't matter," she replied, and I think she meant it then. "Just so long as it is Adam."

She did not forgive Tom Langley. He came once or twice to the camp, diffidently, muttering an apology to Dan but with his eyes pleadingly upon Rose. She would turn away and go to the tent, staying there until after he had left. And soon he knew that she was unforgiving, and so he did not come back. She had learnt about the fight between Adam and Tom, as most of the Eureka had learned. She was proud of Adam for fighting, but she did not understand why he should fight, and then go.

"But he *won*," she kept insisting. "There was no shame. Why did he have to go?"

"There are some fights that are never won," Dan said.

Pat understood why he went, and approved. It was the kind of action he craved himself. "He had to go. He's a seaman," was what he said.

Perhaps part of our trouble was that affairs were troubled on the goldfields, and that Pat was part of them—Sean also. Pat no longer, on the way to the pubs on Main Road, made those amiable visits to the fires of other families on the Eureka, eyeing the daughters and causing some heartbreak. There seemed no time for that any more. The drinking was not amiable, either. He knew that Larry had no sympathy with the groups that sought reform by violent means, and so the drift between them hastened. They barely spoke to each other now when Larry came back from Melbourne. Pat's idols were the men who were emerging to lead the various reform groups—Vern, Lalor, one of the Humphrey brothers. Belatedly Bentley was brought up for a further examination before the magistrates for Scobie's murder; this time he was indicted and tried, and in the end sentenced to hard labour. The diggers were too far gone in their grievances to be appeased by this move. Three of the diggers, Fletcher, McIntyre, and Westerby, were brought to trial for the burning of Bentley's pub. They had all been chosen and arrested arbitrarily—one of them was known to have been nowhere near Bentley's on the night of the fire. Commissioner Rede of The Camp, simply needed men to make an example of; they were the ones chosen. They were tried in Melbourne, safely away from the inflamed tempers of the goldfields, and sentenced to six months' hard labour.

The little time Pat could spare for us from his meetings, he spent haranguing us as if we were the guilty magistrates. He was impatient with Dan's wish to make haste slowly.

"You talk like Larry—afraid!" A few months ago there would have been no words on Pat's lips like these for his father. But he was reckless now; the old rules didn't seem to apply.

"We should take hostages," he said. "We should take hostages from among the troopers and police and hold them until those bastards in Melbourne let Fletcher and the others free . . ."

I saw that the spirit of lawlessness and agitation was not easily confined. It crept into places it was not meant to go. Con listened to Pat's outbursts and he was infected—not with the political fever of the moment, but with his own brand of mischief. Perhaps Rose's constant bickering egged him on; whatever he did she made objection to, and so finally he did things to justify her criticisms. He was inattentive when I tried to give him lessons, often absent when he was wanted to help with some task. The children on the Eureka suddenly found a leader. He invented a game called "Diggers and Traps." They chased each other up and down the mullock heaps, and around the pit shafts; the noise of their shrieks grew deafening at times. Con wore a constant array of cuts and bruises, and once a black eye, from the fights he got into with other boys.

Boxing his ears Kate would cry "This place is ruining him —like the rest of us. I wish to God we could get away from it."

But he had a lot of the child left in him still, had Con. In his mind I was still apart from the family, and it did not shame him to bring his tears to me. They were not so much tears for his stinging ears and the bruises, as for the vague fears and uncertainties we all felt.

John Langley hired another man to drive the second dray. We were civil to him, but that was all we had the heart to be. He slept and took his meals down at The Star on Main Road.

" Sure I can't be bothered fussing after strangers," Kate said. There was a wariness and a caution in the Maguires now that had not been there when they had picked me up on the road to Ballarat. They did not give themselves to easily.

As the weeks passed Adam was less in our talk, but I don't think he left our thoughts. Larry missed his companionship on the long journeys, though he did not let himself say so—or that he had been hurt by Adam's going. Rose moped now, when at first she had raged. She took no trouble about her dress ; her hair hardly saw a brush.

" A disgrace !" Kate said. " You look like something out of the bogs."

" Who's there to see me?" she replied, with a grand and despairing indifference to the whole of Ballarat crowding about her.

I felt the shadow of Adam between us the night that Mary O'Casey's child was born. Kate helped her through the labour —it began in the early afternoon and lasted until just before dawn. In these last few weeks we had prepared the sheets and cloths, and sewn baby clothes. Now all that remained for us was to keep hot water ready, and to try to find the doctor. He came and made a brief inspection, and left. " Everything is normal," he said. " The rest's best left to you women." Like most men he thought that way.

It was a hard labour, and Mary O'Casey was tired even before it began. Her screams frightened Rose, who clung to me as we waited and tended the fire. " I don't want children, Emmy !" she said at once.

" Of course you do."

" I don't—I'm afraid." And she covered her ears to shut out the cries.

But when the baby was born she helped wash it, and afterwards she rocked it gently in her arms. " It's a darling thing," she said. " I wish it were mine—and Adam's."

And miraculously the baby's cries were hushed when he lay in Rose's arms, and she bent to coo at him. I was jealous of that—and the thought of Adam that was in both our minds.

We gave up even asking Larry if there was news of him.

"I heard he'd shipped out on *Swallow*—he's got a mate's berth. It's a small sloop—coastal trade."

Coastal trade—that meant that he would return to Melbourne. He might be back in Ballarat. Each of us, Rose and I, counted this possibility. But only Rose spoke the hope aloud.

II

I was on my way back from Sampson's when I saw Adam's face in the crowd about the stage which was just putting down its passengers on Main Road. I saw the back of him first—the big shoulders straining the seaman's jacket, the old cap on his head, the canvas bag hoisted high. Unmistakably Adam, and I flew through the crowd towards him.

"Adam!"

He turned, and he seemed to drop the bag in the same instant. I was swept up in his arms, my feet off the ground, and he was hugging me with a big man's strength and joy.

"Emmy! Little Emma!" He kissed me—on the cheek—but I didn't care about that at the moment.

"You're back!" I said. "Oh, it's wonderful!" Then I stopped. "But you've missed Larry—he's gone on to Barrandilla. Mr. Langley thinks its time they started some contracts out that way."

"I know," he said. "I've just seen John Langley. He told me about it."

"Then you're going on to join him . . . ?"

He shook his head. "No, Emmy—much better than that. I'll tell you as we walk."

I shook his sleeve with Rose's imperious gesture. "No! Tell me now!"

He picked up his bag again. We were holding up the traffic, the people pushing around and past us. He steered me towards the side of the road.

"The *Swallow* put into Melbourne three days ago. I had the job as mate because the regular man was sick, so I was paid off as soon as the cargo was landed. I was high and dry again, Emmy, so I thought there couldn't be any harm going to see Langley. Not begging, mind—just asking what was available. That is, in ships—not stores. He knows everything that happens in Melbourne."

"Yes—yes!" For once I didn't like his patient deliberation.

"He asked me to his house . . ." And here his eyes lit with an excitement and satisfaction that was foreign to him almost. "He gave me wine . . . And, Emmy, he offered me the *Langley Enterprize!*"

"Offered you the *what?*"

"The *Langley Enterprize!* The first Langley ship! He's starting to build his own fleet. Just coastal schooners in the beginning. If it goes well he'll build his own ship to carry wool to England, and a return cargo of merchandise. And I get the first of them! Do you hear me, Emmy?—I get the first of them!"

"You mean—captain?"

"Captain it is!—nothing less!"

And there on Main Road I flung my arms about him for the second time, not caring one bit about the gaping people. I had seen happiness in his face—more than that, I had seen joy. It was the face of a man who has got the one thing in life more important to him than any other thing. Adam was changed from the person I had known; he was a whole man now, complete, the marring clamp of bitterness lifted from him. And so I kissed him.

"It's the best news!" I said, when I had breath to speak. "It's the best news I've ever heard! Oh—just think of it, Adam! Your own ship—yours!"

"I can't sleep for thinking of it," he said. "I didn't believe it at first. John Langley isn't a man to hand out prizes for nothing. I learned he'd made enquiries. He'd rounded up the four other survivors of the *Julia Jason* and heard their stories. Then he decided to make the offer."

"And why not?" I said, indignant that there was any doubt that it should have been made.

He shrugged, but he was too happy to be very serious about it. "It's a risk—taking on a man who's lost a ship. The crew doesn't have the same feeling about him. Once you've lost a ship you have to be twice as good a captain as any man they've ever sailed under, or they'll give you no respect. Better be in hell than running a ship where the men don't trust the skipper."

"You'll be four times as good."

And he smiled down at me, lacking no confidence now. "I will, Emmy. I will."

Again he took up his bag and hoisted it on his shoulder. We started along Main Road, heading back towards the Eureka—and I so proud I could have burst to be walking like this beside him. So many eyes turned to him, the tall sunburnt man with a look of sheer happiness on his face. He sent cheerful greetings to the men he knew, and bows to the ladies when once he used to stride along this street and see no one. The shame of the *Julia Jason* was gone from him. He wanted the world to see him, and acknowledge him. He held his head up like a man who wanted to meet the world.

"And so," he said, "I thought I should come . . ."

"What was that, Adam?" I quickened my step to keep up with him. I could tell from the way he walked that he would have liked to run all the way along the Eureka to the Maguire camp.

"I thought I should come," he repeated. "The *Enterprize* won't be ready for two months. I told Langley I would come here first. I told him Sampson might need some help if there's trouble, but I suppose he knew I was coming to help the Maguires . . ."

"Trouble . . . ?"

He looked at me, puzzled. "Yes—it's all over Melbourne about Hotham sending up detachments of the 12th and 40th regiments. And a lot of arms and ammunition . . . They seem to expect some kind of uprising. Langley told me to stay clear of those hot-head rebels—that they'd all end on the gallows where they belonged."

"Yes" I said, understanding now. From the moment I had seen him there on Main Road all the thought of trouble had slipped from my mind. But he brought it back, and it stayed there unhappily. It was not only the grievances of the diggers that agitated them, but the refusal of the authorities to recognise that they even existed. The dignity of the autocratic government in Melbourne was offended by the delegation of diggers that came to demand freedom for the men sentenced for the burning of Bentley's pub. No one could demand anything of Sir Charles Hotham, they were told. The rumours of the threat to take police and troopers as hostages spread and took hold. Hotham became enraged. He dismissed the delegation and ordered reinforcements to Ballarat. We knew that they were already on the way.

"Those fools in Melbourne think it's beneath them to listen to some honest men speak," I said. "But they don't understand how things are here on the goldfields. Something will break soon . . ." Then I looked around at him. "I'm glad you're here. I wish Larry were too."

"When is he due?"

I shrugged. "A few days . . . who knows? There are some outlying towns from Barrandilla. He said he wanted to make a sweep of it . . . he said he'd be straight back if there was trouble. That was before we heard about Hotham sending

the extra troops. But then—nothing may happen. It may come
to nothing in the end. That's what Larry says. He can't just
wait here . . ."

" And Pat?"

" Pat wants trouble—he's looking for it." I knew that it
was true, though for the first time I spoke the thought aloud.
" He wants it almost to spite Larry." I was surprised when I
said that, but Adam nodded.

" Families are like that. Pat has to find his own way. It
isn't Larry's way."

We walked on, Adam hailing some of the people he knew
at the camps along the Eureka, and I wishing that my great joy
at seeing Adam had not been so quickly clouded by this
trouble that faced us. It would have been easier to bear
whatever came, especially now that Adam was here, if the
Maguires had been as they were when they first arrived in
Ballarat, if the split had not come between Larry and Pat.
But I could still take comfort from Adam here beside me.
His height towered above mine. I felt his strength, something
calm and solid in the midst of the conflicts of the Maguires.
I glanced sideways at him. His face was not troubled, not as if
he were thinking about the rumours and reports that he said
had brought him here. He looked expectant, the look of a man
who can hardly wait for the end of his journey. Then the
thought of Rose came to me, and I believed I understood
his look.

It was altogether a different Adam who had returned to us.
He was the captain of a vessel, no longer the humble driver of
a wagon. I began to understand why the thought of trouble
could not oppress him, why the look of excitement and
anticipation was barely held in check. I had to face the fact
that this could be the look of a man who had come to Ballarat
to get a wife.

And in my sudden wretchedness I wanted to turn away from
him, to hide my own face. Most of all I did not want to be
there at that moment when he met Rose. I did not think I was
strong enough to bear that. So I sought an excuse to leave
him.

" Adam . . . there's something I've forgotten . . . back at
Sampson's. You go on. Tell them I'll be back soon."

" Don't go . . ." he said. He had halted. " I'll go back
for whatever it is later. No need for you to have the extra
walk."

I wondered that he didn't see the misery in my face. I
looked for a deliverance, and mercifully it came.

It came in the sudden increase of movement about us on the Eureka. The shouts that passed from camp to camp, the men that came up out of the shafts in response to the cries.

"A meeting! A meeting over on Bakery Hill!"

We often heard that cry these days. The various reform groups, the moderates as well as the extremes, called meetings whenever they felt there was need to unify their supporters. Sometimes they were spur-of-the-moment affairs, but this one had been better advertised and organised. The men were finishing work for the day, and they started to come along the Eureka in a steady stream.

"Let's get back to the camp," I said. "Like as not Pat will be going to the meeting." I hurried Adam on, knowing now that his first encounter with Rose would be lost in the flow of people past the Maguire camp.

Pat was coming up from the shaft, and Sean followed him. Pat saluted Adam as he passed—a friendly enough greeting, but absent-minded. He seemed to take Adam's presence there as natural and expected.

"Glad to see you!" he called. "You're here in time for the fight. I hope you brought a gun!" And then he was gone. A moment later Sean passed us running after Pat. Kate came forward to meet us. There was a moment's embrace for Adam, then the urgent, hoarse whisper.

"Go you and see what Pat's after doin'. His father's not out of the shaft yet."

"Rose . . . ?" Adam said.

Kate shrugged. "Who knows?" She was reaching for Adam's canvas bag. "Go now, quickly."

And so we turned back and joined the stream that flowed to Bakery Hill. The men came from all over Ballarat. They knew of the reinforcements coming, and the meeting had an urgency that no other I could remember had possessed. Some ran towards the meeting-place, others came with less haste but just as deliberately. They passed the word to one another, stopping by the shaft-heads to wait for mates to come up and join them. The cradles down at the creek fell silent, the windlasses worked furiously as the men came to the surface. I could see that the crowd of diggers was swollen by the men who spent their days in the hotels, the onlookers. The crowd grew and thickened until there were about ten thousand people gathered about a kind of platform on Bakery Hill. It was the biggest crowd I had ever seen in Ballarat. Some of them, like myself, were afraid, most of them angry.

I caught Adam's arm, and he bent to listen to me. "Pat will be up front," I said. "We should try to get there."

And shamelessly I used my small privilege as a woman to get through that crowd. I squirmed and pushed, tugging at men's sleeves until they realized it was a woman who wanted through, and then Adam would follow in the space I made. That way we managed to reach almost the front ranks by the time the meeting was being called to order by Peter Lalor. Pat was not among the speakers, but I glimpsed him directly behind the platform.

After a time there was quiet enough for Lalor to speak. He talked of reinforcements from Melbourne, the rejection of the plea for the release of the jailed men. With each word he uttered the passion of the crowd mounted.

"Our freedom is threatened. We fight for it, or we see it die!"

The roars of assent echoed in the valley. I found myself trembling, and, unaccountably, I also was shouting and waving my handkerchief.

"I say the licences must go! We must be done with them completely and forever because they are the symbols of tyranny. Who's with me?"

Again the great shout went up.

"I say we must refuse to carry them; we must join together to enter The Camp and rescue everyone arrested for not having one. If we do this together we're strong enough. Are you with me in this, men?"

The hats went up in the air by the hundreds, and the shouts and whistles and cries seemed to shake the hills about us. There was a movement and a surge, I stood on tiptoe to try to see what Pat was doing. A miner's elbow slashed into my face, and without Adam's rock strength behind me, I would have gone under the restless heels. Thus I missed the moment when Pat broke from the group on the plaform to make for one of the fires the crowd had surrounded. Then I felt Adam's hands over my elbows, lifting me above the heads of the mass. I saw the moment when Pat thrust his licence into the fire and then held it aloft, burning. He waved and flourished it, and in a few seconds was swept aside in the rush of men who clamoured to burn their licences also.

For a while Bakery Hill looked as if a group of madmen danced there, the burning papers brandished above their heads like the lights of freedom. Those who had merely come to watch went away quickly; others pocketed their precious piece of paper and they too went away. But enough of them stayed for the lights to flame there in the dusk, enough to tell the whole of Ballarat—the watchers on Specimen Hill, on Black Hill, in the Gravel Pits, the watcher in The Camp too—that their anger was beginning to shape, to have direction and purpose.

We were a subdued group around the fire that night. Not even Rose, her eyes aflame with pleasure at Adam's return, dared break into the general feeling of tension that gripped us. For once she was patient; she seemed willing to bide her time until Adam should speak. She heard the story of the *Langley Enterprize* and she reached the same conclusion as I had done —that Adam had come to ask her to marry him. She was proud; she had been prepared to take Adam on whatever terms he might have offered himself, but now he came with position and a little money, and she would not need to be humble. I could see her, almost visibly, planning how she would overcome the obstacles of the next few days—the chief of them, of course, that Adam was not a Catholic, and there would be difficulties over that. But she was confident; I saw no sign of doubt in her. But I was glad, even so, that Adam waited. Nothing is ever quite certain until it is spoken. Without reason, some small hope survived in me and continued to live, that Adam had come for me and not for Rose.

But the currents that passed between the three of us, Rose, Adam and myself, were lost in the more forceful matters of the moment. Adam unwrapped a long roll of canvas and revealed a rifle. He had always carried one when he drove with Larry, but it was nothing like this.

"I spent my month's wages on it in Melbourne," he said. "I reckon I didn't want to come here with no way of making some account of myself."

Pat and Sean bent over it to examine it. "It's a Winchester," Adam explained. "Almost new."

Pat laid his hand upon it. His voice was harsh, strained—the way a man might talk of a woman he desired, I thought. I saw his knuckles go white in that tight grip of possessiveness. "Adam—I want to buy it, I haven't got the money . . ." Then he gave a laugh that croaked in his throat. "Larry's the one with the money!"

I waited to hear Adam refuse. I saw the strain on Kate's face as she waited also. Then Adam said:

"I don't sell guns, Pat." Then swiftly he handed over the rifle. "Take it!"

"Do you mean this?"

"No!" Kate rose and she seemed to claw the air as if she would take the gun. God forbid!—you're putting trouble in his hands with that cursed thing. And he's only a boy . . ."

Then, for once, Dan overruled her. "Hush now, Kate. It's no boy we have here, but a man."

"Is it as a man then that you'll leave him to go to the devil?" Her hands now gestured pleadingly. "Holy mother, if only Larry were here."

Pat's face whitened; he looked at her in a rage of jealousy.

"Damn Larry! Aren't I enough. Can't I take care of you as well as he? Why is it always Larry? Why . . . Why!"

III

Pat seemed driven and desperate. The next morning he refused to go down the shaft, and we knew it was because he wanted to be on the surface if there should be a raid by the police. He had to flaunt his lack of licence; he had to make sure that Kate knew what he was risking. Adam took his place down the shaft, and Rose sulked because she had looked forward to the day spent with Adam. Bickering, acrimonious words passed between her and Pat until she took herself off to visit Lucy O'Donnell. Then Pat worked on silently, breaking the pile of quartz into small lumps and winding the buckets to the surface.

The cry we all waited for came over by the Gravel Pits. "Traps! Traps!" Pat dropped his pick and rushed towards the tent. I stood tensely, watching him, knowing what would happen. I heard him curse, and then he was out of the tent again.

"Who has it?" he shouted. "Who has it now?"

"What?" Kate said.

"You know right enough! My gun—my *gun!*"

Kate shook her head, slowly wiping flour from the damper she was mixing from her arms. "I haven't laid a finger on it," she said. "But if I had it now I'd break it over your head before I'd see you . . ."

He looked helplessly around the camp. "Where have you hidden it? Why do you have to meddle . . .? *Where is it?*"

"The devil take it," Kate said, "an' you too before I'd tell you that. Is it murder on your hands you want, Pat Maguire? —for that's what it'll be."

"The devil be damned—and you too," Pat shouted. Not even the shock that came into her face at these words halted

100

him. He began to search among the packing cases in a frenzy of anger and frustration, strewing the contents out on the ground. Kate gave a shriek as a case full of china went crashing down. "You're mad!" she screamed. "You edjit, you!"

"And you're a meddlesome old woman." He kicked a stool out of his way savagely. "Don't you know enough to keep your hands out of a man's business?" He looked over towards the Gravel Pits, pausing for just a moment to listen to the sounds that came from there.

"Damn it, I'll be too late!" He started to run, joining the other men who had thrown down their picks and were heading towards the Gravel Pits.

"If God's good you *will* be late," Kate called after him. The tears were flowing unchecked as she stood and watched Pat's figure leaping and darting between the mullock heaps and shafts. "You're a fool, Pat Maguire!" He was too far away to hear this. She turned back to me.

"Where did you put that old gun, Emmy?"

"How did you know?"

She gestured impatiently. "Who else would have thought of it before time? God be thanked you did."

"I put it back in Adam's canvas wrap. I thought that would be the last place he'd look."

She nodded. "Good girl! Go you now after him and see if you can't talk some sense into his head."

"Go after him—me?"

She gestured towards the shaft. "Who else? He's left the three men down there and it'll be more than I can do to raise the bucket and the weight o' one o' them."

"I'll help."

"No time. Go now!"

And as I ran I heard her calling for Rose. "Where are you, Rose? Mother of God, she's only here when she's not wanted!"

There was nothing I could do. A large crowd had gathered on the Gravel Pits, and the police had already arrested some of the men who did not produce licences. Commissioner Rede had come expecting trouble. His men were mounted, as always, but now over the crest of the gully we could see the reinforcements come—the troopers he had had waiting in reserve at The Camp. One of the leaders, a German called Vern, had been taken, and at once the crowd closed in and dragged him back. In among the diggers someone fired a rifle in the air. Its answer was a volley of fire over the heads of the crowd from the police and soldiers. Now they moved in closer, with bayonets fixed and flanked by the mounted troop. I felt a sense of fear suddenly in the crowd, a slight falling back at the sight of the bayonets. All at once the men around me seemed to become aware of the uselessness of the rocks in their hands—which were all the weapons most of them carried. We all fell back a little farther, and drew together. Now no one broke ranks to try to take back any more of the arrested men. We had to watch them being handcuffed to the troopers' harness.

Rede knew the mood of the crowd as well as any of us. He had the advantage, and he used it. He gave an order for another volley to be fired over our heads. It underscored our capitulation; I felt the indignity as much as anyone, the feeling that we were being pushed against our will and against justice and right. It is easy to make a tyrant of a man in your mind at a moment like this one. The Commissioner began to read the Riot Act, and we, who were ordinary people, seemed transformed by it into a lawless mob. By the time he had finished reading his men had assembled the prisoners and were ready to withdraw back to The Camp, leaving the Gravel Pits to us. In the bitter humiliation of the moment for the first time I was one with Pat.

I knew where to look for him. He had been in the front rank of the crowd, and had almost offered himself for arrest. I saw him being led off, and on his face was, strangely, a look of triumph. I felt a blazing pride in him then, because he was not humiliated or defeated.

And so, without knowing quite why, I joined the small group of women who marched to The Camp alongside their men. I even heard myself add to the string of insults which we heaped on the mounted troopers. They were helpless to turn us women away, and we made the most of it. The diggers grinned as they listened to the catcalls and boos we gave, and their heads came up. We must have appeared a mob of screaming harpies as we scrambled to keep up with the pace of the troop —unlovely, our faces streaked with sweat and our dresses hitched up clear of the ground.

I drew level with Pat. " Pat—it's me, Emmy."

He slewed around, dragging against the bridle to which he was handcuffed.

" Greeneyes . . . ! " he said, his mouth cracking in a grin.

I marched with him all the way to The Camp. He did not tell me to go back. Perhaps he guessed about the gun, and knew why I wanted to walk with him. At the gates of the stockade fence around The Camp they held us back. And so we stood there and jeered as we watched them chain the men to the logs.

IV

All day the diggers waited on the Eureka and Bakery Hill for the military to come back on more licence hunts, but they were left alone. The first of the reinforcements arrived from Melbourne, and as the baggage train passed along the Main Road near to the Eureka the diggers cut out the last cart. The driver was beaten and a young drummer-boy was shot in the leg. There was no sense of prudence left now, only the knowledge that they had defied the military but were without arms to meet an attack. I watched Lalor on the Eureka trying to bring some discipline into the men, and some knowledge of what they faced. He separated them into groups and gave instructions for drilling. There was a German blacksmith among them who started fashioning crude pikes for those who had no guns, making them from any piece of metal they brought to him. Those who had no guns to drill with used broom handles.

They sent out messages to the whole town appealing for money and weapons, and beyond that they sent riders to Mount Alexander and Creswick and Clunes asking the diggers there to join them on Bakery Hill. And they started throwing up a stockade of pit slabs roughly piled together, a low, three-sided barricade enclosing a drilling-ground of about an acre. It was temporary, they said. Tomorrow it would be better. On the open side, on the higher ground, it ran close to our camp. But we were luckier than some others who had their tents and pit-shafts arbitrarily enclosed.

Through the afternoon we watched the drilling, the shaggily bearded figures with the clay-caked moleskin trousers and the cabbage-tree hats marching solemnly up and down in the full heat of the afternoon sun. We did not smile at what we saw, though they looked ludicrous with their shambling gait and the imperfect obedience to commands. Sean was among them. He had found the rifle, and he shouldered it proudly. It was a shock to see how much like Pat he was, and how much of a man he had suddenly become now that he no longer stood in the shadow of his brother.

At the end of the day Lalor called them together to take the oath. Some of the women had made the diggers a flag ; it rose now, silken and beautiful on an eighty-foot flag-pole, navy with a cross in white satin, and eight-pointed white stars worked at the intersection and at each end of the cross. It was a solemn thing to see that flag wave above us on the Eureka. Even those who went out of sympathy with Lalor and his men, and those who wanted no part of his quarrel with The Camp drew nearer to watch.

Lalor climbed on a tree stump, the butt end of his rifle resting on his foot. In the light breeze the flag rippled above him. It was the hour of dusk, the hour when the campfires glowed suddenly in the gathering night. The white satin of the cross caught the red glow from below, and seemed to reflect it back into the faces of the men upturned to look at it.

Lalor quietened them with a gesture. "Let all divisions under arms fall in, in their order, around the flag-staff. I order all persons who do not intend to take the oath to leave the meeting at once."

We waited in silence while the men shuffled forward and regrouped. We, the onlookers, moved to the back, but did not leave. Finally Lalor stepped down off the stump, uncovered his head, and knelt. Around him, about five hundred men, Sean among them, did the same. Lalor raised his right arm. He spoke the words and the men repeated them.

"We swear by the Southern Cross to stand truly by each other, and fight to defend our rights and liberties."

*　　　*　　　*

It seemed unreal to us that Sean ate his meal at a fire within the Stockade that night.

"Play-acting," Kate sniffed. "All these grown men play-acting at being soldiers. 'Twill come to nothing in the end. And Sean ought to be heading for his bed at this moment instead of that sentry nonsense."

"Well, I'll have Pat out of The Camp tomorrow—tomorrow for sure," Dan said. "They made excuses this afternoon that there weren't magistrates to hear the cases, but they'll never dare hold them all through tomorrow. It'll be a matter of paying a fine . . ."

"You'll leave Pat where he is, Daniel Maguire. He's safer inside The Camp than out of it. He can do no harm to himself or anyone else where he is, so leave him."

"Chained to a log? That's not the way I want to see my son."

"Then you don't know your son. A taste of that kind of thing might have him thinking that rebellion isn't all it's cracked up to be. He'll come to no harm. I've been down myself and they passed in some food I took him and a blanket. He's better where he is than that pig-sty of a lock-up." She rose and started to light candles for us to take. "Now go to bed, all of you—to-morrow it will be all finished and done with. Sure the thing will fall apart for lack of food and the whisky in that Stockade of theirs. They'll all be back with their womenfolk tomorrow like lambs—and lookin' pretty stupid too."

She began to rake the ashes over the red embers, and thus firmly took away from the affair of the Eureka Stockade any vestige of romance it might have had for us. We went to bed meekly.

As she went to tuck in Con where he lay alone in the tent where he usually slept with Pat and Sean, I heard the thin, young voice speak to her sleepily. "Tomorrow Tommy O'Brien and me are going to get up a troop of our own . . ."

* * *

By the morning it seemed that Kate could have been right. With the sun up, and the realities of the day upon us, the Stockade looked pitifully inadequate and the defenders were, like her phrase, "playing at soldiers." Lalor had them drilling immediately after breakfast, and we could see that their numbers were only about half what they had been the night before.

"Got some sense into their heads, I see," Kate said. "It'll not be long before Sean's back here lookin' for somethin' to eat, and that'll be the end of the great rebellion."

By mid-morning, when the men came up out of the shaft for their tea, the stories were making the rounds.

"It doesn't look good," Dan said. "Some of the men went out last night and requisitioned food and money and ammunition in the name of the Committee of the Eureka Stockade. Most of what was collected never saw the inside of the Stockade. They kept it themselves."

"Sure what did you expect? Aren't rebellions always half made up of people who want something for nothing?"

More rumours came as the morning went on. We heard various tales—that some of the group in the Stockade wanted to take over the funds in the Bank. We knew that the stories had reached The Camp and Commissioner Rede when a detachment of troops took over the Bank and started to sandbag it.

"Sure he's overdoin' the thing," Kate said. "Just like an Englishman. When you look at the few bits o' pikes the boys

105

here have got and all those guns . . . An' it the only stone building in the town, too."

Lalor sent a deputation to The Camp to demand the release of the prisoners taken in yesterday's raid. Rede treated the demand as if it were an ultimatum. But all of us, even the diggers who kept away from the Stockade, suffered in the humiliation of the dismissal. The day was a see-saw of events for and against Lalor. The appeals for help that had gone out to the surrounding gold-towns began to bring in some volunteers. But they had expected a well-armed and fortified Stockade, and food and whisky to provision it. When they saw what actually existed—with none of the excitement of a fight to enliven it—most of them turned back. And with their going some of the Ballarat men left too, ones who had taken the oath. But the hard core that remained were in earnest about what they meant to do. They drilled with more precision, and they had more weapons. A gradual trickle of arms was coming in.

Even so, perhaps it would have fallen apart, as Kate said; perhaps we might have been left in peace on the Eureka that night if the news hadn't reached us ahead of the men on the road. Governor Hothom was determined to suppress the lawlessness on the goldfields, the report came; he had dispatched additional reinforcements from Melbourne. The remainder of the 12th and 40th regiments, with two field pieces and two howitzers were heading for Ballarat.

"There'll be no tame ending to it now," Adam said. "This is a fight."

v

After the midday meal Adam hired a trap from the livery stable on Main Road and took us—Rose and myself—hunting for arms and ammunition. We were bonneted and gloved and dressed in our best, I in the green plaid, Rose in a blue muslin that might have been for a garden party, and which added unfairly to her beauty. Adam had told us to dress up, and Rose never needed bidding twice to do that. Her hair was smoothly brushed under her bonnet; her gloves were clean and so were her stockings, and men never noticed such things as the layer of dried mud along the edge of a petticoat. She looked enchanting, demure, gay, and she smiled at the world as we drove along Main Road. There should have been more to see her, but Main Road wore an unusually deserted appearance. As soon as the soldiers had begun sand-bagging the Bank, the prudent merchants had closed their own doors and checked their weapons and ammunition. But it was Saturday, and the hotels still did business. Rose smiled and bowed to acquaintances from her seat beside Adam. Her possessiveness was an innocent, unconscious thing. She couldn't have known how it hurt me.

"It wasn't easy getting away from Muma. I finally told her that Mrs. O'Donnell needed me."

"She'll know the truth when we get back," Adam said. "She won't love me for doing Peter Lalor's errands, but they're desperately short of everything they need in the Stockade. I have his written authority to ask for help. I thought we should try Clunes and Arrarat, and round Creswick Creek. There must be some who would contribute—even food or money if they won't part with their weapons. I could understand a man not wanting to give up his gun at a time like this."

"What use will we be?" I was feeling apart from them both, an unwilling chaperone on a jaunt.

Adam chuckled. "Decoration, is what you and Rose are, Emmy. You both give me a nice air of respectability. The women won't be afraid of me when we drive up, and the men will know I'm not one of those Ballarat ruffians . . ."

I pulled my bonnet a little forward to shade my face from the sun. It was very hot. "It's not your fight, Adam. You're not one of the diggers. Why do you have to do this?"

He fussed unnecessarily with the reins; he was usually a quiet driver, not showy. "Everything's my fight if it concerns the Maguires." He said this with a kind of nod to us both. "But I'm *for* the diggers—at least I'm against The Camp. I suppose I'm against everything that smells of tyranny. This is a new country—clean, free—or trying to be. In America we know about that. We know about trying to keep free . . ." His voice trailed off into an embarrassed silence, as if he believed that these were ideas which might be acted upon, but rarely spoken of.

Rose did not leave him alone in this silence. She leaned towards him, twisting sideways to try to see completely into his face. She loved him very much, and she wanted every part of him, every thought; she had to tie herself with him in those thoughts.

"I do believe, Adam, that you're turning into an Australian."

He didn't smile at that. "I'll be a Nantucketer till I

die . . ." he said. " You don't change a man's breed. But my children . . . yes, they'll be Australians."

I thought about Adam's children. Probably Rose did also. I thought of them as the countryside rolled out before us, the fresh green of spring gone now, and summer already burning the edges of the land. It was a lonely place, remote, aloof. Even where we caught the traces of man—the occasional homestead which seemed to be sunk panting in the heat, the fenced sheep-runs—they were only slight and tentative marks on the land. They seemed to make no deep impression, not here by the road or on the rolling hills that gave way to the blue distances. They were only the first feeble efforts to inhabit, to subdue, to populate and own this earth. It would need a lot of Adam's sons, and other men's sons, to fill this immense country to the limits of its horizons. Then the thought came to me of the forty thousand or so people in Ballarat and their hunger and need for land. Many of them would have left the diggings if the land had been open to them. This was part of the feelings that had built the Stockade on the Eureka. But when Adam and others like him talked of their children I knew that they would not wait forever in their canvas towns and in the slums of Melbourne. They would spread out and take this land ; in the end they would take it. I was stirred by a feeling of excitement of certainty in this conviction, a feeling that I would be part of the movement and spread, and this made sense of my place here on the buggy.

The whole afternoon's work yielded very little to us. We were not good at begging—even if it were in Peter Lalor's name, and for the men in the Stockade. The news of the trouble at Ballarat moved quickly, even in these lonely distances. Most of the people we talked to had heard of the Stockade ; in some places others had been before us asking for help and we got sour answers, in others our story was listened to carefully, and we got perhaps a sack of flour or a little ammunition. Money was short ; in the end none of us got to the point of asking for it. Always in the outlying places—whether it was a prospector's tent or a lonely homestead—if there was a woman there we were eagerly invited to step inside and have a cup of tea. And while we drank it the woman would snatch hungrily at our talk, and fix mesmerised eyes on our dresses and bonnets.

One woman, with three young children at her skirts, said flatly: " It's more than four months since I've passed a word with another woman. My man don't take me into town."

108

And she gave us a box of ammunition. " Joe'll carry on when he gets back and finds out what I've done. But I don't care. It's been worth it to talk to you . . ."

The one prize of the afternoon was a musket. It was of an ancient make, but it came supplied with ammunition. It was given to us by a prospector we came on by chance. He and his mule were heading out into the emptiness beyond Mount Alexander, and he was making early camp when we drove up. We shared a cup of tea with him, the eighth we had drunk that afternoon. He was a London Cockney, wiry and shrivelled by more than twenty years in Australia—looking for gold most of them, and taking a job as shepherd to earn his grubstake each time his money ran out. We guessed he was a ticket-of-leave man ; he talked of England—or at least of London—with the nostalgia of a man who has not left it voluntarily. He plied me with questions about London ; I answered them as well as I could. We expected nothing of him beyond the cup of tea. The talk was a small gesture of kindness to a man who was heading out into the sort of loneliness that none of us had ever imagined. But as we were leaving he suddenly dived into the tent and came back with the musket. He handed it to me.

" Perhaps the Yankee here will teach you how to use it. Looks like you might need it on the Eureka. Don't need moren't one meself to shoot them wallabies and snakes."

He stood out in the middle of the road waving us out of sight. I pictured him still standing there staring after us until the dust settled ; and when he went back to cook his supper I knew he would be reciting aloud the place names of London we had exchanged, the way lonely people do.

Before we turned back to Ballarat Adam pulled off the road once again. There was nothing to be seen—not a house, not a tent, not even the cold ashes of a one-time camp site—nothing to be seen but a few tall gums near at hand, and one side of the valley, tree-covered, going into purple shadow as the sun moved behind the hills.

" What for, Adam?" Rose demanded.

He lifted us both down quickly.

" I thought it was time you both learned to handle a weapon. If there's trouble the men may not have time to look after you. We'll try it here—away from your mother's sight."

From under the seat he produced a bundle wrapped in soiled calico. When he pulled the calico away there was a polished wooden box lined with blue velvet ; in it rested two slender pistols, identical, sawhandled and very plain.

109

"Duelling pistols," he said. "I bought them in Melbourne. They're a beautiful pair. Look . . ." We bent over the case and his finger traced the tiny engraved characters. *F. Innes—Edinburgh*. "Only one shot each before you have to reprime them—but for a woman one shot's all she's likely to fire."

Rose touched them, lifting one of them out of the case. Her arm dropped suddenly at the dead weight of it. "I saw some duelling pistols once," she said. "They were much prettier than these—silver and mother-of-pearl."

"Show-pieces," Adam said contemptuously. "Just one glint of sunlight into your eyes off that fancy silver and you're a dead man." He took the second pistol out of the case. "Here, you try it, Emmy."

I shrank away from them both. I looked at the pistols with deadly loathing and fear. Already in Adam's hand, in Rose's hand, I saw again the like image of that hated revolver with which I had shot Will Gribbon. I did not want to touch them; I wanted no part of them.

"I don't like firearms," I said tonelessly. I took a step back from them.

Adam shrugged. "As you wish—but I think you should learn for your own protection." He turned away; he was disappointed in me. I knew that, but I still could not make myself touch those guns. I watched in silence as Adam selected a gum tree and fixed the square of white paper he had brought on to it. Then he measured back twenty paces. "You won't have to fire from this distance if there's trouble on the Eureka," he said to Rose. "But it won't hurt for you to try something harder. These guns are deadly accurate. If a woman can lift one to aim on target it's almost impossible to miss . . . Feel the balance," he urged her. "It's beautiful, isn't it?"

But when she tried to raise the pistol to cover the target her arm wavered with the weight of it. She lowered it. "It's too heavy."

"It's made to be that way," he said. "When you fire the dead weight will keep it from being thrown to the right. You don't have time to aim . . . the pistol feels the aim for you."

He instructed her in the loading and firing mechanism. Rose enjoyed this, she placed her fingers wrongly so that Adam had to place them for her. They practised aiming with the pistol half-cocked. Adam stood beside her, close to her, teaching her how to line up her shoulder and hand and eye. Momentarily she leaned back against him, and he did not move away.

She went wide of the target the first two attempts. Adam reprimed the gun and gave it back to her. The third time she hit the target, and the fifth time she was close to the centre.

"One more try," she said, laughing with nervous excitement and pleasure in her skill. This time she reloaded herself, anxious to show Adam how well she had learned from him. It was one of those occasions when Rose was at her best—all the intelligence and concentration which she usually didn't bother to bring into play were called up now. She wanted Adam's admiration, and she would have it. She loaded, aimed and fired with an intuitive, natural skill.

She couldn't wait for Adam to check the target. She raced to it herself, the wide blue muslin skirts floating, an incongruous sight beside the deadly weapon she held.

"Dead centre!" she cried. Perhaps it was not quite so, but no one was going to deprive her of the pleasure from that small lie. She turned and rushed back towards Adam, the lightness and grace of that run beautiful to watch, her whole body exulting in what she had done.

"Wonderful! Wonderful!" he said, and his hand caressed her arm for a moment. "You've got the makings of a first-class marksman, Rose."

"Let me try again!"

He shook his head. "Not now. We can't waste ammunition. But later, when this trouble's over, I'll show you how to use a rifle. A woman should know such things, no matter what they say. One of my grandmothers once stood off six Indians from their cabin in Connecticut when she was alone with two babies. She was a crack shot . . . it's a story they tell in my family as a kind of joke because her husband was a Quaker. We always wondered if he would have helped her shoot if he'd been there."

Abruptly, rudely, I broke in. "Let me try!" I held out my hand for the pistol.

They turned, surprise in their faces. It could have been that they had even forgotten that I was there. I gestured again towards the pistol that Rose held. After a glance at Adam she parted with it reluctantly.

I was impatient as Adam again went over the firing mechanism; I could have recited by heart all the things he had previously said about it to Rose. I knew only one thing—that I must get this act over and done with. However much I feared and hated it I must do it or I would show myself as a coward before Adam. I could not so easily hand this

111

triumph to Rose, or let her bask alone in Adam's admiration.
I might loathe this gun I held, and all other guns, but because
of Adam I would hold this one steady, without letting my hand
tremble, and listen to him recite the mystic ritual of the
weapon—the balance, the aim, the tiny squeeze on the hair-
trigger. But still he must have sensed my fear because he said
these things without enthusiasm, expecting them to fall on
unhearing ears, to be wasted.

He stood behind me as he had with Rose to show me how
to line up shoulder, sight and target. But there was no reaction
between us other than a terrible coldness. Then he stepped
away from me.

I lowered my arm, and raised it again to take fresh aim. Its
balance and swing was miraculous, almost feeling its own way
into line with the target, its dead weight holding it there as I
pulled the trigger. I heard the report, saw the piece of wood
and paper leap away from the tree.

Adam was silent for one stunned second. Then he ran
towards the tree. It was a moment or two before he spoke.

"Dead centre," he called back. There was no possibility of
a lie from Adam. He started to walk towards us slowly.

I despised the violent trembling that possessed me. The
acrid smell of gunpowder was in my nostrils, the hated smell
that was the smell of death for me. The smoke from the flash
seemed to lie like visible clouds under the evening shadows
of the trees. Adam looked at me strangely as he approached.

"You never shot before?"

I shook my head, lying to him. "A lucky shot," I said. I
handed the gun back to him.

He did not even suggest another try. There was a grave
silence between all of us as he carefully put the pistols back in
their velvet. He handed me the slim, polished box.

"You take it, Emmy," he said the words with no pleasure;
they were something he was compelled to say. My own lack
of pleasure in that shot had taken away his own. Beside my
forbidding, dampening fear, Rose's joy and excitement must
have seemed to him a human, warm emotion. But it was to
me he gave the guns.

The only talk on the road back to Ballarat was between
Adam and Rose. I clutched that beautiful, tenderly polished
box on my lap, and I wished that I had the courage to toss it
far into the dry scrub by the side of the road.

I did not sleep that night. It was a warm night; we lay with the flap of the tent thrown back and when a faint breeze stirred it touched my face. I could see a little segment of the sky. The same familiar stars looked at me as on other nights when I had been wakeful. They were growing familiar to me, these southern stars. The wind also carried the sounds of the men's voices from the Stockade. We were close by one of its barricaded walls, close enough to catch the murmured talk of the sentries. The fires glowed all night within the Stockade. I did not think much about the trouble that might come to us because of the Stockade. Instead, I thought of Adam, and the pistols within that little box close by my mattress. I thought of Rose, sleeping so peacefully. I wanted to be glad that she and Adam could love each other, that she could love enough to lift her from her self-absorption. I wanted to be glad because I also loved Rose. I would have to pretend it to others. With myself I had to face the truth.

Just before dawn I got up and went and poked the embers of the fire to life. I hung the billy-can over it to boil, and then decided to make enough tea, and take some cold bacon and damper to go around the men who would come off sentry duty with Sean at four o'clock. So I put on my boots and a long shawl around my shoulders. It was simply a gesture to propriety which required my shawl; the night breeze had died already. By the time the sun was up the heat haze would have begun to rise.

The false dawn had come by the time I had the tea made, and the bread and bacon in a basket. Before I left the camp I went back into the tent and quietly took one of the pistols from the polished box. I laid it with the other things in the basket, not quite sure of why I did it except that I knew it would have pleased Adam if he had known. They were all still sleeping as I went. The stars were pale, and were low at the horizon now. Out of the darkness the things about me were beginning to take shape and outline. And then as I approached the open end of the Stockade the sentry challenged me.

"Halt—who goes there?"

"You know right well who it is," I said with a touch of irritation. "Haven't I been making tea not ten yards from you for the last half-hour."

He waved me on with his rifle. "It's orders, Emmy," he said. "We're supposed to say it—though God knows I've been straining my eyes out into the blackness since midnight and not able to see a bloody thing, and wondering what I'd do if someone did come up." It was Jim Wilson, a man I knew from serving him and his family at Sampson's shop. They had a claim over by Black Hill.

"I've brought some fresh tea," I said. "I'll have a mug of it for you when you're through."

"Thanks," he said. "I could do with it. Well—it's the last night in this place for me. I've more to do with my time over on Black Hill. The family won't get fed by my standing round here like a fool . . ."

I nodded and passed on. The men were being awakened at one camp-fire to go on sentry duty. I headed towards them and acknowledged their low-toned greetings. They held out their mugs eagerly for the tea.

"You shouldn't be here on the Eureka at all, Miss Emmy," one of them said. "When those reinforcements they're sending from Melbourne come it won't be safe."

"That's so," one of them agreed, speaking for me. "I heard Dan Maguire saying last night he would be movin' the women-folk. Ben Sampson would probably give you lodgings . . . Sean was saying that was where you'd probably go."

"I don't know anything about it," I said. "We're safe enough on the Eureka. I can't see Kate Maguire leaving when her men are still here."

"That's the style, Emmy." This from Rory Mitchell. "We've got guns and we're as well able to fight as that lot down in The Camp. Didya see the gun I got off Tom Langley? A repeater . . . finest I ever saw." Affectionately he touched the rifle beside him.

"Tom Langley? Is he here?"

"Was here 'till midnight. Might have stayed, for all I know. He took a turn on the barricades. Strange coot, that one. Seems funny to have a Langley here in the Stockade. By rights he ought to be on the other side of the fence. Any more damper there, Emmy . . ?"

I was at home among them; I caused none of the upset or disturbance that Rose's presence would have made. I was Emmy to them all, comfortable, expected, safe, handing out bread and bacon and tea, listening to the gossip of the night in the Stockade, and waiting for the dawn to come, waiting until Sean would cross the compound. I was supposed to admire

114

their guns or their prowess. "Emmy, did you hear about the time when I beat Charlie Furgess in ten rounds over at Creswick? It was a twenty-pounds' purse. Marquess of Queensberry's . . ." "Emmy, I wrote her a letter to Melbourne, told her about puttin' by a hundred and forty pounds in the Bank. An' she says, 'Come to Melbourne and then I'll marry you, but I ain't comin' to the goldfields.' So when I get a hundred and fifty in the Bank I'm goin' . . ."

The sky towards the east lightened. The talk went on, and we heard no warning from the men at the Barricades. Just a single shot, close by. Then an answering volley that was disciplined and organised. It crashed like thunder on our ears.

"An attack!"

They were gone as soon as the words were spoken, and I was alone at the fire. They ran towards the barricades, shouting, picking up their weapons, calling to the sleeping men around them. A ragged round of fire sounded from the barricades, scattered shots. People were coming from the tents now, confusion, fear and sleep in their faces. Looking out beyond the barricades it was possible to distinguish the attackers. Several lines of infantry were drawn up, and on the flanks were the mounted troops. There might have been three hundred in all, and we inside the Stockade were less than a hundred, with fewer guns than men. Some of those who came out of the tents carried their only weapons—the pikes they had made themselves, and they ran with foolish gallantry with them towards the barricades.

There were some families within the Stockade, and the screams of the terrified women and children brought me to my senses a little. I reached for the basket and the pistol folded within the cloth. There was no time to feel fear now as I took it in my hand.

I did not know how the first flames began in the Stokade—perhaps a lamp overturned in the confusion—but a tent near me was on fire. It was the Foley tent; Sarah Foley stood before it in a kind of trance, barefooted, her hair tumbled on her shoulders just as she had come from her bed. Her four children were around her—the youngest, a baby, was on the ground at her feet, howling, his face crimson with rage. One of the girls was holding a smouldering rag doll in her hand. I went to them quickly.

I took hold of Sarah Foley. "Matt?" I said. "Where's Matt?"

She looked at me dumbly, shaking her head. "Dada's

gone," the eldest girl said. "He's gone with the others over there—and left us." She started to cry now, holding out the doll for me to look at.

"We've got to get out of here—across the Main Road. It's safer back there . . . they won't come that far."

"Uh . . . ?" Sarah Foley's mouth fell open. Her eyes were fixed on the burning tent. The smoke billowed over us; the screaming, angry baby started to crawl away. I looked around desperately for help, but there was none for such inessential matters as the Foley family. It was harder to see now. The smoke hung in the motionless air, but I needed only my ears to know what was happening. In quick precision one volley after another came from the military. From the barricades came only single shots and the cries of men in pain and confusion.

A bullet struck the ground near Sarah Foley's feet. She screamed; I think it was the first time she had been really aware of anything beyond the burning tent. She turned to me.

"What'll we do?"

"Get out of here. We can't do anything until it's over . . ." I picked up the baby, and dumped him into her arms. "Here —take little Matt—and Mary." That was the second youngest who had been clutching her mother's nightgown all along. I gave her a push in the direction of the open end of the Stockade, where the Main Road ran by it. Another bullet whined close to us, crashing into a box of supplies belonging to the Foleys. Sarah looked at it dazedly, and hung back.

"My things . . . help me get my things, Emmy."

I waved the pistol at her, not realising what I held in my hand. "For the love of God, go!" I gave her shoulder a thump to knock some sense of reality back into her. She started to stumble towards the road.

The other Foley boy was screaming now, and had started to fight his sister for possession of a ball she had salvaged from their belongings. I boxed him smartly on the ear. He stopped screaming in sheer amazement.

"Now shut up, and come on—both of you!" I shook the girl. "Here, you take your brother's hand, and don't let go, or you'll get some of the same."

The dead weight of the pistol hampered me. I had only one hand free, but I didn't realize at the time how impressive the sight of the gun was. They obeyed meekly. I caught the girl's hand and started to run. She dragged her brother along with her.

For a few minutes we were forced to crouch in the shelter

of a mullock heap. The military were moving up on the sides of the Stockade, and this was a period of vicious crossfire. Other women crouched there with me ; ones who had not left as soon as the shots were heard, who, like Sarah Foley could not believe in the world of violence that had suddenly crashed in upon them. I could see it in their eyes, the staring unbelief, the stunned refusal to accept the fact that the men, the husbands, the friends, the strangers on the other side of the barricades could be foolish enough to bring this havoc. We could do nothing to stop it, or to help. We could only retreat and know that we would come back to the chaos of the wounded and the dead.

The firing grew spasmodic. Down at the front of the Stockade the military were forcing the barricades. The screams we heard now were not from the women, but from the men. The word ran among the women.

" Bayonets ! "

We gathered up the children and ran. Threatening and pulling I got the two young Foleys away from the Stockade, and finally across the road. Out of danger, the children started to scream again. The boy in his fright, aimed a kick at me, and just as swiftly I boxed his ear again. Mrs. Foley seemed to lapse back into her panic-stricken trance. The women from the camp-sites here came to help us, to try to hush the cries, to soothe the fears. We were out of range of the fire, or what was left of it. The resistance in the Stockade seemed to have died.

Many of the people from the tents surrounding the Stockade had rushed here. I looked for the Maguires among them, but there was no sign of them that I could see. I asked the woman who had taken Mary Foley from me.

" Mrs. Simmons, have you seen the Maguires?—any of them ? "

" Kate Maguire is back with Flahertys. I haven't seen the others."

" Adam Langley? Have you seen him?" I couldn't stop myself asking that.

She shook her head. " In the Stockade probably—with Dan."

So I turned and ran back across the road to the Stockade.

When I entered again the fight was finished. There was no one left to offer resistance. Those who could had fled, the wounded lay where they had fallen. It was a bare fifteen minutes since the first shot had been fired. Now the soldiers and police were pouring across the barricades unchecked, and

I saw that they passed over the bodies of dead men. The air was filled with smoke, several of the troopers ran from tent to tent with flaming tar sticks, and the roar and crackle of the burning canvas was loud even in the midst of the cries. There were still women and children within the Stockade—confused, not understanding exactly what had happened and where they should go. And there were those, like myself, who had come deliberately, searching for their men in the chaos of the pit-slabs, the burning tents and overturned wagons. I could not see Adam. I started to pick my way through the debris and the fallen men, trying to close my ears to the groans of the wounded, trying not to recognise any face but his. I turned away from the familiar faces I saw on the ground, selfishly letting myself think only of Adam.

As I came to the centre of the Stockade a mad, wild cheer suddenly broke from a group of soldiers around the flagpole as one of them cut down the diggers' flag, the Southern Cross. For a moment I saw it under their feet. That was the end of the Stockade. The mounted troops now rode through freely. One of them came close enough for me to feel the rush of air of his passing. They took no notice of me: I kept the pistol under the shawl. An isolated shot sounded now and again, from the military, but there seemed no one left to shoot at.

The real horror began then when they were sure the Stockade was theirs. They began to use their bayonets on the diggers who lay on the ground, stabbing at both the dead and the wounded. Sometimes they struck more than once, in a kind of frenzy. Close to me a man was slashed in the throat; the blood gushed out bright and swift. I heard my own voice scream, but the sound was only part of all the other screams, the cries of agony and grief. I wheeled in panic, wanting nothing now but to get away from the sight of the slaughter. I stumbled then against the projecting edge of a pit slab, one of a pile near the head of the digging. The blow knocked the pistol from my hand, but the shock of it also brought me to my senses. I looked about me with more awareness.

A man lay downwards across the pit-slabs. His shirt was blood-soaked from a wound at the back or the shoulder —I couldn't tell which. He looked grotesque in that awkward, outstretched position. I knelt beside him, and the stickiness of the blood was on me at once, on my nightgown and on my hands.

"Adam!"

He wasn't conscious. It took all my strength to turn him over, and the movement started the flow of blood more strongly. But seeing that blood flow was like feeling life flow back into my own body. I did not know the half of my love for him until then.

The pain brought him a moment of consciousness. He half-opened his eyes.

"It's me, Adam. It's Emmy! You'll be all right now. I'll bring someone to help you."

His eyes held no understanding of what I said. I thought that he might die there, where I watched him. I looked around desperately for the help I had promised him.

I had an impression of someone standing above me. As I turned the soldier put his hand on me and tried to pull me to my feet.

"Out of the way—it's against the law to aid a rebel."

"Leave him be! Don't touch him!" I wriggled from his grasp, my hand searching desperately among the slabs for the pistol. As I felt it in my grasp, I tried to cover it with the spread of my shawl. The man bent over me; I was aware of his bulk menacing Adam, of the smell of gunpowder from his tunic. More than that I was aware of the bayonet.

He tugged at me again to try to pull me away from Adam. I did not know what his real intention was; there was never any way to tell if he had meant to kill Adam as he lay there. But I could not afford that chance. I cocked the pistol, and still on my knees, I turned and fired its single shot into the man. He was so close that the gunpowder burned us both.

So for the second time I watched a man die from a gun that I had held. He crumpled slowly, as Will Gribbon had done. I dropped the pistol and raised my hands to fend him off Adam and myself. I grabbed his shoulders as he sagged towards us and thrust him sideways. I think he was already dead then. But the weight of his body was enough. As he fell the bayonet struck my forearm and slashed through the flesh right to the bone.

The wound bled badly, and I had to use my strength quickly. I tugged two of the pit slabs out of the pile so that they projected and formed a kind of screen over Adam. It was inadequate, but it was all that I could manage in that little time. The first mad dash of the troopers was over. They were moving more carefully now, taking prisoners. I had no way to cover Adam except with my own body. So I lay quickly over him, my face just level with his chest. My nightgown covered his legs, and I spread the shawl over his face. My nightgown now was soaked with blood, and I prayed that the troopers would think me dead, and so leave me.

We lay close together in the cold darkness of pain. It was not the way I had dreamed of lying with Adam. But he was mine then; even if we died, he was mine for these moments. I had paid for him with that shot. I would never be sure, completely sure, that the soldier had meant to kill Adam. I could never pretend that I had shot him accidentally. Not the fear of guns nor the horror of killing had weighed in that moment. Nothing had weighed beside Adam. I did not want to bear the thought alone; I wanted Adam to help me bear it. Pressed against him like a lover I sheltered him and drew comfort from him, until the darkness became more real than he, and I let myself slip into it gratefully.

Chapter Eight

Eternal rest grant to him, O Lord, and may perpetual light shine on him . . . He shall not fear the evil hearing . . .

These were the words I woke to after they had found Adam and myself in the Stockade and brought us back to the Maguire camp. These were what I remember best. The flap of the tent was open and I heard the words clearly but did not understand them. My arm was bandaged and it pained me.

Afterwards Rose came; she gave me water and wiped the perspiration from my forehead. Her hands were very tender on me. There was no impatience.

"What's happened?" I said. "Adam . . .?"

"He's alive. He's all right." Her voice was dry and calm.

"Then what . . .? I heard that out there."

"Sean—Sean was killed at the barricades. A bullet in his throat. Thirty-three others killed with him. They're all to be buried before sunset."

There was little sound on the Eureka that day except the sound of hammers as the coffins were made. Each camp produced its own carpenter. Those coffins were rough and clumsy; the gaps in the planks showed the white sheets that wrapped the bodies.

A terrible stillness seemed to descend on the Eureka and Bakery Hill towards evening. All day the activity had somehow masked the grief and held it back—tending the wounded took time, preparing to bury the dead was a task for those who did not want to stand still to think. But the activity finished at that mass grave—still too shallow, so that they had to mound up the earth over it—and the quietness was felt, it seemed to me, through the whole valley.

They left me alone when the burial parties moved off the Eureka, alone except for Adam in the tent close by. He had, Kate said, only moments of consciousness. The bullet was still in his shoulder; and the doctor had not had time to attend to him yet. There were others more seriously wounded on the Eureka. The loneliness pressed in on me now. I felt the sting of tears upon my cheek, and I left them there. I thought of Sean, but I could not picture him one of the company down there at the cemetery in one of those crude coffins. The priest had been that morning. I remembered the words.

May now the bright company of angels meet your soul; may the triumphant army of glorious martyrs conduct you . . . and thus placed among those happy spirits . . .

I whispered the words to myself to ease the loneliness. " Bright company of angels . . ." And Sean would be as young and beautiful as any of them, I thought. A strange kind of angel he would be though, full of talk and argument. No, that was Pat; Sean never talked when there was Pat to talk for him. He could be a listening spirit. But for all the peace these words conveyed, they still had a vague sound to them. I had a need for a more solid, human comfort. What pressed upon me was the weight of the man I had killed that morning. I could not be free of him. I did not know how to bear this, and the burden of the loneliness as well.

I gathered up my strength. " Adam . . . Adam, are you awake? Can you hear me?"

It seemed a long time that I waited. But he answered me at last. His voice was faint, questioning, as if he wondered if he had dreamed the sound.

" Emmy . . . ?"

That was all he said, but it reached and soothed me.

II

Afterwards I was able to put together the story of the Eureka Stockade, to fill in with what was later knowledge, to learn the pieces I had not seen at the time.

They said that Sean had been the first to fall at the barricades. I don't know if this was true. It is what they said. Dan had finally, when it was all over, found his body half buried beneath the pit-slabs where the barricades had been broken down. He bore only the single wound where the bullet had entered his throat. The military were making prisoners of the wounded then, sending for carts to take them away. There were also the bodies of their own four dead soldiers to gather up. They were collecting weapons from the prisoners, and trying to take them away from those who had merely come to search among the wreckage of the Stockade for their own dead and wounded. Dan had carried a gun ; he gave it to Tim O'Donnell when he bent to lift Sean. Together they walked from the Stockade ; a trooper tried to stop them, demanding the gun and ammunition.

"You'll get nothing more from us," Dan said. He extended his arms with their burden, and the gesture revealed the dead face of his son.

Tim O'Donnell told me that the trooper held his ground only a moment longer ; then he stepped aside and let them pass.

That was the mood of Ballarat at the time. When once the fifteen minutes of skirmish was over, the feeling of the people was with the diggers. And as the reports began to come in from Melbourne, from Geelong, from the whole country-side, we knew that they, too, were with us. The military reinforcements and their big guns arrived from Melbourne, and they were not needed. They crept in like men ashamed. The fugitives from the Stockade, and particularly the leaders, Lalor, Vern and Black, were being sought and rewards were out for them. But they were sheltered and hidden, and no one would give them up. The military seemed almost not to expect it. There were plenty of wounded lying in the tents all over the leads in Ballarat, but no one come to try to arrest or harass them. They did not attempt to search the tents. The people would not have stood for it.

Eventually I heard what happened to Rose during the firing on the Stockade. Kate whispered it to me. "Tom Langley brought her out of it. Sure, she was running like a wild thing, up and down, he said, looking for Sean."

We did not speak of this to Rose. She seemed to blame Tom Langley for taking her away. She had some notion that she could have saved Sean if she had been allowed to remain. And we heard the ugly story, too, that Kevin O'Neill had accused Tom of cowardice when Tom had tried to lead Rose from the Stockade. Kevin had demanded the gun Tom was carrying, and three minutes later Kevin was dead, shot through the chest. The gun was among the weapons captured that day by the military. It was a Westley Richards—a notable weapon, they tell me. The news got into the Melbourne papers that Tom Langley was involved in the uprising at the Eureka Stockade.

But these were only the small things beside what happened to the Maguire family because of the way Sean had died. They were quieter in their grief than I had expected, and it went deeper. Kate once spoke of it.

"Something changes when you leave your first child in a foreign place," she said. "It isn't foreign any more because you put a piece of yourself there in that earth."

And so Sean's dying made them a part of this country; they owned it and had rights in it because of what he had done.

III

The day after the episode of the Stockade, Dan was permitted to pay a fine, and Pat was released from The Camp. It was strange how remote the reason for his arrest seemed; to be arrested for not having a licence now appeared a small thing when Sean had died for it. Pat came back to us quietly, and this became him. There was not the outburst of wild bitterness we had expected. The Irish on the Eureka, who had suffered by far the greatest number of the dead, had not held wakes. The magnitude of the loss was too great for that, and too close. So when Pat rejoined us at the camp he was silent. He took his mother briefly in his arms, and for a moment laid his hand on Con's head. Rose flung herself into his arms, and clung to him, sobbing.

"I tried to take him out, you understand, Pat! I tried to go and get him—but Tom came and took me away! I would have taken him out for you, Pat! I tried!"

He stroked her hair. "There, Rosie—there . . . You did your best."

When she was quieter, he detached himself gently. There was a physical contact between them, but no more. Pat belonged to himself, and whatever grief he felt was tight inside him.

He said to his father: "Well—I'll be getting back to work. We're one man short, but I'll work for two." He finished the mug of tea Kate had given him, and then he went down the shaft.

That evening, while they ate dinner, and Adam and I still lay in our tents, Larry came back. I could see only the outlines of their figures against the fire, but I could hear the words.

123

"I've heard," Larry said. "I got the word at Barrandilla last night. I know about Sean."

There was silence around the fire, then Pat's low voice. "Well—so you've come back, Larry. When it's too late."

"I came as soon as I could. I've been driving since dawn . . ."

"But you left here . . . you left when you knew there could be trouble."

"I didn't know it would go as far as this—or so quickly. I thought I would be back before anything could happen. And *you were here* . . ."

"No, I wasn't here. I let them lock me up because I thought that was a fine thing to do to show them what I thought of them. And so between us we left Sean. If either one of us had been here he might not be dead. We left him, both of us. I left him for a useless piece of paper. You left him for money. Remember that, Larry—for money! We're both of us guilty, but my hands are cleaner than yours."

They spoke no more after that. I heard only Kate's weeping.

IV

The days must have been long and monotonous and yet troubled for Adam. I knew that he was troubled; it showed in his face, the long silences, the halting attempts at conversation with me when he both sat in our enforced idleness. The bullet had come out of his shoulder cleanly, and the wound began to heal. I did less well. The bayonet wound festered, and it gave me pain. The doctor said it would leave a scar; as it started to heal at last I saw the new flesh puckering. Adam watched the progress of that wound also. It was part of what troubled him. As soon as he was able to leave his bed he could have absented himself for most of the day from the camp. But he stayed there, and he always seemed to be present when Kate bathed and dressed the wound. I did not like his eyes on it, but there was nothing I could do.

We spent most of our days in each other's company, but we were not really together. I avoided Adam when I could, or put a barrier between us with an artificial busyness which did not much deceive him. Because my arm was in a sling I could not cook or sew, but I gathered together the children around us on the Eureka who could be spared from working on the cradles and give them lessons. Adam tried to join us—he offered to help, and I rejected the offer, almost curtly.

And when I held him off, at arm's length, as I did, Rose was always there, waiting to fill the empty hours with talk, to listen to him talk, to beguile him and hasten away the long days. She was very demure, very gentle in her charm. To him she did not show the openness of her desire, but a woman could see it, as I did.

For myself, I did not want Adam to look at me. I did not want now to be reminded of what I had done on the morning of the Stockade. It is not an easy thing to admit to the world that you can give your life readily for a man who is not your lover or your husband. So now I was cold to him, and distant, trying to deny that it had been anything but an ordinary act, which any woman would have done. But it was not so, and Adam knew it. He knew how I had feared to use that pistol; he knew that only some extraordinary force had moved me to fire it to kill a man. These were things I could not deny, no matter how my actions tried to. I was aloof with him, and awkwardly self-conscious, and it did no good.

So we were not an easy group there about the Maguire camp. Larry had gone back to Melbourne, but that did not ease the black mood of grieving that was on Pat. All of us grieved, but Pat's was a hard and driving thing that would permit him no peace. As he had said, he did work for two men, and into him had come a kind of strength and endurance that belonged to a hardened man. Almost nothing of the young Pat seemed to have returned from The Camp. He was silent and taciturn; he drank more, but he didn't seem to show the effects. He was absent from the camp each night until long after Kate had gathered everyone to family prayers. But he was up first each morning chopping wood for the fire, and he was ready to go down the shaft before Dan had finished his breakfast.

We grew afraid of his silences, and it would almost have been a relief to hear the old rebellious talk back again. He never spoke of the Eureka Stockade, and he had no more to do with the men who had fought there. He found his companions in the pubs along Main Road. He was gambling, and winning, because he had money enough in his pockets for drink.

Kate grieved somewhat less for Sean because her mind was filled with her worry over Pat. She was patient, though, and she said little to him. To us she said: " Sure God help him—he's thinking he's the one should be dead."

125

Finally, Adam found a way to say to me what he thought had to be said. We were going down to Sampson's—Larry was due back from Melbourne within the next day or two, and we had to prepare lists for him of goods that were in short supply. When Adam asked me to come with him I made an excuse about not being able to write.

"I'll begin to think you dislike me, Emmy, if you keep running away from me—or that I've done something to offend you."

"What could you possibly do to offend me?" I said shortly.

"Well, then—get your bonnet and come."

We walked down the Main Road together, mostly in silence —an embarrassed silence, I thought it. I was tongue-tied, and furious with myself that I had no light chatter for him. Ben Sampson greeted us with a sardonic raising of an eyebrow. "Well, if it isn't the pair of rebels!"

"Oh, hush," I said. "What if people heard you? What if they came to arrest Adam?"

"Rubbish!" Ben answered. "They'd like to be rid of the prisoners they've already got. There isn't a newspaper in the colony that wasn't down on their necks over the Stockade business. They'd like to forget it ever happened. You mark what I'm saying—when those men come to trial there won't be a jury in the whole country who'll convict them. So stop your worrying, little Emma. Adam wasn't a ringleader, so they'll not trouble him."

That he winked at Adam with great deliberation, making sure I saw him. "Not that I wouldn't mind having our Miss Emma so worried over me—and rushing into the Stockade after me like that." He saw my discomfort, and he stopped.

"Well," he said, "I guess we have some work to do, don't we? What are your plans, Adam? Will you be making more trips back here, or is the Langley ship ready?"

"I wish I knew that," Adam said. "I wish I could be sure that John Langley was still willing to give me the *Enterprize*. Langley is on the side of law and order—especially where his property is concerned."

We spent an hour with Ben. This time he himself wrote the lists, usually my job. "I miss your quick fingers, Miss Emma," he said.

He was very kind to me, not teasing as he usually did. To please him I smiled at his jokes, and didn't protest when he gave me a Paisley cotton kerchief to use as a sling. "Better than that calico thing you've got," he said. "There now—that looks better. You'll have every woman on the Eureka fancying herself a bad arm for a spell when they see your style."

Ben's company was a help to Adam and myself, but he lapsed back into the old silence once we were outside on the street again. It was evening, almost the meal-hour here in Ballarat. The diggers were finished in the shafts for the day; some of them were on Main Road to buy supplies, others in search of company. The shops were doing a brisk trade. It was a hot, still evening; the thought of the mutton chops and damper at the Maguire camp was not attractive.

"Let's go and look at Heath's," Adam said suddenly. Heath's was the place everyone went to when they had money to spend on luxuries, or when they merely wanted to spend a half-hour planning what they'd buy when they struck pay-dirt. It was not a place Adam ever went; he was not a man who was very interested in things just for the sake of possessing them. But he urged me forward now, and I was glad of the break in our silence. But I drew back still from his proffered hand; he said nothing, but he let his hand drop. We walked quickly across the street to Carl Heath's.

I looked over the merchandise with a professional eye. Of all the goods that came into Ballarat, Heath imported the very finest. Many of the people came into the shop for just the same reason as we were there—only to look. Carl Heath was ahead of his time in that he didn't urge anyone to buy. He knew they would be back. Elihu Pearson had done this in the London shop, I knew the trick.

"He keeps a good stock," I said to Adam. "He's sure of himself. You notice he doesn't bother with frying-pans and cheap cotton prints and scrubbing brushes. They're the kind of things we all have to have, but we'd rather forget about them. People come here to enjoy spending their money, or planning how to spend it. It's like . . ." I paused, uncertain of how I should say it. "It's like coming to buy a dream." I pointed swiftly. "Now that silk dress is a dream, or part of a dream. Only someone who's just struck it rich would come in and buy that."

I walked over and stood before it. It was on a dressmaker's dummy, a soft, shining blue silk with lace at the throat, a delicate impractical thing that had no place on the dusty

127

streets of the diggings. I touched it reverently. "It's the very best silk," I said. "I know—I've handled this kind before in Elihu's shop."

"It's a beautiful dress," Adam said, behind me. "It would look nice on you, Emma."

I shrugged. "I told you it was a dream. It's not for wearing. It's for making people want it. Besides, it's too big for me."

"Could you fix it? Could you make it small enough?"

"Of course, if I were foolish enough to buy it. But no one is *that* foolish."

"Could you fix it for a wedding dress, Emmy? I'd like to buy it for you."

"It costs a fortune, and it's——" I wheeled around to face him. "Did you say a *wedding* dress? Who . . . whose wedding?"

His face was calm, determined, I thought. He spoke the words quietly. The sun-strained eyes in the tanned face were no easier to read than ever before. He spoke the words, and I had never known Adam to speak anything but the truth. But I did not know what was behind the words.

"Whose wedding did you think I was talking about? Your own. Your wedding."

So I finally had to speak the words for him. "Do you mean," I said carefully, "that you are asking me to marry you?"

"What else? You must know that I want you to marry me."

"No," I shook my head. "I didn't know that at all. How could I possibly know that? I thought . . . I thought it was Rose."

I watched his face very closely. It did not flinch as I spoke her name. His eyes betrayed nothing, nor his mouth. He did not look away from me. But when you love a man as well as I loved Adam you do not miss the shadowy things, the feeling of a tightness coming on that face, the suggestion of the hollows deepening under the cheek-bones, so that you are afraid to look at the hands to see if they clench.

"Emmy, it's *you*. I'm asking you to marry me. Can I say it plainer? Is there some other way to say it?"

I wanted it said a hundred different ways. I wanted it said, not here in the crowd at Carl Heath's shop. I wanted it said to me alone, with his arms about me, with his lips on mine. I wanted the thousand intimacies of two people in love. But I was not to have them.

I looked at Adam and I saw all the things I loved. I saw the body that I had tried to shield with my own, its height and strength, and the handsome face above it. I knew his gentleness and his honesty, the fierceness of his righteous anger when he was aroused. He was a plain man, Adam Langley, not subtle, not conniving, not skilled much in talk or in charm, except that women's eyes turned to him whether he knew it or not. There was the curious kind of innocence of an honest man about him. I knew him very well, because I loved him. But I did not know the very core of him; I had not been able to reach in and touch the passion of him. This was what I wanted, and did not get.

My long hesitation was painful. He swallowed hard. "Emmy it's not much I'm offering you. If John Langley doesn't give me the *Enterprize* I'll be looking for work again. There's no home to take you to. I haven't any money but the wages I earned last month. And if I get the *Enterprize* I'll be away a great deal—you would be alone. Being married to a sailor is a lonely business, Emmy. It needs a special kind of woman to live that life."

"A special kind of woman . . ." I repeated the words slowly. "I'm not special, Adam. I'm just Emmy Brown."

"You are special. You're clever . . . and wise, and understanding." He shifted awkwardly. "I don't know how to say these things, Emmy."

He looked humble, this great towering man. I did not want him to be like that. I did not want to be reminded that I had given him his life, and that now he was trying to pay it back. This kind of honesty can be too devastating, too painful. Pretence would have been better, but Adam and I were not good at pretending.

I took a deep breath. "Yes—yes, I'll marry you. The sooner the better."

It was done. I was going to gamble on being able to reach what was in the very heart of Adam, on being able to bind him to me so that the vision and thought of Rose was forever shut out. He was asking me to be his wife because he felt it was owed to me. He would make me his wife out of a sense of obligation. What he didn't know was that I too had passions, and a will and a heart. I could fight for him in a way that Rose did not understand. I would fight for him, and love him, so that in the end I would give such a conviction of love that he would never look back to this moment and regret it.

I put out my hand and touched his arm, tightening my grip so that he would feel the confidence and the strength.

"Yes—as soon as possible." His hand came up and touched mine, as if we sealed a bargain. "I'll make you a good wife, Adam."

"I know that." He smiled at me then for the first time. We were nervous with each other.

I gestured, half-laughing, at the dress. "And I'll start by saying that we've no business to be standing here looking at this dress. A poor man's wife doesn't buy silk dresses."

"Poor or not, we'll start as we should. You'll have no less than any other woman on her wedding-day. Silk is for the bride . . ."

I was proud when he said that. I felt wanted and cherished as he summoned Carl Heath to take the dress off the dummy. We bought it just as it was, without trying it on. I hurried Heath through the business, as if the whole thing—dress and marriage—might vanish if we were not quick. It was the loveliest dress in Ballarat, I said to Adam, and I would make it fit. It had long sleeves, and I thought, though I did not say it, that they would hide the bandages, and later, the scar. There was a darker blue trimmed bonnet which Carl Heath insisted would set off the dress, and it did. There were no blue slippers, but there was a pair of white satin ones, just a trifle too big, so Heath stuffed the toes.

Heath knew me from Ben Sampson's store. He looked curiously from Adam to me as we tried the shoes.

"If you're not in a hurry, Miss Emma," he said, "I could order a pair from Melbourne just your size."

"We're in a hurry," Adam replied. "Wrap them up."

Adam paid, and he carried the parcel from the shop, awkwardly, because his arm was stiff. I walked beside him with my head held up, waiting to see someone we knew in the passers-by, waiting to say that Adam and I were going to be married. I felt I had to establish some firm claim before the moment when we had to face Rose and tell her.

"Adam, when will we be married?"

"Day after to-morrow. Larry should be back from Melbourne to-morrow. We could ride back with him." He turned to me, remembering. "That is, if you're well enough to travel."

"It's very quick—I mean to get married."

"You said the sooner the better," he frowned. "Do you need more time?"

He must know, as well as I did, that once the announcement was made, the sooner we left Ballarat and Rose behind, the better for all of us. " No," I answered quickly, anxiously. " I don't need more time."

"I'll talk to the Methodist minister, to-night. Will a Methodist minister be all right for you, Emmy."

I nodded. Any minister would be all right so long as he married me well and truly to Adam. It was the only advantage that I had over Rose, not being a Catholic.

I turned to help him settle the parcel more securely under his arm, warning him not to crush the bonnet. It was a proprietary gesture, acted out for all the strangers who passed us by. It was a little pause, the hope that Adam would finally say that he loved me before we went up the hill to the Maguires. I knew he was a simple man, and honest. He did not say it. Perhaps he never would. That was the chance I had to take.

II

Every one of the Maguires looked up as we approached the camp. It seemed for a moment that they already knew. The activity seemed to stop. Kate was finishing preparations for the evening meal ; she halted with the wooden spoon poised. Dan and Pat were washing, their faces and arms streaked with soap. Con ran at once to meet us, obviously curious about the parcel Adam carried. Rose stood and watched us, as if she had been waiting for our return. There was a tenseness in her body which communicated itself to the others.

Adam did not look at Rose as he spoke. He said it quite simply. " Emmy has promised to marry me. We're going to be married in a day or two. She's coming back to Melbourne when I go."

I didn't want to look at Rose, so I watched Dan as he slowly took up the towel. He seemed to be pondering what he should say. He was the first to speak.

" Well, now—a wedding! That's just what this family is needing. Do you hear that, Katie?—a wedding! And it's our Emmy and Adam—well, what could be better?"

His voice urged them, and he started to move towards us. Suddenly they were all there, kissing me, shaking Adam's hand. I heard Kate's voice huskily in my ear. " God bless you, child." Surprisingly Pat was there, the lather still on his face, his hands and arms dripping. He kissed me on the lips. " Good for you, Emmy!" It was a strange thing to have said. Con hugged me about the waist. " I don't want you to go, Emmy," he said. He had nothing to say to Adam.

131

They made a good show of it, but I felt their shock just the same. They were not like those outside the family who had automatically paired Adam and myself together after they learned what happened in the Stockade. They knew better than that. They might not have wanted a husband who was not a Catholic for Rose, but just the same they knew the power of her feeling for Adam, and the extreme of her passion when she was thwarted. And they had seen Adam's eyes on her too often, as I had. What Adam had said did not change that, and they all knew it. So in the end, instinctively, we turned to look at Rose.

Rose didn't even try to hide what she felt. Perhaps she wasn't able. In later years she grew better at it, but now she was just a young girl, unskilled, still naïve in a fashion. She stood as if she were frozen. All the colour had drained from her face ; her features seemed to sharpen, to lose their look of youth. Her eyes were staring in unbelief, wide and grown darker. There was no colour in her, just the black of her hair and the white skin. Her lips opened on a sound, but she couldn't utter it. This single movement, though, broke the rigour of her body. She turned and ran to the tent.

" Rose . . ."

I think I died a little at the sound of the desperate appeal in Adam's voice. If only, I thought, it had not been Adam who had called Rose back. But it had been Adam, calling that name almost invountarily, and I knew that I would go on hearing it, its tone, its longing, for a very long time.

There was a stirring in the group. Then Adam himself seemed to know what he had done. He turned to me with a gesture that half asked for forgiveness, and yet begged me to pretend that nothing had happened.

And so I began the game that lasted for a long time. I lifted my head and smiled at the faces about me.

" Adam's bought me a silk dress to be married in," I said.

Rose did not leave the tent all evening. She was still there at the time when we all went to bed. She sat hunched on the mattress, her hair in a tangled mess on her shoulders, and she was waiting for me. The tent had been in darkness ; she blinked in the light of the candle I carried. Her eyes were dark-rimmed with fatigue ; it suddenly seemed to me that Rose had lived longer hours than the actual passage of time. Her expression was no longer unbelieving. A kind of fury lived there.

Her lips were thin. The words came harshly when she spoke.

"What made you do it?"

"Do what?"

"Adam is mine! You know I love Adam!"

"*You* love Adam. Does he love you?"

"Yes! You know he does!"

"Then why did he ask me to marry him?" I felt myself trembling, but I made my tone firm. Rose must find no weakness here, or she would use it. This had to be said between us. Something had to be established once and for all. Rose was making claims, and I was going to deny them. I was going to deny every voice that said, loud or whispered, that Adam loved Rose. I was going to take what had been offered, take hold of it and keep it. I had thought that I could give Rose anything, but I could not give her Adam.

"Why?" repeated Rose. Though the tone was rough, she kept it low. In these few hours she appeared to have learned a kind of wisdom; she was no longer quite so young as the girl who had stood out there and let us see her shock so plainly.

"I'll tell you why," she went on. "He thinks you saved his life. He thinks he owes you that. You've let him know that you're sick with love for him, and he's going to marry you because there's a debt to pay."

"That isn't true! There's no debt."

"He thinks there is, and he's paying it. What else has he got to give you except this? And what have you got to give him? . . . *you!!* What have you got?"

The words were cruel, and cruelly meant. I felt sick as I listened to them. I looked fully at Rose, and as much as I wanted to deny it my eyes told me the sense of what she was saying. The difference between us was there, sharp and clear, for anyone to see. Rose had pulled off her dress and tossed it on the ground. Her arms and shoulders were bare, and her petticoat revealed the full perfection of her breasts. Her anger gave her beauty an intense, wild quality. Her skin was warm and faintly damp with perspiration. There was never a woman more ready for love, and any man would know it. I felt myself shrink inside at the thought of this, but I wouldn't let my eyes leave Rose, or waver.

"I have plenty to give Adam. I've got loyalty and love. Yes, I love him! I love him in the kind of way you don't know about—don't understand. All you see is that I'm not pretty. You don't see anything else. I've got a brain, and I can use it to help Adam. You've never done that, and you never will. Adam *needs* me. Perhaps he doesn't know it yet, but he will. I promise you he will!"

Her lips curled in a grimace of contempt. " Is *that* what you think will hold a man? You suppose a bit of sewing and cooking and adding up your old figures in a book will be enough? A man wants something in his bed that's more than skin and bone. He doesn't want a clerk or a cook—he wants a woman!"

"Yes—he wants a woman, and he chose me. Do you understand that, Rose? He chose *me!*"

" He chose you, but he doesn't really want you. He chose you because you're safe—you're the kind he's always known before. You're like his mother and his sisters and all those other drabs he's used to back on that place he comes from. But *me*—I'm something under his skin. You think you're the only one who could be for Adam? There are other ways of doing him good besides washing his shirts. "I'll be good for Adam—but he doesn't understand that yet. A man's sense and his inclinations go different ways. It's *me* Adam wants in bed. Does anything count beside that? He may marry you, but he wants me!"

I slapped that passionate, greedy face with all the strength of my anger. The blow left red marks on the warm soft flesh.

" I've listened to enough of your filthy talk," I said. "I'll hear no more of it. You've made a mistake, Rose. You've gone too far."

I sank down on the mattress opposite her. Her rage and frustration seemed not to have permitted her to feel the blow. I think she was glad to have had the power to goad me to such an action.

"I've loved you, Rose," I said. " I've given you—you, the whole family, all of them—as much love as I have. But there's one thing I can't give you, and that's Adam. He belongs to himself. He's not something to be snatched at, and taken— not something to be fought over by two women. Adam belongs to himself. And marriage counts with a man like Adam. Never forget that, Rose. In the end he chose me!"

" And he'll regret it. A year from now he'll wish he'd never seen you. And that's when I'll be waiting."

We faced each other for some time in silence. Finally I said to her, very quietly; " Rose, when Adam and I leave here I don't want to see you again—ever. I've loved you—but I love Adam more. And a year from now he won't regret it, because when I hold Adam's child in my arms *then* he will love me."

I snuffed out the candle, preferring the darkness to seeing her face. Mercifully she said no more, just lay back on the mattress in her petticoat. My arm hampered me; and it was difficult to undress; always before Rose had helped me. But it was understood that this was finished now. From now on we were alone and apart. For the first time we lay down in this tent and neither spoke to the other. Neither hand brushed the other in the final sleepy gesture of affection.

When I woke the next morning Rose's bed was empty. May God forgive me for my suspicions because I looked at once to see if Adam was still there. He sat by the fire, tending it, drinking his tea and talking to Kate.

Before he had finished breakfast Larry had arrived. He had been on the road since dawn, he said. In the commotion of his arrival, in the talk and telling of the news, Rose's absense was hardly noticed. And no one wanted to underscore it.

"Rose is sulking," I heard Kate say to Dan. "Leave her be."

So they tried to make the usual fuss over Larry's arrival, listened to the gossip from the capital, and Kate selected the largest from Larry's supply of hams for the wedding feast. But for all that the arrival was strangely quiet. Pat finished his breakfast and went down the shaft immediately. His going seemed to point up the change that was in all of us since Sean's death. Nothing was as it used to be. There was both a sense of hurry and of emptiness. Larry stayed only long enough to unload the provisions for the family's use, and then he too went. The business of the goldfields seemed grim, and a feeling of further change hung over us. The Methodist minister had agreed to marry Adam and I the next day at noon. We would leave that afternoon with Larry for Melbourne. Kate suddenly took to scolding Con unnecessarily that day. She seemed to need reassurance that she still had some family about her.

Before he left for Sampson's Larry had kissed me lightly on the cheek. "You didn't wait, did you?" he said. "If you'd only given me time I was meaning myself to ask you to marry me."

They all smiled when they heard that; it was the kind of compliment always paid to a bride. And yet I knew the grain of truth in it. It was my kind of woman Larry would marry—sensible, hard-working, above all, useful. Ambitious men with a long way to go, like Larry, did not marry idle beauties. The truth depressed me.

But there was little time for self-pity. Kate was engulfed in a frenzy of baking—the hams, the bread, the fruit cake for which she was famous on the Eureka—and all of it to be done in the tiny camp oven. She sent Con to Sampson's for more whisky and butter. I protested the trouble and expense. "Especially now—well, you can't feel like making a celebration with Sean not here."

Kate halted in the task of adding the flour. "Now, lookit —I'm told in the Protestant part of the Bible there's a piece about there being a time for marrying and a time for grieving. They're mixed up together, the way they always are. Sean treated you like a sister. We couldn't have him shamed by a miserable wedding-party."

"It should be his sister's wedding-party. It should be Rose who's getting married, shouldn't it?—to Adam?" I had to say it.

Kate looked at me from under lowered brows. "Rose has come to the time I always said she'd come to—the time when she couldn't have what she wanted. "No——" She waved a floury hand to cut me off. "She's my own child but I'll not be denying the things that are in her that men don't want. Those are the things that Adam doesn't want."

"But if he loves her?"

"Love, is it?—Ah, now, that's different. It can last a day or a year or forever, they say. From what I see when I look around me it's more likely to be a year than forever. Have patience, Emmy. Wait for Adam to find it out."

"And if he doesn't?"

She shrugged. "We all take our chances."

We said no more about Adam or about Rose—there wasn't time. And then Kate had already said the last word on it. Rose stayed away from the camp for the midday meal, and I was grateful, because it was easier to believe that all would be well between me and Adam so long as Rose was not there to look at, to cause a kind of stirring among the men wherever she moved. Adam and Larry were at Sampson's all the day, and the camp was strangely empty. No one wanted to talk about Rose or the reason for her absence.

"Oh—she had some new friend over on Black Hill— Kathleen Burke she said her name was. She'll be there," Kate said in answer to Dan's question.

"Then she should be back here helping."

"Sure she'd only be under my feet."

They left it at that. After the meal Sarah Foley arrived to start fixing my dress. She had seemed slightly timid with me

136

since the morning I had swept her and the children out of the Stockade. Matt Foley was one of the men taken prisoner by the military and shipped off to Melbourne for trial. Everyone on the Eureka had taken collections of food and money to support the Foleys since then. Sarah Foley now fingered the blue silk of my wedding dress with a faint wistfulness that had not a great deal to do with wanting it. She was still in her twenties, but already old, and with four children clustered about her, fragile silk dresses were no longer part of her dreams. "You'll look grand in it, Emmy," was what she said.

It irked me somewhat to see another woman sew on my wedding gown, but with my arm still in a sling, there was nothing I could do to help her. I kept the Foley children busy for the afternoon—it was not difficult because they remembered well the ear-boxing, and the pistol I had waved. I stood patiently for the hem to be measured, and the waist to be lifted and taken in. Mrs. Foley was an expert needlewoman, but even so I wanted to snatch away the dress, to permit no one but myself to touch it. I suppose she sensed this, and when she was preparing to leave, just about sundown, she unwrapped a nightgown from a roll of calico and rather shyly placed it in my hands.

"I've nothing else to give you," she said. "I sewed it myself before my own wedding—that's ten years ago. I wanted *one* nice thing—you know the way it is. Sure I only wore it the once. I've washed it and bleached it in the sun. It's nice and fresh." It was fine lawn, trimmed with Irish lace, an exquisitely useless thing in the baggage of a digger's wife.

"My grandmother made the lace," she said. Then she gathered together the children, put the baby across her hip, and left quickly, declining Kate's invitation to stay to supper. Kate watched her go thoughtfully. "Sometimes I wonder why any of us came here—when it ends up in a couple of tents for a home, and hungry children, and a man in gaol in Melbourne." She brushed a wisp of hair from her forehead. "Or a son in his grave before his time."

It was not until we were ready to eat supper, with the smell of the baked hams and the spiced cakes heavy on the air, that we thought about Rose still being absent.

"'Tis enough now," Kate said. "You'll go to the Burkes' the minute supper's over, Pat, and fetch her back. She's making a great edjit of herself, so she is."

Pat went and he came back without Rose. "She's not been there all day. They've not seen a sight of her."

Dan got to his feet at once. I had never seen his face so

137

stern; the craggy lines that had been more pronounced since Sean's death seemed to deepen still more. He tugged at his beard. "She has to be found if it takes all night. I'll not have her bring more trouble on her mother. Boys, we'll split up. Ask everyone you see. She has to be somewhere in the town."

Larry had already begun lighting a lamp to take with him. "And the place to start is the pubs on Main Road," he said shortly. He handed a second lamp to Adam. "Come on— we each take one side of the Road. And if I get her in one of those whore-holes I'll break her neck."

We did not find Rose that night. Kate and I sat alone by the fire, Kate having forbidden Con to join the search. "We will stay," she said. "There must be someone here if she comes back."

We drank tea, and talked a little at times, and kept the water hot against the men's return. I tried to speak of Rose only once.

"It's my fault," I said. "I've driven her away. If I had let her have Adam . . ."

Kate forgot her worry in a flash of contempt. "And do you think Adam's a parcel to be passed around between the two of you? Holy Mother, he's a *man* and he knows what he's about." She shook her head, returning now to her sober tone. "Nothing drove Rose away but what's in her own soul. And God knows what that is, because I don't any more."

Dan was the last to come back to the camp. It was almost four o'clock, and the first of the sunrise colours was streaking the sky against the hills. He swayed a little in his fatigue, and his giant shoulders were hunched. As he stood in silhouette he looked old and tired; I had never thought to see him so shaken.

"I'll have to tell the police," he said. "I don't believe she's in the town." After that he said nothing, drinking his tea noisily, holding the pannikin between his two hands as if he needed the comfort of its warmth. When he finished he rose. "Come on, Kate. We'll get a few hours' sleep."

His hand rested briefly on my head. "You should have been in bed a long time ago. A bride needs sleep on her wedding day."

"I couldn't . . ." I found my head against his chest suddenly. I did not let my tears fall, because they were useless in this trouble. But I could not speak. All I wanted to do was to cling to Dan and feel his great strength and his gentleness.

He stroked my hair. "It's a bad thing Rose has done to you on your wedding way," he said. "But a wedding there'll be, whether Rose is here to see it or not!"

III

Whenever I thought about my wedding day in the years afterwards I was never myself I saw at the centre of things, but Rose—Rose triumphant, defiant and a little desperate.

It began like no other day, of course. There was a wedding to be got through, though the gaiety was gone from the event. Dan had said the wedding would be as planned, even if Rose had not returned by that time. No one argued against his wishes. Both Adam and myself knew that the sooner we left Ballarat the sooner Rose might come back. We made arrangements to go by stage to Melbourne that afternoon because now Larry must stay here.

"Set out the food, Katie, and call in the neighbours. We'll not be sending Emmy off without a little feasting."

But still it was a preoccupied group that followed Adam and me to the Methodist chapel. At any other time they would have been uneasy about the ceremony in this nonconformist church, been a little guilty about their own presence at it. But now they stood behind me solidly, dressed in their best clothes—Dan and Kate, Larry, Pat and Con. Rose's presence was more weightily felt than if she had stood there also.

Adam showed nothing, not the anguish he must have been in, nor the desire to hurry too much and so be done with it. I remember only his great courtesy. He had brought no clothes with him suitable for a wedding, but he stood up in good serge, straining the shoulders of the coat he had borrowed from Ben Sampson. He looked almost a stranger to me, out of the familiar seaman's peaked cap and the old jacket. I liked the other Adam better. But he smiled at me, and the stranger vanished; then he took my hand, and it felt warm.

Ben Sampson, who had been brought up in the Wesleyan religion, was the only one fully at ease—or pretending to be. He roared out the "Amens" to the prayers with great gusto, looking very religious, and smelling of whisky. He winked at me while we waited for the ceremony to start, and I couldn't help laughing. Adam laughed also—mostly out of nervousness, I think—but it relieved the tension, and the minister, Mr. Scott, had a smiling pair to marry, after all.

They waited until we were outside the severity of the Methodist Chapel before they threw rice. For a moment it was possible to forget Rose; there was laughter and the sun shone. Adam held my arm; he kissed me well and lovingly. The excitement and pleasure mounted in me; the sun caught the light in the blue silk, I felt my cheeks flushed and I knew that I was experiencing one of my visitations of prettiness. I had left the arm sling off, and the sleeves covered the bandage nicely. I wanted no one reminded of that wound. The blue bonnet was gay, and so was I. Adam held my hand all the way back to the Maguire camp, and I kept my head high, happily acknowledging the greetings of the neighbours who fell in behind us. Jimmy O'Rourke was waiting outside the church to fiddle us on our way. So in the end we had a bridal procession back to the camp.

I was kissed by everyone, and the dress was inspected, and Adam's hand was shaken. He stayed close by me. No one mentioned Rose, and Adam looked nothing but the happy bridegroom. Dan began to dip the ladle into the buckets of whisky punch he had prepared. Finally the hands were raised, grasping the tin pannikins, the tea cups and whatever else they could find to hold the punch.

"The bride and bridegroom!" Dan cried.

They drank the toast down. There were some individual toasts: "Emmy" and "Adam!" I heard a few say. Someone called—Mike Healy I think it was—"To the prettiest bride on the Eureka!" which wasn't the truth, but they gallantly drank to that also. Jimmy O'Rourke's fiddle started to scrape again in a flashing reel.

Adam's arm went about my waist. "Come on, Emmy."

We took a few steps, and the people parted before us, clapping their hands. We stumbled on the rough ground, and recovered, laughing. A few other couples started to join in. I heard Pat cry, "My turn now, Greeneyes." But I held fast to Adam, and I thought my heart had to burst with happiness and pride. We danced over the mullock heaps in an undignified gallop.

Then the fiddle faded away in a dismal sour screech. Our momentum carried us on a moment or so, but by then I was conscious that no one else danced. We turned together and looked back to the camp-fire.

The crowd seemed to fall away a little and we could see through it clearly. But I heard the voice, and that was all I needed.

"Isn't there a toast for us, too, Dada?"

Rose stood there, bareheaded, in her simplest cotton gown, and she clung to Tom Langley's arm. She held her head high and defiantly. She looked straight at Adam and myself.

"Tom and I were married last night over at Clunes. Isn't anyone going to drink our health too?"

I looked immediately up at Adam's face then, because I had to see for myself. It had gone deadly white, and it held a look of undisguised pain such as I had never seen there before or since.

IV

We left Ballarat that same afternoon on Larry's wagon since there was now no reason for any of us to stay. We remained just long enough to witness the second ceremony of making Rose Tom Langley's wife. Dan had insisted on this.

"I want no part of this business," he said to Tom, "but since you've made her your wife, let her be so in God's sight."

"We were married properly," Rose answered sullenly. "By a minister in Clunes. It's in the records there."

Dan looked at her with hard eyes. "Have you gone so far, my daughter, that you think of records as being marriages? It's no marriage until the priest says the holy words."

Rose made no further protest, but Tom did. "I refuse," he said. "I've no need for these Papish superstitions."

"You've married her now, and you'll have to take what comes with her. Her religion is part of it." He gestured to Con. "Go over and see if Father Smyth's at the church, Con. Tell him we'll be to see him in ten minutes."

Rose changed her gown and put on a bonnet, and all of us went with her and Tom to the church. Our neighbours on the Eureka had drifted away long since, though they looked at us covertly now as we passed. Some of them were angry because Rose's arrival at that time had cheated them of the party; they knew enough to know that there would be no celebration over this second wedding of the day.

In view of the marriage the day before at Clunes, Father Smythe waived the rules that usually surrounded the celebration of a mixed marriage.

"It's done now," he said. "We must make the best of it."

They were a sullen, uncomfortable pair who stood before the altar, waiting for Father Smythe to get ready. Rose fingered her mittens, and Tom coughed nervously. He had the look of a man dazed and stunned, afraid to believe his good fortune, and perhaps already beginning to question exactly what it was that he had got. He stared around at his unfamiliar surroundings without comprehension, at the crudely coloured statues and the crucifix. Beside me, Kate wept.

"To think my only daughter is being married in this hurry-up way . . . with no banns read out . . . and no mass. It's as if we had something to be ashamed of. I wouldn't have believed that Tom Langley could take advantage of a young girl's innocence this way . . ."

Rose turned to her savagely, and she looked neither young nor innocent. "If you must know it, *I* did the asking!"

The simple ceremony went forward. For appearance sake, Adam and I had to be there, but I wished we were not. I did not punish myself further by trying to see Adam's face; I'd had enough of that. I knew I had made a mistake in agreeing to marry him, and it was now past undoing. In spite of the almost certain knowledge that he loved Rose I had gone ahead with it. I had gambled and I began now to believe that I had lost right from the beginning. The die was cast then for the years ahead as together we listened to the words being pronounced over Rose and Tom; the pattern was cut. We suffered equally in these moments, I think, and one of the hells of our marriage was that we were never able to speak to each other of this torment.

There were no festivities afterwards. I changed from my finery into a sensible cotton gown for the dusty road. The canvas bag I had brought with me to Ballarat was swollen by the acquisitions of these months, mostly gifts Rose had given to me. It hurt me to look at them. They represented the flowering of a friendship and of a love. For the sake of Adam I had lost them, and I had snarled and twisted our three lives.

I closed up the bag quickly and went out of the tent for the last time, to join my husband.

We rode out of Ballarat, Larry, Adam and myself on the front seat of the dray. And Rose went to spend the second night of her wedding among the silken fineries of the Palace Hotel on Main Road. In at least that desire she succeeded.

We made a good show of talk on the road after we left Ballarat behind. It was the only thing to do. Adam and I were both going to make the best of it, and we began right then. Larry only mentioned Rose once.

"We've always spoiled Rose—being the only girl. Tom will do the same." And then later, he said, "it will be lonely at the camp to-night. Only Pat and Con left now."

I was not sorry to leave Ballarat. I was both harder, and stronger than when I had made my way up this road four months ago. I was also more vulnerable. With learning to love the Maguires, and then Adam, I had opened myself to a whole host of new joys that could also be hurts. I was no longer sufficient to myself. I had found that I had been needed, and in turn I had needed others. But Ballarat for me would always be the story of Rose and Adam, and I wanted peace from it. So I did not regret it, nor look back.

We drove past sunset into the dusk. Adam had wanted to stop earlier, but Larry insisted on going on, so that it was almost dark my the time we stopped and Adam lifted me down from the dray.

" I don't know why we didn't stop by The Digger's Arms." Adam grumbled, as he tried to pitch the tents in near-darkness. " It's the best spot along this part of the road."

I never forgot that Larry did not even glance towards me then, nor had he when we passed the tavern a few miles back. " I never liked the place," he answered. " I never stop there if I can help it."

Larry retired to his tent immediately after the meal and left us. I was coming out of the shock of what Rose had done to us, and the urge to fight had reasserted itself. I would not give up Adam so easily to that shadowy figure who mocked us both, who had seemed to sit like a fourth at our fire that night.

So I was not shy with Adam, nor timid. I had wanted his hands on me, and when they came I welcomed them. He knew well how to hold a woman, with strength and firmness. I left Sarah Foley's lace-trimmed nightgown on the bare floor of the tent, and Adam's warmth did not let me feel the lack of it. We seemed well-matched, and as far as I could tell, he was happy. My own happiness was that he did not let Rose come between us here. And the first pain was good too, because it was given by Adam, and after there was the exquisite pleasure and peace. Our meeting was swift, and I don't think he knew that I was not a virgin then. He lay close to me, and his breathing grew deep and easy.

" I love you, Adam," I said softly.

" I love you, Emmy." He spoke the words at last. I believed them ; perhaps he did too.

But when I woke in the first uncertain light of the morning, to lie gloating a little in my good fortune, I heard the name that he murmured in his sleep, and it was not my name.

BOOK TWO: 1855

Chapter One

John Langley, Tom's father, was to remain an almost mythical figure to me for some time after we came to Melbourne. I saw his name frequently—I seemed never to be able to get away from it. It was on the brewery drays pulled by the great matched pairs of greys which were one of the sights of Melbourne; it was on the stores and warehouses that dominated a whole block in the busiest part of Collins Street, it was on the warehouse down at Hobson's Bay and on the ship's chandler's stores there. His name was painted on the lighters that plied up and down the Yarra between the city and Hobson's Bay. I did not pick up the *Argus* a single day, it seemed to me, that I did not read some pronouncement of his, either as a leader of commerce or as a member of the Legislative Council. I had a sense of John Langley long before I met him; it was a partially wrong impression, but it was a powerful one.

It was John Langley, also, who gave us our first home.

This didn't come about because he was a generous man—I knew enough of his public character to know that he was the kind who preached hard work and one's own efforts as the only means by which a man should expect to advance himself. He urged the virtues of thrift and industry, and he did not make life easy for those who worked for him. In the final judgment, I suppose, it was because Adam's name was Langley that we found ourselves setting up house in those three small rooms at the back of the Collins Street warehouse.

We took a room at the Bull and Mouth hard by the Bourke Street Eastern Market, and Adam tried the very first day to see John Langley. I remember watching him go, wearing his good suit and a smile that was more encouragement than confidence in the interview. He came back holding his cap, as if he wanted to throw it away, and looking angry.

" He wouldn't see me. He sent his clerk to tell me to come back to-morrow."

It went on in that fashion for nearly a week. There was nothing to do but wait. The country was still stirred up about the events at the Eureka, and the names of most of the men who had participated were known. We had no hope that John Langley didn't know the part that Adam had played. We took a trip to Hobson's Bay to look at the *Enterprize*. We didn't go aboard, just looked at her from the dock, the neat lines of her, the new paint, the superstructure that was almost completed, Adam gazed at her like a man in love. There had been no look on his face for me like this—nor for Rose neither.

"Some day I'll have my own ship, Emmy."

"I nodded. "Yes." I had no idea how this would ever be, but he said it like a promise. We went back to the Bull and Mouth and Adam sat all evening, whittling endlessly at his pieces of soft wood and from his expression I knew he was thinking of the *Enterprize*—or not the *Enterprize* but his own ship. I had no reason to fear a ship as I did Rose, so I was content to have it that way.

Finally John Langley saw him. He was summoned, not to Langley's office at the warehouse, but to his home, farther along on Collins Street. I waited all afternoon for him in the stifling summer heat, with the flies buzzing and the noise of the Bourke Street traffic for company. At the end of the afternoon I heard his footsteps on the stairs; they came at a run.

He caught me by the shoulders, and almost shouted his pleasure. "It's all right, Emmy! Do you hear?—it's all right!"

"You still have the *Enterprize*?"

His face was exultant. "I still have it!"

He clasped his hands together behind his back as he paced the room as he talked.

"He wanted to throw me out. I think that's what he's been trying to make up his mind to all this week. And yet he can't because he's beginning to believe that Tom is lost to him. He's a stubborn old man and he won't admit how much he wants Tom back. But with Tom not here he needs someone of the Langley name about him. So the *Enterprize* is mine, though, I suppose Tom would say I was stealing it from him."

"That's foolish."

He nodded. "I know it. Tom couldn't captain the *Enterprize*, so I'm taking nothing I'm not due."

"The marriage?" I said. "Did he talk of the marriage?"

Adam shrugged. "What do you expect. He doesn't like it—he doesn't like it at all. He had very definite plans about the sort of person Tom should have married. Tom's sister,

Elizabeth, married very well, he reminded me . . . a nobleman's son. It was Tom's duty, he said, to do the same."

"Yes—and look where Elizabeth Townsend is today!" I said hotly. "Back here with her father with neither husband nor child to her name. A pretty sort of marriage that is! They say Elizabeth's a poor sort of creature. At least Tom has married a *woman*——!"

I stopped short, astonished to hear myself defending Rose. But this was the smallest truth that I could say of hear. It was what she had so cruelly pointed out to me. But now I repeated it, and I knew its importance.

"Did he . . . Did John Langley ask about her?"

"No. He has his own ideas of what she is. He doesn't like the Irish. Not the immigrant Irish. He thinks that Tom has married some ignorant little girl from the bogs, and a Catholic to make matters worse. He talks of annulment. But he knows he only talks. It's a hard thing to do with a twice-repeated ceremony before witnesses. . . ."

It was the first time he had spoken of the marriage. I felt his dejection, the flat tone of finality as he had talked of the two ceremonies. Heaven knows how often he thought about it, all the time he did not talk. I was jealous now of the moments of silence because I feared that they belonged to Rose.

"But he knows Larry," I said. "He trusts him . . . he knows what kind of man he it. Could Larry's sister be so different?"

"Where business is concerned a man's usefulness is what concerns John Langley most. He doesn't care about the person. Larry half-expectetd to have his business with Langley stopped after the marriage, but it's gone right on. The only difference is that Langley has given orders that Larry is never to be permitted to see him. They negotiate entirely through Clay, the head clerk."

"What a twisted old man," I said slowly. "Not honest enough to make a clean break with the Maguires—hanging on to Larry because of the money he brings. No wonder Tom left . . . how he must hate his father."

I sat down in the rocking-chair again by the window, staring out at the spaces of the market-place that were now emptying as the dinner hour approached. I was troubled about John Langley. I sensed a hand of possessiveness falling over Adam. I almost wished that he had lost the *Enterprize*, and that we were free of John Langley.

I said, half-musingly, "I begin to see why Tom wanted to

be with the Maguires so much. I used to wonder why he would stay on the goldfields when he had so much here . . . Poor Tom!"

"Poor Tom?" Adam's voice was harsh with contempt. "He ran off to the goldfields in a fit of spite when his father sent away a servant he got in the family way. Everyone knows that story."

"They say John Langley put her on a ship for England without Tom knowing it. Perhaps he meant to marry her."

"Marry her! That's not likely. Tom's not that kind."

"He married Rose."

"Rose isn't a servant girl." His rebuke was stern and passionate. I shrank from it. This was Adam at his worst, the severe, puritanical side of his inheritance coming out, arrogant, unforgiving. At moments like this he utterly lacked compassion. In two ways he hurt me then—to judge Tom for his behaviour without understanding any of its causes, and then, in a sense, to upbraid me for speaking so of Rose. I knew he carried an unreal picture of Rose in his heart, a romanticised ideal of beauty and innocence. He was telling me now that I must not besmirch that ideal with my sharp, unkind tongue.

I stared at him in a long silence. It was the first time we had had words since we were married. I learned, eventually, not to speak of Rose except to praise her to him. But at that time I was not so agreeable, and my lesson had not been learned. I was angry with him.

He sought his pipe and filled it. He glanced at me several times while he lit it, and I think he felt contrite. I had not expected him to speak first, but he did.

"John Langley isn't such a hard man," he said. The words were an overture, an offering of peace. "You'll find that out when you have dealings with him.

"Thank you—I hope I don't have dealings with him."

"Well—there's the matter of the house. There's not many would be troubled where you were to live while I was away on the *Enterprize*. Not with the city as crowded as it is, and rents sky-high. He's letting us have it for a song!"

I sprang out of the chair. "What are you talking about, Adam Langley? What house? Where . . . ?"

He looked at me in triumph, withholding for just a moment his piece of news, confident now that I would have to be nice to him, that I had no excuse to glower at him any longer.

"He says is only small, Emmy. Three small rooms, he said . . . and they'll need cleaning and fixing up."

I grasped his lapels and wanted to shake him. "Where?"

"Behind the Langley Stores. At the back of that little lane that runs between the Stores and the warehouse. Where the stables are. Of course, it's not much, but I thought that just for the time being we'd make it serve . . . just till we can get enough money to find a house of our own . . ."

I continued to smile at him, and to nod at his words, but a sense of foreboding touched me. I could not say precisely why, but I did not want to live in a house owned by John Langley, at the end of a little alley that was called Langley Lane.

"He gave me the key," Adam was saying, "so get your bonnet and we'll go and see it now."

As we walked across the market place, Adam holding my arm in exactly the right degree of proprietorship and smugness expected of a new bridegroom—as if Rose Maguire's name had never been mentioned between us—he continued to talk about the house.

"Of course it will be only temporary. I don't approve of rented houses. A man should own the house he lives in."

Well, that was Adam, a mixture of passion and caution, urging himself towards all the virtues that had bred and continued his own hardy, thrifty race. But he had their fire too, the sudden flaring of recklessness that could stake everything on a chance for fortune or to cry out against an injustice. Who would have imagined, to see him so respectable, so nearly pompous, that evening, that he had been one of those who had rushed to the defence of the Eureka Stockade. But that was Adam.

The shadows fell deeply in the Lane between the Langley Stores and the warehouse. The shuttered shop-front looked grim and unfriendly, the loading-bays of the warehouses were closed and dark. There was always the smell of horses in that lane; they stood there all day harnessed to the Big Langley drays. It was littered with chaff and manure. We made our way along there to the back of the Stores, where the Lane widened a little into a kind of courtyard. Directly facing the opening from the Lane were the stables for the horses that pulled the Langley drays.

"The house was used by the watchman," Adam said. "Then the old one died, and the new one had his family at Flemington and didn't want to move them. The old man lived here alone for about twelve years, Langley said."

The house was very small, a wooden one, unpainted, almost

148

leaning against the wall of the Stores. It's single door opened directly into the yard, and the two curtainless windows were piled around with boxes. Across the yard the blank wall of the warehouse towered over it a full three stories. Adam shoved aside some boxes and unlocked the door; it opened grudgingly with a squeal of the hinges, and Adam had to push hard against the newspapers that were stacked behind it. We squeezed past it to get inside.

There were three rooms opening off a little cubby-hole of the hall, and they were full of the old man's accumulation of junk. There was a sour odour of old rags, and in the back we heard the scamper of rats. In the front room there was a rusted bedstead collapsed on the floor; the mattress had been eaten by the rats. There was a fireplace with an oven set in the brick beside it; there was a pump for water, and a bucket standing under it. Adam pushed his way through the rubbish and began to prime it. After a time a jet of rusty water shot out on his trousers.

" Well, it works," he said looking hopefully at me. I went to help wipe the water off him with my handkerchief. But he didn't let me do that. He caught my wrist and forced me to look at him.

" Emmy—will it do? Can you live in this place?"

I shrugged. " Have you forgotten I've just come from the goldfields? This place has a roof—from the dampness in here I'd say it probably leaks—but it's a roof, and I suppose it can be fixed. That's all I need to begin with."

He suddenly threw out his hands in a gesture of despair that indicated the uneven floors soaked with rain-water, the sagging door-posts, the rusty pump and the rooms piled high with newspapers, rags, old iron pots, and broken, discarded display stands from the Stores.

" It won't do," he said. " I can't leave you in a place like this."

" It will clean up," I said. " The rubbish will burn. With a good scrub down and two cats in here, you'll never know it's the same place."

He looked at me, half doubting, and yet appealing. " Could you manage, Emmy?"

" Yes," I said.

He pushed his cap back on his head. " If you could . . ." he began slowly. " If you could manage here it would make a big difference—just in the beginning, you understand. If we could save some money, Langley has promised that he'd let me buy into the cargoes I'm handling. The profits are fat,

149

Emmy, if I can make that first step. And then . . . after that, with some money saved, there's a chance I could borrow enough to buy a sloop. Just coastal trade. But my own, you understand. My own vessel, Emmy." He looked at me, and his face was rapt. "Think of it! My own vessel."

I realized that he was listening to his dreams spoken aloud, and that this was the first time he had cared to share them with me. He was a long way off in the future, impossibly remote it seemed to me. But he was there already, in his thoughts; he had it planned and his foot was already set upon that path. But the beginning, for him, lay here in this dismal little shack. If we stayed here it represented the beginning for him, the first step. I loved him too well to lay any shadow across the bright dream.

We locked up and walked back down the alley where the gathering dusk was already blackness.

"We'll call her *Emma*," he said.

My mind busy with what had to be done to get those filthy rooms habitable, I answered him absently, "What—the house?"

"The sloop," he said. "We'll call the sloop *Emma*."

II

I suppose there were the best days of our marriage, the weeks when we cleaned up the little house in Langley Lane, the weeks during which the *Enterprize* was finally made ready for sea—the best, I judged, because the dreams we had then counted more than the accomplishment. We were happier in what still had to be achieved than what could be looked back on.

The morning after we first inspected it we went back to the house to begin our task. We hired neither carpenter nor scrubwoman; we could do what needed to be done ourselves. In a way I liked going back to the hard, familiar things we had shared in the goldfields; it was good to see Adam wearing the old breeches and flannel shirts as he crawled on the roof to replace the missing shingles. Both of us forgot what discomfort we still felt from our wounds. I rolled up my sleeves and was no longer afraid to show the bandage.

It was strange how quickly we made friends there in Langley Lane. The first were the cats. A young black and white cat brought her kitten, an all-black male, to our door the first night we stayed there, attracted by the smell of cooking, I suppose. She walked boldly in, her tail high, her paws lifting daintily. She inspected the house, and then went out and brought back the kitten, a feeble thing who wobbled on his shaky legs.

"There," Adam said, "you have the cats. Now, if the rest would come as easily . . ."

The kitten was called, simply, Black. The mother we called Digger.

The other friends were the teamsters who drove the drays for John Langley. At first I hadn't liked to see them there, waiting in the lane and the stable yard all day long, chewing tobacco and spitting, their rough voices and their laughter echoing off the high walls. While Adam worked on the roof I began to drag out the boxes and rubbish into the yard. Some of them watched me curiously, but they said nothing, at least not until Watkins, the night watchman at the Stores, came out and tried to stop me lighting a fire there to begin burning the rubbish.

He knew of the arrangement with John Langley that we were to have the house, but he was the sort of man who was pleased to know that someone of the Langley name was living in what amounted to not much more than a shack in Langley Lane. He had already dubbed us "poor relations."

"See 'ere, Mrs. Langley, you can't do that! Might set the 'ole place on fire. Dangerous, it is!"

Adam stopped his pounding on the roof, and one or two of the drivers straightened from their leaning positions against the wall.

I drew myself up. "And what do you expect me to do? Live here with it?"

He shrugged. "It's no concern of mine what you do with it, Mrs. Langley. Pay someone to take it away—do what you like, but you can't burn it 'ere. Might get out of 'and."

One of the drivers drew nearer, walking softly, speaking softly. "'O says the lady can't burn it, Watkins? Ain't no 'arm."

"I say. I 'ave my responsibility to Mr. Langley . . ."

I did not know then the running feud that existed between the drivers and Watkins. But it existed, and I was the beneficiary.

"We'll tend the fire," one of the other men said. "Buckets of water an' the lot. Won't come to no 'arm.'"

The fire kept going all the day as the men hauled the crates for me, and fed the newspapers into it. As each wagon was ready and the driver was called, another seemed to take his

151

place. The task was passed from one to the other and they took it willingly. All they had to do was mention Watkins's name, and the men went to work. From the rooftop Adam, at first offended because there was a suggestion that someone was taking over what he considered his duties, finally saw the joke of it. He grinned at me, and waved his hammer, and sent over to the Crown for pints of ale all round. And finally the supervisor of the warehouse appeared and told me that he didn't think Mr. Langley would like his men drinking ale on the premises.

So by the end of the first day we had made friends of the drivers and the distant enemies of those in authority. And by the end of the day I was " Miss Emma " to most of the men who stood around in Langley Lane.

After the roof was mended, Adam spent a good deal of his time at the dock where the *Enterprize* was being finished. " She's a good ship," he said. And he worked on it with his own hands. " My grandfather would have liked to work on her. He loved a good ship."

So I was alone often now at the little house. We had bought some furniture at auction sales, enough to begin with. The pump worked well now, and the chimney had been swept. I sewed curtains and a white cover for the big brass bed we put in the back room. Adam liked it. He was full of memories of the house in Nantucket wheret he was born.

" My mother sewed big quilts, Emmy. Coloured ones— they used to look best in the winter when it was all white outside with the snow."

And he would examine our old, worn floors distastefully, and tell me about the waxed pine ones of his home. I began to feel that that house was also my rival, and so I polished lamps and candle-sticks, and the fire irons and every other thing that could be polished.

" It needs some paint," Adam finally said. " Before the *Enterprize* sails I'll paint it white." And he did paint it, with much advice and some help from the drivers. They came to my door regularly now to inspect each new thing that was done. One of them kept me supplied with fresh eggs and milk from the country. They had a proprietary feeling towards the house, and Watkins did not come near us again.

Adam said, laughing, " You won't be lonely when I'm away. You'll hardly miss me."

One of the drivers, Higgins, said to me, " My Missus says she's tired of hearing about Miss Emmy's house, and it's about time I washed some windows for her."

The house was painted, the front door was mended, the broken step replaced, and then the letter came from John Langley. It took note of the repairs we had made to the property in Langley Lane.

We wish to remind you that these repairs have been effected entirely at your own discretion, and in no way constitute a claim against the owners for reimbursement.

" Mean old man!" I said. " I wouldn't touch his money."

" It's the way he is," Adam remarked. " It's his way of saying we have no claim of any kind on him."

" As if we would want it! He can keep what he has, and welcome to it!"

There was a letter of our own written the night before the *Enterprize* sailed. Adam sat at our big table and wrote it carefully, and addressed it to his family in Nantucket. He wrote of his marriage, the house, and then finally the line I remember best.

And tomorrow I take command of a vessel for Mr. Langley—the " Langley Enterprize "—trading between ports on the Australian coast.

That was the letter that went back to Nantucket Island to be passed from hand to hand, to wipe out, a little, the stigma of the loss of the *Julia Jason.*

I lay in Adam's arms that night, and wished that the letter had carried news of a grandchild on the way. There was not one yet, and Adam would now be gone these two months and more.

Larry was in Melbourne when the *Langley Enterprize* sailed. He came with us to Hobson's Bay that morning, and he was standing beside me on the dock when the sloop slipped off with the tide down Port Phillip. The sails lifted prettily ; she had the look of a dainty, light craft ; Fast but tricky," Adam said. Adam had saluted me from the poop ; he was unsmiling, not letting the excitement and pleasure of this moment show before the crew. They were a mixed lot, he had said, dragged out of every pub in Melbourne to make the complement. And they would need handling. I judged him able to handle anything as he stood there on the deck of the *Enterprize* that morning.

" Trust old John to name her so," Larry murmured beside me. " The *Langley Enterprize* . . . He must have his stamp on everything."

I put away my handkerchief, and turned to go. It was fiercely hot on the dock. " I expected to see him here this

153

morning—his first ship—to see her sail. Even to wish Adam well."

Larry shrugged. He's paying Adam, so he *expects* him to do well." Then he nodded briefly. " But he's here all right. Didn't you notice the carriage? Over there."

The carriage was drawn by a pair of beautiful chestnuts and it was turning as I looked. I had only the quick impression of the occupant well back within its shadow, a tall hat and a pair of white gloves resting on a cane. The newly-painted wheels flashed in the sun as it bowled off.

" But he didn't get out!" I said. " He didn't go aboard . . . ?"

" But Adam knew he was there, just the same. That's what he intended."

I felt I hated him for the moment. " Not even to shake his hand . . ." I said with bitter anger. " He treats him like a lackey!"

"That's how he treats everyone." Larry took my arm. " Let's go, Emmy. Old John saw me here, and he'll be sending by noon to enquire why the dray isn't loaded."

Chapter Two

I found the time heavy on my hands during the weeks Adam was gone. There was only a certain amount that I could do in those three rooms, and it was soon done. The stove was blacked till it shone, and the rest of the curtains for the windows were made, the brass was polished every second day. I felt idle and useless. There was a sale at Langley' Stores, and I spent a morning picking over the dress lengths, trying to find the best for the least money ; I chose a sprigged muslin with a little lace for the sleeves, and when it was finished, in a fit of extravagance, I gave away the old grey gown that spoke too strongly of Elihu Pearson. I made the muslin to the most stylish pattern I could find, and I even bought a parasol with a frilled edge. I walked in the afternoon on Collins Street like a lady of fashion, the parasol tilted to shield me from the sun, and my gloves tightly buttoned even in the heat. The first two afternoons it amused me to do this, to browse through the books I could not afford to buy, to window shop and pretend that none of the merchandise interested me. Then I grew bored with it, and wondered how some women managed to spend their lives this way, and at the same time to make other women envy them.

The drivers in Langley Lane stayed my friends, and I was lonely enough to welcome the few minutes' conversation we exchanged ; the cats were well-fed and sleek. Black had grown so that he was hardly a kitten, and he had started to show his independence of Digger. I talked to them to break the silence of the long days. It was very hot. There were bush-fires burning near Geelong they said. One of the drivers was almost trapped in one of them—or that was the story he told in Langley Lane.

Larry came to see me each time he was in Melbourne, a very discreet call that did not last long because he was conscious of Adam's absence, and the fact that there might be gossip about his calling. It was very different from the old freedom of the goldfields, and I was saddened to see it go. We were almost formal with each other, Larry sitting on the edge of the chair holding the tea cup and saucer stiffly. I pressed him for news of Ballarat, of everyone on the Eureka. "Everything is the same," he would say, in the maddening way of men who do not know that nothing is the same from one day to the next.

Even such short visits left me more lonely than before, missing the Maguires, missing the company of the Eureka. I felt idle, too, as I remembered how full and busy the days had been. I longed for Ben Sampson to come through my door and drop a load of ledgers on my scrubbed table. I wanted a man to disarrange this tidy woman's world I dwelt in. I wanted Adam back with me.

II

I lay in bed, half-asleep in the heat that never seemed to leave the house trapped there among the tall buildings. It was past my hour to rise, but there seemed nothing to get up for. The cats had jumped up on the bed, and I hadn't the heart to send them away. Black nudged me with his nose, reminding me that it was past breakfast time ; Digger was more patient, lying peacefully in the patch of sun that already was making the bed too warm. I stirred lazily, and listened to the voices of the drivers out in the lane, the rumble of the huge drays, the shouts of the men who loaded the bales of hay. It was another day without Adam.

Then there was a different voice, familiar, loved. I flung the bedclothes aside, dumping the astonished cats on the floor, and raced in my bare feet to the door. I flung it open.

" Kate! "

She smelled of Cologne and curling tongs as I buried myself in her arms. Her rich warm voice in my ear.

" There, Emmy! What's to cry about! Aren't you glad to see me? "

She drew me away from the open door, and closed it on the interested spectators out in the yard.

" I see you have some friends," she said. " Like watchdogs they are. I almost had to fight my way through them. The likes of them, fancy, asking me what I wanted of you . . ."

I sat her now in Adam's big chair and scuttled round to poke up the fire and put the kettle on. I kept looking back at her in wonder, hardly daring to believe that she sat there. Her bonnet was askew, and her dress was damp with perspiration. The cats were rubbing round her, but she seemed to happy to mind them now. She did not like cats.

Then I went back to her and squatted before her, and again my arms went around her. " Oh, Kate, I'm so glad to see you. It's been terrible how I've missed you all. What brings you here? Have you given up at the Eureka? Larry didn't say anything . . . ? "

And now the excitement she had been holding burst out.

" Gold, Emmy! That's what brings us! "

I sat back on my heels. " I don't believe it! "

She laughed. " Believe it or not—it's there. A nugget— one of the biggest they ever took out of the Eureka. Fifteen hundred and twenty ounces. They paid three guineas the ounce. And then a man bought out the claim for fifteen hundred pounds. And we're rich! "

Then suddenly she put her face into her hands and burst into tears. We cried together for a few moments, the way women do, sniffing and trying to talk. She produced a heavily scented handkerchief and handed it to me. Then she blew her own nose vigorously.

" We tried a new sinking—after you went. It was . . . well, the other one seemed cursed, somehow. All the trouble of Rose, and Sean going. I said we should work the claim that was filled in Sean's name. Give him a chance, I said. Dan didn't want to, but Pat did. It was good right from the beginning. We put three hundred pounds in the bank before we struck the nugget. And then I said, ' That's it, Dan.' So he sold. And now we're here."

Her eyes filled with tears again. " Sure I haven't had time to get used to it all—I'm a bit shaky—the journey, and all the excitement. They came from the newspaper to find out about it. They asked what we were going to call it—you know, like those names they gave the other big ones—you remember the 'Welcome' and the others? So I spoke up. I said, it's called 'The Sean Maguire Nugget.' And he wrote it down, Emmy, and he's putting it in the newspaper. The Sean Maguire Nugget! It'll be in the Melbourne papers, too. Two men came round last night just after we got to the hotel and were asking questions. Sure I don't know what I said to them in all the fuss."

My hands shook a little as I made the tea. We sat facing each other in the two chairs, and we talked about it—how it had happened, what it had looked like when it had come out. We had all seen the small ones, the bright shine of metal not quite lost in the surrounding quartz, but this one—"A sort of monster, it looked," Kate said. I didn't quite believe it, still. If it had happened the first week we had been on the Eureka I could have believed it; anything had seemed possible then. But after you have endured the grinding work, the monotony, have settled to the routine of bringing up only enough to pay expenses, you almost start to forget the big ones, the hope of sudden fortune that brought men across the world. I could see that Kate didn't believe it either. She was scarcely aware that she had left Ballarat; the creases were still in her dress from the long months of being stored in a box. The curling tongs and the Cologne had come out but that was an automatic gesture.

"What will you do now?" I said.

She looked troubled, bewildered. "What we always said we'd do. We'll get a hotel. That's the only thing we know about." She set down her cup, and I realized for the first time how much older she seemed now than when I had first seen her on the Ballarat road. Her face had a worn look; the lines running down from the corners of her mouth were deep and those under her eyes were not there only from laughter, as I had once thought them. There was much grey now in her hair. There was a grease spot in the middle of her bodice.

"It's all different now, though. At times it doesn't seem worth it. There's only Con with us now."

"Pat?" I said. "What about Pat?"

Her lips trembled, and then she stilled it. "He stayed behind. He took his share and he stayed behind."

"What for?"

She shrugged. "How's anyone to know that? How's anyone to know what's in his mind these days? He just said he was staying, and that's that."

" And Larry?"

" Larry gets his share. It's in the bank for him already. We put everything in the Ballarat bank and we draw on the money here. Larry made us do that. He said we didn't spend all these months digging just to give our money to some bushranger." She sighed deeply, and her expression was puzzled again, and uncertain, as if she were suddenly too old to grasp the pace of events that flowed past her. " I thought Larry would have come to Melbourne with us—you know, to celebrate a bit and help us find the hotel we want. But not a bit of it. He says ' Go to Duggan's Hotel in Melbourne and wait there for me. Don't talk to anyone, and don't buy anything until I come.' And then he went off on the rounds to Mount Alexander and Bendigo as if nothing had happened. All this money, and he treats it like a five pound note."

Then she shrugged, in acceptance. " So we did as he said. He's younger than we are. He knows the way of this country —he knows what's best for us to do."

I took water from the stove into the bedroom to wash and dress so that I could go back with her to Duggan's. My heart ached for a sight of Con and Dan, and I was glad the sprigged muslin was so becoming, because I wanted them to see the evidence that these months had been happy ones for Adam and me. Kate had made herself another cup of tea while she waited. She drank it, and kept the cats at bay with her parasol, and we talked through the open door. But she avoided all mention of Rose, as if she were careful of my feelings. So finally I had to ask.

" And Rose?—is she coming to Melbourne?"

" My fine Rose is still sulking at the Palace because the high and mighty John Langley hasn't sent for them. He just ignores them. Oh—and she's in the family way."

III

I found the Maguires altered. I had expected an exuberance of spending, a joyful embracing of city life again. They tried— even to convince themselves that nothing had changed, they tried—but the effort showed. Dan wore his Dublin clothes again, and looked more handsome even than I remembered him, but his face was now deeply, and it seemed, permanently tanned, and his hands bore callouses that they would carry for a lifetime. He talked about Ballarat to whomever would listen —to acquaintances in Duggan's bar, to complete strangers

outside the livery stables. He talked as a man homesick. In
her fashion Kate tried also. She went shopping, though never
to the Langley Stores, but more for the sake of something to
do than for the old joy it had once given her. Con had
completely grown out of his clothes during the months at
Ballarat, so there was a legitimate reason to buy for him. He
hated his new clothes.

"Do I have to be stuffed up like this? I liked it better the
other way."

He kept all his mementoes of the Eureka in a special trunk
and took them out each day to examine them.

"Sure why are you wanting that stuff for?" Kate would
demand impatiently. "Haven't I just bought you much
better?"

But she did not insist, and I noticed that when Con left them
scattered about the room at Duggan's, Kate herself put them
away carefully—the soiled old cabbage-tree hat, the broken
head of a pick, even the bullet cases from the Stockade.

"Sure, it's all he has, and the lad's lonely for his friends
back there."

We were all lonely for them, I think. I noticed how often,
when we were together, the conversation would start "Do you
remember that time when Mary Healy . . ." or "I wonder
did Timmy Mulchay ever find out who got off with the half
of the sheep he bought that time?"

We spent more time in my house than in the stuffy velvet
draped rooms at Duggan's. Kate even got over her reluctance
to walking down the lane between the two Langley buildings.

"It's a free country," she would announce loudly enough
for the drivers to hear, " even if this part of it does belong to
high and mighty Langley." She always wore her best clothes
when she came to call, flower-trimmed bonnets and fringed
shawls and gaudy parasols; I think she hoped to encounter
John Langley himself there one day. She would incline the
bonnet and the parasol grandly like a duchess to the drivers,
who all raised their hats to her. She walked down that lane
as if it were carepeted in red for her.

I saw the spirit reawaken in her at those times.

Larry came back to Melbourne at last and he marshalled us
all around like children while we inspected the few pubs whose
licences were for sale. Kate turned up her nose at all of them.
She wanted to build her own, and couldn't get it into her head
that the one nugget wouldn't any more buy even the land on
which these buildings stood . . .

"You had to be here before they drove through the first street to be able to pay their prices, Muma," Larry explained to her. "If I owned a single lot to-day I wouldn't have to work again for the rest of my life. They say John Langley got his the day of the first auction. They say he only paid sixty pounds for that corner."

"Then good luck to him and may it bring him joy," Kate retorted. "He needs it—the sour old thing."

Finally they negotiated the lease of a pub near the Horse Sale Yards in Bourke Street. It was a derelict place, very run down, but Larry looked at the crowds of people who passed its doors, and he pronounced it right.

"You'll make it right, Muma," he said. "You'll bring the people in."

And she was flattered enough to try. He had the good sense not to restrain her in anything she wanted to buy, not any of the engraved mirrors or the mahogany or the brass. Not even the little alcoves she ordered built and draped with the favourite red velvet.

"Sure won't the gentry be coming to look at horses? And won't they want a nice decent place, private-like, to make their bargains. They'll get what they want at Maguires'."

"Muma, this is Australia! Don't you know there aren't any gentry here?"

She snorted. "You sound like Pat talking. No gentry? With every second Paddy from the bogs hurrying to be mistaken for gentry just as soon as his purse and his fine silk hat will let him?" She laughed. "Don't fuss yourself, Larry boy! There'll always be gentry!"

They called the pub simply Maguire's. There was never any thought of hiding their light under another name for that family. "I'll have none of your 'Shamrock' or 'Harp '," Dan said. "Maguire is a proud name. No reason not to let everyone know it." And Larry was pleased to have his name displayed in yet another place; he had bought a big new dray, as fine as anything John Langley owned, and his name was in gold and green on the side, painted by Melbourne's best sign-painter. I think they were actually in debt again before the pub opened its doors.

They did nothing in a small way. They opened the doors on sale day in the market, and at the noon hour the drinks were free, the whole front of the pub, gleaming with new paint, was decked in flags and bunting—even the Union Jack. Larry insisted it be there, though Dan tried to hide it.

"You're Australian now," Larry said. "Never forget it."

"It'll take more than a flag to make me anything but Irish, boy," Dan answered. "You know an awful lot for your years, Larry, but there are some things you've yet to learn."

Kate took her place behind the bar on opening day, but she made me stay upstairs in the living quarters. "You've Adam to think of, Emmy. He has a position to build and it wouldn't do to have his wife seen here in the public rooms." So the busyness and the fun finished for me on opening day; I wasn't even allowed to help in the kitchen where they prepared the sausages and the ham, and cut the big cheeses. Larry had hired a man to do that, another to wash glasses, another to clean. "It must pay for itself, Emmy, or it will never work. If the place can't support a few in help, then it's not worth having."

I was disappointed, because I had looked forward to filling in the days here, but I knew what he said was the truth. We were no longer on the Eureka, and the willingness to work now counted less than making the right appearance and impression. So I sat upstairs in the sitting-room with Con, with a pile of Kate's petticoats to mend, and I made Con read aloud to me from his books. He was as restless as I—the smell and the noise of the sale yards drifted through the open windows, the dust settled on Kate's new curtains. Downstairs the piano tinkled, and the roar of the noontime rush on the bar was a small, continuous thunder. Every instinct in me rebelled sitting here placidly while so much happened right under my feet; I knew part of the reason why Con sweated so over the difficult words.

And then the Langley driver, Higgins, arrived. "A message from Hobson's Bay, Miss Emma. The *Enterprize* has docked."

I put on my bonnet and hurried down the stairs with him; out of pity I had to take Con with me, though I wanted no one else at this moment. Kate was waiting below with a mug of ale for Higgins.

"How did you know he's docked?"

"A message came to Mr. Langley. He sent the head clerk to tell me to find you at once. He says I'm to take you to Hobson's bay by wagon."

I stopped short. "*John Langley* said that?"

"Yes, Miss Emma."

"There'll be two moons in the sky to-night!" Kate said.

And so it happened that I was driven to Hobson's Bay in one of the big Langley drays, behind one of the famous matched pairs of greys. Con was almost beside himself with excitement. The greys each wore a great silver headpiece with silver bells and I think Adam heard us before he saw us. The dray rumbled on to the dock, and I was out of it and running towards Adam. He came down the gangway to me. Our meeting was decorous, because of the hands who watched eagerly, but later in the cabin there was no lack of warmth. I felt his arms about me with real desire.

"Dear Emmy," he said, leaning his whole strength on me for a moment. And then, "It's good to be home."

Home, he said, and I whispered the words inside me, loving it, rejoicing that he used it of me, and the place to which he came. I pressed closer to him, trying to make him feel my gladness until the clatter of Con's boots on the companionway made us draw apart.

We sat at the tiny mess table that was used by Adam and his first mate, Mr. Parker. Parker had withdrawn, after being presented to me, to supervise the landing operations, so that Adam was free, for the time being, to sit at the table and talk to us, and drink a little wine. There was much to tell him, mostly of the Maguires, while Con roamed around the crowded place, examining Adam's mahogany enclosed berth, the tiny galley, the cupboards with racks for the dishes and glasses. But the captain's private toilet enclosure interested him more than anything else. He looked at Adam with awe, as if he had just realized what it meant to be the master of a ship, even a small one like this. "Like being a king," he said. I looked quickly at Adam and I knew by his face that a part of this was true, that once you have ruled in this small, creaking world for a time that there is nothing again that can be like it. And as I saw the polished perfection of this cabin—this miniature domain of shining wood and brass whose neatness and order could not be disturbed even in a storm because of the confining racks and bars and screws that held it all in place—I began to understand more of the man I had married. This was the world to which he had grown up. As a small boy he must have been brought like Con, to welcome his father home from a voyage. And just as I strove to make our house in some way resemble this, Adam's mother must have done the same. These things fashioned a man, and gave him standards that was hard to match elsewhere. I understood a little more his occasional rigidity, the inflexible turn his mind sometimes took.

He did not ride back with us on the Langley dray. There was still much unloading to be done before dark, and it would go on through tomorrow as well. He would be home tonight,

162

he said, and then he added. " I have to make a report to Mr. Langley first—at his house."

Above Con's head he looked at me. " I had a note bidding me to dine. I replied that I was already engaged."

" Oh, Adam! You shouldn't have done that! It would have been a good opportunity . . ."

" When I'm in my home port I don't accept invitations to dine that do not include my wife."

He was stiff-necked and stubborn, but he was also right.

I left the curtains drawn so that he would see the lights as he came down the lane. It was very quiet as I waited for him. The Maguires would not be free until after closing time ; Kate, with a nice understanding, had sent word that they would see Adam tomorrow. I had sent Con home, and so I was alone when I heard Adam's whistle in the lane.

He had some bottles of wine, a pair of gloves bought for me in Sydney, and a brass knocker for the door. We laughed at the knocker—a heavy ornate thing that was vaguely ridiculous on that flimsy little house.

" Well," Adam said, as he screwed it into place, " people may say we haven't anything of our mansion but the front door knocker, but at least we have that."

He talked about John Langley. " He was very civil," he said, as if he didn't like to admit it. " Then he should be—the voyage was very prosperous. We made a lot of money, just carrying cargo for other firms, apart from what he ordered for his own warehouses. He talked about buying another ship— bigger, this one—to take his wool home to the English market. He doesn't like to pay a middleman he said."

I wet my lips which were suddenly dry. " Would you— would that be your ship, Adam?"

" We didn't discuss it. It's for him to say, of course. But I'd like it."

I made no protest. This was part of our marriage bargain ; I was to be prepared to see him go for long periods of time. It was expected that I would have nothing to say against it ; Adam had been brought up that way ; he knew no other. He was still too young as sailors go to want to stay close to the home port.

I told myself that night that I would be prepared to see him leave me many times if the homecomings could always be like this. We were very close, and there was both passion and peace between us. I believed, in a comfortable, languid daze of love, that Rose was forgotten. I knew that I would keep him and that he would love me so long as Rose left us alone to our own quiet concerns. We would build and grow on what we had so long as the disruptive force did not enter our lives again, so long as her beauty did not torment him. I could withstand all his other rivals—his ambitions, his drive for power in his own world of ships, the restless urge for travel and movement. I did not really fight these things; I was a complement to them. I was something solid and substantial for Adam to count on, as durable, as functional, as much his property as that door knocker he had bought. I would become, given time, so much the centre, the anchor of his life that he would include me with every thought. I told myself these things as I went to sleep that night.

*   *   *

We woke next morning to the heat and the sunshine, the noise and the dust from the lane. I didn't mind any of this— they were friendly things to me now. But Adam frowned up at the stained ceiling as he lay there.

"Emmy, don't you want to leave this place? It isn't right for you to be here. I made a hundred and fifty pounds from the voyage. It could start us in a little house somewhere out from the city a bit."

It was a temptation. It would remove us a little from the Maguires, and thus from Rose if she should come to Melbourne. But Adam was not meant for a little house " out a bit." He belonged in the heart of things, as I did. I felt my fear again of those empty, dusty silences of the bush, the fires that roared in and consumed, the loneliness. I thought that I would take the noise and dust of Langley Lane, and I would be on hand every time the *Enterprize* docked. I would not become the wife in the little house " out a bit."

I said to him, " We'll only leave here when we have so many children that they push us out."

IV

Adam worked by day on the *Enterprize,* unloading, loading the new cargo. He was bound for Hobart, Launceston and up to Sydney again. Everything went into that hold—silks and tobaccos from the Langley warehouses for the Van Diemen's Land merchants, six prize merino ewes and one ram from Langley Downs for a buyer inland from Sydney at Camden who wanted to introduce the Langley strain for experiment;

from Sydney, Adam would bring back a thoroughbred, purchased for John Langley by his Sydney agent, which was bred from one of the famous New South Wales sires. I studied the cargo manifest and I traced the destination of each shipment on the map Adam brought me and I began to see the landscape of commerce—the silk ribbon brought to Melbourne from Hong Kong and finally sold in the post office store in a township eighty miles from Sydney, the cotton from Calcutta gathered into the Langley warehouse and reshipped to the Swan River Settlement in Western Australia where a cargo of wheat was shipped in payment, and that in turn joined the big grain cargoes leaving Sydney for Liverpool where a return cargo would be taken on—iron goods, household pots, fire irons, farm implements, hatchets, sail maker's sewing machines, a cargo of bed linen and printed calico, part of them coming to the Langley warehouses and starting their slow distribution through the whole continent. We were on the edge of the earth here—thirteen thousand miles from London—but we needed a kettle to boil water in, and they needed our wool for the Yorkshire mills. And so we existed and paid for ourselves, and sent them gold, and men like Adam were the movers and transformers, changing a world gradually.

And now, these days, the time was short. It ran out in great gushes and was gone before I knew it. In the evenings we visited the Maguires, we listened to a band concert in the Botanic Gardens by the Yarra, we went to a theatre. We, and all the rest of the country gladly got the news that the men on trial for the participation at Eureka had all been acquitted, and their names were now in the colony's history. It was a good time to look back on, but hardly a week after he landed, I was on the dock to see Adam go again. Kate stood beside me this time—Larry had been upcountry all the period of Adam's stay—but I knew that soon no one but myself would trouble to come down to Hobson's Bay to wave the *Enterprize* and Adam off. It would be just one of many sailings, a part of the pattern of what Adam's life was to be, and mine.

But John Langley was there. I recognised the carriage, the tall hat, the gloved hands and cane. He did not emerge, and the carriage was gone almost as soon as the *Enterprize* had slipped her moorings.

It was unseasonably warm weather at the end of March, and when Kate presented herself at my door at noon one day almost two weeks after Adam had left she was hot and angry. I was surprised to see her there—this being Tuesday and sale day at the Yards in Bourke Street, and this the hour of the biggest rush at Maguire's She nearly swept me aside as she entered, her face flushed and irritated, her mouth pursed. She went straight to Adam's chair after giving me a perfunctory kiss ; she dropped down on it heavily, and loosened the strings of her bonnet and the top buttons of her gown.

" Well, it's hot enough to roast you in the sun, and didn't I have to walk all the way over here from Hanson's Hotel, and never an empty cab in sight! Or the devil bit of notice would they take of me if they were empty."

" What's the matter," I said.

" What's the matter, is it? Trouble, that's what's the matter. And where is trouble if Rose isn't in the middle of it?"

" Rose?" My voice was cold. " Is she in Melbourne?"

" Indeed she is, and I'm almost wishing she'd stayed out of it. She got here yesterday afternoon with Tom, and a merry time I've had of it since then. I haven't been home all night, what with her crying and carrying on."

" Is there something wrong with her."

" Nothing more than is wrong with most women some time or other. She's sick because of the baby, and you'd think she was going to die to hear the moans of her. 'Tis nothing but the usual sickness and I kept telling her it would wear off in time, but she just throws herself around on the bed and that makes her sick again, and poor Tom nearly has a fit . . ." She paused for breath.

" Did you call a doctor?"

" I did. He examined her and told her to pull herself together and stop acting like a baby—and Madame ordered him out of the room. Called him a stupid old fool to his face. I don't mind telling you *that* story will make the rounds pretty quick. Madame won't find it easy to get another doctor. Tom asked the management to send up a maid to take care of her. The poor little girl was so frightened she was shaking. Rose called her a clumsy edjit, and threw her out. Oh—she was in grand form, I'm telling you."

" What are you going to do?" I needn't have asked; I could see it in her face—the plea, the look of defeated helplessness.

" Emmy, would you go . . . ?"

I turned away; I went and poked at the low fire in the range, filled the kettle with water and set it on it. Kate said, " You know what it's like on sale days at the pub. And we're one man short today to make it worse." That may or may not have been true, but Kate was capable of saying it to increase the pressure.

Then I looked back. " Do I have to go? Is she sick enough?"

There was more concern now than irritation in her face. " I don't know how sick she is—it has the life worried out of me in case she does harm to the baby with all this carrying on. I told her she deserved to be thrashed, but what can you do with a woman who's that way? She needs to calm down. She needs some sleep. That's a hard journey—those roads are like to shake your insides out."

I shrugged. " What could I do?" I was trying to keep myself hard and cold against the image of Rose.

" Talk to her . . . she's always heeded you, Emmy."

I flung out my hands. " Heeded me! My God—she would have walked over me if she could have had Adam."

Kate's face tightened. " She's come to her senses now."

" I hope so," I said flatly. She did not want to be reminded of that; she fidgeted with her parasol.

" Will you go, Emmy?" she asked. " Just for an hour or two? Maybe you could get her mind off it . . . it's her first, after all. It's frightened she is, I'm thinking."

I sighed, and I knew I would have to go. What else could I do? Kate had far more owed to her than this small thing. At least it seemed a small enough thing that I agreed to do. I went into the lane and asked one of the men, Thompson, to try to find us a cab; as I rode with Kate to Hanson's in the full heat of the day with the sun pouring through on to the hot upholstery, I didn't know that this was the first of many such journeys. If I could have known I would have drawn back.

II

Hanson's was the best hotel in the city. It was far grander than any place I had ever seen, and while I waited for a message to be sent to Tom I sat very straight in a massive chair and tried not to appear overawed.

Tom seemed rumpled and harassed as he came towards me. "Emmy! Thank God you've come!" And he bent swiftly and kissed my cheek. After that I would have done anything for him; we were suddenly, then, part of the same family. He took my arm and led me up the broad staircase to the first floor.

"It's the journey," he said. "It's overtired her, and in her condition . . ." He looked uncomfortable, even guilty as he spoke, and I felt a rage sweep through me at Rose who could make him feel this way when he should have felt only pride.

I didn't spare her to him. "Some women," I said, as he opened a door for me, "don't deserve babies."

Their sitting-room was a corner room that seemed to me only a little smaller than the foyer downstairs, and just as heavily burdened with the magnificence of sofas and draped velvet curtains. Tom led me through it, the bedroom door opened for me, and then stopped.

"Rose, it's Emmy," he called softly.

The room was almost in darkness, the small gap in the drawn curtains admitted only a chink of light and no air. It was unbearably hot and everything smelled stiflingly of Cologne and perspiration. As I stood blinking in the darkness there was a restless movement from the bed, and a white-gowned figure sat up and leaned towards me.

"Emmy!"

For a moment I couldn't answer her. All the distrust of her was back; I felt again the soft insidious power of that voice, the plea that reached me directly and strongly. I wanted to turn back; I wanted to close my ears and my heart to that voice, and yet I could not. These months of separation had made no difference. I had not broken free of her. Rose was one of the few people to whom I had ever given love, and I was not able to take it away.

Jerkily I walked to the window near the bed and flung back the curtains on their rods. The light flooded in and there was a cry of protest from the bed.

"No, Emmy—no! It hurts my eyes!"

I looked at her lying back blinking in a huge rumpled bed; she was only part of the disorder of that fantastically disordered room. She was swollen-faced from weeping, her skin was pale and clammy; her eyes seemed pale and black, but they were red-rimmed. She was not beautiful at all, just a girl who was frightened and unsure of what act to play next.

She licked her lips and said docilely, "I'm glad you've come. I feel terrible."

"You wouldn't feel so bad if you'd done what your mama wanted. You have to eat, and get some sleep."

Her nose wrinkled in distaste. "Yes, I know—Muma said all those things. But you know Muma and I always fight. I was so glad when she said she was going for you. I hoped you'd come. I knew it would be all right if you came . . ." There was no reference to the things we had said to each other on that last night we had been together in Ballarat. They had to be put aside, if not wholly forgotten. It was better so.

Her gentleness was disarming. I felt myself respond as I had always done. She looked miserable, and I wanted to comfort her. I touched her sweating forehead, and ran my hand back over the tangled, knotted hair. "It was the journey," I said. "You'll be better when you've settled down again—when you've eaten and rested."

"A doctor came," she said plaintively. "He said there was nothing wrong with me. The old fool."

"There's nothing wrong with you that time won't fix," I answered. "Come now, Rose—sit up. I want to get this nightgown off."

She submitted, complaining. "I'll look hideous for months now. I'll look a sight. I'll never get back to my right shape again. I didn't want the baby . . ." She started to cry, a loud sobbing that I was sure Tom could hear in the next room. I took her by the shoulders and shook her.

"May God forgive you!" I said. "That's a terrible thing to say!"

"Well, it's true! I didn't want . . ." And then, as she watched my face her voice trailed off. She shrugged. "It doesn't matter—it's done now."

She was quiet while I bathed her, and changed her gown, and brushed and plaited her hair. Perhaps the anger in my face kept her silent; I know that my hands seemed to be clumsy because I longed to slap her. She glanced at me a few times from under those thick lashes, that soft beguiling look that in Rose was almost irresistible.

"I don't mean all the things I say, Emmy. You know how I am. I said things last night to Muma just to shock her—and you looked so severe I thought I had to say them again. The devil seems to get into me at times. I can't help myself . . ."

I nodded, and went on with the brushing, and I felt myself relenting towards her. It was useless to fight with Rose.

She looked better when I had finished—at least cleaner. She made no objection when I ordered cold chicken and champagne for her. I ordered two glasses; I had never tasted champagne myself. It seemed a miraculous world to me in which I had only to pull a bell-cord for these things to appear; I was determined to enjoy as much of it as I could.

Rose ate the chicken eagerly. "I didn't know I was hungry," she said. "I've been vomiting—nothing left in my stomach."

She waved a chicken leg at me. "It wasn't just the baby that made me sick. There are other things . . ."

I put down the champagne, not sure from the first cautious sip whether or not I liked it. "What things?"

She shrugged. "Everyone says I'm to be calm—and rest. How can I?—we left a mountain of debts behind in Ballarat, and we have about five pounds left to pay for all this until Tom gets next month's money from his father. We *had* to leave Ballarat. They were going to bring charges . . . we only got out because I told the manager that Tom's father had sent for us, and that he would settle all the bills." She giggled weakly. "The Langley name is useful for *some* things."

"How are you going to pay them?" The thought appalled me; I looked at the champagne and realized that I was guilty also.

She shook her head. "I don't know." She said it like a child, hopefully, looking at me as if she expected an answer to the problem.

I grew angry again, to think of this deliberate courting of disaster. They were fools, both of them. "Then why are you staying here? This place costs a fortune!"

She opened her eyes wide. "But Tom wouldn't let me stay any other place. He says they're not fit to live in. And in my condition . . ."

"Rose—you're tiresome! It isn't any use play-acting like this with me—pretending you've never been in worse places in your life." I laughed at her. I couldn't help it, it was so ludicrous. "Remember—I'm Emmy! I shared a tent with you on the Eureka."

She pouted for a second, and then she laughed too. "What's the harm in it? Besides . . ." she shrugged and her gesture indicated all the rich furnishings about her, "I like places like this. I don't want anything different."

"What does Tom say?"

"He doesn't say anything. He gambles and tries to get some money back." She made a little grimace which seemed to indicate that we both understood the situation and must condone it. "Poor Tom—I don't think he's a very cool gambler. He loses a lot of money. At least, I suppose he

170

loses it. He doesn't tell me . . . but we couldn't have *spent* all that money he says we owe in Ballarat."

I said nothing, but I looked at the fine lawn gown she wore, trimmed with deep lace. I had brushed her hair with a silver-backed brush, and the Cologne bottle was crystal with a silver stopper. The room bore many more traces of a gigantic spending-spree in the Ballarat shops that catered to the tiny luxury trade. Rose followed my gaze about. "Well . . . Tom did buy me a lot of things. It was lonely after Dada and Muma left. There wasn't anything to do . . . we used to go shopping every afternoon just for the fun of it. I didn't know Tom didn't have the money to pay for all these things."

She may not have known then, but she knew now and she was still determined to have what money would buy for her—a little release from loneliness, from boredom, a moment's novelty. She would go on with this, if I knew Rose, and if John Langley did not pay for it, then in the end Dan and Larry probably would. I was going to try not to let that happen.

"Rose," I said slowly, "how much do you need all this?" I indicated the room, the array of her possessions. "Could you manage with less? If Tom got some kind of work would you try to live on what he earned?"

She shrugged. "Tom—work? You don't know him very well. He's a gentleman, Emmy. He hasn't been trained to do anything but manage the family properties . . . and buy horses." She gave a little strained laugh. "What would you expect him to be?—a shopkeeper?"

"His father's a shopkeeper. The best in Australia. It wouldn't hurt Tom to go behind one of John Langley's counters, or learn to keep his books."

"You expect too much from Tom. He is as he is—and half of it is his father's fault. Don't try to reform him, Emmy. It's a waste of time." Her voice was sharp.

"Then you?—what would you do to get out of this tangle."

"Me? What could I do? I'm not able to do anything."

"Yes you are. You could go and see John Langley. You could tell him that you're going to have a child, and that John Langley's grandson should not be born in a hotel with his father dunned by half of Victoria for debts."

She gasped. "I wouldn't dare! I don't want to! Why should I go and suck up to that old man?"

"A bargain isn't a surrender," I said. Then I looked at her straight. "What else can you do? This won't be your last child, Rose—not unless you keep Tom out of your bed, and I don't think you'll do that. You'll breed well, Rose. You have the look of a woman who breeds. Are you going to live in a little cottage with six children dragging about you? Are you going to be poor because Tom's too proud and too educated to work for a living? Are you going to be old when you're twenty-five, Rose, and have men pass you in the street and not notice that you're there?"

She winced. I got up from my chair and came and took the tray from her. "Think about it," I said. I did not return to my own champagne. I had no need for it now.

There was silence in the room for a long time while I folded clothes and put them in drawers, hung others, emptied the portmanteaus that spilled their contents. At last her voice came to me, muffled, uncertain.

"What makes you think he'd take us in? He's shown no signs of wanting us so far."

"He doesn't, I suppose, know you're going to have a child. Unless that doctor's spread the tale about. You have the one thing John Langley can't buy. He has only one son, and through him only one hope of heirs. A man does not build what he has done in this country to see it pass into strangers' hands."

"You seem very sure," she said. "How do you know this?"

I shook my head. "I can't be sure. I only feel it. No one paints his name in letters so high as Langley does. No one paints it in more places. He has made it a great name in this country. And Tom is his only hope."

She shivered. "I don't like it. Suppose he refuses to help? Suppose he throws me out?"

"Will you be worse off than you are now?"

She lay back against the pillows, and her fingers drummed a little tattoo on the covers. Now that she had something to think about she looked better, less like a sulky child. "There would be conditions," she said. "He would want things. We'd probably have to live with him . . ."

"Perhaps not," I said. "There's Langley Downs, and the place at Hope Bay. He might find you a house here in Melbourne, since he already has Tom's sister living there with him."

"He'd want more than that. He'd want the children, and not me."

"And cause a scandal? I don't think so. You forget that he's never met you. He pictures some little girl straight off the farm . . ."

172

Her interest sharpened. "Yes, that's true. He doesn't know me." And I saw that triumphant smile play about her lips that told me now, as it had in the past, that she was already imagining a conquest.

Then she jerked her head around sharply on the pillow to look at me. "Emmy!"

"What is it?"

"What about Tom? Would he consent to my going to his father? He's very proud." For a moment a look of compassion touched her face. "He's very weak, I know . . . but he's not all to blame. *I* spent the money, too."

"Don't tell Tom you're going. Say nothing until it's all done. Can he refuse then? It's his child as well as yours."

She shook her head. "You're so hard, Emmy! I didn't know you could be so hard. It's like offering to give my child away."

Furiously I turned on her. "You don't care two raps about your child, and you know it! And neither does Tom! The least you can do is give it a chance for a name and an education. If you can't give it love you can give it these things."

"You've no right to say that! I could learn to take care of my baby . . . It would love me, Emmy. I know it would love me."

"*You* take care of it? You can't take care of yourself! What you mean is that your mother would take care of it. She'd try to, because it was her flesh and blood. She'd make room for it, and all the others, and give them love. But she's too old to begin again, Rose. She's too old now."

"Then you could help me. You're good with children, Emmy. Perhaps it could live with you . . ."

I put my two hands to my head, which was aching now. The heat of the room was oppressive and the argument wearied me. I held my hands against my temples and tried to calm myself before I spoke, to keep from flinging back at her her arrogance and her stupidity.

"Perhaps I might even have agreed to take your baby, Rose —I might even have been that much of a fool. But it isn't possible."

"Why isn't it possible?" she said fretfully.

I took my hands away from my head. All the things we had not spoken about Adam were said then.

"Because Adam and I are going to have a child."

173

The heatwave ended with the stirring of a cool wind at dusk that lifted the chaff and papers in Langley Lane and rattled the loose windows. It was the last heatwave of the season; the next morning was crisp with the feel of autumn, though the sun was warm. I opened my door wide and dragged my chair over to the broad shaft of sunlight. I rocked a little as I sewed, and enjoyed the warmth of the sun in my bones. Sometimes I put my hand wonderingly on my stomach, though of course there was nothing discernible to touch. The baby, if it were a baby, was there only a few weeks. I had had only slight evidence for the declaration I had made yesterday to Rose—but I had made it in a gesture of defiance, to prove my right to Adam, to hold my own, to prove my own womanhood in the face of the abundance of hers.

She had been sobered by the news, grown a little pale, a little tightness appeared in her mouth. But she was surprisingly gentle.

"Go home, Emmy," she had said. "I've kept you too long."

Then she lay down quietly in the bed and turned her head away from me. There were no loud sobs now. I thought, as I looked at her, that her body shook with weeping, but I was never sure, for she made no sound. I left her then, and came back to the quietness and the peace of this little house. Here, in this place, Adam was my own. No part of Rose had touched our lives here. I felt reassured. And when I woke in the morning I was violently ill for a time, and through the vomiting I could have laughed for joy. I sang as I did my housework that day, uncaring of the audience out in Langley Lane.

Con came for a few hours—ostensibly to have a lesson in arithmetic from me, but mostly to gossip and ask unanswerable boys' questions. Next week he was starting at a private school in Swanston Street.

"A private one it will have to be," Larry had said. "The parochial ones aren't much better than you'll find in Ireland. He can't go to the good ones—Scotch College wouldn't take him because he's Catholic and his father runs a pub. We'll have to make the best of what he can get. And you'll keep an eye on him, won't you, Emmy?"

I had said yes, as I always did to Larry. I had my doubts about Mr. Woods' school in Swanston Street. I heard he drank, and was murderous with the cane when his pupils misbehaved. But he was a fine Latin and Greek scholar they said. What he didn't know about arithmetic and ledgers I would teach Con. I began to sense what waited for Con in this country if only he could be prepared. So when he was idle, and wanted to talk, I forced him back to his books.

"Sometimes you're nice, Emmy," he said, " and sometimes you're as cross as Rose."

"Don't be impertinent! And let me see all those problems worked out in twenty minutes."

The pencil squeaked hideously on the slate, and he murmured something about three men and forty-seven feet of ditch. Weakly I put a piece of freshly-baked cake by his elbow to help him forgive me for those forty-seven feet of ditch.

Five minutes later he said, "Larry got in this morning. He said to tell you that Ben Sampson asked to be remembered to you." I nodded, pleased by the message. "And Larry said would it be convenient for you to come around this evening to help him sort out the orders and write them up for the Langley people to fill. The new man he has can't write, and he has to remember all the orders or get the storekeepers to write them for him. Larry wants to find a new man."

"Would Pat do it?"

"Larry says no. He says Pat doesn't want to work for him, and in any case they'd fight the first week. Pat got a new claim, but he isn't working it."

"What is he doing?"

"He spends all his time down on Main Road, Larry said—drinking and gambling. He's won some money. He's luckier than Tom—Larry said the whole of Ballarat is talking about the money they went away owing."

"Con . . . you shouldn't listen to such talk. You're too young."

He looked at me coolly. "Then why are you asking me, if I'm not supposed to listen to know the answers?"

I subsided, and he ate his cake in triumph.

It was late in the afternoon, Con was gone and the sun had shifted out of the courtyard when I heard the commotion in the lane. I could hear the voices of the drivers raised in protest, and then after some argument I heard the commands to the horses to move, and the rumble of the huge wheels on the paving, and the stamp of the great feet. One of the drays backed up into the stable yard to make room for the passage of another vehicle, the driver, Higgins it was, glowering and muttering.

"If you wan't going t' see Miss Emmy I wouldna done it," he called to the occupant of the carriage.

And Rose, waiting for the coachman to come and help her down, leaned out and called back with equal gusto, "And you keep a civil tongue in your head, my man!"

She stepped down from the carriage, an unforgettable figure in that dingy yard with her tartan dress tightly fixed and its enormous skirt held out by at least six starched petticoats. I think there was not a wider skirt in the whole of Melbourne that afternoon. She wore a tiny hat perched forward on her forehead, almost the first of its kind seen here, and her rich hair was piled in glossy, tidy curls at the back of her neck. She swayed gracefully towards me, the skirt billowing.

"They expected me to *walk* through this filthy place," she said, by way of explanation of Higgins's angry shouts.

I turned my eyes from her to the carriage. "This is John Langley's carriage," I said.

She took my arm, and leaned closer; her eyes seemed to snap with sly amusement. "Come inside. I'll tell you about it."

"It's done," she said, as soon as I shut the door. "I've seen him, and it's arranged. We're to go and live with him in Collins Street—oh, just until the baby's born—and he's to settle the debts."

She didn't look at me as she said this; she moved about the room restlessly, peering into the mirror over the mantel, touching my sewing basket, even lifting the lid of the stew pot to see what was inside.

"Sit down, Rose, and tell it to me properly. How can you concentrate when you're fluttering about like a bird."

She sat down unwillingly. "I don't need to concentrate. I told you—it's done!" Now her face darkened with resentment.

"How did he receive you?"

"Well enough," she said. Then she shrugged impatiently. "Oh, does it matter? You might as well know the truth. He was polite, but I felt as if I were someone he accidentally brushed against in the street and didn't expect to see again. He was better after we had talked for a few minutes. I spoke out straight to him about the debts. I said it was time he and Tom came together—that Tom should be helping him in the management of the properties. He said nothing—nothing, Emmy—until I told him about the baby. Then it was over very quickly, as if it were a bargain. I suppose it was a bargain. He's to have the say where the child is concerned—education, nurses, everything. And we "—her voice shook a little—" we are to have everything provided. A house, an allowance, a carriage. Even a trip to London, he said—after the second child is born."

" The second . . . ?"

" The second child, Emmy. That is what he said. And I —I agreed. I agreed to everything!" Suddenly her face crumpled, and she couldn't hold her lips steady. " Oh, my God, Emmy! How am I going to tell my father? What can I say to him."

" Nothing! Say nothing to him. Why do you have to load your troubles on his shoulders? Hasn't he had enough? You will just tell him that in future you and Tom will make your home with John Langley. What else does he need to know? Isn't it enough that you torture and shame him with the stories of the debts you and Tom left behind in Ballarat? Must you make it worse for him by making it known that you and Tom aren't fit to be parents of your own child? You made your agreement with John Langley, and because of your children you won't ever have to worry about how to pay for the roof over your head, or your next meal, or even for the new gown that you buy but don't need. Now stick to your bargain—for once, stick to something without whining. If it's on your conscience, keep it there! Don't pass it to your father, or Larry—or me!"

She sat with her head bent, twisting her hands in her lap. She was more composed now, though her face was pale. She did not look like the girl of yesterday. Her eyes were no longer red-rimmed. She was three months gone in her pregnancy, and the added fullness suited her without distorting her shape. She was ripe and mature, more beautiful, I think, than before she married. I did not wonder that John Langley had spoken so frankly of a second child. She seemed made for bearing children. And as I thought of the children she would bear I was not sorry for what I had engineered. Other hands would feed and care for them, and she would still be there to give whatever love she was capable of giving to them. Or, as she put it, she would be there for them to love.

She raised her head and looked about her, examined the room carefully. " You know, Emmy, you're very lucky!"

I thought she taunted the simplicity of this room, the near-poverty. I felt myself flush. " What do you mean—lucky?"

"I mean this." She looked back at me directly. "This is quite enough for you, isn't it? You don't want anything else but a shack like this at the end of a dirty lane? You're quite happy with it. You have enough pots and pans, and a spare dress or two, and that's enough. You're lucky. You'll have your child, and that will be enough. Your not cursed with wanting anything else."

She rose to her feet languidly; her voice was calm and matter-of-fact. "And you have Adam. We mustn't forget you have your Adam."

I watched her go to the door and I made no move to follow her. She was hateful and evil, I thought—a monster of cruelty. I wanted her gone. She had entered even into the peace of this house and taken it away from me.

"I must go back to Tom," she said, still calmly. "He doesn't know, poor Tom, what I've arranged." With her hand on the latch she paused. "It's funny, isn't it, Emmy, that some people are called 'poor' no matter how rich they are. I mean—Tom. He's 'poor Tom'—he always will be. Strange, I never thought of that three months ago."

Chapter Four

It happened that I first went to John Langley's house on Collins Street, not as Adam's wife, but as Rose Langley's friend. Even after she had left my house that day, having said what she did, I knew that we would go on being friends. A part of me still resented the fact that she could say "come" and I came, but Rose was a part of the Maguire family and from them I would never be willingly separated. I resigned myself to the fact that Rose would say outrageous things, and I would make myself forget them. I began to see that I had an influence of a kind on her, more than her family, more than Tom, and I must use it to make her do things she did not want to do, to make her conform to the behaviour expected of Tom Langley's wife. I don't know why Rose accepted me in this role of guide and confidante—perhaps her loneliness drove her to it, or perhaps it was the fear of losing contact with Adam. For whatever reason, the pattern was established, and those about us soon came to accept it. God knows I did not want it. I would gladly have been rid of Rose because I was haunted by the thought that she yet might take Adam from me. I did what I had to do for the sake of Kate and Dan, for the sake of what I owed them.

A sweet and repentant note arrived from Rose hardly more than an hour after she left my house that day. She always knew how to disarm me, how to melt my determination that this time would be the last she would insult me. The note was vague; I think if I had asked her what she was repentant about she would not have known. There was a postscript.

Please come and help me move to the Langleys'. We
go tomorrow.

I went; I may have been a fool, but I was growing used to being a fool where Rose was concerned.

I was there mainly to bolster her in her first encounter with the Langley household, because no one could have helped much with the chaos of their moving. When I arrived at Hanson's they were half packed. There were two trunks and a carpet bag to hold belongings that wouldn't have fitted into five trunks. Even during her two days in Melbourne, Rose had acquired more possessions, and now they spilled all over the room in a grand confusion of boxes, paper wrappings and baskets. There was one thing to be said for Rose; she never did things by half measures. The Langley carriage came to Hanson's for them, but Tom had to call for another cab to carry the overflow of the luggage. When the Langley manservant opened the cab door the boxes and paper packages spilled out like the odds and end from a gypsy's caravan. Rose didn't appear to notice them.

She hardly waited for Tom's arm on the steps. In the open doorway stood a woman whom I didn't need to be told was Elizabeth Langley. Mrs. Townsend was her name, but everyone in Melbourne talked and thought of her as Elizabeth Langley. I learned later that she preferred it so. She was tall, like Tom, and good-looking, though her finely modelled features were handsome rather than pretty. She wore a very plain gown, skimpy sleeves and skirt, severe in the neckline and without ornament. I thought she looked more like a governess than the mistress of this splendid house.

It was mid-afternoon, the fashionable time on Collins Street, and, I believe for the benefit of those who might be watching, she leaned forward and pecked Rose on the cheek. But her eyes were not friendly. Tom she also kissed, even more swiftly.

"Well, Tom."

"Well, Elizabeth . . ."

That was all the greeting they gave to each other after the months of separation. Her attention was now on me, and she scrutinized me questioningly.

" This is my friend, Emmy Langley."

Almost reluctantly she gave me her hand. Her nod was very cool. " I believe my husband has had the pleasure of meeting you," I said, to break the silence. Her look suggested that it had been no pleasure.

" Yes, Captain Langley was here on business with my father." She turned abruptly to Rose. " You will want to see your rooms."

Rose had courage when she saw clearly what it was she wanted. In full hearing of the manservant and the two maids who had come to help bring in the luggage she spoke up.

" Oh—I understood that I was to *live* here, Elizabeth, not just have rooms. I would like to see the rest of the house first. Tom—you show me. Come along, Emmy!"

I saw gratitude in Tom's face for a second, and fury in Elizabeth's. Rose put her hand in Tom's and with that gesture he suddenly was her husband and the heir to this house, not some stranger whose presence was barely tolerated. He led her forward eagerly, no longer the prodigal. And in that one swift moment Rose had established her place in this house.

I knew it would be a long time before John Langley deserted this house on Collins Street to follow the fashionable spread to St. Kilda and Toorak. He would stay here while the city traffic and noises increased about him, while the buildings crowded in, because he had built this handsome bluestone house for permanence, and because he intended to remind people that John Langley remained in the heart of things. There would be no quiet withdrawal to the pleasanter suburbs for him. He had his study on the ground floor, only a few feet from the iron railings that separated the house from the street. The dust of the city drifted in, and the voices of the passers-by, and I understood, even before I met him, that this was what he wanted. His house looked to me like a smaller version of the great establishments I had passed daily in Berkeley Square, around the corner from Elihu Pearson's shop in London—the iron railings, the columned porch, the marble steps, and the graceful circular staircase rising from the entrance hall. The furnishings were delicate, not in the taste of the present day. Later I learned from John Langley the names of the men who had fashioned these things—the Hepplewhite chairs, the Adam mantels, the china of Josiah Wedgwood ; I was ignorant of these names when I first saw them but I was conscious of the effect of uncluttered charm and a kind of intimacy I had not associated with the thought of John Langley.

Elizabeth followed us on our inspection of the rooms—the dining-room on the ground floor opposite John Langley's study, the double drawing-room on the floor above that, the bedrooms on the third floor, and on the next floor the servants' rooms.

"The nursery and the schoolroom are up there," Tom said, indicating the last steep flight.

"Well, we won't worry about them before it's time, will we?" Rose said. "Emmy, come and help me unpack. I'm so glad we have a front room, aren't you, Tom? I like to hear things going on about me."

She flung up the sash of one of the windows that looked down into the street, and leaned out, her hands resting on the sill. I saw Elizabeth's mouth open in protest; it occurred to me that it was possible since the house had been built no one had ever leaned out of its windows and surveyed Collins Street in just this way. Rose looked as if she owned the world at that moment.

Elizabeth began taking some keys off a bunch she carried. "I'll leave these for you. They belong to the tallboy and the wardrobes. Now, there are things I have to attend to . . ."

Rose turned quickly from the window. "Oh, but you mustn't go now. There are . . . I have something to show you. Quickly, Tom—the carpet bag! No—no, it was in that hamper." She put her hand to her forehead. "*Where* did I put it?"

Elizabeth was moving towards the door. "Put what?" Tom said.

"The brooch—the brooch we got in Ballarat for Elizabeth." Rose was flinging the contents out of a wicker basket and Elizabeth stood transfixed by what had happened to that immaculate room in the space of five minutes. She didn't see Tom's face, the raised eyebrows, the look of startled inquiry. Rose finally tipped the whole contents of the carpet bag out on the bed.

"Here it is!" Rose advanced towards Elizabeth with a small box in her hand, a jeweller's velvet box whose lid hung by one hinge. "It got broken on the journey—those carters are so careless—but the brooch is all right. You see—it originally came from Simmons here in Melbourne." She hesitated for only a moment as Elizabeth took two steps backwards; I wondered then if Rose was about to receive a direct refusal. The other woman's face was tight and suspicious. Suddenly Rose took the brooch out herself and reached for Elizabeth's collar. "See!—how handsome it looks with that gown." She pinned it swiftly on the tight, high collar. It was a small circle of gold set with a dark blue opal.

Elizabeth fingered it, looking almost as if she had been stung by Rose's touch. She backed away.

"I'll leave the keys," was all she said. But she did not hand back the brooch, which was what I expected her to do.

"Don't worry about the keys," Rose said lightly. "I never lock anything up."

But Elizabeth had gone. Rose shrugged, and spread her hands in a gesture of helplessness.

"Well—I tried to be friendly."

Tom spoke in a low voice. "Why did you give her that, Rose? It wasn't meant for Elizabeth. I bought it for you!"

"Oh, don't fuss so! It's only a little thing. That hideous dress!—she needed something to help it."

"You had no right to give it without my permission."

Rose shrugged again. She was already set in her habit of disregarding Tom, and today she had started to pity and to patronize Elizabeth Langley. She turned back and began to poke half-heartedly among the tangle of clothes on the bed.

"Come on, Emmy. Let's decide where to put these things. I'm tired—I want a rest. I want to be fresh this evening when Mr. Langley gets home."

She had already decided that there was only one person who mattered in that household. She made this decision early, and it served her in the years ahead.

She glanced over at her husband, still standing as he had been when she had given the brooch to Elizabeth, the look of hurt and humiliation still on his face. "Tom, don't just stand there! Ring the bell and tell them I want some tea." It seemed impossible that she was the same woman who had given him her hand so confidingly a few minutes before to be led over the house. But by little crumbs and scraps she held Tom to her.

She smiled across at him. "There—don't fuss over the brooch. Think of the fun we'll have going to choose another one . . . and ring for the tea, my darling."

For the rest of the afternoon she was amiable and good-humoured, so that we didn't really mind that she lay on the bed while Tom and I put away all their belongings. She

laughed often about little things that seemed to amuse her;
Tom was happy, and the time passed swiftly.

I I

Finally Tom went downstairs, reluctantly I thought, and I
prepared to leave. As I began to put on my bonnet, Rose
suddenly sat up.

"Emmy, don't go! Stay to dinner."

I shook my head. "I can't live your life for you, Rose.
You'll have to face him my yourself—now or sometime."

She nodded slowly, her expression sober. And then, as if
she regretted the admission, she said, "I'm not afraid of him,
mind."

"No." I tied the strings of my bonnet.

"But there's no reason why you shouldn't stay. I mean—
you would enjoy it. It would be a change from that . . ."

"I don't stay anywhere without invitation," I said.

"*I* invited you. This is my home. I won't be under that
woman's thumb—or his either."

I nodded. "But you don't have to prove it the first night.
Gently, Rose . . . gently!"

She flung aside the covers. "Then stay until I'm dressed."

I sat down and untied my bonnet. "Very well." I looked at
her as she rang for hot water to be brought and began to strip
off her petticoats, wondering why she continued to need me.
She was sure of herself, and strong enough to have taken this
household in this first afternoon and ordered it to her liking.
She did not fear Tom or Elizabeth. There remained John
Langley. As she washed, her humming had a nervous, strained
sound, like someone whistling for courage. She took ten
minutes to brush her hair, something I had never seen happen
before.

"No—not like that, Rose. Knot it low at the back."

She tried it. "I look like a scullery maid. It's terrible!"

"No—it's right." I had never spoken to John Langley, had
never seen him face to face, but I knew from the look this
house wore, that he would admire the plain and the simple. I
was suddenly conscious that Rose was representing me as
much as her family. I wanted her to do us credit. "A little
over the ears—yes, like that!"

She did not seem pleased with the result, but she accepted
my decision, just as she did over the gown. I watched her

183

stand before the wardrobe and she hesitated between a gown of a sort of peacock blue, which was new to me, and a green silk she had worn once on the Eureka. Neither would do for this occasion; later she could wear them, but not tonight. I went over to the wardrobe and laid my hand on one and pulled it out—a dark wine-red.

"This one," I said. "This is the one to wear."

"That!" Her nose wrinkled. "Tom insisted on buying it, but I don't care for it. It makes me look old."

"Older," I corrected. "Perhaps that would be a good thing —for tonight."

She nodded slowly, and took the dress from me. When she had put it on she turned to me, humbly for Rose, and said, "What jewellery shall I wear?"

The dress was of striking simplicity and I knew why Tom had liked it so. It needed beauty like Rose's to set it off—the deep colour of her black hair and the whiteness of her skin. She was unaware of the effect she created, though; I saw her mouth turn down a little as she looked at her reflection in the mirror.

I searched through the jewel box. There was nothing of very great value—a turquoise necklace, a coral bracelet and brooch, a pair of tiny pearl earrings. I recognised them all from the display case at Heath's in Ballarat. The opal brooch she had given to Elizabeth had been the best piece of the collection.

"Wear the earrings—that's all."

She gave a low wail. "Nothing else? Not the necklace? —at least the necklace, Emmy!" She gestured at the low-cut neckline of the gown. "I look so—so *poor*."

"One day," I said, and I felt a great sureness about my prophecy, "John Langley will give you diamonds."

I was proud of her as she preceded me down the stairs. She no longer looked a young girl, not raw and uncertain. She may have been nervous, but she did not show it. She did not look, either, as if she had ever had anything to do with the tents on the Eureka or with Maguire's pub on Bourke Street. She might have been walking down a circular staircase all of her life. The new way of dressing her hair revealed the exquisite set of her head on her shoulders. She had always possessed an unerring grace in the way she moved; now she seemed to respond to the setting in which she found herself, to play up to it. In the wine-dark gown, without ornament, she was almost regal. I felt the satisfaction of having helped to create the essence of this moment and I had my reward in the look that suddenly crossed John Langley's face as he stood at the foot of the stairs and watched Rose come down towards him.

"You are welcome . . . Rose."

She nodded, as if the welcome was her due. "Thank you. Emmy, this is Tom's father. My friend . . . Emma Langley."

John Langley bowed over my hand, civilly but no more. "Adam's wife is always welcome in this house."

Rose waved her hand airily. "Emmy was my friend long before she was Adam's wife."

I looked at the old man who was Tom's father, the face that I had glimpsed briefly in the carriage, the man whose presence was felt daily in my life. He was thin and tall, but still handsome; his hair was white and his side-whiskers were a bristling grey. So were his eyes grey; I had expected them to be brown, like Tom's, since he resembled his son. But they were a grey, without light, stern, disciplined. In his faultlessly cut black coat with the silk lapels, the immaculately laundered shirt, he might have been any gentleman on any of the fashionable London streets. But I felt the long-ago callouses on the slender hand he gave to me, the wind and sun had weathered his face permanently so that I was reminded of the tales they told of him—how he had worked along with his own servants in the first years in this country clearing his land, splitting fence-posts, mustering sheep, making with his own hands the bricks for the first chimney in the first house at Hope Bay. And at nights he had read Virgil by the light of the fire before he went to sleep. For the first years he had left his wife, with Elizabeth and the infant Tom, in Van Diemen's Land across the Straight until there should be a house and property fit for the lady he had married. I thought it was an infinitely lonely face that I looked at now.

"Elizabeth told me that you were with Rose. I gave instructions for another place to be laid for dinner."

"Thank you," I said stiffly, "but I must go. There are things waiting . . ."

"I would esteem it a pleasure if you would stay."

The words were a polite formula. He did not seek pleasure in my company; for a moment I thought that he was nervous too. I had to remind myself that he was human. For him, as well as Rose, this was a moment of strangeness, the hours ahead would seem long. Then Tom, who had been standing by the morning-room door, came towards me.

"Do stay, Emmy." If his fathers face did not present an appeal, Tom's did, and I nodded.

At that moment a gong sounded loudly here in the hall, and I started. So did Rose. It was the first time I had ever been summoned to a meal in this way.

"Won't you lay aside your bonnet and shawl, Mrs. Langley?" John Langley said. "I insist on punctuality in my servants—which means my family must be punctual also."

He offered Rose his arm to the dining-room. I took Tom's, thus leaving Elizabeth, who had just appeared at the door leading from the servants' quarters, in the rear. We marched in almost solemn procession to our places, locked in a silence which we waited for John Langley to break. I glanced across at Tom and to the look of frozen stillness in his face, and I remembered the eagerness with which he had shared our tin dishes and our stew across the camp fire on the Eureka.

Elizabeth had taken her place at the end of the table facing her father, but it was he who gave the signal for the man-servant to begin serving. She had changed her gown, but the change made no difference; this one was of a dark blue, still tight to the neck and wrists, and in place of the plain linen collar she wore one of lace, a gesture to the hour but not to her own adornment. And then I saw the little opal brooch pinned there. Her hand strayed to it sometimes self-consciously, and her eyes were often on Rose. I recognised then that Rose, hardly even trying, had touched some part of this woman that was closed to most.

I learned during that first meal at the Langley house that the rich inhabit a lonely world, that their money does not buy them ease with strangers and with those less endowed. This would have been the reason why John Langley accepted Rose. He was growing old in his enclosure of pride and wealth; it was a cold place, and he may have come to realize it. As I looked from Tom to Elizabeth, who seemed almost paralysed by their father's presence, I began to see the prize that Rose may have been to him, the unexpected boon in his son's unpromising marriage. She was endowed with an enormous vitality which turned Tom and Elizabeth, by comparison, to pallid dummies. She was not the raw, ignorant girl he had feared, and he knew how quickly the tricks and mannerisms of the rich are learned—as Rose and I both learned them that evening. The food was set on delicate plates and our glasses were filled with wine. Both of us discovered from the Langleys which knife and fork next to pick up; we left our wine almost untasted, and it was changed with the next course.

"I brought my chef from London, Miss Emma," John Langley told me.

I knew that I was meant to admire the excellence of the sauces, the subtle flavour of the meat, but remembered that I left that table hungry. John Langley believed in moderation in eating, going against the fashion of his time, and he imposed his beliefs on his household. His manservant, I learned, had instructions not to offer second helpings.

John Langley, of course, set the pace and tone of the conversation, what there was of it. It mostly consisted of instructions.

" You'll share an office with Lawrence Clay at the Stores," he told Tom. " I've given orders to have another desk moved in there."

" Clay won't like it," Tom said. " It's his great satisfaction in life, having that office to himself."

" Then he must learn to do without it," John Langley proceeded to say what was next on his mind. " We're going to Langley Downs the day after tomorrow. I haven't sent any message that they're to expect us. It keeps them up to the mark if we come unannounced."

" Should I leave the Stores so soon?" Tom said. " Old Clay gets upset when the routine is disturbed." His thought was not for Clay; I saw him gaze longingly at Rose, who wasn't even looking at him. He didn't want to go to Langley Downs.

" What Clay thinks is no concern of mine. What matters is that you should . . ."

He was interrupted by Rose, and from the frown that met the interruption, I knew that it was not something that very often happened to him. She turned to him, her face lit with interest. " Oh, yes—let's go to Langley Downs. I want so much to see it . . ."

" In your condition, my dear Rose, it is unwise to go anywhere. You must make no journeys until after the child is born. We cannot risk its welfare."

He knew what he was buying in this bargain, I thought. He might be gracious to Rose but his real concern was the child she would bear. He would overlook almost anything—the fact that she was Irish, Catholic, a publican's daughter, so long as she produced healthy children that her body gave promise of. I believed that John Langley had wiped this generation off. His children had disappointed him; he was determined his grandchildren would not. I think he had weighed Rose's background against the dash of new life and vigour she would bring to the Langleys, and he had come down in favour of the latter.

I have engaged a personal maid for you, Rose, who has also had some experience in nursing. She is coming to you tomorrow."

"I prefer to select my own maid."

"She comes with impeccable references," he answered her, and that was the end of the matter. He looked across at Elizabeth, then. She actually grew paler, I thought, as he began to speak. "You will instruct Rose about the management of the household, Elizabeth, and in due course she may take charge of the keys. It's only fitting that a married woman should run the housekeeping."

The colour rushed into her white face. "*Married, Papa!* —have you forgotten that I am married?"

He first of all made sure that the manservant had withdrawn before he offered his taunt. He thrust his head forward and peered down the length of the table like an old tortoise. "Married!—I count no woman without husband or child as married."

"You are unfair . . . unfair!" she said. She half rose, and her mouth worked nervously. "It wasn't my fault! You arranged . . ."

Rose spoke quickly. "Perhaps it would be better to leave things as they are for the time being." She gazed down at her lap with the kind of delicacy that in Rose I knew was pure sham, but it had its effect on John Langley. "This is such a large household . . ." She fluttered her hands helplessly. "In my condition it would be a big task to take on. Perhaps after the baby . . ."

"To be sure," he said hastily. "To be sure . . . whatever you wish."

Then he decided that we had eaten enough and he rose. As we slowly left the dining-room I saw the look that passed between Rose and Elizabeth. A debt was owed, and the obligation was acknowledged. Elizabeth would remain the housekeeper here. That is the way Rose wanted to be, but Elizabeth thought it was a favour granted. An improbable bond had been formed between the pair, a conspiracy to save each other from John Langley. Elizabeth wore almost an air of triumph. Although she was weakened in her father's eyes because another woman was going to bear the first grandchild, she was stronger for having gained a champion in Rose. For such desperate reasons of mutual self-help this alliance was made.

Mr. Langley took Rose's arm on the stairs up to the

drawing-room. The three of us trailed behind, listening to their conversation, or rather to the old man's monologue.

"You must, of course, see Langley Downs when you are able—and Hope Bay, too. They are my greatest pride. If there was nothing else they would be sufficient in themselves. Both of them were pioneering efforts. I was the first man to settle on that part of the coast where Hope Bay is—the first to make anything permanent out of what was just inhabited seasonally by whalers. I brought the first merino sheep into the colony. Others men dispute that claim, but they are liars!"

He sat Rose on the same sofa with him, and he went on talking. "I helped to build Hope Bay with my own hands, and I cleared the land for my sheep. I knew farming, of course— I had a fine farm on the Sussex Downs but agricultural reform and the demands of farm labourers for more wages convinced me that I would be better to start over again out here. I sold out and came to Van Diemen's Land—Tom was born there. All the good land was taken, so I ignored the Governor's regulations that there was to be no settlement in this part of the country and I came and settled my flocks and herds here. It took me ten years of fighting with the Colonial Secretary to have my claims settled. I opened up this country . . . I helped make it possible for people to come here! And the scoundrels tried to tell me that I had no right to my lands. As if I had not earned them with my work and sweat . . ."

Tom and Elizabeth had chosen chairs that were beyond the range of their father's immediate view. To me the story John Langley told was new and fascinating, but for them it was many times told, and always against them. There was a look of pained endurance on Tom's face as he listened to his father talk about work and effort, of achievements which were by now legends in the colony. Every word was a reproach that seemed to strike him physically. I knew why he had left this house. It seemed hardly his fault that he had had only sufficient strength to leave but not to achieve anything for himself. I began to regret that Rose and I together had brought him back here, and yet even as I thought of it I knew that, with or without me, he would have come back. Rose was his undoing here; she was his love and his burden. For her sake he would stay and endure, and so long as she was even kind to him, he would count his freedom well lost. I pitied him, but I knew I wasted this pity. John Langley had ruined his only son long ago with just such talk as I listened to now, and there was no helping him.

Rose was wise enough to make a good audience for her father-in-law. He was not a man who could unbend enough to boast to strangers, and his listeners had all long ago been exhausted. He enjoyed a new one.

"Everything you see in this house was selected by me, of course, on my visits to London. The original furniture I brought out is still at Langley Downs. Mostly oak—though there are some pieces as fine as these. The piano out there, though, is not so good. This instrument was made by Pleyel."

I guessed that, for Rose as for myself, it was the first time to hear the piano-maker's name, but as I had noted earlier, we both learned quickly. She clapped her hands together.

"How Wonderful! Could I try it?"

Without waiting for his permission she rose and went to it, and I wondered which of the Irish songs it would be, and how the old man would take it. But she was cleverer than that. She tried a few chords, and then she sang.

"Drink to me only with thine eyes,
And I will pledge with mine . . ."

And for the first time, then, I saw John Langley smile. Only once after that did I ever hear Rose sing an Irish song. And that song was meant for Adam, not for John Langley.

Chapter Five

The autumn came very quickly, with chill winds and rain that lay in great pools in Langley Lane; the house that had been too hot in the summer was warm now, shielded from the winds by the height of the buildings about it. The smell of the horses was still there, but it was a warm, homely smell. I kept a kettle on the range most of the time to make tea for the drivers of the Langley drays. Whenever I was away, at the Maguires or at the Langley house, their faces would greet me as I returned, as much a part of my life there as the welcome from my cats. The men would warm their hands on the big mugs of tea I passed out until the loaders called to them that a dray was ready. And when autumn advanced into winter and they knew that I was going to have a baby, small presents for it began to appear—little caps and a jacket and even a shawl, knitted by the wives I had never seen. Adam used to joke about it.

"What will you do at the christening? This baby will have more godfathers than he can shake his fist at."

190

Adam was not there for long at a time—trade for the Langley warehouses was brisk between all the coast ports. But his voyages were often short, just to Sydney and back again as quickly as he could reload. Whenever the *Enterprize* was sighted coming in to Williamstown a message went at once to John Langley or Lawrence Clay, his chief clerk. And in turn I received the news, and the invitation to use whatever of the Langley vehicles was free to take me to Hobson's Bay. When John Langley learned that I also was going to have a baby he gave orders that I was to have transport whenever I needed it. I was grateful, but not mistaken about his reasons for doing this. In certain ways I was useful to John Langley, and he knew it.

My usefulness was to Rose, and thus, indirectly, to him. In these months while she waited for the baby to be born Rose was a trial to everyone. She was impatient and fretful, and while she was enormously healthy it pleased her at times to play the invalid. There was some kind of amusement, I suppose, for her in turning that well-ordered household upside down to satisfy some impossible whim. She plagued Tom with complaints about how dull her life was, and to Elizabeth she complained about the laziness of the servants. It needed all of Elizabeth's tact to keep anyone in service in that house after a few weeks of Rose's demands and abuse. John Langley was not unaware of the tantrums and the tears, though Rose kept the worst of them from him, and Elizabeth never complained of trouble in running the house. But he said nothing, not even when Rose was late to meals, or did not appear at all. His voice was sometimes edgy, but his harshest words to her were very mild. "Tranquillity, Rose, is very important to a woman in your condition. You must think of the child."

"Think of the child!" Rose would rage at me afterwards. "That's all he ever does is think of the child. Sometimes I wonder whose it is! What about thinking of me? He won't let me stir from this place. He won't ever let me go for a ride to Brighton for some sea air because I might be 'taken' too far from home. He doesn't know what he's talking about—it's not due for three months."

It was in this way that I was useful to John Langley. He knew me as a companion for Rose who was not afraid of her, and from whom she sometimes took advice. She had no friends in Melbourne, and in an uncharacteristic way he recognised that she needed some woman other than Elizabeth to talk to. We went shopping together often—John Langley permitted her to charge all her purchases to him, and she used

191

the privilege recklessly. I restrained her when I could from too many heavily-trimmed bonnets and elaborate parasols, and I made her walk past the jeweller's shop when she would have lingered. She never went to the Langley Stores though.

"I can't bear Tom hovering about me every time I show my face. Besides, it's bad for his position with the clerks."

She did not really worry over what Tom's position was at the Stores. It did not interest her. He spent his days there when he was not required to accompany his father to Langley Downs or Hope Bay or down to the warehouse at Hobson's Bay. He had position; he was "young Mr. Langley" but that was all. There was no authority to go with the roll-top desk in Clay's office. He did not understand bookkeeping, and he didn't want to. He made no effort that I could see to learn. He was always available to step out to the Crown for ten minutes when the salesmen of other companies called. But it was Lawrence Clay who gave the orders to the salesmen. The only time Tom had handled an order he had specified what the salesmen suggested instead of what Langley's could sell. They were overstocked and had to let the goods go at cost.

I knew of these things because Tom had taken to strolling down the lane on the way back from the Crown, and knocking at my door to see if I were at home. Then he would sit in Adam's chair, sometimes with his boots propped against the range and one of the cats in his lap, and he would talk to me. Mostly the talk was of Rose; he had little else to talk about. After half an hour or so he would look at the clock, sigh, place the cat gently on the floor, and return to the Stores. From what he told me of the work he did there, I guessed that he wrote a few figures in a book, and played with a pen until the earliest moment when he could leave. He stayed later when his father was in the Stores, but most afternoons he was in the Crown again by half-past four.

Whenever Tom was missing and Clay needed him, or John Langley was expected in his office and Clay wanted to spare him his father's disapproval, he would send one of the clerks for him. "He'll be at the Crown or at Miss Emmy's house."

Thus, to the clerks at the Stores, as well as the Langley drivers, the old watchman's house at the end of the Lane became Miss Emma's house.

John Langley himself walked down that lane one day and knocked on my door. I never understood fully what brought him there; curiosity was too ordinary an emotion to associate with him. I gave him tea, and he sat in the chair Tom so often used, looking about him carefully, examining the new shelves Adam had put up, the cupboards built against the wall.

"I hope you don't expect me to reimburse you for the money you've spent here," he said. "This land is too valuable to be occupied forever by this house—in time it must come down for an extension of the Stores."

"We expect nothing," I said stiffly. "Adam wanted to make us as comfortable as possible for the time we were here."

He nodded. "Well, you're getting a bargain. Houses aren't to be had for this rent anywhere within twenty miles of the city."

He inspected the three rooms before he left, like any other landlord—he looked at the fresh paint, the cupboards, the mended floor boards. He even fingered the bed cover and the curtains.

"Did you sew these yourself?" When I answered that I had, he seemed pleased. My growing knowledge of John Langley was making me aware that the rich can take a large amount of pleasure out of quite small amounts of money saved. On the way out he stopped by the kitchen table where I had been working on the ledgers for Larry when his knock had interrupted me. He ran his old, lean finger down the colums, adding swiftly. It was typical of him that he had not bothered to ask my permission before looking at the books. He always assumed that anything remotely connected with him was his business.

"You're a fair bookkeeper, Miss Emma," he said, " but it's not women's work."

"Why not?" I answered. "I don't make mistakes. I write a neat hand."

"Women have no place in business," he said. It was pronounced in his usual tone of finality, but for once I was inclined to argue.

"I think you're mistaken. Take the Stores, for example. You could use women there."

"We have a few female clerks—who are, I may say, generally inefficient and given to being ill at inconvenient times. If we could hire sufficient men I would dismiss them."

" Men wouldn't take the wages you offer women—you get only what you pay for, Mr. Langley. And I say that the Stores need a woman."

" *A* woman, Miss Emma?"

" Who does your ordering for the drapery and millinery?— Lawrence Clay, who hasn't studied pictures of the latest fashions since he entered the business. Why, he's still ordering the kind of bonnet the Queen wore to the Exhibition four years ago because that's the last time he ever took notice of what a woman was wearing. The cloth he stocks gathers dust on the shelves because it's not the fashionable colour this year —he has black parasols when women want green . . ."

"Lawrence Clay has served me faithfully for almost twenty years. I have no reason to question his efficiency."

"Mr. Clay is admirable in every respect except that he happens not to be a woman where a woman is needed."

He smiled a wintry smile that seemed to mock me. "Nevertheless, Miss Emma, a woman's place is not in business."

He turned his attention back to the ledgers, thus dismissing my argument. He tapped the open page with his forefinger. "This young man—this Maguire—he will go a long way. He wants to be another Langley. He will not accomplish that much. He has come too late for that. But he will go a long way."

I looked at him questioningly. "Yes," he said, "he has the feel of it about him. You can almost smell it in some men."

"Then why . . . ?" I stopped. "Forgive me. It is not my affair."

"Why do I not meet him? Why do I refuse to see the Maguires? Because his kind is not my kind, Miss Emma. They are the usurpers—the newcomers who must be taught that they cannot have everything just because they make some money. I said he would go a long way. I did not say he would make a gentleman. It takes more than money, and I will hold the line for my kind against their kind for as long as I can— in every way I can. Let them fight! It's good for them!"

"And what of Rose?—a Maguire?"

"Women are different. They are creatures of environment, Miss Emma. Their sons can be moulded, can be shaped to better things."

He left me then. I sat and thought about the Langleys and the Maguires, wondering if John Langley had come here for the express purpose of telling me how he felt towards Rose's family. Perhaps he had meant me to carry the information to them, that his acceptance of Rose did not mean an acceptance of them. He was a shrewd man and he had seen what was written clearly for the future—that this was Australia, not England, and that he and his kind would not forever 'hold the line' as he put it, against the Maguires' kind. He made his mistake in thinking that the Maguires would care. I thought of Kate in her paradise of Nottingham lace curtains above the proud green and gold sign of Maguire's Tavern, and I knew that she would not care if she never set foot in the beautiful austerity of John Langley's drawing-room. And the grandchildren of both, I believed, would probably mix happily in either world. It was the ones in between— Tom, Rose, Larry, Con, Pat—they were the unsure, the bedevilled. I sat and rocked for a time, Digger, the mother cat in my lap, thinking about this, my hands idle except to play gently with Digger's ear. I also wondered what place my own child would have in this new world that was being formed from the struggle between the Langley kind and the Maguire kind.

One tangible result of John Langley's visit was that Watkins, the watchman, had orders to see that the lane between the buildings was swept clean of manure and straw every evening after the warehouse closed. This was a source of great satisfaction to the drivers, who stood to watch him at his task and cheer him on derisively. Watkins also removed his hat each time he saw me, and came to my door each day to remove my garbage. This the drivers liked less, and they generally had the garbage taken away before Watkins could present himself.

The Maguires laughed when I told them, and then Kate pulled a wry face. " You watch out for that Langley man," she said. " He's the having kind, that one is. He wants to own everything he touches."

I smiled, but I was reminded of what I had felt when Adam had first talked of going to live in John Langley's house. The feeling of his possessiveness had lessened as I came to know him, but I realized then that it was not that the threat was less, but that I had grown accustomed to it.

I was not the only one who ran back to the Maguires to escape the presence of John Langley. Almost every day that I walked along towards the Horse Sale Yards I glimpsed the elegant, and in Melbourne, rare, closed carriage that John Langley had ordered for Rose's use standing outside Maguire's. She came back instinctively when the ordered, silent house of John Langley grew too much for her, when the passivity in which Elizabeth and Tom dwelt was too much for her own spirit to endure. She came back to fight with her mother, play chequers with her father, to tease Con and interrupt his studies, to wonder aloud what Pat was doing up in Ballarat.

" I wonder if they've had snow there yet," she would say. " Larry said there would be snow soon on the high ground.

They say it doesn't lie here the way it does at home." The colony was full of people who said "at home" and meant somewhere else.

Rose would wander restlessly about the room, unable to sit still even though she was now heavy with child. She had kept her hair drawn back in the knot from that first night at the Langleys', and to me she seemed more beautiful than ever. Her hands, I noticed, when she played chequers with her father, were as white and soft as she had told us they would be, and now she wore her first diamond.

"Muma," she would say, "after the baby's born we'll have a holiday at Brighton. You and me, Muma—where we can get some sea air." And then, "Emmy, after the baby's born I'm going to buy six new dresses all at once and you must help me pick the stuff to make them."

She did not mind talking about the baby before Con, and once, when she had caught him to her in a moment of playfulness, he felt the baby stir. The shock of it registered in his face, and then a wide grin of surprise came. Kate snatched him away.

"Rose, have you no shame!"

"Oh, Muma! Con's old enough to know. He's seen plenty of it in Dublin and on the goldfields. What do you think you're making of him?"

It must have been strange for Con in those days to realize that soon there would be two babies to take his place as youngest. It may have been that he was glad to see that place slip away from him. He was growing taller and the childish roundness was leaving him; it may have been that he was glad to see Kate's attention focusing on someone else.

"When Rose's time comes I'll be with her," Kate would state firmly, "and be damned to John Langley."

The preparations that Adam and I made for our baby were necessarily less elaborate than those made at the Langley house. There they had set aside two rooms for the baby and the nurse was already engaged, and a pile of towels and sheets and baby garments waited.

"We didn't need all those things on the Eureka," Kate sniffed.

Adam made the cradle for our baby himself. He spent countless hours working on it during his nights in port here, and there was love in his hands. It was polished and beautiful, an old-fashioned cradle on rockers—high, so that I wouldn't have to bend over it.

"We've had a cradle like that in our family for a hundred years," he said.

He carved a wooden doll and painted it with a dark green soldier's coat. "I don't want any English red-coats here." And then a bear with jointed head and paws, painted dark brown. "A New England bear."

He was very happy about the child, and I think in those months he loved me. We never talked of Rose, except casually, and though I watched his face closely it did not show the tension, the extra awareness that had once been there whenever her name was spoken. It happened that he did not see Rose for all these months. He never went to the Langley house, and whenever he was in port Rose kept away from the Maguires. I began to feel that I was winning him away from her. Perhaps she too conceded this. The last time she visited me before her confinement she ran her hand lingeringly over the silken wood of Adam's cradle.

"You're very lucky, Emmy." And this time she meant no taunt.

II

It was spring, and the air warmed perceptibly; I was six months pregnant and Rose was near her time. I remember it was the first day that I left the door of my house open to the sun and the soft wind. I was sitting sewing, with the cats at my feet when John Langley's shadow fell across the floorboards.

"Miss Emma—will you come to the house at once? Rose has been in labour since this morning."

"I laid down the sewing. "Is she bad? Is there any danger?"

He shook his head; it was almost a gesture of helplessness. "The doctor says not. The nurse is with her, of course . . . she was pain."

"Pain she must expect? What can I do for her?"

"I don't know. She wants you—she keeps asking for you."

I hardened myself. "I don't think I should go. There is my own child to consider. I don't think Adam would want it."

"Miss Emma—I would be grateful." And he meant it. "Just a few minutes. Perhaps it would calm her. She screams —and in between the pains she throws herself about." I knew how he hated to concern himself in what was completely a woman's affair; but he valued the child more than he valued
197

his detachment. I knew what he thought—that we, the women, were a silly, emotional lot not fit for the precious children we bore. Perhaps he was right. "You know how it is with Rose," he said.

Yes, I knew how it was with Rose; she would never be different. Not in anything. It would save trouble if I gave in now and went to her, because in the end she would get me there, in one fashion or another.

"Only for a little while," he urged again, humbly.

But I knew Rose better than he, so I fed the cats, and locked the house, accepting the fact that I would be away until the baby was born.

Kate was there, a bed-sheet pinned about her, fighting with the nurse. And Rose was fighting with both of them. She gripped my hand when I came to the bedside. "Thank you for coming, Emmy." It was one of the few times she ever thanked me, and the realization of that made me believe that her fear was real. She seemed feverish, and I think the pains were bad when they came, though I knew it was not beyond Rose to scream louder because she knew that John Langley was listening. Kate clucked in disapproval.

"Sure, you shouldn't be here at all, Emmy—the way you are! It isn't as if this great lump of girl hasn't got plenty of help . . ."

Whatever she had she seemed to need me. She had me sit by the bedside, and she kept hold of my hand. To us both the labour seemed very long; I had expected Rose to bear her child with supreme ease, but it was not so. I sat there through the afternoon and most of the night. When Kate tried to take me away there came anguished protests from Rose, and her nails dug into the flesh of my hand.

"Don't you understand!" she screamed at her mother. "I don't want you or anyone else. It's Emmy I want!" My back was on fire with the ache of sitting there, and my hand had long ago gone numb. The doctor dozed in the bedroom across the hall with Tom for company. The nurse told me that John Langley waited downstairs in his study.

"I never did see such a fuss over a baby," she said, sniffing disapproval of Rose. "And this one is as healthy as an ox . . ."

The pains came faster, and the child was finally born in the early morning—a straight, strong child, a girl, whose cries seemed to fill the whole house. John Langley heard them from his study, and he was outside the door waiting with Tom when the nurse came with the baby wrapped in shawls. I don't know what he said of his granddaughter, but I did know that all his thoughts had been fixed on a boy. Rose, when she learned it, spoke dejectedly. " Now he'll want another one at once—a boy!"

I was sitting slumped in the chair drinking the tea which Kate, in defiance of all the household rules, had been to the kitchen herself to make. On his way out the doctor paused. " Go home to bed," he said.

Rose was washed, and went to sleep immediately. The house was quiet now. I went downstairs on John Langley's arm. Tom walked beside me and handed me into the carriage.

" I'll ask Rose's mother to call on her way home, Emmy," he said. " You look so tired . . ."

" I'm all right," I said. " Don't send her. She's been up all night too."

The cats greeted me with hungry cries when I put the key in the door. While they ate I rekindled the range, which had gone out. The drivers had not yet arrived for work, and it was very quiet out in the Lane. The early morning air was fresh ; I flung the windows wide and left the door partly open. While the kettle boiled I went and changed into my nightgown and turned down the bed.

I was lifting the kettle to pour the boiling water into the teapot when the pain struck me. I was able to set the kettle down without spilling the water. That was the last conscious thing I did before Higgins found me later lying by the open door.

III

I did not make it anyone else's task to tell Adam that I had lost the baby. When the word came that the *Langley Enterprize* was about to tie up at Hobson's Bay I sent around to borrow Rose's carriage, and I went myself. The weakness from the miscarriage was still with me, but it was not that which made my legs, my whole body tremble as I approached the gangway of the *Enterprize*.

Parker, the mate, was supervising the unloading. He told me Adam was ashore at the office of the Langley warehouse. I waited in the cabin, and I dreaded the moment when I would hear his steps on the companion ladder. I knew I was afraid at that moment. With the child I had been secure, wanted, perhaps loved. Without it I was afraid, and desolate.

He stood and looked at me, and his eyes went immediately

199

to the flatness of my figure. Protectively I put my hand to my stomach to ward off that look.

"I lost the baby, Adam."

He came to me at once and put his arms about me; I felt my failure in the gentleness of his kiss on my cheek, the kiss of pity and compassion, but not of love. I felt my heart grow cold, telling myself that if there had been love there would have been a sharing now of the loss, a joining together. He seemed to take the disappointment on himself and to bear his own grief separately and privately, apart from me. He was sorry for me, but would not permit me to be sorry for him. "Poor Emmy . . ." he said.

"There'll be other children, Adam."

His answer was, "My poor Emmy."

I turned away from him, breaking free of his arms, from the pain in his face. "There will be others," I repeated. But I felt as if I had been robbed of Adam as well as my child.

Chapter Six

I found that I was not able to stay away from Rose and the baby. Each day, on some pretext or other, I walked along Collins Street and rang the bell at the Langley house. Sometimes Rose was at home, sometimes not, but I climbed the stairs to the nursery without question from any of the servants, who were used to me—even expected me. I would hold the baby, play with her, say the things to her that I suppose I would have said to my own child. To do this only partly stilled the sense of longing; eventually I would have to lay her back in the cradle and leave. Perhaps I only hurt myself by these daily visits, and prolonged the pain, but I was unable to stop going there.

In the bad moments, when I was full of my misery, I would blame Rose for my losing the baby—blame her for demanding that I stay with her all through the night when her own child was born. Then I would blame myself for being stupid enough to give in to her demands, for caring so little for myself. But thoughts like these were cold comfort, and I did not stay with them for long at a time. Alone now, without Adam, without the thought of the baby to fill my days, I began to need Rose as much as she needed me. I wanted her companionship, even the frivolous, bored gossip she indulged in. Most of all, I suppose, I wanted her child.

She was generous in this, as in most things—but I knew the child did not mean very much to her except as a hold over John Langley. Her motherhood was a careless, haphazard thing, and her baby was a toy to her because she never had to care for her. She would visit the nursery as a way of passing time, she would rock the baby a little in her arms, and then hand her back to the nurse, thankfully, I thought. And yet, in the perverse way these things go, Rose had an instinct with children, a natural way of pleasing them. For her the baby never cried, seemed to recognise her mother, to know her arms and the pleased smiles and gurgles were a sign of it. Rose would sing a lullaby to her, dangle a gold watch before her eyes and laugh to see the baby's tiny hands try to reach for it; she would press the child against her and put her face down to her daughter's. I used to think that the baby's first recollections must have been the feel of silk and the perfume Rose wore.

She was called Anne. Rose lost to John Langley over that and the baby's baptism—or perhaps she didn't care enough to fight for these things. The child was called by the English name of Anne and was baptised in the Church of England. I recognized it as part of John Langley's fight against the Maguire kind.

Rose defended herself, shrugging. "How else does she have a chance? I want her to belong to the right people. I don't want the door shut in her face . . ."

None of the Maguires attended the christening, and Kate never saw the baby in the long lace robes that Tom and Elizabeth had worn. "Sure, do you suppose I'll stand there and see the poor wee thing signed over to the devil? And never will I step foot in the Langley house again!"

But Rose continued to go to Maguire's, and no one denied her this. Kate did not welcome her, but she did not forbid her either, and Dan, with his quick look at Kate, would always rise to take Rose in his arms.

"And how is it with you, Darlin'? And when will you bring the little one along to see us?"

In time she did bring the baby to the pub, and John Langley could do nothing to stop it. She came without the nurse, always stopping at Langley Lane to pick me up, so that I could manage Anne if she grew fractious. Kate was not able to resist her first grandchild, and Rose gained new acceptance through Anne. The child was fussed over, and held high in the air, kissed, sung to, and rocked. All the discipline of the nursery was destroyed. She learned to reach for Dan's beard, and Con let her tug quite fiercely at his hair. She was a small queen here in these crowded rooms above Maguire's pub, and she soon knew it.

Some months after Anne was born I heard Kate say, as she held her in her lap, "Isn't it time now for your own house, Rose? You said he promised it after the baby came."

Rose shrugged. "Well, I don't want it now."

"Don't want it? Are you mad? When there's a chance to get away from that creature . . .? To get this innocent little thing out of his hands?"

Rose rustled her skirts defiantly as she swept by Kate to go and stand at the window. She parted the lace curtains and stared down into Bourke Street. "I couldn't have a house like that one—and *that*'s the kind I want. He wouldn't give me enough money for that. I couldn't have as many servants and the carriage. Besides, it suits me to have Elizabeth to do the housekeeping. I'd make a mess of it—we all know that!"

"I never heard of a woman who didn't want her own house to run—to be her own mistress in."

"I *am* my own mistress." The tones were loud and ringing. But what she next said was muffled into the lace curtains; we were meant to hear it, but not to question it.

"Besides, who would want to live in a house alone with Tom?"

I lowered my head over my sewing, and Kate pretended to be absorbed in the baby. But nothing could blot out the restless swishing of Rose's skirts as she began her pacing back and forth across the room.

For me also it was an unhappy and restless time. The days were too long and far too empty. My house was too clean, with no one to disorder its unnatural neatness. I knitted socks for Adam until he had too many, and made fine linen shirts. I even knitted caps for the men out in Langley Lane; they didn't want them—I knew they accepted them with embarrassment only because they knew my need for activity. I continued to do the books for Larry, but they were too easily done, and there even came a time when there was no more mending to do for Kate and Dan and Con. Rose had her own maid, so had no further need of my services. My hands were as empty as my days.

And as for Adam, he seemed a stranger. He was a kind, gentle stranger. I did not know his thoughts—he never spoke of the baby; I only knew that he worked incessantly. While the *Enterprize* was in port he supervised all the loading operations himself, and when there was no more to do he would come home and take out his carpenter's tools. He made cupboards and shelves, and even began to rip out and replace the worn floorboards. He put down fine hardwood and spent many hours waxing it and bringing a rich shine to it. He did things to that house that were far too good for what it was—three coats of paint and window boxes set at each window. We were like two puppets in a doll's house. It was almost with relief now that I saw him go ; but each time I was still there to wave goodbye from the wharf at Hobson's Bay, and to meet the *Enterprize* each time she docked. It was a ritual, and we performed it. We skirted around each other, observing the forms of our life as it had existed, but the life itself was gone. I could not have believed that the child could have made such a difference. We were lovers, but it was a performance full of passion but no heart. I prayed for a child, but there was no easy pregnancy this time. Each month there was the hope, and the disappointment, and each month Adam seemed farther away from me.

We were saving money, the *Enterprize* carried full cargoes, and Adam's commission was handsome. He simply brought the money to me, with no sign of pleasure at having earned it, and I deposited it in the bank. He never enquired about the total deposited there ; he left it entirely in my hands—I could have done with it as I pleased. He worked hard, but it was not for money he worked.

And then, early in 1856, John Langley announced that he was laying the keel of his second ship. She was to be larger than the *Enterprize*—314 tons burden, and would carry a crew of 34 men and boys. Adam was to be her captain. She was to be named the *Rose Langley*.

II

The naming of the new ship was a measure of the relationship between Rose and John Langley. It proclaimed to that world of colonial society that there was no discord between Langley and his daughter-in-law ; it said that she was more than accepted, she was approved. I had sensed this for a long time, even before Anne was born, but now it was a proclaimed fact.

Rose's instinct with men was never surer or more successful than with John Langley. She stretched past his aloofness and disarmed him. Instinctively she reached into the core of his

203

loneliness and found her place there. By this time, with the maturity that had come to her with the baby, she was a very beautiful woman indeed. It would have been a strange man who could long have resisted her overtures of friendliness, her seeming guileless pleasure in his company, the bright glow of charm and spirit she brought to that formerly half-dead house. He must have known her faults—only a fool could have missed them. But like many of us he overlooked them. She caused disturbances in his orderly life, she was vain and greedy and sometimes noisy. But she changed her gown carefully each evening before he came home, buying now only the colours he liked, wearing his gifts of jewellery with pride and a show of great pleasure. She was waiting in the hall when his carriage returned at the end of the day; she poured his Madeira for him, and refused to let him drink his port alone with Tom in the dining-room after dinner. She took his arm to the drawing-room, and she never refused, not once, to sing for him when he asked it. She learned the songs that pleased him, and these were the only ones we heard. Night after night I sat in that drawing-room with them and watched her work at the task of winning his confidence, his admiration, and finally, I suppose, a kind of love. I had never seen Rose work at anything before; always the act of charming and captivating had been natural and effortless. She was growing in a certain kind of wisdom.

She was the centre of that household because she was its buffer against the tyranny of John Langley. Time and again, I had seen her turn his attention away from some imagined mistake of Elizabeth's, some fault or slackness of Tom's he had discovered. Even the servants formed a grudging alliance behind her, although her whims and the perpetual chaos of her possessions made work for them. She could sweeten John Langley's temper and change his mood. He seemed not to take it as a sign of weakness to smile, to pay her compliments, to listen to her chatter. She was to him the daughter that that poor shadow, Elizabeth, had never been. He found a spirit he could not break or intimidate and it delighted him. People began to speak of a mellowing in John Langley; it was true only of the areas in which Rose touched his life.

I saw much of this because for the first year that she lived in the Langley house Rose did not go into society, and I was her only companion. Elizabeth might have been Rose's companion if Rose herself had permitted it. She was fascinated and absorbed in the study of someone who was not afraid of her father; the novelty of it astonished her and she gave

Rose unstinting admiration. Rose was polite to her, kind when she remembered to be, and bored with her.

"Fussy old maid!" was her description of Elizabeth. "Poor thing, she's frightened every minute her father's in the house. She'd hate him if she dared to."

Elizabeth was jealous of every thing and person who came close to Rose—of Tom, she was jealous, of Anne, most of all of myself. She would have been jealous of her father if it had occurred to her that it was possible. She lived a strange life, hiding behind Rose, sheltering beneath the force of her personality, offering to her the love and service that no one had ever asked of her. Rose accepted only that part which she needed.

"She seems to be everywhere," she complained to me. "Sometimes I have to close the door in her face to keep her out. She's like a dog—always at my heels."

In the places where Elizabeth wanted to follow the doors were closed very firmly—the places that represented Rose's freedom beyond the house. Elizabeth was rarely seen with Rose in the carriage. She never came to Langley Lane, or to the Maguires'. Rose shrugged off Elizabeth's bewilderment at this treatment.

"It's as much as I can do to act like their idea of a lady when Papa Langley's about. I can't do it for Elizabeth too."

Once she said to me, in a voice that was nearly a whisper as she stared about the quiet luxury of her bedroom, "Emmy, sometimes I think these walls are closing in on me—as if the door is shut and I can't open it. Sometimes I tell myself that I'll have to get out of here or I'll die."

And we knew, all this time, that John Langley expected her daily to announce her second pregnancy. He desperately wanted to see his first grandson, and Rose knew this power she still held over him.

III

There were people standing on Collins Street watching the carriages draw up when Adam and I arrived at the Langley house. Every window was lighted and we could hear the sound of the music as we walked towards the house.

"Old John isn't doing it by half," Adam said. He flexed his fingers to try to soften the new white gloves and make them easier on his hands.

"To do it my half would spoil the whole effect," I answered. "He wants to introduce Rose to Melbourne society and if he gives less than the best people will regard her that way. He's more than a year late in doing this and he has only the baby as an excuse . . . He had *better* do his best."

We pushed our way through the crowd around the Langley steps. They parted reluctantly, cockily contemptuous of anyone so humble as to arrive on foot at John Langley's reception. In the hall we parted, Adam to go to Elizabeth's housekeeping room at the back which had been turned into a cloakroom for the men, and I to go upstairs to Rose's bedroom where the women were leaving their wraps. I watched Adam as he threaded his way through the people milling about in the hall—so handsome he looked, so straight and tall, and his shoulders broader than any man in sight. I saw more than one woman glance at him in those moments. His dress suit was new, but he wore it well, more comfortably than the gloves. But I knew, as I climbed the stairs, that he had not wanted to come at all.

The invitations had gone out long ago. Adam had looked at it on our mantel and said, " No point in getting new clothes. I'll probably be in Sydney or Hobart the night it's held." He was reluctant ; he still avoided the meeting with Rose.

If he had been a less honest man he would not have been here. It would have been easy for him to delay sailing from Sydney until he was certain that he would miss the reception. John Langley was not to know how long it had taken to assemble the cargo. But Adam was of that New England breed who expected value but gave value in return, and so he had sailed as soon as the cargo was complete, and there had been the rush after he had landed at Hobson's Bay to find the tailor to make him a suit, and I had written a late acceptance of the invitation, I had previously declined. I didn't want to go either. But if I were going I determined to go in style, and so I had cut the neckline of my blue silk wedding gown as low as was proper, but left the long sleeves to hide the scar. I had made a dark blue wrap and lined it with a light blue that matched the dress. I wore my hair piled high, and a tall comb in it, and I had some satisfaction as I turned from the mirror.

Adam had said to me as I picked up my gloves, " You look handsome, Emma."

What he meant was that I looked chic—I did not look like Emmy Brown who had tumbled into the Maguire dray, nor did I look like the washed-out little girl who had landed here in Melbourne from the immigrant ship. Since that time I had won a husband and lost a baby—and, yes—I had twice shot a man and seen him die. I looked older perhaps, than I should have looked, but that was no disadvantage because there are some who are gauche in their youthfulness, and who are better to leave it behind. I was one of those. As I mounted the Langley stairs that night I looked better than I had ever looked in my life before, and I met the cool stares of the other women without wavering. I knew no one here, and no one knew me, but I would have died before I let anyone think that I cared.

Adam was waiting for me on the landing outside the drawing-room when I returned from leaving my wrap. He fingered his gloves again, and the snowy immaculateness of his cravat, and then he extended his arm for my hand and together we stepped into the receiving line. The line moved slowly because almost no one had been formally introduced to Rose before—though she was well enough known by sight—and I had plenty of time to study her. She was wearing the gown I had chosen for her an incredibly soft green that only her complexion and colouring could have worn successfully, and the back and shoulders she displayed must have been the most beautiful that Melbourne had seen in many a year. Around her neck hung the diamond pendant that John Langley had given her for this occasion. She wore neither flowers nor ribbons—I had not let her spoil the simplicity of the gown with the unnecessary ornamentation. At times I was very jealous of Rose, but even jealousy would not let me spoil beauty where I had a chance to create or enhance it. She was as much my creation as she stood there that night as she was the creation of John Langley's money.

She was flanked by her father-in-law and by Tom, but almost no one noticed Tom. Beside me I saw Adam's hand flex and unflex, and I wondered if it were entirely due to the gloves.

At last we were before them, and going through the formal greetings. I don't remember what was said, except that as our name was called, Rose turned swiftly from the last guest who had held her attention, and as her eyes fell on Adam her expression altered quickly. The laughter, the pleasure went out of it. She gave him her hand quite coolly and properly, but I had seen that look on Rose's face too often not to know the substance of what it meant. Rose looked like this when she was wanting something, when her eyes had fallen on something she desired and did not yet possess. As I was reminded that in her short life Rose had got everything she had ever wanted except Adam.

207

"Well, Adam . . ." she said.

And he replied, "Well, Rose . . ." They were appraising each other and trying to seem detached about it, but I knew that Tom hung on every shade of expression, as I did. What the rest of us said I will never remember.

We moved on into the drawing-room, and into the press of people about the door, the sounds of the music just under-scoring the bigger volume of talk, the scent of lavender and verbena in the air. As we squeezed with exaggerated politeness through the people, I had a chance at last to look into Adam's face. He had the look of a man who has been struck, and the shock still registers. And as I smiled the smile that is automatic as one steps into the midst of a party, I knew that the year and the months since Adam and Rose had last seen each other might not have existed. I had won nothing of him back from her. Just by a look and a word they were drawn again.

There was more talk than dancing that night, and the world we saw represented a mingling of two societies that did not often come together in Melbourne in those days. John Langley was one of the " Old Guard "—the ones who had defied the Colonial office and the Governor's edicts from Sydney and had come and taken and settled the land. They were the aristocrats of this world, the men of entrenched privilege and position. Some of them had been, like John Langley, lesser gentry in England, gentlemen farmers who had been able to bring some money, and servants with them in their venture. Others had come from much less but the fact that they had been among the first conferred rank on them. It conferred wealth in the form of land and the right to graze sheep. Then there were the others, the ones who had come in the Forties to make money on the land boom and speculation in Melbourne. Some men and their fortunes had vanished when the boom had collapsed ; others had held on and when the golden tide swept across Victoria they were doubly rich—rich in the real estate they held and rich in the trade that suddenly came to their doorstep. But they were not of the " Old Guard." Very few combined squatter, farmer, and merchant as John Langley did. He belonged to both worlds, and he had bidden both worlds, all the power and wealth of Melbourne, to come and meet his daughter-in-law. Some of the old squatter families dared to stay away because Rose was, for all her Langley name, one of the gold-digger, immigrant Irish. But more had come—willingly or unwillingly, they had come.

We moved among them, and I was surprised to see how

many knew Adam, knew of me by name. They talked of the new ship. "I hear you're to captain the *Rose Langley*, Adam —she'll be a fine ship." And then "Well, I hear Old John is laying down another keel."—with a nod towards Rose in the receiving line—"It's well named." It was cruel to hear Adam's name so often, and inadvertantly linked with Rose's. I discovered, though, that I had a small identity of my own. Some of the wives of the men Adam knew through handling their cargoes nodded to me in recognition.

Melbourne was really a very small place, and no man was wholly anonymous. Adam talked for a while to a man who imported hardware, a plain man who seemed about to choke behind the stiff formality of his collar; his wife reached out her hand to me—a hand in a glove to tight that it wanted to burst from its skin like a sausage. She was not given to genteel delicacies. "I 'eard you lost your baby. Poor thing!" She meant it kindly.

We walked on, and in the crush we met Larry. He looked extraordinarily handsome in his dress suit—handsome and a little gipsyish with his curling black hair and the deep tan of his skin.

"Are Kate and Dan here?"

"They wouldn't come. Only births and deaths are the exception to crossing this threshold."

"And you?" I said.

He shrugged. "I'll go anywhere there's business." He gestured about him. "And all of Melbourne's business is here tonight—the small and the big." And then he laughed. "And could I let them say that Rose got no support from her family?" He gestured about the brilliantly lighted room, the throng of people, the squad of extra servants hired to circulate with the trays, the silk curtains and wallpaper, the lovely oval mirrors, the gleam of the crystal lamp-brackets. "This is it, isn't it, Adam. This is worth trying for?" He winked and laughed again. "I'd change my seat on the dray for this any time."

"Are things going well?" Adam said.

Larry nodded. "John Langley will have competition before he knows it. I've got my eye on a little space here." He spread his hands expressively. "How would it look, Emmy? —Lawrence Maguire, General merchant."

"Wonderful—how proud we'd all be . . ."

"Well, I'd better go and find myself a rich widow so that it can happen all the sooner . . . And where better——"

Elizabeth was about to pass us in the crowd. I was

determined she would not slip by. She looked tired and almost dishevelled; all the work of the reception had been hers. As a gesture to the occasion she had put on a gown of a dull blue that did not become her; it had a scooped neckline which was neither high nor low, and she wore Rose's brooch pinned there.

"Elizabeth, I want to present Rose's brother, Larry. Larry—Mrs. Townsend." She looked at him with some hostility while he made the most elegant bow possible in that crowded place. All the Maguires were graceful, I thought.

"May I compliment you, ma'am, on the brilliant success of this evening." He smiled with an almost outrageous charm. "I can appreciate the amount of planning it required."

Clever devil, I thought; he knew exactly how this household worked. And there was Elizabeth, ordinarily so cold with men, actually blushing like a girl. "It's Rose who is the success," she said, without a trace of wistfulness. She gave me what was nearly a friendly look. "Have you ever seen Rose look so beautiful?—have you, Captain Langley?"

"No—no, I haven't," he stammered.

She was jostled then by someone trying to squeeze past, and so Adam's confusion was not noticed, except by myself. "Of course," she said a trifle irritably, "they all swarm about her—all those men. I mean, they'll wear her out. She's not quite recovered . . . from the baby. She never thinks that she's not strong. But she isn't—she has to rest." She looked as if she would gladly have pushed all the people back from Rose.

When Elizabeth had gone, Larry looked after her in some puzzlement. "I didn't know Rose had found such a champion. It isn't usual. You, Emmy, are the only woman she's ever kept as a friend."

"She doesn't need women—she has enough men," I answered tartly. And then I put my hand firmly on Adam's arm, for once making my claim forcibly. "Come, Adam—I see they're going to supper. I'm hungry."

"And I," Larry said, "must set about finding that widow."

It was not a widow we saw him later take to supper, but she was the daughter of a rich grain merhcant who supplied agents all over the colony and had partners in Sydney. I wished for Larry's sake that she had been pretty, but Eunice Jackson had never been that. She was a big girl, strong and wholesome, and she wore a gown on to which there couldn't be fitted an extra inch of braid or ribbon, not another piece of embroidery. She wore a mess of flowers in her red hair, but the pearls around her neck were real. Melbourne gossip said that Sam Jackson was searching for a husband for Eunice who was a step or two up the social scale. So far he had found no one. Now his daughter looked at Larry with mesmerised eyes, and laughed at everything he said. And Larry, I thought, looked as much a gentleman as anyone in sight. I watched him across the room as he found a seat for Eunice and saw that she was settled comfortably, brought her champagne and food from the buffet, picked up the handkerchief which she dropped several times. It was hard to know that under those gloves his hands were calloused, as were the hands of half the men present. There hadn't been time yet, in this country, to make an aristocracy, but everyone here tonight was trying for it as hard as he could.

Later Adam seemed to come out of his trance a little, and he was gayer. Maybe it was the champagne. He bowed to many people, and introduced me, and I heard the warmth in his tones. An old woman in a purple gown, dyed hair and a heavy necklace of diamonds tapped his arm with her fan as we passed.

"*There* you are, Captain Langley." She turned to me. "He brought me down from Sydney on the *Enterprize* the other day and he tried to tell me he wasn't related to John Langley." Adam presented me, and I recognised the name of one of the big landed families of New South Wales. She tapped his arm again.

"Sweet wife you've got, Captain Langley. Sweet gal!" And then she leaned over to me and whispered loudly so that Adam should overhear. "And you're a lucky woman. Handsomest man I ever laid eyes on!"

After a while we danced. I had never danced anywhere but on the *Eureka* and it was no preparation for John Langley's polished floor. But Adam led confidently, and I followed easily. We moved together well, I thought.

"You're light, Emmy," he said. "Light as a feather."

He smiled at me, and I smiled back, and we moved to that music as two people should. I began to hope that that look between Rose and Adam had been only a mischance, a thing, perhaps, of my imagination.

But I was wrong. She would not let him in peace to forget her. When John Langley led Rose to the piano later in the evening, proud to display her accomplishments, she said plainly enough what was in her own heart.

A crowd had gathered politely to hear her sing, the ladies seated, the men standing behind them. I remember Adam's hands resting on the back of my chair as she went through the repertoire of songs that John Langley liked best. Along with the rest of her her voice had matured; it was still utterly true and bell-like, but it was richer in the lower register. The applause that greeted the songs was more than polite.

And then, for the last song, she broke from the pattern. It was a song that was a mocking little slap in the face to the Langleys, a reminder of who she was and what she had come from. It was the only time I heard her sing an Irish song there.

She looked directly at Adam, a beguiling, enticing woman, superbly confident in her powers.

I know my love by his way of walkin',
I know my love by his way of talkin'
I know my love by his coat so blue,
And if my love leaves me what shall I do? . . . what
    shall I do?

The look to Adam disregarded me. For Rose I simply was not there, seated on the chair between them.

. . . Bonny boys are few,
And if my love leaves me, what shall I do?

Chapter Seven

The first time I saw Langley Downs was on one of the golden-blue days of the Australian spring when the air seems to sing in your nostrils and you are twice as alive as you have ever been before. It was also a day more than six months after the reception John Langley had given for Rose, and it was two years since the morning I had looked from the window of The Digger's Arms and seen the Maguire dray. Now there was more beauty in this land than I had found before; my eyes were accustomed to the browns and greys, the faint blues, and I had ceased searching for the lush greens. The wild flowers were subtle, not thrusting or riotous. They were sensed, rather than seen. They were a feeling in the air, a tangy, wild perfume carried on the wind which made me forget there was any other way to smell flowers. I saw the tender new red leaves uncurl on the eucalypts.

Rose and I rode in the buggy that morning, and up ahead was the barouche with Anne and her nurse, and Rose's maid. Ahead of them, and leading the procession was John Langley, very straight in the saddle still, though he had been travelling

212

all day. Rose had chosen deliberately to stay behind the barouche even if it meant riding in the dust it left.

" I feel I have some peace here. It's private—the last of the line."

Occasionally John Langley rode back to point out some feature of interest in the small hamlets we passed through, or to name the man to whom some of the homesteads and runs belonged. It was sheep country, wide and grassy, rolling in low hills, lightly treed along the creeks.

" The best sheep country in the world," John Langley said. Perhaps he exaggerated, but with the soft wind blowing and the freshness of spring on the land, I was prepared to believe him.

Rose managed the buggy very well, with style, occasionally with dash. It had been a present to her from John Langley, and it had pleased him mightily, the lover of good horses, to see how well she learned to handle the chestnut mare who always pulled it. She called the mare Taffy; there were always plenty of good horses where John Langley was, but this one Rose loved. In the beginning a groom had occupied the seat with her when she drove about Melbourne, shopping or paying the calls that became the usual thing once the reception had introduced her to the kind of women who stayed at home to receive calls. She was a notable sight in those Melbourne streets, and she knew it. The buggy suited her much better than the closed barouche. Then she started to leave the groom behind, which was forbidden by John Langley but whose order she disregarded. This gave her the kind of freedom she had never known in her whole life; she began to use it recklessly.

There wasn't any serious talk at first—it didn't seem possible that anyone would dare behave as she did in so small a place as Melbourne. The talk increased and it concerned her and Charles Greenley—a man in his thirties, just out from England with some money to invest. He was " Looking around " he said. He had rented a house at St. Kilda for six months, and it was inevitable that he would be introduced to John Langley, and, since there was frequent entertaining now at the Langley House, that he would meet Rose. After that they were seen a few times walking together in the Botanic Gardens and even as far away as Brighton. But where was there to go in Melbourne? Rose had made herself conspicuous in her buggy, and it was not surprising then that it was recognised as it stood one day in the driveway of Charles Greenley's house. I did not know who it was had the courage to tell John Langley, or if it was that Tom simply could not endure any longer the sympathetic smiles and the nods behind his back.

There was one short, sharp interview between Rose and John Langley, and then a message came to me to ask if I would go with Rose to Langley Downs for an indefinite stay. Surprisingly, John Langley was very gentle with Rose, or was it, I wondered, that he couldn't bear to admit his judgment had been at fault.

" Rose had been doing too much—too much entertaining, not enough rest. She should be quiet for a time, Miss Emma."

So I agreed to go. There was no reason not to ; Adam was away and even if he came back while I was absent I did not think it would make much difference. It seemed almost a good thing to me if I should escape the strain of our forced intimacy for the few days he was in port. We played our game quite well, I thought, and we never admitted to the strain. We were considerate of each other, and kind to each other's failures. Kindness, when you want love, is almost the worst thing. Occasionally, when we were bidden to the Langley house, Adam saw Rose, and always I had the impression that it would have needed only a word from Adam and Rose would have left everything, even her child, for him. This could not have appeared so to the other people who saw them together, because Adam was always welcomed by John Langley, and even Tom, in time, began to drop his attitude of mistrust and suspicion towards him. So I was the only one who saw, or imagined I saw, the strong bond between these two, the bond of people irresistibly and forever drawn to each other. I didn't know through what torments Adam lived in his soul, but I believed that only the unshakable idea of what a man like Adam believes to be right held him back from Rose. And as for Rose, I believe she waited—and she thought that Adam, sometimes, like all other men, would crack.

I think, during those months after the reception, they never exchanged a single word in private ; they had nothing but the communication of their senses. When they were in a room together this was powerful enough for me to feel. It may have been the frustration over Adam that drove Rose into Charles Greenley's arms.

As a result of this I was on my way to Langley Downs as a kind of guardian for Rose, someone to relieve her boredom, to restrain her if that was possible. My ears were safe for whatever she would say. In a sense I was grateful for this trust.

214

"To think I'm being sent here like a child in disgrace," Rose said bitterly to me. Her eyes were narrow and angry as she watched the figure of John Langley up ahead.

"You can thank heaven you have Langley Downs to run to," I answered shortly. "And John Langley to protect you. If he left you to the gossips they'd tear you limb from limb." And then I added, "I suppose you know Charles Greenley is leaving? He's going to Sydney."

She nodded. "Poor Charlie—I ruined things for him, didn't I? I didn't mean to. It just happened." Then she turned to look at me. "How do you know so much, Emmy? You don't go out in society?—you don't meet people. How do you know what happens?"

"I have ears—and eyes. What do you think the teamsters out in Langley Lane talk about? and the barmen at the pub? . . . and the shopkeepers I deal with. I know most of what goes on in Melbourne."

"Then why didn't you tell me people were talking?"

"I did tell you—you weren't listening. You *knew* they were talking, but you didn't care."

"You're right," she said, and her expression seemed to harden. "I still don't care."

II

At Langley Downs I thought that John Langley seemed different in some ways. He was mellower, or at least less stern. Perhaps it was that Tom and Elizabeth were no longer in evidence to irritate him with their inadequacies. Here he met up with the ghost of himself twenty years ago ; he was a younger man and this was the place of his greatest efforts and triumphs.

"Everything in Melbourne," he said to me once as we walked together in the garden, "everything that is there could be bought with money alone. This—Langley Downs and Hope Bay—this needed work and faith."

I came to enjoy our walks together. Sometimes in the evening we paced the wide veranda which surrounded the house completely, smelling the night scent of the English flowers which were grown here with much pride and labour. I learned something of the history of this house, and I thought I knew in a small way the younger man who had lived here, who had built it for his wife, who had buried her in the lower part of the garden and made a rose garden about her grave.

"There were no graveyards then," he told me, "and no churches either. But she was buried with reverence." He did not say she was buried with love, but I knew that he had respected her as he did not respect his children.

It was a big, plain square house of whitewashed brick, solid, two-storied with the veranda around both the upper and lower stories, and french doors that opened from each room. In the hot months the veranda and the open french doors shaded and aired the house. It was far less elegant than the house in Collins Street. The furniture was mostly oak, brought out with Langley from England, darkened with age and use, massive and plain. It suited the character of the house and the land about it. The bed-covers were all white, and the curtains were hand-woven linen that belonged with the rough cast of the walls. I felt at home in this house. By the standards of this country it was old, and I felt the currents of its life. If John Langley's ambition had stopped here he and his children would have been happier. He must have sensed what I felt about this house, because he responded to it, and we became friends as we took our walks. I inspected his newest imported rams with him, and listened to him explain their fine points, I walked the mustering paddocks and the shearing-sheds and the dipping troughs. My neck and hands were sunburned again as they had been on the Eureka.

The difference in our stations and rank was great, or it would have been if the barriers of English society had existed here. But need was a great leveller. In a strange way I knew that John Langley needed me—not only for Rose's sake now, but for his own as well. They were happy weeks, those first ones at Langley Downs. Rose and I complemented each other in John Langley's need. I was the companion of his walks, the one who listened to his plans for the future, for his grandchildren. Rose was the companion of the drawing-room, the one who sang the airs he liked, whose chatter could amuse him at times. I was the one to talk to, Rose the one to look at.

While we were there John Langley left us for three visits away from Langley Downs—once he took the long trip down to the coast of Hope Bay, and twice he went into Melbourne to stay for a few days. As usual, when there was no man about to play with, Rose was listless and bored. For so early in the season the weather was hot, and we spent the afternoons sitting in the shade of the veranda. Anne slept in her cradle upstairs, and even the servants were quiet at the back of the house. A deep silence lay on the land; the sheep that scarcely seemed to move grazed in the home paddock, and at that dead time of the afternoon there was not even a breeze to stir in the trees. I had my sewing, because it was a long habit with me, but Rose had nothing for her idle hands.

Once she turned to me and said, " My God, Emmy, I think I'll go mad. I'm dying here—I'm smothering! I'm smothering in sheep and virtue. I miss . . . I miss Charlie!" She threw her head back. " Charlie is my darlin'—my darlin' . . ." she sang mockingly.

" Hush, Rose! You must put up with it—you *must!*"

" Oh, it isn't that I loved him," she said. " He made me laugh. He made me forget . . . all the things I want to forget."

" You must live with them," I said. I didn't mean to be cruel. There was nothing else for her. " You must somehow bear them. They will grow easier in time." I suppose we both spoke of the same thing, but neither of us spoke it outright.

Those afternoons on the veranda were long and trying for both of us.

The one release Rose had was in the new horse that John Langley gave her. He was a grey three-year-old, a thorough-bred, and Rose almost worshipped him. He was by way of a thank-offering from John Langley to Rose for agreeing to leave Melbourne and Charles Greenley behind, he was a bribe to stay on here at Langley Downs until Melbourne had found something else to talk about. She learned to ride him with great courage and eagerness. The long history of the Irish love for horses was in her blood, and what she did so well she did, it seemed to me, by instinct. The coachman and the grooms marvelled at her.

" Never a hand wrong," the head groom commented to me. " She never puts a hand wrong. It's as if she was born knowing that creature."

She rode every morning while it was still cool. She was supposed always to be accompanied by a groom, but Dancer, as she called her horse, could outpace the groom's mare easily. After she had some schooling she began to take jumps; in that awkward side-saddle she took jumps that men did not go at easily. Soon the home paddocks would not contain her.

" Rose, I forbid it," John Langley said. " It is unsafe—there are unsavoury characters about—bushrangers, horse-thieves—all these types who've wandered off the goldfields." He seemed unaware of the insult he offered with this reference.

"Bushrangers, is it?" she said. "I'd like to see any of them catch Dancer. But I can handle a pistol, you know. I was once shown how."

And she did strap on a pistol in a holster, and when the news of it spread about the district, it caused another mild scandal. Rose shrugged. "It seems I shock them whatever I do—so I might as well do as I please."

John Langley tried to persist in her prohibition, but he was lost in pride at the sight she made mounted on that horse. "If only Elizabeth had ridden like that," he said to me.

I also took riding lessons while I was at Langley Downs, but the results were very different. I was a little afraid of horses, but I was learning that the woman who cannot stay in the saddle for a few hours is at a disadvantage in that country. So they found the slowest, quietest old mare in the stable, and she and I were quite content to jog about the home paddock, the stable boy only a few feet behind, bored probably, and watching with envy the luckier groom who was supposed to attend Rose, who did attend her until she gave Dancer his head and left the groom behind. Some days John Langley rode out with Rose, and she was forced to stay at his side. She liked best the times when she was alone, when she recovered the freedom that seemed lost to her.

"Oh, Emmy, it's wonderful! I belong to no one when I'm out there alone. It's the one time I feel something for this country—I want to ride and ride to the horizon, and when there's a new horizon I want to ride to that, too. But I always have to turn back."

She was not interested in Langley Downs as a sheep run, in the fortune that was won there. All she cared about was the broad acres, the miles of grazing land almost free of timber, the empty spaces for Dancer and herself to run.

III

"Crinolines are bigger," Rose said, "and bonnets smaller." She yawned as she turned the pages of the magazine. "I must have a new habit made when I get back to Melbourne . . ." We were alone, during one of John Langley's absences, and we sat in the drawing-room waiting for it to be time to go to bed. Rose kept looking at the clock. Everything in the house was closed and shuttered for the night except this one door to the veranda which we had left open to catch the breeze. The servants were gone to bed; outside in the hall there were candles ready for us to carry upstairs. The unearthly silence of night in the country was about us; Rose hated that silence —that and the blackness of the empty miles without a single light. It oppressed her. I glanced up from my book and saw that the magazine had fallen from her hands and she just sat staring at the open doorway and the darkness beyond. Her expression was grave, almost sad; she often wore this look now when her face was in repose; I was touched by it, and troubled, because I knew that in the little space of these few years Rose had passed far beyond being satisfied by a riding habit or a hat or even a diamond. For a time Dancer could make her happy, but there were still many empty hours left that could not be filled by her child, or her husband, or any other thing in her life. Perhaps she thought that Adam could have satisfied all her longings, but if she did, she was wrong in that. She did not know the man I knew—how unyielding he could be at times, how hard; she did not know his heritage, his love of simplicity and order and decency. In a little time together, I thought, they would have driven each other mad. Perhaps Adam's own good sense told him that, and only his heart denied it. But Rose, she had no sense; she had instincts and desires that betrayed her, and left her as she was in these moments, a woman whose face was shadowed with pain and a non-understanding of herself.

Her startled gasp roused me, and her mouth feel open. Then she hurled herself from her chair, the magazine thudding to the ground.

"Pat!—oh, Pat!"

He had come to the doorway, as quietly as a shadow, and just stood there. Now we were both hugging and kissing him, and he was half laughing with his arms about both of us. Then he held us back a little, and looked from face to face.

"Rosie . . .! Greeneyes . . .!" He put his head on the side. "Well, when I looked in the door and saw these two grand ladies I thought I'd come to the wrong place. Sure, I'm never have known the pair of you, so fashionable you've become!"

Rose pulled him forward into the room. Her expression was radiant. "Pat, you tease! *You* haven't changed at all! What brings you here . . .? Larry said he heard you were heading for New South Wales."

"Brother Larry doesn't know everything. I'm by way of being a neighbour of the great John L . . . about eight miles from here. I bought a little place owned by a man called Sweeney—Matt Sweeney. It's only a few thousand acres. Not big by Langley standards. Matt started out here when the first settlers came through. He's a thorn in the side of John L. and his big neighbours. He has a nice little bit adjoining the Langley property, and Old John would pay a lot to get his hands on it."

" You devil! " Rose said admiringly. " I suppose you did it on purpose."

He shook his head, but he laughed at the same time. " I swear the thought never entered my mind."

I tugged at his sleeve, laughing too, in spite of myself. " I don't believe a word of it! But it's wonderful to hear you've got some land of your own at last—what you've always wanted, isn't it, Pat? "

" It is," he said. " You're right." But he didn't sound too sure, and I felt a small coldness in my heart, wondering if perhaps he was afflicted with the same malady as Rose, the eternal restlessness, the dissatisfaction.

" Then why haven't you shown yourself before this? " Rose demanded. " Why do you have to come sneaking here at this time of night? "

" Didn't I just get back from a trip to Adelaide," he said. " Just today. I and two others took a bunch of horses into the sales. I've been up into New South Wales a bit . . . there's enough jobs about the country if you're roaming. You don't have to stay any place longer than you feel like."

" Then you're not going to stay here and farm? " Rose's expression drooped a little.

He shrugged. " You know the way it is with me, Rosie. I just wanted a little share in this place. Just some place I could come back to once in a while. A place to put my feet up. It can't support two partners full time . . . it doesn't pay enough."

" But you'll come often when you're here, Pat? " Rose urged. " We've missed seeing you. You've never been to Melbourne to see Maguire's Tavern . . . or anything. You've never seen my baby."

" Sure I can read, can't I? Don't I know all about Miss Anne Maria Langley baptised in the Protestant Church? And I know all about her mother—and the fancy new gowns and the diamonds and the carriage. The papers don't let me forget my little sister, Rosie."

" Come and I'll get you something to eat," I interrupted hastily. I could see they were getting ready to bicker, and I pulled at Pat's sleeve to distract him. " Don't tell me you're not starving—I've been trying to learn to ride, and I know that eight miles shakes your insides down very nicely."

But as I turned towards the door he took me by the shoulders and turned me back to face him. He seemed to look into my face for almost a minute.

"You look wonderful, Greeneyes." He surveyed my dress and my hair. "You've turned into a handsome woman, little Emmy." And without any hesitation or shyness he put out his hand and touched my cheek gently. "Little Greeneyes . . ."

We carried a meal into the dining-room—cold lamb, bread, cheese, apple-pie. John Langley had left the key of the wine cupboard with me; I selected a bottle of his best whisky and I mentally dared him to make an objection. It was the gayest meal I remember since those early weeks on the Eureka. We laughed, and exchanged news, and the bread crumbs scattered over the polished oak. It was a long time since I had seen Rose eat so heartily. In the middle of it, Mary Anderson, the housekeeper here at Langley Downs, appeared, candle in hand, her nightcap still neat on her tight curls. The noise had aroused her, and she was inclined to disapprove.

"It was not Miss Elizabeth's habit to entertain at this time of night."

Rose's eyes darkened with annoyance. "This is *my* home, Andy. And this is my brother."

She was the only one dared call the housekeeper Andy. The woman stood in almost the same relationship to her as Elizabeth Langley did, ready to forgive her most things in return for a little notice. She subsided.

"Well, I'm sure, Miss Rose, it's perfectly all right. It's just that Mr. Langley . . ." She looked at Pat. "The trouble was I didn't hear you arrive. I didn't hear the dogs . . . or your horse."

He half bowed to her over the whisky. "I'm a bushman now, Miss Anderson. One of the things I've learned is not to make noise."

We stayed up very late talking, Pat telling of stories of cattle mustering, of the vast properties he had seen in the west of New South Wales where the grazing was scarce and it needed thousand of acres to support a few hundred head of cattle. He had crossed the Murrumbidgee, and travelled up the Darling. He told us of the formidable country he'd seen in the mountains in New South Wales, the deep gorges where the cattle sometimes strayed and a horse had to be better than a man to keep his head and his footing. He was harder and tougher than on the Eureka, the camp fire was now his permanent home. He had learned skills that none of us had dreamed of. There was a sense of violence and power in his hard-muscled body.

When he went it was as quietly as he had come, kissing us both. " There'll be a moon," he said. " I'll be back at Sweeney's in no time at all."

" We'll come tomorrow," Rose said. " We'll be over early."

His brow wrinkled. " I don't know that you should, Rose. Matt—well, his wife left him, and it isn't much of a place for women. I doubt if there's anything fit to eat."

" We'll bring our own," I said, and it was settled. I knew that Kate would never forgive me if I failed to bring back a report of the Sweeney place. And I knew, from Rose's face, that if I did not go with her, she would go alone.

" I don't like it, Miss Rose," Mary Anderson said. " Matt Sweeney's an ex-convict. It was back twenty years ago he came here. From Van Diemen's Land. No one goes to the Sweeney place . . . I don't know what Mr. Langley will say about this."

" It's not Mr. Langley's concern," Rose answered.

Rose insisted on riding Dancer, because she wanted to show him off to Pat, and so I had to drive the buggy. I could manage it fairly well so long as they put a quiet horse in the shafts, but Rose was impatient with my slowness all during the journey to the Sweeney place. She kept riding ahead of me, and then coming back.

" Can't you hurry, Emmy? We want to be there before it gets too hot."

" I'm doing better than I hoped, so just be patient."

We came at last to the Sweeney place, down a road deeply rutted with cart tracks and bounded by broken fences.

" Don't they say you can always tell a farmer by his fences? From these I wouldn't think much of Mr. Matt Sweeney."

" Oh shut up, Emmy! "

We were within sight of the house now, and it was a sad affair, a little square, unpainted wooden house, with the usual veranda around three sides. Honeysuckle and wisteria climbed on every veranda post, softening the ugly lines of the house, somewhat, but threatening, in its monstrous overgrowth, to pull the veranda down with it. There was the remains of a garden, littered with rusted buckets and tools. There were several apple trees, with a bench built around one of them.

"There was a woman here once—you can tell that," I said.

Rose was silent until Pat, hearing the horses, appeared in the open doorway. He waved at us, laughing, "Welcome to Sweeney's Manor."

I saw the tears of rage stand out suddenly in Rose's eyes. "Pat—how could you do this? How could you waste your money on a place like this?"

He lifted her down, and tethered the horses in the shade of one of the trees. His expression was calm and patient, and his voice quite gentle when he turned back to us.

"You don't understand, Rose. I met Sweeney when he left here to go prospecting for a bit around Bendigo. He said there wasn't anything left for him because if he didn't produce some money, the bank was going to have this place. He told me about it—slap in the middle of some of the sweetest sheep country God ever put on this earth. He said the big squatters were going to have it—Langley and his friends. So I thought this was one time when they weren't going to have what they wanted. I gave him the money and he paid up the interest on the loans. It's free and clear now, and Matt has another chance."

"Another chance at what?" Rose demanded. She did not seem to expect an answer, because she flounced past him up to the veranda.

We inspected the few rooms of the house, which seemed to be furnished mainly with empty bottles and well-thumbed books. "Matt is a reader," Pat explained unnecessarily. Then we met Matt himself, a dried-up little man, brown and hard like a nut, grinning at us cheerily. He looked at us both with appreciation.

"This is a treat—a real treat," he said, bowing. "My woman left me—can't blame her, I can't put up with myself sometimes, but there hasn't been a woman here since, as you can see."

Rose sniffed the stale air of the house, and her nose twiched without any regard for Matt's feelings. "We brought a picnic basket," she said. "We'll eat outside."

He was a fumbling little man, who drank too much, and had no notion of how to work, but he had a way with him. He told us stories in which he was always the butt of the joke, and It was a very gay lunch we had out under the apple tree. Rose warmed to him, as I did, as no one could help doing. He was shiftless and likeable, and he took such pleasure in the fact of our being there that it would have been churlish not to let him enjoy himself. He sprawled in the uncut grass at our feet when the meal was through, smoking his pipe and staring up dreamily into the tree.

"What it is to have women about," he sighed. "There's nothing takes the place of a woman, Pat, boy . . ."

"Why don't you get married, Pat?" Rose said abruptly. "It would be good for you. Larry's been courting Miss Eunice Jackson these last six months. Her father doesn't like it—Larry being a Catholic—but Eunice is going to wear him down. She's rich, you know. She'll have all her father's money since she's the only child."

"Be damned to Larry and whatever arrangements he makes! Women aren't a business with me. What I'll look for is a woman, not a dowry. He can tie himself down if he wants to, but that's not for me."

"There's nothing wrong with what Larry's doing! Miss Jackson's a nice girl, and she's very fond of Larry. He'll do very well for himself—and he'll make her a good husband."

"Don't mistake me, Rose. I didn't say wrong for Larry—wrong for *me*."

She grew angry. "You don't know what's good for you."

He laughed. "I wouldn't say you were much judge of what's good for anyone, Rose. Don't pass out advice to me—look at yourself! I *know* what my life is, and it's not one I can share with a woman. I have to be free. I must know I can go tomorrow, if that's what I want . . ."

Rose got to her feet slowly. "It's time we went, Emmy . . . if we're to be back before sunset."

Then she looked down at Matt, still sprawled on the grass—at Pat beside him.

"Men don't know how lucky they are. All there is for me is to have another baby—and another—until even John Langley is satisfied."

It was the sort of thing that a woman says only to another woman, but Rose would never pay much attention to such rules of propriety. All the way home she was quiet, seeming to want only her own thoughts; she rode docilely beside the buggy the whole way.

IV

Rose visited Pat almost every day at the Sweeney place, even after John Langley returned. She made no secret of where she was going in fact she seemed to take some pleasure in her father-in-law's discomfort.

"Sweeney has been a thorn in the side of every responsible
224

grazier in the district for years," he said. " His farm methods are a disgrace. He won't keep his fences in repair and his inferior stock is forever getting mixed with mine . . ."

" But *Pat* is there, you see," Rose would say with a kind of mock innocence. " It isn't *Sweeney* I go to see."

He could not prevent her going; he could do nothing but insist that she take a groom with her. Rose bribed the groom, James, to stay behind in the little township of Forbes Corner, while she went on alone. I didn't try to stop this; there seemed a dangerous pressure building within Rose and my senses told me that this small rebellion might ease it. She seemed to enjoy being with Pat. They argued half the time they were together, and there were some quite violent quarrels, she told me. But she always went back there the next day, and when she would return to Langley Downs in the evening at the last possible moment before dinner, she seemed relaxed and almost happy. She sang as she changed her gown for dinner, and chattered to me of what Pat had said, and what she had said. There was no more picnics for me under that apple tree. I knew that one of us had to stay behind to keep John Langley company, to placate his annoyance at these visits. But I watched Rose ride off on Dancer on those bright mornings with a feeling of envy. John Langley was irritable and touchy until she returned.

He had had news for me when he came back from Melbourne.

" I've given instructions that if the *Enterprize* should dock while we are still here, Adam is to proceed on here. There is a great deal we have to discuss. The next voyage is a long one. I'm sending the *Enterprize* to Calcutta with a cargo of grain which Adam will take on in Sydney. From there he goes to Singapore. He's buying a mixed cargo there for the Stores— whatever is available at a good price. It is cheaper to do that than send him all the way to England . . ." He launched into a discussion of the values of the entrepot trading posts of the East, which, from the months of listening to him and Adam speak on the subject, I could follow without difficulty. Many times in the Langley drawing-room I had heard him attempt the same discussion with Tom, a discussion which always died after the first few minutes. Elizabeth, with her head bent over her embroidery frame, would only nod her head. I think it was in desperation that John Langley had first turned to me as a listener. On this occasion, when he had finished with the matter almost two hours later, I felt I could have gone and bought his cargo for him.

He had added, almost as an afterthought to the news about Adam, that Tom would come with him.

"That was said for me," Rose remarked to me later. "That's to warn me that it's time I started being a dutiful wife again—and Charlie Greenley is forgiven and forgotten."

They arrived at Langley Downs, Adam and Tom, one day about noon, when the heat haze had begun to blur the line of the horizon. I was on the veranda on the shady side of the house with John Langley when Rose's voice reached us.

"It's Adam! . . . Adam . . . !"

It was for all the world like the times when she used to herald his return with Larry on the Eureka. That same glad cry, the tone of possessiveness that seemed to announce that he had come for her alone.

As we turned the corner of the veranda she dashed out into the blazing sun to greet him. From her behaviour it was hard to believe that Tom rode beside Adam. I saw her arms go up towards Adam in an automatic gesture, as if she could not have restrained herself. It was John Langley's voice that arrested her.

"You are welcome, Adam . . . Tom. Have you had a good journey?"

Rose seemed to freeze, her arms still outstretched. She couldn't have heard, as I did, the short intake of breath that preceded John Langley's words, but she heard his tone, that was almost a command to her. I think it was the first time that he became truly aware that there might be danger for us all here. Then Rose seemed to come to her senses; slowly she lowered her arms and went around to Tom's side. She stretched on tiptoe to receive his kiss as he leaned down to her from the saddle. There was no word of welcome, only a forlorn, tight smile.

I spent the afternoon with Anne in the garden; she was crawling now, trying to pull herself to her feet. Her long, cumbersome skirts got dusty as she crawled in the grass to make an inspection of the flower beds. I carried her down to the rose garden where John Langley's wife, her grandmother, was buried. I watched the wonder and delight in her face as I bent and held her for a moment near a bloom, and she caught the full warm scent. "Emm . . . Emm . . ." She put her arms about my neck, laughing. Mine was the first name she had learned to say.

As I played with her on the veranda I could hear the steady

226

murmur, the rise and fall of John Langley's and Adam's voices as they talked of the coming voyage. I would have liked to be with them, but of course it wasn't fitting to sit down deliberately to discuss business with a woman. Anne grew sleepy, and I carried her up and laid her in her cot. As I kissed her she still smelled of rich pungent sap of the flower she had crushed in her hands. She slept immediately and peacefully. Anne was a good baby, a gentler, quieter child than you would have expected from Rose.

I stayed for a time in the room with her. The afternoon was so still, without a breath of wind stirring, that from where I stood by the open window I could hear the soft rhythm of her breathing. The stillness held the land fast, in the way that Rose hated, and that I had grown to love. The formal, English garden was only a little trifling thing holding back the sweep of the land in which there was not even a single house to tell me where the Langley acres ended. From where I stood at this high window you would have thought they had no end. You could begin to understand why John Langley had given his first and greatest love here.

The voices were below me now. John Langley and Adam paced the walk that led to the rose garden—a wide hat on the old man against the sun, but Adam was bareheaded. Their strides matched evenly; both were tall men. Heads bent in discussion, and hands clasped behind, they seemed alike, though I had never thought of them being so before. My eyes lingered on Adam, and I told myself that now, in this new atmosphere, away from the house in Langley Lane, things would be different between us. After the empty months of grieving for the baby, now, in these last weeks, I had experienced a force rise in me again. I had seen the instant recognition of it in Pat's eyes, I had sensed it strongly during the hours of talk with John Langley. I was past grieving now, and I was ready to take hold of living again. I wanted to be used—as a woman, a wife. I was past living through another woman's child. I wanted Adam and my own child; I told myself that I would have Adam again, wholly and completely, here at Langley Downs. In spite of Rose I would have him. I never felt more sure of myself as I did then.

The languid afternoon air seemed to explode about me in brightness as I watched Adam pace the walk. There was too much energy for me to contain.

"I love you, Adam," I said aloud. The sudden surge of joy and certainty was so great that I thought it must surely

communicate itself to him, and that he would look up and
salute me. But he did not; the pacing continued, the low,
earnest sound of their talk, as even and steady as the child's
breathing behind me.

v

I first became aware of the voices that night as I lay and waited
for Adam to be finished with his business with John Langley
in his study and to come upstairs to bed. I lay patiently, but
still filled with the hope and the promise that had come to me
that afternoon, thinking of Adam but content now to wait out
these last few minutes. I was full of my own thoughts and
the first sounds were ignored, but they rose in volume and
hammered insistently, in their ugliness, on my ears. Like all
the bedrooms at Langley Down mine opened on to the
second-floor veranda; Rose's was next to mine. It was a warm
night and her door was flung wide to catch the breeze, as mine
was. Until now we had each occupied the rooms alone, and
only an occasional snatch of song had reminded me of her
presence. Now it was impossible to shut it out. She and Tom
were quarrelling, and their voices, rising sharply, were clear
and inescapable.

". . . why can't you be like other women?"

"Other women? What have I to do with other women?"

"Nothing, I suppose. That's the trouble. Other women
would be happy with what you have . . . a child, a home.
Why aren't you? Why do you always have to run like this . . .
run and leave them behind? All this visiting Pat at Matt
Sweeney's place—It's just like the excuses you used to make in
Melbourne to get away to see the swine Charlie Greenley."

"Oh, God, can you never understand, Tom? I can't sit all
day and sew or read books. I'm not made that way. I'm . . ."

"Too well I know how you're made!" A bureau drawer
was slammed violently. "It's the men for you, isn't it, Rose!
That's what interests you. Always the men . . . a husband
isn't enough!"

"A husband like *you!*" I heard the cruel, tormenting
laughter, and I shrank from it, as Tom must have done. I
burrowed down into the pillows and put the sheet over my
ears, not from any sense of guilt at overhearing what I had,
but because I couldn't bear the bitterness, the accusation in
both their voices. But the sounds were still there, undeniable.

"I'm the only husband you have," Tom said. "And you
228

had better learn that, Rose. Sooner or later you'll have to learn it. You can't always have what you want. At some time you'll have to decide to make do with what you have."

" I don't know what you're talking about!" Her tone was petulant.

" You know right well what I mean. I mean Adam."

At the sound of that name I sat bolt upright in the bed, straining now to hear every word.

" Adam . . . ?"

" Yes, Adam. Who else? God knows, I was fool enough to feel almost glad when you started after Charlie Greenley because I thought that it meant you had forgotten Adam. But I should have known better . . . right from the beginning on the Eureka it was Adam you wanted. It still is."

" You're wrong, Tom! You're wrong!" She seemed shaken.

" Not wrong—stupid! But not so stupid as not to see what's before my eyes. Do you know how you behaved when Adam came today? Do you suppose any of us missed that? We're not blind!—not children!"

" But it isn't true. I haven't seen Adam for months . . . why I've never ever seen him alone! Don't you know that, Tom? We've *never* been alone . . ."

" Since when did that ever stop him from being with him in your heart? And if Adam were not the sour-faced Puritan he is he'd admit it too. Adam always makes himself do the right thing—but he's a man for all that! Don't you think it's just as conspicuous the way he avoids you as it would be if he sought you out. Adam is afraid. You know that—and you think you'll win yet. You think you'll wear him down."

I sat there in cold anguish and heard Tom say for me all the things I had never dared to say for myself. He spoke my doubts and fears and made them certainties. I held my face in my hands and knew that all my joy and hope was destroyed.

They were silent for a time. I had expected that Rose would deny what he had said, but she did not. I wanted her to deny it even for the sake of the small crumb of comfort. Then I could have made do with the notion that Tom and I had tricked ourselves, had been deceived because of our jealousy. But it was not to be so. I had heard the rage and despair in Tom's voice ; now I heard his plea, his cry of torment.

" It need not be this way, Rosie . . ." he said. His tone was lower now, and all the words did not reach me.

" If you only understood how I love you . . . even knowing you, I love you . . . if you would just let yourself be

229

loved . . ." The next words were softly spoken and I did not hear them. The cadences were tender, pleading, the tones of a man who begs. I hated Rose for the shame she brought to us all when Tom must beg this way.

But when she answered him I heard her clearly. I think my ears caught the words because I had listened too often to Rose when she spoke this way. I almost knew what she would say before the words were uttered.

"Be kind to me, Tom—I can't help what I am. *You* can help me." Now the plea was in her voice. I knew the sound of it—dangerously persuasive, irresistible to a man, to anyone who loved Rose.

"Oh, my God, Rosie! If you would . . ."

"Come here—come close to me, Tom."

I heard no more of their words, just the rise and fall of their voices, and the silences that were more eloquent and spoke louder. I heard too much, even so—the movements of their passion that made even that solid old bed creak, the little cry from Rose that was almost a laugh of triumph and delight, the low tones of Tom's voice, the violence and the urgency.

I could stand no more of it, and I got up and went and sat on the stairs outside my room. I held my head in my hands waiting for Adam, thinking about Rose and fiercely envying the she could win any man when it suited her. She would soothe Tom's fears and lull him to sleep, and he would be tricked into thinking that he had possessed her. She was reckless and impulsive, but always in the final moments she had an instinct for self-preservation with her husband and with John Langley. I hated her for being able to trick us all, and still hold us.

I saw the light from Adam's candle on the bend in the stairs, and so I stood up and went over to the window on the stairwell. I would not let him see me distressed. I would give Rose no more importance in his eyes than she already possessed.

"Emmy! What are you doing out here?"

I turned and smiled at him, holding out my hand. I wore the nightgown that Sarah Foley had given me on the Eureka, with the real lace and the fine lawn. I had brushed my hair for half an hour, and I knew in the candlelight it looked red. I had scented my wrists and throat.

"I couldn't sleep," I said. "I thought I'd wait here for you."

He half-smiled. " You're a strange woman, Emmy. Sometimes I think I don't know you at all . . ."

" Perhaps you don't. Perhaps you've always let yourself think of me the way you saw me on the Eureka. There are a lot of different Emmys . . . if you would let me show them to you. If you would let yourself see them, Adam."

I moved in close to him, and reached up and kissed him fully on the lips, and there was joy again in me when I felt his response. He put his free arm about me and pulled me against him hard, and his mouth on mine was searching.

" Emmy . . . my little Em . . . come to bed. I've been away a long time. Too long, little Emmy."

But when he opened the door to our room I heard again the sounds that had driven me out. I felt Adam's whole body grow tense and in a kind of fury he went to the french doors and closed them. There was almost a frenzy in the way he took me then, a loving that had little to do with tenderness, but may have contained much of frustration. It was not the first time I felt I was being taken in place of Rose. I accepted his loving for what it was, and gave back a kind of frenzy of my own, compounded of my need to satisfy him, to hold him, to keep him—my need to keep him from Rose, to bear his child. We slept in the exhaustion of our passion.

VI

I finished the last sentence John Langley had dictated to me, read it over, and then passed it to him to be signed. It was addressed to the Langley agent in Singapore, and it was the very last of the letters, lists, notes and buying instructions that I had taken at John Langley's dictation in these past three days and which were to go with Adam on the next voyage of the *Enterprize*. It was hardly yet seven-thirty in the morning ; we had breakfasted by candlelight more than an hour ago. Adam had had the final conference with Langley, and was now in the stable packing his saddle-bags for the journey back to Melbourne.

John Langley handed the letter back to me. " Thank you, Miss Emma," he said. " That's the last then." He permitted himself the luxury of looking relieved. " If you hadn't been here to do this I should have had to go back to Melbourne with Adam . . . my eyes and my penmanship are not what they used to be."

Then he frowned as if he regretted having said such a thing; as if an admission of failing eyesight was somehow a weakness. To spare him I pretended not to have heard. I stood up quickly.

"I'll take this to Adam now. It will save him unstrapping the saddle-bags when he comes around to say goodbye." I wanted a chance to say goodbye to him myself, privately.

The morning already had a feeling of heat in it; the sky was cloudless but the haze would soon appear on the horizon and Adam would have many hours riding in the sun. I walked quite slowly along the path to the stables, wondering how I would say goodbye to him. It would be many months before I saw Adam again and I did not feel sure about this leave-taking. He had seemed in these three days to have belonged more fully to me than at any time since the period when we had waited for the baby to be born. But I had questioned whether our physical love-making had meant any more than a desire to cover the panic we had both felt in the closeness of Rose's presence. She had been devilish during this time, ceaselessly provocative, playing the game of the devoted wife to Tom, touching him when he was near, kissing him before all of us, singing especially for him in the evenings—and all the time watching to see how it affected Adam. The strain had been great, but it was worse when Rose realized that the sounds of their love-play could be heard in our bedroom at nights. I don't know what relief from her own torment she may have found in torturing Adam in this fashion, but she did it deliberately, and I believed, with cruel intent. She seemed to say that if she suffered, then he would also. I was glad to see him go from Langley Downs this morning.

The groom who usually tended Adam's horse approached me on the path. I thought he seemed startled to see me.

"Good morning, Miss Emma. Captain Langley's all saddled up. He'll be around any moment now. I'm just taking his canteens to be filled . . . it'll be a hot one today, I'm thinking."

"Yes, James . . ." I went to pass on, but he stopped me.

"Miss Emma——" he was fumbling nervously. "I was wanting to talk to you about maybe sending my little Betsy down to Melbourne for some schooling. Miss Anderson was saying that you could maybe help."

"I'll talk to you about it later, James. I must take this to Captain Langley."

"Yes, Miss Emma . . . but . . ."

"Later . . . I'll talk to you about it later."

232

A moment after that, when I was within sight of the stables, I realized why he had tried to delay me. A furious rage rose in me as I saw Rose, her hair tumbled on her shoulders, and the ruffled hem of the loose wrapper she wore trailing in the dust, framed in the stable doorway. She vanished into the dimness as I turned the corner by the kitchen quarters. I started to run.

Adam still had his hand on the buckle of the saddle-girth when I came upon them, as if she had surprised him. I prayed that it was so—that there had been no arranged meeting between them. Rose was standing very close to him, her face upraised to his.

"Rose—you're mad to come here like this!"

"I couldn't help it. I can't let you go this time, Adam. I *can't*."

"What are you talking about?"

She put her hand on his shoulder. "You have to take me with you, Adam. I've tried not to say this to you, but now I have to say it. I can't stay here any longer. I have to go with you."

"Now I *know* you're mad. You've taken leave of your senses. It isn't possible." Slowly his hand came away from the saddle girth.

"I could catch up with you on the road," she urged. "It could be managed. We could go together—to San Francisco, Adam. We'd have money—I have my jewels to sell." She shook his arm with fierce urgency. "Don't you see it *is* possible."

He looked down at her, his face tight and hard. "You would do this to me, Rose? Even to the end you have to play your game. You have to prove that every man within sight is yours, don't you?"

She shrank back a little from him. "What are you saying? Don't you understand that you're the *only* one. You're the only man I ever cared about. From the first moment I saw you."

Now Adam's hands came up to take her shoulders. He shook his head. "You don't know what you're doing."

"Yes, I do!" she said in triumph. "I know full well what I'm doing." She stood on tip-toe to him now. "Kiss me! *Kiss me, Adam.*"

He seemed to hesitate for a second or two, but at last he bent and his lips did go to hers. Their bodies seemed to fuse together. And then I found my tongue.

"Well, Adam? Are you going to do what she says? Are you going to take her with you?"

They fell apart, but it seemed to me that their arms left one another reluctantly. After the first surprise there was no confusion in Adam's face. He answered me directly.

"No, Emmy, I'm not. Whether you believe it or not, even if you had not come at this moment, I would not have taken her with me."

He pushed past Rose, and led the horse forward by the bridle. When he reached the doorway he paused and spoke to me again.

"There is no apology I can offer you, Emmy. No words would mean anything now. All I can say is that I would not knowingly have hurt you."

Then with a swift movement he mounted, and without looking back again he started on the path that led to the front of the house. I stood watching him, thinking over his words, and then at last I turned away from the brightness of the sunlit yard to where Rose still stood in the shadow of the stable.

"I can't say I'm sorry, Emmy. It wouldn't be true. If you had not come I would have had him . . . , yes, I think I would have had him."

"You don't understand Adam," I said, as calmly as I could. "You never will understand him. He has slipped away from you again. You have lost him, Rose."

She shook her head. "No—not lost him. I have not lost him so long as we both live. A part of me is Adam, and that can't be lost."

I left her, and turned and followed Adam along the path. I said my goodbyes to him dutifully under John Langley's eyes, and my lips met his without visible quivering. He raised his hat to me in a final salute, and I stood on the veranda to watch him until he was out of sight. The last of Emmy Brown seemed to go with him, the last of the foolish, hopeful, naïve girl that had met and loved him back in the Eureka days. I was fully a woman, fully changed and aware of what I faced in the years ahead as I turned to John Langley and said:

"I would like to talk to you. I have a proposition to make."

BOOK THREE: 1862

Chapter One

Every afternoon I seemed to work against the clock to be finished with the papers on my desk before the children came. While I drank my tea they had the little cakes and milk that I had ordered always to be put out for them, and they told me the happenings of their day. If there was no one waiting to see me I walked back home with them and we went up to the schoolroom together. I helped bathe them, and I read a little to them before bedtime. Sometimes this part of the routine was not possible. If too much was left unfinished on my desk, if Ben Sampson or Lawrence Clay had matters to discuss with me, then I had to stay. Or there might be a summons from John Langley, though he rarely interfered with my time with the children. The hours with them were the part of the day that I lived for, and he knew that.

Ben Sampson put his head into my room. " Miss Emma— Mrs. George Hathaway has just sent word that she'll be in the store tomorrow morning to choose the material for her gown for the Governor's Ball, and she would think kindly of your assistance." His shaggy eyebrows were raised as he said it, waiting for my comment.

I dipped the pen in the ink again and finished out the column of figures before I answered him. " That means, of course, that both you and I, Ben, must be prepared to spend two hours and take every roll of stuff in the place before she thinks she has her money's worth. Sometimes I wonder if *we* get our money's worth—I mean in time and trouble."

He wanted to gossip a little, so he stepped inside the room. " Well now, you know better than that, Miss Emma. She wants to make sure she gets the best advice in Melbourne on what precisely is the most fashionable colour to wear this year, and how she should have it made. And four dozen other ladies will see Mrs. George Hathaway getting advice from Miss Emma, and they will tell twelve dozen other ladies and we will end up selling every yard of that *peau de soie* I told you would never sell because it was too expensive."

I massaged my stiff fingers as I talked. " I enjoy it, though,

Ben. I don't really mind taking down the whole shop for them —we all get value in the end. I like it better than sitting up here counting pennies."

"Well, if it's any satisfaction to you you'll be sure that you've dressed half the women at the Governor's Ball—what with selling them the material and the lace and the fans and telling them what style to have it made up in, and recommending which dressmaker to go to."

"Well, it *is* satisfaction. But I liked it better in the old days when you and I between us sold every yard of ribbon that left the shop, and did the ordering and the books with one eye on the door and between waiting on customers. I liked the struggle better than the success . . ."

He interrupted me. "You're the cleverest woman in Melbourne, Emmy," he said, for once not calling me "Miss." "And it's a damn' shame you're not at the Governor's Ball dancing with the rest of them. You could do it, if you wanted to. All you'd have to do is push John Langley . . ."

I shook my head. "My customers don't want to meet their draper at 'Toorak.' Besides, I don't *want* to go—you must know that now."

He scowled at me a little, and tugged at the end of his moustache. "You waste yourself, between this store, and those books, and the Langley children and fussing over the Maguires."

"What else would you have me do? Sit at home and knit, Ben? You know I'm as little fitted for that as Rose is, even though I disguise it better." With the pen I pointed to the seat in front of the desk. "Sit down, Ben. It's spring coming too early has put you out of sorts." He looked tired more than out of sorts, but I did not say that to Ben because he was very vain of his masculinity, and hated the suggestion of age. He dyed his hair and his handsome moustache to hide the grey and I could not say he was wrong to do it. Ben was a great success with the women who came to the store. I rang a bell on my desk, and Susan Higgins, the daughter of the man who had been my first friend among the drivers in Langley Lane, answered it. Susan was barely seventeen, and I was supposed to be training her, which meant she followed me about and tried to learn what she could.

"I'll have some tea now, Susan—and you can bring a fresh pot when the children came. And bring the whisky for Mr. Sampson."

I could order whisky to be served to a gentleman in my

office and there would be no scandal because Melbourne knew by now what Emma Langley was. It was nearly six years since this shop had opened its doors, and in that time some power had gathered to me, and a degree of trust. It was true that it was still the Langley Stores—it was merely a two-story extension of the bigger building next door, the run-down shoemaker's shop that I had persuaded John Langley to take over and finance as the new millinery and drapery department, with its separate entrance and the silk curtains dressing the window, fresh grey paint and its upholstered high chairs beside the counters so that a lady might spend an hour trying on hats or gloves in comfort. I had done no more than separate the laces and ribbons from the gun counter and the moleskin trousers of the larger store, but I had made a feminine world in this little annexe where women came and spent their money with some feeling that they were getting the latest in fashion and some help with their choice as well. Heaven knows, I had only the same ladies' magazines from London and Paris as they had to get direction from, but no one in Melbourne studied them more carefully than I. And no one else in Melbourne had Ben Sampson to stand there, handsome in his frock coat with the silk lapels, and assure the customers, when there was any doubt, that this particular shade of violet was all the rage in New York. Dear Ben, as if he knew any more than I did what was the rage in New York.

Ben had come in answer to my letter to Ballarat six years ago when I had asked him to help me start this annexe to the Stores, which I had persuaded John Langley to finance. It had been a doubtful venture then; nothing less than complete success would have satisfied Langley, but he had trusted me. He had done more than that—he had gone against the feeling of his time that women were never to be permitted to join in business. Perhaps he had recognised the desperation that had made me make the proposal at the time of Adam's visit to Langley Downs. He would not admit what he must have known to be the truth about Rose but I think he had seen that I was driven to asking for something to fill my days. I did not really care how he had viewed it—a compensation, a bribe, a payment for what Rose had done; what mattered was that the money and the backing of his name was forthcoming, and I had a purpose to my life and an outlet for my energies.

Without bothering to reply to my letter, Ben had come himself from Ballarat. He had stood with me in that ramshackle shoemaker's shop whose lease John Langley had controlled and watched the traffic going by on Collins Street, seeming to count the heads.

"I don't pretend to know how you persuaded old Langley to let you into this, Miss Emma, but it's a better gold mine than the one Dan Maguire struck. I'll be in it if you want me."

"What about leaving Ballarat?" I said.

"Oh, to hell with it! Ballarat's as dull as Sunday since the mining's been taken over by the big companies—and I've nothing there but a few boards nailed together and some stock I can sell in three days. I've a little bit of money I can put in this with you if there's room for it."

"There's room," I said. "The less John Langley puts up the less he'll own. And he's a businessman, never mistake that, Ben. When he takes a partner he requires that the partner put up every penny he can lay hands on—it's a kind of insurance that the partner's risk is always greater than the Langley risk. It's his way of making sure you don't trifle with the venture. I'm putting all our savings into it."

"Adam agrees?"

"Adam doesn't care what happens to his money. I believe he's even forgotten there *are* some savings. Don't worry—I'll have his agreement just as soon as the *Enterprize* is back again." I tried to take up again the notes and measurements I had been making when Ben had arrived. But he caught my arm and turned me back to him.

"I don't like the sound of that, Miss Emma. Is there some trouble between you and Adam?" When I didn't answer he pressed me further. "I've been thinking that this is not something for a young married woman to be going into when she should be thinking about husband and family . . . I wouldn't have taken much notice of your letter if you hadn't said that John Langley himself was behind it, and I've never had reason to think you a fool."

"And I haven't become a fool, either. I know that Adam will agree."

He shook his head. "That isn't what I asked. Is there trouble, Emmy?"

I pulled my arm away from his grasp, but I found that I was unable to lie outright to him. He had known me too well to be deceived.

"Don't you ever ask me that again, Ben Sampson, because it's none of your business."

He put his hand on my head, as if I were a child. "I won't
238

ask again. You're quite right, Emmy. It is none of my business."

Within a week he had sold out in Ballarat and was back with me. The agreement was drawn up with John Langley, and we ordered the men to start repainting the outside of the shop. It was old weatherboard beside the bluestone of the Langley Stores, so we could paint it to suit ourselves. We chose a pale grey picked out with a white trim. " Unserviceable," John Langley said, " you'll have to keep it up . . ."

" But smart!" Ben added. " The smartest shop on Collins Street."

Ben and I painted the inside ourselves, leaving the upstairs offices to their original grime until we could afford to furnish and redecorate them. But we hung the two windows on Collins Street with grey silk with a white fringe, displayed one hat and a single nonchalantly draped glove, and opened our doors to business. The main legend on the glass said The Langley Stores, and in neat gilt letters in the lower corner, Ladies Dept. Moved from the cramped quarters of the main store, our stock looked miserably inadequate for all those empty shelves, but we somehow created the illusion that space was elegance and we held to this until our first shipments started arriving from England. In those days Ben and I were the whole staff outside of a young boy who ran errands, delivered parcels to our customers, and hopefully waited to open carriage doors. The first six months were lean. Ben and I often wondered if we had misjudged our market, if the chic bareness of our shop was too austere for the frontier tastes of this city. But your shelves and our counters began to fill, and finally the day came when we had to hire our first assistant saleslady, and a month later, two more. Ben paraded the aisles with his hands behind his back and did far more work behind the scenes than he appeared to. I made myself two gowns of black silk, discreet, but of an almost ferocious stylishness and dressed my hair in the latest fashion ; I did not compete with the customers, but I hoped my appearance suggested that my advice was to be trusted. I rather disliked the way I looked when I was dressed for the shop, but it was good for business.

A year after we opened the aisles that Ben walked were crowded with customers each day from noon until well after four o'clock. It had become a recognised thing to do on the afternoon stroll on Collins Street to look into Langley's ; often it was just a way to pass an hour and no sale was made.

But I trained the saleswomen to patience, and eventually the strollers became customers. I learned the most important women in Melbourne and I waited on them myself, and whenever there was a new customer one of the girls would always come to fetch Ben or me to wait on them. By such flattery and patience we built up our clientele, and we started to show a profit.

And in six years Ben and I had made money and John Langley was richer. Melbourne still did not know whether I was a partner in the shop or merely employed by John Langley; it took note of the fact that my name was Langley but I had none of the associations with the land that would have made my being "in trade" acceptable in the highest circles. And there was the undeniable fact that I still lived in what was little better than a painted shack at the end of Langley Lane, and in my few hours away from the shop I seemed willing to act as a kind of unpaid nursemaid-governess to Rose Langley's children. Society put that beside the evidence that I was one of the few people who could be said to be close to John Langley, and that he welcomed me to his house. They didn't know where to place me, so I was left alone. Melbourne society respected me, but did not court me.

I was content to have it so. I doubted though, that Ben believed this. His face always screwed up sceptically when I denied that I wanted to follow any of my customers to the parties for which they shopped for dress lengths and gloves at Langley's. Ben fussed over me, and I liked it; we had a rare companionship of understanding and mutual affection, relaxed and unguarded. John Langley had never taken to Ben; he tolerated him, but no more than that. At times I flattered myself that Langley was perhaps sometimes jealous of Ben; he mistrusted the fact that at past fifty Ben was still attractive to the women who crowded our aisles. He mistrusted his dyed moustache, and his habit of spending his evenings drinking in the better known pubs. But Ben had style. His long figure in the black coat, the way he wore his cravats, his manner of bowing or of snapping his fingers to warn the boy to open the door for a departing customer all had a certain dandified elegance to them—a slightly vulgar elegance, but effective. You didn't stop to notice often that the craggy face was almost ugly. Like my stylish black silk dress, Ben was good for business.

Susan Higgins came back with Ben's whisky and my tea, served in the Crown Derby china John Langley had given me a year ago on the fifth anniversary of the opening of the shop.

It had been as much for his benefit as mine. He sometimes came to drink a cup of tea with me while we talked business. He detested thick earthenware.

While I sipped my tea and flicked my eyes back to the books spread on the desk, Ben poured a second whisky.

"Emmy—I feel my age. That's what's the matter with me."

It was so unusual for him to mention his age that my attention went back to him at once. "What is it, Ben?"

He sighed and put down his glass. "It makes me feel old to know that even if I did go back to the States I wouldn't be any use to them—except maybe in some office writing out forms. I was once a damn good shot too. They could have used some good shooting at Bull Run."

When the war had broken out between the States Ben had hung a portrait of Abraham Lincoln above his roll-top desk down on the ground floor where the customers could see it. This annoyed John Langley intensely since he sided with the South. But he had never yet reached the point where he had asked Ben to take it down. And Ben himself seemed to feel a kind of guilt because he was away from the fighting. I suspected that he wanted to stay just where he was, but he filled the days with his sighs about the Union cause, and his dreams about the glory that he might have won. The thing that was upmost in my mind when Ben talked of the war was that the blockade of the Confederate coast by the North would mean less cotton for Manchester, and eventually less cotton to sell in the shop. I did not say this because it would have hurt Ben's feelings, but he must have heard the rumblings from John Langley on the subject.

I looked at him closely. "Ben—I need you too."

He tugged at his moustache in the way he always did when he was agitated or pleased. "I'm glad you can still say that, Miss Emma. Of course I'm an old fool and I like to hear a woman say she needs me. But sometimes when I see the way you run this place, when I see what you can do with old Langley I wonder how long you'll need a man about you—any man."

"I'll always need you," I said, and I meant it. "You know as well as I do, Ben, the things that a woman may not do for herself. The business has to have you—*I* have to have you here."

He nodded. We knew our respective roles very well, and understood them. It did not matter between us that in this shabby, untidy room upstairs I was the one who looked after the books and made the decisions on quantities, and colours, and prices of what we ordered and later sold. This was supposed to be a man's work. As long as the customers saw Ben downstairs they could feel reasonably sure that I had not stepped out of my place as a woman. Those who worked for us knew the difference but there was a kind of conspiracy not to let the knowledge of it go too far. The masculine world of commerce could be only deviously brushed by the skirts of a woman. Every year, as Melbourne became less and less of a frontier town, women were pushed more firmly back to the place men thought they should be and I had to tread more softly.

"There'd be no need to rely on me if Adam had the sense to take a shore job," Ben observed morosely. "It's not good for you to be alone for so long at a time."

"I married a seaman, Ben," I reminded him crisply. "I didn't expect him to turn into a farmer. If I had children no one would remember that I was alone."

I gave him one long look that warned him that I would have no more discussion of the matter, and then I went back to the books. Ben was the only one to whom I would speak of this hurt, but then, there was very little about me that Ben did not know or guess. He even knew of the time when I had been briefly pregnant and had lost the child after carrying it a little more than a month; he was the only one beside Adam who knew this. Sometimes the pain and the longing for my own children and Adam's children grew beyond bearing and I had to speak of it. Ben received my words, heard them and did not deny them, and he held his silence. I had no fear that he would ever recall them for anyone else's ears, even at the times when he drank too much. Ben was my helper and my friend and my confidant, and it would have scandalised any of the women in the shop below to know to what extent this was so. We never saw each other outside of the shop but his protection and his care was there like a cloak.

He rumbled something into his glass. ". . . and it wouldn't hurt Adam to know that Harry Seymour is out there making sheep-eyes at you every time you pass the warehouse. It beats me how he ever gets any work done the way he's forever watching out of the window to see when you leave here, and then popping out the door to bid you good-evening. I swear one day they'll hitch a team to him and never notice— he's getting to be such an institution in the Lane . . ."

In spite of myself I laughed. "You hold your scandalous tongue, Ben Sampson. There's not a thing in the world that's wrong with Harry Seymour except that he's newly arrived here and lonely and he doesn't know a soul outside the Langley warehouse. He was telling me, poor man, that he lost his wife before he came out here. She was only twenty-four . . ."

"Not much younger than you, Miss Emma," Ben said. "I'd watch out for Mister Harry Seymour if I were you—him and his melancholy brown eyes."

"I like Harry Seamour's eyes," I said, just to tease him.

"Well, there's no accounting for the taste of a woman," he answered shortly. "He looks just like a cow mooning over you . . ."

I smiled a little as I bent over the books again, though I took care to hide the smile. I didn't mind Harry Seymour's admiration, nor the fact that Ben grumbled over it. Sometimes when I felt I had lived too long with my rustling black dresses and the ledgers, it needed the gentle appealing smile on Harry Seymour's face, or Ben's touchy jealousy to remind me that men could find me attractive. As I grew older it had been a curious discovery to learn that beauty was not always the reason why a man was drawn to a woman. I had grown surer of myself with the years.

We sat in silence for the next ten minutes, or at least Ben held his tongue because he recognised the sudden tension in me that always came when I knew that the children were due to arrive and my tasks were not completed. My eyes raced down the columns of figures, and the scratch of the pen on the paper was rapid and loud in that quiet. With all my haste the day's entries were not done by the time I heard their footsteps on the stairs and the light high voices that reached to me.

Being brought up in John Langley's house, they were well-mannered children. Mostly Anne remembered to knock and wait for permission to enter, but to-day the knock was perfunctory and there was no pause before the door was flung open and they all rushed in together.

But it was James, Rose's eldest son, who got the words out first.

"Miss Emma—Grandpapa said Anne was to have a pony of her own but I had to wait another year to have mine. He said I was to learn to ride Anne's and then we'll see . . . that's what he said—we'll see!"

Anne's face was flushed and angry; she was normally a clean and tidy girl, but this afternoon I could see the tear-streaks on her cheeks.

" And James ran to Mama, and of course she said that he should have a pony of his own—that she would get Papa to buy him one. It isn't fair, Miss Emma!"

She rushed towards me, and almost automatically my arms went out to receive her. But James was beside her, pulling at my sleeve, demanding my attention.

" I should have a pony, Miss Emma, because I'm a boy. You won't say anything to make Mama change her mind, will you? Miss Emmy, it's important . . ." His tugging at my sleeve grew urgent. I put my hand on his shoulder soothingly.

" We'll see, James . . ."

So I held them both, but my eyes went to the doorway where the two younger brothers had paused. They were sufficiently under James's domination to know that they must wait until he was ready to let them speak. They were three and four years old, and they clung together in a kind of mutual defence pact against their elder brother.

" Henry . . . William . . . do you have no kiss for me to-day?"

They came forward with a short rush, almost pushing James away from me. They still kissed me as babies do, moistly, with their arms tightly about my neck.

While they jostled each other about my chair my eyes went over their familiar, beloved faces. Each day I searched those young faces, jealous at the thought that a single day's growth and change might escape me, and I would not witness it. They were my handsome, lovely, darlings, beautiful in their quick alert expressions. They were all the best of Rose and Tom, but I felt I was mother and father both to them.

" Anne," I said, " little girls shouldn't be seen on the streets with dirty faces. Here—we'll clean those tears off." With my own handkerchief I wiped at the tear-streaks. She knew I was not scolding her; she seemed to relax a little under my hands. There was a very special feeling in me for Anne. She did not know that she was the baby born on the day I had lost my own, nor did she know that she was given the love that I was once able to give to Rose, and could no longer. But she did know that with her my hands had a special gentleness, and that I was, in a sense, her shield against her mother.

" But Miss Emma . . . What about the pony?" James exclaimed. " Are you going to say to Grandpapa that I should have it?"

At five years James had a bold, startlingly handsome face, and at the moment he looked like some angry angel-child, sure of himself, self-righteous almost, trumpeting his claims to heaven. He was John Langley's first grandson, and for the five years of his life he had enjoyed all the privileges of that position. He was arrogant, intelligent and spirited. He was the child of those nights of Rose's passionate abandonment to Tom after Adam had refused her and left her behind at Langley Downs on that visit six years ago. I was sometimes reminded that perhaps Rose had unknowingly already been pregnant with his child when she had begged Adam to take her away.

So for me there was another memory each time I looked at James. I loved him too, but differently from Anne.

Ben turned back from the cupboard where he had put the whisky bottle out of sight.

" Good afternoon, Miss Anne," he said, and bowed formally to her. She returned the greeting promptly with her short graceful curtsy. Except in moments of stress her manners were always impeccable, a fact that John Langley took great pride in. When she came to understand this, she doubled her efforts in this direction ; against the competition of her three brothers, against the unacknowledged rivalry with her mother, she had to find every advantage she had. With the birth of three handsome, healthy grandsons, John Langley had long ago forgotten the first disappointment he had felt that Anne had not been a boy. He was proud of her beauty and her good sense. She was a gentler version of Rose, a female thing whom he could love and admire without feeling the bewilderment and frustrations that marked his relationship with her mother. Like her three brothers she was dark-haired and white-skinned —a Maguire to look at, rather than a Langley.

" Good afternoon, James . . . Henry . . . William." Ben shook hands with each of them in turn. He always grew especially elegant in his own manners when the children were present, and he put away the whisky and sufferingly drank tea with us. Now he sat down and took William on his lap while the child rolled down his stocking to show him a slight graze on his knee.

" James pushed me down . . ." he explained, his face upturned to Ben, waiting for, and getting the sympathetic head-shake.

I held my finger up to my lips. " Hush, William . . . it isn't right to tell tales . . ."

" Oh, he's a crybaby," James said contemptuously. " Even my mother says that!"

They talked on, spilling out the small news of their world until Susan arrived with the fresh tea-tray. The nurse who always accompanied them on their afternoon walk had instructions to wait downstairs, and so they had a sense of freedom with me here that was lacking somewhat when we all returned to the schoolroom in John Langley's house. As each of them had grown beyond infanthood they had brought small possessions to this room—a favourite toy, books, the wooden animals they had tried to carve in imitation of the ones that Adam still fashioned for them. An accumulation of these was all about us here, and each day the children went naturally to their own things.

"I've learned the next page, Miss Emma," James said. "I'll say it for you."

He dragged a chair into place near mine; then he went to the bookshelf and took down the large-print copy of the Bible he had left there. He opened it on the desk between us, and pulled himself up on to the chair. He cleared his throat.

"The earth is the Lord's, and the fullness thereof . . ."

I watched his finger travelling along the line. "James, you're not reading it—you're just saying it from memory!"

"Just as good," he said. "I can *almost* read it. I made Annie say it over to me seven times last night until I could remember every word. Seven's lucky, isn't it, Miss Emma?"

He had learned to read at this desk—or almost learned, as he said. I glanced across at Anne, who was quietly tying the ribbons of a bonnet on the doll whose clothes she had sewed here in the afternoons. William had slid down from Ben's lap and drawn him over to the table in the corner where Henry was working on the simple jig-saw puzzle that was left there permanently for them. Under that table in times past Henry and William had built blockhouses and made forts out of the heavy ledgers. Susan Higgins had helped them make paper soldier's hats from the discards in the waste-paper. They learned the art and theory of war from the map of the United States hanging on the wall to which Ben had fastened the little flags that represented the Union and Confederate forces. It did not please John Langley that his grandsons sympathized with the Union because they had their teaching from Ben, but he did not attempt to interfere. Perhaps he knew, as we all did by now, that these children were getting an education of sorts in this untidy, cluttered room; in the midst of the confusion of ledgers and teacups they were learning of the world in a way they could not learn it from the colourless woman who was their governess. John Langley's success had come because he was a man of parts. He wanted his grandchildren to be the same. I think this was the sole reason why he did not forbid their weekly visits to the Maguire grandparents. Having watched the failure of his rearing of Tom and Elizabeth, he was perhaps now wise enough to know what good came to these children from the hours spent hearing Ben's talk and mine, in sensing the atmosphere of this store, of the hours spent in the parlour above the Maguire pub in the Horse Sale Yards. There were no plans made to send them to school in England, as their father had been, and their Aunt Elizabeth. John Langley meant to fit them for the world they would inherit.

Beside me, James leafed the pages. He came to another familiar place and his shrill voice rang out again, clearly, authoritatively.

"*By the rivers of Babylon, there we sat down, yea, we wept, when we remembered Zion*—where is Babylon, Miss Emma?"

Anne answered him, contemptuously. "It's right there—in the Bible!"

"I know better than that—the Bible isn't a *place*!"

But Anne wasn't listening. She had caught the sound of the voice that drifted up the stairs—almost, without actually being able to hear or smell them, the sound of Rose's voice brought also the sound of the rustle of silk and the smell of the perfume she wore.

"Here's Mama!" she said. A little of the tension returned to her; she hastily wiped her face once again on the skirt of her doll's petticoat. Then the door opened, and Rose stood there.

"Well—and how are all my darlings!" She held out her arms to them and they came running—Anne, James, Henry and William—all fighting for the kiss that she placed on each cheek. Then over their heads she looked at me, the triumphant, amused look which was to remind me that she was their mother, and that all she had to do was open her arms to them. She had never lost her knack of charming her children. If she gave them no more than ten minutes of her attention each day, for them it was a magical ten minutes. When Rose was with them there was never tears or irritability; they strove with each other to have good reports to give her, to show her the latest things they had made. If they behaved badly she left them; if they behaved well she was sweet, and sometimes she sang for them. To their eyes, as to other people, Rose was very beautiful. Her silken clothes, the jewels, the strange exotic smells of the perfumes she wore all carried an aura of unreality. They almost didn't believe in their mother; there was a sense that she might vanish, as the splendid illustrations vanished when the picture books closed.

Having kissed them, and received their homage, Rose was all briskness again.

"Emmy—so annoying—I seem to have lost one glove of every pair of white ones I possess. I haven't a pair to wear to-night . . ."

"I'm sure you'll find plenty downstairs, Rose," I said dryly.

She shrugged. "Well, of course, if you'd rather I was waited on by one of those stupid girls who don't know where anything is . . ."

I rose. "I'll come immediately." Then to the children I said: "Drink your milk—and don't eat too many cakes. Anne, I leave it to you to see that everyone behaves. You may pour a cup of tea for Mr. Sampson . . ."

Rose gave only the slightest nod to acknowledge Ben's bow as she left. She was always very cold with him, and he took a malicious pleasure in mentioning the Eureka as often as possible in her presence. There were very few people in Melbourne these days who ever reminded young Mrs. Langley that her first days in his country had been on the Eureka.

Downstairs in the shop Rose seated herself on one of the plush-covered chairs and languidly inspected the display of long white gloves I placed before her. I didn't have to ask the size. I knew everything about Rose by heart.

"They're to wear with the watered blue silk," she said.

I nodded. "Yes." I had helped her choose the silk, or rather I had chosen it for her. Rose bought everything she wore at Langley's, and she selected nothing without my approval. Perhaps she didn't really need my help—what we both needed were these opportunities to show those who were interested that we were friends still. There are many things that can be done in public to imply friendship, even where none exists. After that day six years ago in the stables at Langley Downs there was little left to us that was not mere form and show. What lingered in me for Rose was affection for the memory of the girl who had been kind to me on the road to Ballarat. What I felt now was not love for Rose, but for Kate and Dan Maguire. And I felt love for Rose's children. She clung to me in a curious way—a thin shield against the scandalous idea of a woman who has no other woman as a friend; she clung to me because I was still the frail link with Adam. That was all that existed between us now.

"They're the finest kid," I said to her. "This is the best we've ever stocked."

She turned them over. "Yes," she said, but she was bored with white kid gloves as she was bored with most of her possessions. "They're for the Crestwell reception to-night."

"Then you won't be at Eunice and Larry's dinner?"

She shrugged. "You know how Papa Langley is. He always says one's outside social obligations come before family ones."

That wasn't quite what John Langley meant, but she made it sound as if it came from him. "I'll have little Miss . . . Miss . . ."

"Margaret Curran," I said.

". . . Miss Curran over to tea some afternoon."

"I think it will not be the same, Rose. Eunice and Larry are taking a great deal of trouble over this dinner. After all, it's Con's engagement party . . . And he's going off to Sydney so soon."

"Yes," she said. "That's true. It's always hard to think of little Con being old enough to be married." Her voice was softer. "I suppose it's because he was the only one younger than me." She lifted her eyebrows, shrugging. "It's hard to believe I'm getting older myself . . . I don't think about that."

Then roughly, as if she wanted to close the subject, she tossed all the gloves into a heap. "Send me six pairs—all the same. Perhaps out of the six I might manage to lose a left hand instead of always a right. You'll have them there by this evening, Emmy?"

I nodded. I knew that her barouche waited outside for her, but it was one of Rose's little mannerisms never to carry a package if she could avoid it. It was one of the ways of showing that she was a Langley. As she stood and prepared to leave I looked at her carefully, up and down, taking in the details of her face, her hair, her costume. As always she was well turned out—the clothes were of my choice, the care of them belonged to the two maids who were now solely employed in looking after her wants. As always, though, there was the individual touch of dishevelment that was still curiously attractive, as if the spirit of the woman was stronger than the clothes we put on her. She always dominated what she wore—even the necklace and earrings of emeralds that John Langley had given her. She had never been dimmed or subdued by any circumstance; she never would be. As I looked at her I tried to console myself with the thought that she would grow heavy with the years; that the ripeness of her looks would grow over-ripe. But it was not yet so. Now, in her middle twenties, she was more beautiful than she had ever been.

She felt my scrutiny, and her eyes glinted a little as if she guessed my thoughts. Her voice was arch, amused, as she asked her question.

" Is there news of Adam?"

She had grown naïve with the years. She could ask her questions now in public without the agonized, betraying look that had once gone with them. She could enquire casually, as if he were no more than any other distant relative. We played this game often, Rose and I—she perhaps to hurt me a little, to underline my lack of security with him, I perhaps to flaunt my possession of him.

" Thank you—a letter yesterday written from Cape Town. They had a week of violent storms on the passage from West Australia. But everything held well—they had only a few repairs to make in Cape Town."

She smiled, nodding. " The *Rose Langley* is a good ship— they built her well."

" Adam is a good captain."

" A captain is generally no better than the ship he commands," she said, and there was a snap in her voice. It was sometimes her pleasure to criticize Adam ; she had never forgiven that morning at Langley Downs.

" Adam will stand with the best—ship or captain."

" You're touchingly loyal, Emmy."

" I have reason to be."

Her eyes clouded, and seemed to darken with anger ; it was anger against me as well as Adam. Since that morning six years ago she had never broken the solidarity of the front Adam and I presented to the world ; if there were cracks beneath the surface she could only guess them, she did not know them with certainty.

The red flush crept into her cheeks. She sought for another way to hurt me. She glanced towards the staircase. " The children must come home with me now—it's quite late enough. They spend entirely too much time in this place. It surely isn't right for children . . ." She took up her parasol and turned away, adding, " I must speak to Papa Langley about it."

With the threat of denying me the children she had her greatest weapon, and she knew it. This, I suppose, was the final reason why I consented to select her gloves, her gowns and her bonnets, why I posed as a friend when she thought she needed a woman friend, why I continued to let myself be used by her.

"I'll send for them," I said.

"Yes, do," she answered, sweeping towards the door.

They were summoned downstairs quickly, and we said our good-byes on the doorstep.

"Aren't you coming with us, Miss Emma?" Anne asked. "I have the map I coloured especially for you to see . . ."

"Tomorrow, darling," I said. "Tonight is your Uncle Con's engagement party and I must go home and dress . . ."

We were cut short by Rose's voice from the barouche. "Children—did you hear me? Come at once!"

They knew from the tone of her voice that she was displeased, and they rushed to obey her. These were the times when the princess from the fairy tale descended to being an ordinary human, irritated or angry with them, just as quick to scold or box an ear as she was to smile at other times. They knew better than to keep her waiting any longer. I did not go near the barouche but stood by the doorway watching them pack themselves in, listening to Rose's shrill commands to them. She gave the signal to drive on without turning to look at me again. The servant who came with the children was left to walk back alone.

II

I had hired a hackney cab to take me to Larry's house in St. Kilda, and to wait for me until the end of the party. I knew I could have had one of the Langley carriages if I had wanted to mention it to John Langley, but I did not. There were some things in which I had to make a small show of independence from the family, although it was only a show.

Larry had built himself what was perilously close to a mansion in St. Kilda, and surrounded it with wide lawns that let every passer-by on the road see its dimensions. He had gone heavily into debt for it, even with Eunice Jackson's dowry to help him, but I knew quite surely that Larry had calculated every penny of its cost as well spent since it advertised his success to the world. I had heard him say that only a poor man was never in debt, and although Larry was not yet a rich man, he soon would be. On his marriage to Eunice, he had joined her father as a partner, and the firm of Jackson and Maguire was known through three colonies now, and would go much further. He had fathered three children by his adoring, complacent Eunice, who was now heavy with her fourth. He was as energetic in founding his dynasty as John Langley had been.

I had heard John Langley say of him: "That streak of restlessness that afflicts Rose is turned to the right channels in him. I pray my grandsons possess it also."

Larry was audacious and successful, always expanding and opening a new store or agency as soon as the last showed the smallest profit. He swept Sam Jackson along with him, reaching into New South Wales and South Australia, picking up partnerships in small concerns, supplying money to make them grow, supplying direction and resource.

"If he lives long enough—and if he doesn't come a cropper —he'll be bigger than Langley's," I had also heard said of him.

The cab now turned into the driveway of the florid, over-ornamented house that Larry had built, the house that cried to the world that it was the home of a man who might do either of those things. It had iron lace hung on all the verandas which surrounded it, and at each end a round, copper-roofed tower. I thought, that with a little more courage, Larry would put peacocks on those smooth lawns—and he might yet. Eunice would have agreed, as she agreed to everything.

Larry himself came to open the cab door; he took pride in his possessions but he was not a proud man and he was quicker than his own servants. I felt his kiss on my cheek as he handed me down; it was the kiss of trust and welcome that had been mine now from Larry for some years, a salute that acknowledged me as an equal with his family. Larry could give me no more than that.

"Emmy—you look dazzling! I've never seen you look so . . . so elegant!"

"That's because you never trouble to come to see me except when I'm dressed for the store." But it was true what he said —I had never had a gown like this one. It was of a delicate apricot silk, cut to emphasise the smallness of my waist, and with a crinoline so wide that I had to move about a room with care. I enjoyed the sway of it as I walked across the hall to were Eunice waited to greet her guests.

"Emmy . . . dear . . ." she said softly, and offered me her cheek to kiss. She was very little different from the girl I remembered at the first reception John Langley had given to Rose. Her hair was as red, and her dress was besplattered with ribbons and flowers. She would have her child in three months, and she had draped herself with a long trailing lace scarf to disguise the swelling of her figure. But it was not something she wanted to disguise too carefully; she knew Larry's pride in his children, and his approval and love was all she sought.

She would go on bearing his children cheerfully and placidly. She was a quiet, rather dull woman, but since their marriage Larry had looked at no other woman. He had sought dependability, and found it; the energy and the dash of passion he would supply. In his own home he wanted peace and no competition—no word but his own. He ruled his wife and his children with the same easy authority.

"Look at our Emmy, will you now, Dan." Kate's arms were about me in an embrace. "Sure, it's a treat to see you out of that old black."

She was heavier than in the Eureka days, though still pretty, and still dressing in her favourite purple. The gowns were as rich, and made no concession to her age; but when Kate smiled and spoke you could forget her age. She was one of the best-known women in Melbourne, though her name would never be on the Governor's invitation list.

After Dan kissed me he said, "Well, Emmy—what news of Adam?"

He nodded as I repeated the news I had given earlier to Rose. His tall frame stooped just a little, but the massive shoulders were still hard and muscled; his beard was grey though, and so was his hair.

"It will be a steam ship for Adam soon," he said, "and then the voyages with be much shorter. It would be good if he could be home more often."

In Dan's heart, I think, there was an instinctive feeling of my loneliness, a reaching forward to comfort me without words. He was the kindest man I had ever known, and that was how Melbourne knew him. Trade was always brisk at the Maguire pub but Dan Maguire would never have money in the bank. It went through his hands in ways he never noticed —loans, gifts, free meals, gowns for Kate, and furniture, books for Con, a pony for Larry's children. For a time Larry had tried to stop the outflow, but his efforts were a finger in the dyke. In the end he even took a kind of inverted pride in what he could not prevent—his father was known as the most generous man in town.

I moved forward then into Larry's red-upholstered drawing-room, with the great red and gold Persian carpet which Adam had bought for Larry in Singapore. The mantel was a chaste white piece startlingly introduced into the dark mahogany furnishings because of the pair of similar mantels that Larry had seen in John Langley's drawing-room. I had never known a man enjoy himself so much as Larry had in the two years it had taken to build and furnish his house. An enjoyment it had been, but not a mania. Larry was not one to be obsessed.

It was a small group who had gathered to celebrate Con's engagement to Margaret Curran, and his entry into the firm of Jackson and Maguire. He was going to Sydney for a year to work in the branch office there, and Margaret Curran's parents had consented to the announcement of the engagement on the condition that there would be no marriage until after the year was up. She was an only child, barely eighteen, and they clung to her. Con was only a few months older. They looked young and beautiful, and full of a kind of innocent hopefulness that was strangely touching as they stood together before the mantel.

"How beautiful you look, Margaret," I said to her, but it was Con who blushed for pleasure in the compliment. They were both of them fair, though Con was darker-skinned than she. She had been born here, during the early boom times of Melbourne, and her father, a lawyer, had made enough in land speculation so that she had never known any of the hardships of this country. Her hands were as soft and white as her face. She was untried in the things that tested the strength of a man or a woman in this land, and yet I had a feeling, as she stood there close to Con and gazed up at him, that she would have dared much if he had asked it of her.

Con answered for her. "I have to remember how she looks, Emmy—a year is a long time."

I did not tell him it would soon pass; I knew how long a year could be.

"I would like to go with Con," she said shyly. "It would not matter for such a short time where we lived . . . we could manage, I'm sure."

Larry had come to join us, and now he took up the conversation. "You don't understand, my dear," he said firmly. "Sydney is not like Melbourne . . . here you have your family and all your friends. You would be lonely there, and Con's salary in the beginning isn't enough to give you the things you're used to having."

"I wouldn't mind," she said quickly, eagerly. "No one's ever asked me if I would like to learn to do without some things." She suddenly, hopefully, pressed the point. "I could manage quite well . . . I can sew, and I've been taking cooking lessons."

Smilingly, Larry shook his head, his expression faintly amused as if one of his own young daughters had made the suggestion of packing up and going off to Sydney. "What?—

254

with no big wedding and no presents, and not having your own house ready to go to? You wouldn't like it at all, Margaret." He shook his head again. "It's for the best to wait, my dear. In another year Con with be in a position to take a loan to build you the kind of house you should have—he'll be ready to settle down here in Melbourne, and you won't be separated from your parents. It's a better way to start a married life— you can trust me on that, Margaret."

"But if she's willing . . ." Con put in.

Larry cut him short with a gesture and a drawing together of the eyebrows that was a warning. "You must think of Margaret, Con—think of what is best for her."

The discussion was finished, and the hope died. Larry was protective of Con, and if he could, he would have planned every step of his brother's life for him. The fact that Margaret Curran would fall in love with Con had not been foreseen, but it was a more fortunate happening than anything Larry could have devised. The Currans were people of means and some position in Melbourne; Michael Curran had been an early investor in Sam Jackson's business, and handled all the legal matters for the firm. The marriage of Margaret and Con was a further strengthening of the fabric of the Maguire prosperity, another step forward in building the esteem of the name and its connections. Therefore the marriage had to be protected against the harsh winds of circumstance. Larry would see to it that no trouble that he could prevent would ever touch Margaret and Con.

I leaned in to say quietly to him as he walked me across the room to meet Margaret Curran's uncle, Judge Curran, "Wouldn't it be better to let them do something for themselves . . .?"

He waved away the suggestion. "They are children yet," he said. "Let me avoid their mistakes for them."

I put my hand on his arm to halt him. "But on the Eureka boys no older than Con had families . . . and some of them died. Sean was hardly older than Con."

His features seemed to tighten; I saw in his face the look that told me Larry would hear no more. He detached my hand from his arm, and his touch was not gentle.

"Look around you, Emmy. We've come a long way from the Eureka."

I thought of Larry's words as we sat about the table for dinner. It was a family party; beside the Maguires there were only the

255

Currans, Judge and Mrs. Curran, the Jacksons, and Sam Jackson's brother who was in the Legislative Council. The table glowed with the shine of the silver and the crystal and the white damask cloth that must have taken a woman a whole day to iron to such perfection. It was a table that John Langley might have set, though the food on it was much more abundant. It was the table of people who have the best to show off and to give away. I did not miss Larry's nod of satisfaction towards Eunice, nor the resulting happiness of her smile. Larry's face, above the stiff white of his cravat was startlingly handsome still, but it was too weather-beaten, too gipsyish, too thrusting and vital to have been mistaken for the face of an aristocrat. But he was on his way, and he knew it. For him and Con, Australia had been two different places, two different experiences. He could soften the way for his brother, and encourage his marriage to a gentle girl who could never have survived on the Eureka. And he could bid me put aside the Eureka and forgot about it, and he was right. His grand-children would boast that he got his start at Ballarat, but for this generation and the next Eureka was best left to the private memories, only to be brought out and examined during the long rides, or over the camp-fire or, in the tired pause when the ledgers are closed and one is too tired to move at once. Eureka was not a thought to bring into the open in Larry's solid, prosperous, mahogany and red-draped dining-room.

Eunice had seated Sam Jackson's brother, her uncle William, on my right. I had never met him before, but he spoke to me of Adam. Adam had handled cargoes for him on the *Rose Langley*, and the old *Enterprize*.

" He's as fine a captain as we have sailing these waters, and John Langley must know it. I know his reputation in Sydney too—he goes to any length to accommodate a cargo, and he doesn't care how long it takes to see that it's stowed properly and safely. I've never had anything smashed that Adam Langley handled. And I remember that time he brought me that special order from Liverpool. He delayed the *Rose Langley* three days in port that time just so that I should have exactly what I specified. After that I said Adam Langley would always get whatever business I had to give." He looked at me closely then. " But he should have his own ship," he said. " He should be an owner. It's the owners who make the money . . ."

I nodded my head, knowing that what he said was right, but how was I to tell him what Adam was, what kind of a man it was who could captain John Langley's ships, bring back the large profits he did with each voyage, and not covet them? How did you explain a man who ran his ship on lines of extreme discipline and efficiency, who saw to the health of the crew and the soundness of his timbers with equal passion, but did it for his own satisfaction? They said that Adam ran a happy ship; it was happy in that it was clean and the crew were well fed, and that no accidents occurred that extra care could have avoided. But Adam was not a soft man, and you did not sail under him for the gaiety of the voyage. He voyaged for the love of voyaging, and not for the love of money. Though in Melbourne they spoke of him as the typical Yankee captain, he was not that. He did not care for the money. He wanted to own his ship, but for the pride of ownership, not for the money. But I could not say that because men were always suspicious of any other man who does not care for money.

So I said, " Yes, he will be an owner . . ."

He nodded, satisfied. " Yes, I heard Larry say there was the chance that he and Tom Langley would go into it together. Is it settled, then?"

" No—not settled. It takes a lot of money to build a ship, Mr. Jackson."

" And old Langley doesn't like anything to get out of his control?" he shrugged. " Why should he? I wouldn't want to lose Adam Langley. I'm thinking Tom will have to use a lot of persuasion to make his father give him that big a loan. John Langley doesn't encourage independence . . ."

Then his eyebrows brushed together, and he drew back a little to look at me. " But my dear lady, I'm forgetting to whom I speak. There can't be much that *you* don't know about Old John, the way he handles his money."

I took up my wine glass quickly, seeking something to shield my expression from him. I did not welcome any discussion of my business connection with the Langley Stores, I did not like to be reminded that I was any different from any other woman who sat at this table. But William Jackson had talked to me as if I were a man, not the way he would have talked to Eunice, with the long scarf insufficiently disguising her pregnancy, not the way he would have talked to Margaret, with her gentle eyes fixed unmovingly on Con, not the way he would have talked even to Kate who had handled money and customers all her life. It troubled me that, as much as I tried to hide behind the screen of Ben Sampson and John Langley, Melbourne still knew who ran the business that was conducted behind the grey silk curtains.

"I know no more of John Langley's affairs than the next person," I said. But the denial was useless, and we both knew it.

He shook his head at me, amused. "And I've said to Sam—'You know, Sam, no one could ever tell it to look at that little woman that she had a head on her shoulders like that.' Why, when you think that most women can't add more than two dress lengths together . . . well, it's a wonder!"

He meant me to take it as a compliment, but he did not himself believe what he said. No man was really comfortable in the presence of a woman to whom he could talk business. He did not envy Adam; he did not envy Adam's return to the woman in the rustling black silk dresses who had ledgers instead of children, who must borrow Rose Langley's children to give her love to. William Jackson did not see the apricot silk and the wide, swaying hoops. He saw only the Emma Langley who knew John Langley and his business better than anyone else seated at this table, and he did not envy Adam. I played desperately with the stem of my glass, shamed and humiliated because I was not Eunice, or Margaret or Kate.

I was glad when he turned to talk to Mrs. Curran and left me to the familiar, uncritical company of Con on my left—Con, whom I had undressed and put to bed on that first night on the Eureka, and who knew more of me than the ledgers.

But even he had to prove that he was a grown man, that he too knew how to pay the gallant compliment though his eyes were still on Margaret.

"Emmy, you look so handsome that if I hadn't promised Margaret first, I think I'd run off with you . . ."

So to him I was the stranger in the apricot silk, and there was little left, except in my own mind, of the child who had done his lessons at my kitchen table.

The meal was over and Larry had already risen with his glass in his hand to propose the toast to Margaret and Con when we heard the sounds of the carriage, and then quickly, the voices. There was laughter, too—deep masculine laughter, and above it the lighter sound that was Rose's voice.

"What the devil . . . ?" Larry said. He pushed his chair aside and went to fling open the doors of the dining-room. He did not like being interrupted in anything that was once begun, especially when it was a speech. He was frowning as Rose came across the hall towards him.

"What is it, Larry? You don't look pleased to see me!

After all, it is my little brother's engagement party!" She laughed at him, and blew a mock kiss as she passed him. She wore a dark crimson cloak tossed back off her shoulders to reveal the watered blue silk ; on her left arm she wore a long white glove, but her right arm was bare. We all turned in our chairs to look at her.

" Good evening—everyone." She walked down the length of the table and paused by my chair, leaning down to kiss Con on the cheek.

" We left the Crestwells' early. We had to come and drink your health—Tom and I."

Con flushed darkly. " Rose, don't play the fool!"

She straightened, laughing. " Oh, did I break into something serious? Well, perhaps that won't hurt. We can't all take life as seriously as Larry does." She bowed across the table. " Good evening, Mrs. Curran—Mr. Curran. Good evening, Judge—and Mrs. Jackson. What a charming gown you have, Miss Curran. Good evening, Dada, Muma!"

" Rose, sit down!" Kate ordered. " You're making a display of yourself!"

She remained standing. " What a pity all the family isn't here. Judge, did you know I have another brother?—a brother that Larry won't invite to his house? He's a drover. Did you know that? When he's tired of droving he comes back and lives with Matt Sweeney. Oh—you must surely have heard of Matt Sweeney! He's that terrible old man who won't drink himself to death quickly enough to please my father-in-law and his respectable neighbours."

Larry was behind her now. He had drawn up a chair and gently pressed her down. Quickly he poured a glass of champagne and handed it to her. Everyone heard Kate's shrill whisper.

" For God's sake, Larry, don't give her more. She's enough taken."

" I'm glad you and Tom could get here to drink Margaret and Con's health, Rosie. It wouldn't have been the same without you." He said it soothingly, to quiet her.

" We brought someone else," Rose said, and she turned back to look at the doorway. " We brought our new neighbour at Langley Downs. This is Robert Dalkeith. Robbie is Andrew Dalkeith's nephew. He would like to drink to Con's health too, wouldn't you, Robbie?"

Beside Tom in the doorway, and partly supporting him, was a man I had never seen before but whose name I knew.

This was the heir who had come to take over Andrew Dalkeith's property adjoining Langley Downs. I had heard talk of him over all the counters at the Stores. He was a bachelor, a little over thirty years old and now I saw him I understood why the talk had been as much of the man himself as of the money he was said to have. And yet there was no young woman on his arm now. He supported Tom, who was drunk, and helped him to walk to the table, but Dalkeith's eyes never left Rose for a second. And she basked in his gaze, without shame, concealing her pleasure from no one.

Con leaned towards me, his face pinched and angry. " God, Emmy," he said softly, " why does she do it? Why does she have to flaunt him here, in front of Margaret? This is the next one, I suppose?—this is the new fool she's got her hands on . . ."

" Hush ! "

Tom was rapping the table and spilling the champagne. There wasn't room at the table for Robert Dalkeith's chair. He was seated behind Tom, and this gave him a clear view along the back of the others to where Rose sat. He seemed detached from the drunken man he had helped into the room ; I thought the expression on his handsome face was almost one of amusement if it had not been cold at the same time. He sat behind Tom and watched Rose, and his whole being was intent on her.

" Listen, everyone ! " Tom was calling. " I have something to say."

Larry interrupted him. " Tom, we were about to drink . . ."

" Have something *I* want to drink to ! " Tom persisted. His voice rose to a volume which was close to a shout, and Larry subsided. " It's just been settled ! Had to come and tell you so we could *all* drink to it. Wanted you to meet my good friend, Robbie, so you could drink to him too."

" Tom——! "

" Don't interrupt, God damn you ! Have something to say. It's settled about the new ship. Robbie here has agreed, and it's all settled. He's to be part owner. Third for Robbie, a third for Adam, and a third for Tom. And to hell with my father."

He thumped the table, and the champagne ran down over his fingers clenched about the stem. " What do you say to that? Isn't that worth drinking to? Come on now, everyone. Fill the glasses, Larry ! "

He pushed himself to his feet, one hand resting heavily on the table, the other waving the glass. " Ladies and gentlemen

—I give you the new partnership! Langley, Langley & Dalkeith!"

There was a slow, unwilling movement of hands towards the glasses, with many glances towards Larry to see what he would do.

Tom looked along the table, and he suddenly cried, " I give you the new ship, ladies and gentlemen. I give you the *Emma Langley*!"

And down the length of the table I saw the glasses raised, and I heard the words repeated . . . *Emma Langley*.

III

The cats stirred and stretched on the hearth to greet my return from Larry's. Black came to rub against my skirts as he had always done, but Digger, old and cranky now, stayed where she was. I lit a single lamp, and poked the range into life to boil the water for tea. While I waited I sat before the fire, and Black jumped into my lap, as he always did. I stroked him absently, and until the kettle began to steam, his purring was unnaturally loud in the stillness.

Alone here, and idle like this, I always felt Adam very strongly in this house. Each of his trips to San Francisco was marked by the Windsor chairs he had brought back ; the tall clock and the thin china from which I drank my tea were from England. The walnut desk in the corner, really too delicate for the heavy piles of ledgers, was also from England. These rooms were a hodge-podge of many styles and periods with little relation to each other, except that they seemed to live well together. Perhaps it was because, over the years when he was ashore, Adam had lined each room with plain pine boards, lovingly finished, and this little house had great warmth, and the kind of human quality that had nothing to do with elegance. They were Adam's rooms, fashioned and made by a man with a reverence and a passion for wood, with a cabinetmaker's eye for the niceties of detail. It was an absurd house to have in a stable-yard, and yet we both clung to it, and so far John Langley had never said the words that would have meant the beginning of tearing it down. Adam lived in these rooms for me when he was not present ; the softness of Adam's character, the warmth was all contained here. Sometimes I looked around here to remind myself that it was so, that he was not always the stranger I imagined him to be. In the long months of his absences it was sometimes easier to know Adam's heart in the warm beauty of the grain of that pine, than in the dutiful, often stiff and uncertain letters he wrote me.

And now Adam would have his ship. As I sipped my tea I thought of what this would mean to him. Even owning only a third of the new *Emma Langley*, it still would be his deck beneath his feet, and I knew that there had been nothing in Adam's dreams that he had wanted more than that. Already he seemed to go further from my reach and grasp. I almost wished that Robert Dalkeith had never come to make this thing possible. Adam's independence upon John Langley had been in a small way a dependence upon me ; he would still carry Langley cargoes, but he was no longer servant to the Langley money. In a sense Adam mistrusted and feared the power of money, the power to command men to his service. He wanted money only to be free of it. I, who belonged among those who made money as John Langley did, must also in Adam's mind have partaken a little of the tyranny that went with it. I remembered very well how he had looked across at me from his seat by the fire as I had worked at the desk, and I remembered how he had spoken.

"It's a rare talent you have, Emmy—to make money. And you're so young still. I wonder what you will be twenty years from now."

I had felt cold at his words, and I had wanted to cry out to him that to work all day at the Stores, to sit over these ledgers at night, was no choice of mine. I had wanted to tell him that the long hours of the day have to be filled, and I had to be tired in order to sleep at night. But since that morning at the stable at Langley Downs when I had listened to him and Rose I was never able to say to Adam the things that were in my heart to say. The words stayed inside of me, locked there. I was too proud to speak, to proud and too fearful to offer my love and have it rejected. So I offered no explanation to this or to any other thing he might have wondered about me. And the silence grew firmer and tighter with the years.

But it was the money and the credit into which I had built Adam's original investment in the Stores that would enable him to become part owner of the *Emma Langley*. And so I thought, as I poured my second cup of tea, that the money-makers have their uses. And again I remembered the way William Jackson had talked to me that night, and I wished again that I was another kind of woman.

There never seemed reason to go to bed when Adam was

not there to share it with me, and so I think I dozed a short while, sitting there with Black in my lap. The rapping at the window startled me; I lurched forward in the chair, and the cat was thrown to the floor. He spat at me indignantly before he went to join Digger at the fire.

"Who . . . who's there?" I realized it was very late, and that the rapping had been soft, almost furtive. I went and stood close to the door, and I had a moment to wonder if those who had warned me about living here in this empty lane had been right.

"It's me, Emmy—Pat!"

I threw the bolts back, and he slipped inside before the door was more than half open. "Pat?—what is it? What's wrong?"

He himself bolted the door. His movements seemed to me urgent and strained but his face was smiling as he turned back to me.

"Now is that any way to greet me? Sure haven't you got a kiss for me, Greeneyes?"

I would have kissed his cheek, but his lips were there instead. He held me too tightly for a moment, and when he released me the movement was too abrupt.

"Have you got a drink, Emmy? Have you got any whisky?"

I went and poured it and brought it to him. He drank half the glass at a swallow, and then he threw himself down in Adam's chair opposite me. His clothes were layered with dust, and under the dust of his face I could see the lines were etched deeply with fatigue. He was usually clean-shaven, but now he wore a week's growth of beard. He reminded me of Dan as he sat there—he seemed to have aged a great deal since I had last seen him—but Dan had never, even in the hardest days of the Eureka, looked as driven as this, or as weary with this kind of weariness. He slumped back in the chair and held his glass towards me. I refilled it, and then went and sat down.

"You're all dressed up, Greeneyes. You look very grand in that—I expect next thing you'll be wearing pearls and diamonds."

"Pearls and diamonds are for Rose, not me," I answered shortly. "And why shouldn't I be dressed up?—it was for Con's engagement party."

He took the whisky more slowly now, and his shoulders relaxed against the back of the chair.

"Yes—Con's engagement party. I had a card—did you

know that, Emmy? My sister-in-law, whom I've never met, sent me a beautiful copperplate card of invitation. Matt Sweeney and I put it on the mantelpiece. Sure, it made a grand sight. It would have been impressive, don't you know, if any of the neighbours had happened to drop in."

"Pat, why do you mock yourself so? If Eunice wrote the card, she meant it to be accepted. You would have been welcome."

"Yes, welcome to see how well my brother Larry had done, how tightly he's married himself into the money here in Melbourne. I would have been welcome so long as I kept quiet and behaved myself. Do you know why I think that invitation came, Emmy? I think Brother Larry had just begun to realize that Matt Sweeney has a valuable property if it were taken care of, and that the old man won't live forever. And Larry thinks that by throwing a little money my way he'll buy himself in. Well, he's mistaken."

"There's no truth in that, Pat. You're inventing that to give yourself a reason to stay away from Larry's house. He has pride too. He's not going to ride out to the Sweeney place to beg you to come. He made the gesture . . ."

"Yes, the gesture. And that's what it was—a gesture. To made him feel comfortable with himself. So that if I don't come it's because I didn't know the way decent people act. Oh, to hell with it, Emmy! I didn't come here to talk about Larry."

"Why have you come?"

"I need help. That's why I've come. And you're the only person I want to ask it of."

"Help?"

"Money is what I need. For Matt—no, not for Matt. He wouldn't need it if I hadn't thrown my money away. I gamble, Emmy. You know that. Sometimes I lose. Sometimes I go to Sydney and spend every penny I have and don't know what's happened to it. That's how it was this time. I had to borrow money on my horse to go after a droving job. And when I got back Matt tells me it's been a terrible season—he's lost a lot of lambs, and the wool prices are off. Well, the poor old devil's got so much drink in him he doesn't even know if there's been a season. The interest on the mortgage is due again, and there's one note that's been called in."

"How much?"

"Five hundred pounds will cover it."

"I'll let you have it in the morning."

He shook his head, smiling slowly. " No questions? No sermons?"

" No one asked any questions of me when you picked me up on the road to Ballarat. I don't remember any sermons, either."

He gestured violently with the glass. " You owe us nothing. It wasn't for that reason I came to you."

" I owe you—Dan and Kate, Larry, even Rose—more than money can pay back. Let's have no more talk of it, Pat."

" It's damn decent of you."

" Not decent—proper. Right." I got to my feet. " Will I make you some tea or do you want more whisky?"

" You'd like to give me the tea, but I'd rather have the whisky. Whatever you choose, Emmy."

I poured the whisky for him, and put the kettle back on the range for myself. When I glanced back at him his eyes were half closed. " Did you come straight here? Where's your horse?"

" I left him at Even's stable. I'll stay there tonight and get the hell out of here tomorrow morning. This town depresses me. It reminds me of Larry. Very sure of itself. Sydney's more my style."

" Will you go back to Matt?"

" Yes—I'll go back and get this mess straightened out, and see that he's stocked up on some grub—flour, sugar, tea—that sort of thing. The old devil forgets to eat when he's got drink in him, and if there's nothing there he's just as likely to let a week go by without baking a damper. He'll be dead of starvation if the drink doesn't get him first. " Emmy . . . ?"

" Yes?"

" If anything happens to me, you'd keep an eye on the old fella, wouldn't you?"

" Happens to you. What would happen to you?"

He shrugged. " Anything. Have you ever seen horsemen rounding up cattle in heavy timber—down gullies that would frighten the soul clean out of you? Have you ever heard the kind of arguments that can get started in a shearing shed at night. They're not gentlemen, most of the boys, and they fight very rough. There are a dozen ways—a hundred ways something could happen to me. And the old fella hasn't got a soul in the world who cares whether he's alive or dead."

" Why do you care, Pat?"

" I'm all he's got. And, God help me, I need that at times. I tell myself someday I'll go back and settled down there, take care of the old man, get the place in shape."

But I knew it was only a dream he talked of, the dream he had to hold before himself to ease the tedium of the long days of driving cattle and sheep. I did not know his world, but I sensed its violence and ruthlessness, the hunger that must be in him sometimes for one thing that was solid and enduring. But the dream had no duration; it was short and fleeting, gone as soon as a new mood of restlessness came on him.

"Will you promise me, Emmy?" he persisted. "Will you promise me that you'll take care of the old man?"

I nodded. "I promise." I could do no less.

"God bless you," he said, quite simply.

Before he left me he kissed me on the lips again, strongly, not like a brother.

"Adam is a fool," he said. "Perhaps one day he'll know it."

Chapter Two

In the next year they built and named and launched the *Emma Langley*. Adam and Tom and Robert Dalkeith owned equal shares in the vessel, Tom having sold back to his father his interest in the Stores in order to raise the money, and Adam put in a large part of our savings to buy his share. For both of them the launching of the Emma Langley was an event of supreme importance—for Tom because it was his first taste of independence from his father, for Adam because the moment had come at last when he walked the deck of a vessel which was his own. Of Robert Dalkeith I was not sure. It often seemed to me that he paid for his share of the *Emma Langley* as the price of his association with Tom, and therefore with Rose.

The Honourable Robert Dalkeith was a strange man to find here in our colonial society. He was the fourth son of a Scottish peer, and a man better suited, I would have thought, to Newmarket and his London clubs than the lonely acres of Rosscommon, which Andrew Dalkeith had left to him. He had little interest in farming, but he knew good horses, and the time he spent at Rosscommon was concerned not with sheep, but with the breeding and training of a stable. Their common interest in horses drew them closer to John Langley, and for a time he enjoyed a certain vogue among Melbourne hostesses, especially those with unmarried daughters. This lasted until the arrival of the first visitor from London who identified him as the Robert Dalkeith who had deserted his wife in London, and had lived with his mistress for a year in Italy. The woman was dead now, and Robert Dalkeith was wandering again. It was also said that Rosscommon had not been left to him at all, but to an older brother; that it had been signed over to him as an inducement to come out here. After that news there was a hurried closing of ranks among the hostesses. He was no longer eligible, and so was invited only to the largest gatherings. There was nothing that could have pleased Rose more. She did not want to have to share Robert Dalkeith.

There was talk about Rose and Robert Dalkeith—not very serious talk, because Rose by now had learned some of the rules of discretion. I didn't know whether Tom heard the stray ends of the gossip and chose to ignore it, or whether his eyes simply did not see any more the truth about Rose because he had long ago accepted it and come to terms with it. It was possible he knew at last that no one man would ever wholly possess Rose, that she would forever chafe against any form of restraint. So he held her but loosely, and seemed resigned to having it so. He made much, publicly, of his friendship with Dalkeith, perhaps to shield Rose, and he drank a great deal. Each month his grasp on the affairs at the Langley Stores, at Langley Downs and Hope Bay slipped a little, and John Langley seemed to give up any notion that Tom would ever fill his place there. In the old man I saw growing a fierce determination to live, to prolong his life and to endure until James should be old enough to take some control of the Langley affairs. It seemed an interminable length of time, and sometimes to me he confided his weariness, and also his hopes.

"James has a great head on him—William and Henry too. They're strong fine boys, and so long as I'm here I'll see that Rose and Tom don't ruin them. But they're so young yet, and I—I am old, Miss Emma. What will happen to them, to the Langley business, in the years between?"

"You will be there to see James take his desk in the Stores," I said, as we drank our tea in my office from the fine china he had given me.

He nodded. "I mean to do that."

But as this worry grew in his mind he drew closer to me in order to share it. He talked to me of the things that should have been for Tom. Although a solid wall existed between the Ladies Department and the rest of the Stores, I knew almost as much of the business that went on that side of the wall as John Langley or his head clerk did. The old man leaned on me—not for advice or decisions, but simply as a listener. I had a feeling that he was trying to impart to me all that he knew, because there was no one else whom he could teach.

In that year James finally learned to read—mostly at my desk, and his two younger brothers grew up sufficiently to begin to challenge him in his domination of them. And Anne began to give a promise of a beauty that would equal Rose's, but of a more delicate kind. She was a slight-limbed creature, graceful, passionate, but less wilful than Rose. John Langley took to joining us quite frequently now in the afternoons, thereby driving Ben Sampson away. Like Rose they were never subdued in their grandfather's presence, only a little quieter. He seemed at times to brood over them; he would have forced them on too quickly if I had not stood in the way.

"Rose has given me fine, strong grandchildren," he said once. "But I don't know if I can wait for them to grow up."

In his stiff, unbending way John Langley did what he could to honour me. When the *Emma Langley* was ready for her maiden voyage, and Adam had returned from a voyage to San Francisco, he announced that there would be a reception at his house as a send-off to the new ship. It was an awkward gesture of goodwill which no one wanted or appreciated. Although the ship was named for me, I was not in a position in Melbourne society where a formal recognition of the naming was called for; Tom, on his part, was angry because he had wanted to give a reception of his own, away from his father's house. Adam, I thought, didn't care about anything but the fact that the ship would soon be his to command, and Robert Dalkeith was indifferent. I thought Dalkeith was sometimes surprised when he remembered the name by which his ship was called; although I had met him several times, I doubt that he knew I existed.

But Adam gave the ship its naming, privately, for me alone, at the moment when he handed me my wrap as we were about to leave for the reception.

"Well, Emmy—here it is. It has taken a long time, but not as long as I thought when I first promised it to you."

The words of my reply seemed to stick in my throat; I was almost breathless. "What did you promise, Adam?"

He looked surprised. "The ship," he said. "I promised you the ship would be named Emma. If I'd been the sole owner she would have been *Emma*. But Tom held out to call her *Emma Langley*. I thought that you remembered I promised you that—the first day we came to this house."

I fumbled stupidly with my wrap, lost in an ecstasy of

pleasure that he had recalled that past day which I had thought was lost to us, that ecstasy and the sudden, swift fear that he had spoken only in kindness—one of the times when his kindness was the cruellest thing of all. I did not want to be hurt, and I did not let myself be fool enough to believe.

"I thought it was you who had forgotten," I said.

The wrap was laid on my shoulders as if by the hands of a stranger. "We must hurry," he said. "It won't do to be late."

The reception was only partly successful. People did not turn out to meet the woman who ran the Ladies Department of the Stores, and the rooms were sparsely filled. There was champagne and flowers and music, and John Langley hovered anxiously about me, a thing in itself so rare that I knew he was disturbed. Tom was glowering and already drunk. As he kissed my cheek he said:

"Emmy, if I'd arranged it myself at Hanson's as I wanted it wouldn't have been like this."

And Rose came forward to kiss me also, the cool kiss we always exchanged in public, and which was all we had left now.

"Darling Emmy—how sweet you look! How the colour becomes you! Doesn't she look sweet, Adam?"

Her eyes went to him in the old way, inviting the comparison between us, mocking him for the choice he had made. It was always thus with Rose. She would not leave him in peace. Every second in his company was meant to show him, over and over, what he had not taken.

"Emmy always looks well," he said. Adam had no subtlety in dealing with her. She discomforted him, and he could not hide it.

She gave him a twisted, strange smile. "Of course," she said, and then she left us.

Kate and Dan did not come. They had never yet accepted an invitation to John Langley's house. In a sense this was right and fitting, and we all recognised it. The two worlds had met and fused in Rose and Tom, and in their children, but the old generation was irrevocably separated, and by mingling now, so long after it mattered, would have been false and unreal. In this way they kept their identity and their dignity, and it was better. Tomorrow, before the *Emma Langley* sailed with the late tide, there would be another gathering. It would be at Maguire's—smaller than this one, noisier and gayer. It would be the true send-off to the *Emma Langley*.

But there was still this evening to be got through—the earnest conversations with the less important merchants of Melbourne to whom I was someone of importance, the distant greetings from those higher in the social scale, but not so high that they could afford to stay away from a Langley reception. Adam stood beside me all the night, answered questions about the *Emma Langley,* was polite where it mattered to be polite, and polite where it did not matter. And he almost never looked in Rose's direction. That was not to say that we were not, both of us, acutely aware of her. She spent most of the evening seated between Tom and Robert Dalkeith, and they laughed and joked and shared a private world that excluded all the solid, dull respectability about them. At one of the times when the laughter rang loudest and the resentful glances of those that it excluded came from all over the room, Elizabeth Langley stood close by Adam and I. Her fingers played nervously with Rose's opal brooch which was pinned, as always, on the lace at her throat. Her face was flushed and ugly, and I was touched by the wretchedness I saw there—the compound of love and jealousy which seemed to be the fate of everyone who came in contact with Rose. For an instant I saw myself in that face.

"Look at her!" she said; her voice was a thin, shrill whisper. "Look at him! He makes love to her under Tom's eyes! Why does she let him?—how can she? How does she dare—I try to tell her, to warn her about men like him. But she doesn't listen. Rose never listens to me."

Beside me Adam wheeled abruptly and put down his glass on a tray with such a violent motion that it overturned and upset half-a-dozen other glasses. He disregarded the crash and the spilled champagne. His face was a clenched, furious mask. It seemed that if he had not put the glass down he might have hurled it at Rose. For the first time that evening he left my side.

"I see that Jim Anderson, my first mate, has arrived. I must speak to him."

The groups of people fell back a little before his swift-paced stride across the room. And I saw that Rose also watched him go, and she was smiling.

II

At the end of the year Con was married to Margaret Curran with the kind of wedding that Larry and the Currans considered appropriate, and the couple moved immediately into

the house that Larry had built for them during the time that
Con was in Sydney. It was neither too modest nor too large
a house for their circumstances, and the firm of Jackson and
Maguire had guaranteed the mortgage with the bank.

" It will do them for the next few years," Larry said to me
at the reception he gave at his house after the marriage.
" They'll have a family by then, and Con will be far enough on
in the business to be able to afford something more in the
Currans' style. Since she's an only child Michael Curran made
a handsome settlement . . ."

Larry had the look of a man who has brought off something
that is highly pleasing to him. He swaggered a little as he
moved among the guests. And he had some reason to, I
thought. The alliance of the daughter of one of the town's
leading lawyers, and the niece of a judge, to the younger
Maguire of Jackson and Maguire had brought out most of the
town's notables. The merchant and professional class was
solidly represented ; the squatter aristocracy felt no need to
attend, except for a few who had had long dealings with Sam
Jackson. John Langley came, and it was strange to see him
and the older Maguires ostentatiously avoid each other in
those crowded rooms.

Kate and Dan were completely happy. This was the first
time they had witnessed the full rites of the Catholic Church at
the marriage of one of their children. This was not one of the
feared mixed marriages, as Rose's had been, and Larry's.
They could look forward to more grandchildren without
thought of the conflict over the different religions.

" It was lovely, wasn't it, Emmy?" Kate said to me. " Everything was right, this time. And didn't the priest say the lovliest
things . . ." Her eyes filled with happy enjoyable tears as she
recalled the ceremony. And then she sighed. " Sure, it just
need Pat to be here."

Larry was beside us, appearing suddenly as if Pat's name
had summoned him there. " Pat had an invitation," he said.
" I went out of my way two weeks ago to ask old Sweeney if
Pat had had it safely. He swore that Pat had been there not
more than a week before, and the invitation was in his hands."
He spoke defensively, as he almost always did when Pat was
talked of. She shrugged. " If Pat chose not to come, that
surely is his affair."

" Ah, but he sent a present!" Kate exclaimed. " Did you
ever see the like of it, Emmy? It puts the lot of them to
shame."

Pat had sent, all the way from Sydney, a great engraved

silver teapot, with heavy scrolled legs and handle. It was flamboyant, and must have cost a great deal of money. This was present that was sent for show, the one for Kate to boast of. For Con, personally, there was an American repeater rifle, of the latest design. Few of them had been seen in this country, Con told me.

"A gun . . ." Dan commented. "Why does he have to give him a gun? Pat's mind runs too much to guns and the like."

"Pat can't be stopped, if he's bent on ruining himself. I hear he's keeping bad company. Nick Palmer told me he was seen drinking a few weeks ago with Jim Dawson and his brother—the same pair that were taken in for shooting that bank manager at Clunes last week." This news was from Larry, as the bad news of Pat always seemed to be.

"Pat is all right," Kate said. "And I'll not listen to any more of your doleful talk—not on this blessed day. Sure it's hard to think it's my baby Con that's married. Did you ever see anything so handsome, Emmy, in his new suit . . . ?"

And so Con, hardly more than twenty years old, was married and safely settled, and I wondered a little as I watched Larry's preparations, listened to the arrangements he had made for Con's future, observed the way he moved to protect Con in every possible avenue and circumstance, if he were not striving to wipe out the memory of his failure to protect Sean at the time of the Eureka. He spread the evidence of his stewardship before Kate and Dan, and seemed to ask their forgetfulness of the other time.

It amused me somewhat to know that Pat's splendid teapot, which dominated the display of wedding-presents at Larry's house, had been paid for with my money. I knew more of Pat than they did. Twice in the last year he had come to my house in Langley Lane, late at night, and he had borrowed money. I did not care about the money—they were each small enough sums by comparison to what I owed the Maguires. I did not expect to see it back again, but Pat would not take it as a gift, and I wounded his pride by offering it.

"You're the only one I can ask, Emmy," he said. "I'd die before I'd go to Larry for it. And Rose never has any cash. I don't want the Langleys to know because it's to keep old Matt going. If I ask my father he'll have to borrow from Larry more than likely . . ."

"Is it such a bad thing to ask me?"

"You're a woman," he said, as if it answered the question.

272

"Now you talk like Larry."

We both laughed, and it was easier between us then. I did not really care whether the money was spent on drink for Matt Sweeney or presents for Con and Margaret. It was my own money, earned from the toil over those ledgers at the Stores. I did not have to account for it to Adam; he had asked only enough to pay his share of the *Emma Langley*. What remained did not concern him. So it was a small pleasure for me to let Pat have what he asked—one of the few pleasures of these years. It amused me a little too, that I should keep the Sweeney place out of John Langley's hands with the money I earned in his Stores. I did not feel disloyalty here. The Langleys had enough, I thought. I grew tired of the efficiency of my own life, and I thought with a faint envy of such a creature as Matt Sweeney.

"The Langleys ought to be able to afford a lily of the field. Isn't that what one is rich for?"

"What?" Pat said.

"I mean Matt—he toils not, and neither does he spin."

"But he's no lily. He'll be dead soon, Emmy. He's soaked in grog, poor old devil, and it would be a cruelty to try to take it away from him. He does nothing with the place—and neither do I. I suppose when he's dead I'll have to come back and take care of it. Either that or see the Langleys get it."

"Could you do that?—could you settled down to farming? I remember—oh, back on that dray to Ballarat—you said you'd be a sheep-farmer. Could you do it, Pat?"

"I could try," he said.

And each time before he left he kissed me in the way he should not have done. I was glad he did; I was glad he wanted to kiss me that way.

III

That was the year, also, when I came into possession of a piece of my own past. Larry was my agent in this, and he did not ask, even then, the questions he had not asked back on the Eureka. Quietly, discreetly, he negotiated, without my name being mentioned, the purchase of the building and the land on which it stood—the place that was known as The Digger's Arms.

The inn was derelict now, untenanted for this last year, and almost worthless. The crossroads at which it stood had never grown to anything more important and all the passing business went to a little township that had sprung up three miles farther along the road. After successive floodings the curve of the billabong near which it stood had at last been cut off. The main creek now flowed some hundreds of feet farther back in the scrub, and the pool that remained was full only when the rain was good. In a dry season it disappeared, and travellers along the road seldom sought it now.

All this I knew, as I had made it my business to know through the years, everything that concerned The Digger's Arms. I bought it cheaply enough, and I made no plans for it, except that time should take it over. I could wait now for the white ants to eat into the supports under the drinking trough, and I could wait until the building itself, bleaching there in the endless sun, should fall down, or until the spark from the camp-fire of some swagman on the road should take it from me.

Chapter Three

There are things, to certain people, which cannot be refused. It was this way with me when Kate asked me to go to Langley Downs. She climbed the stairs slowly to my office one afternoon, her face creased with lines of worry. It was a warm day in early summer; she had grown heavier of late, and the perspiration stood in beads on her forehead and in a line above her lip. I sent Susan Higgins to make some tea.

" I've left Larry downstairs," Kate said as she settled herself. " He's waiting outside."

" Outside? Why didn't he come up?"

" Oh, sure, isn't it better if I say the thing myself. Larry has a way of putting things badly when he's asking for something —especially when it's asking something from a woman."

" What is it he wants to ask me?"

" It isn't for Larry—it's for all of us. He wants you to go to Langley Downs, Emmy. Rose packed up and moved off there this morning—and took the children with her. We want you to go and stay with her."

I leaned back in my chair, feeling my spirits sag, feeling the weight and the weariness of the arguments before me, trying to make her see why I had to refuse but still without saying too much.

" You know I haven't been to Langley Downs for more than seven years. I was only there once—I haven't wanted to go since."

"Yes . . ." Kate nodded quickly, the plumes on her bonnet jerking violently. "But Old John has asked you many a time, hasn't he? I mean—you're welcome there any time."

I had to admit this was so. Each time the children went with their grandfather to Langley Downs I was pressed to go with them. As the business at the Stores grew better and required less of my personal attention, it would have been possible to go for short visits. But I would not go with Rose, and I could not be there without her because the flaw in our friendship would then be visible to everyone. So I made my excuses each time, but John Langley continued to invite me. Now I shook my head at Kate. "I can't go. There's too much here . . ."

She waved her hand to cut me short. "Will you listen to me? She and Tom had a fight. They fought half the night—calling each other everything they could lay tongue to, I'm told—and the end of it was that Rose packed up her bags and the children and went rushing off to Langley Downs this morning. Which wouldn't be a bad thing, mind you, if it weren't for that no-good Dalkeith being at home at Rosscommon at the moment."

I knew what she meant now, the reason for the worry. "Why not send Elizabeth after her? She'll do better than I would as a chaperone."

"Wasn't it the fine sister-in-law that started all the fuss? And wouldn't you know it?—the likes of her losing her own husband and never at rest with any woman who's got one? And my fine Rose just about put blisters on her hide once she got started, so the sister-in-law has no notion to go hurrying after her."

"How do you know all this?" I wanted time now to think about this, to find some way out. The man who would have ended the trouble, who would have prevented it, in fact, was not here. John Langley had been called away to Van Diemen's Land. He had been appointed executor of the estate of a life-long friend who had died, and although he did not relish the thought of the rough sea voyage, the discomforts of a strange bed, the unsettling of his routine, nevertheless he had gone. He considered it his duty, he had told me dryly. I think behind his reluctance was fear, also—the fear of what might happen when Rose and Tom were left without the restraint of his presence. The estate, he had said, was in a bad condition, and he expected to be away at least a month. He had left only a week before.

"There's a wee Irish girl Rose got a position for in the

kitchen there—the only Catholic in that Protestant hole,
believe me. Well, they all heard the fuss, and this little girl
came to me this morning and told me. I'd arranged with her,
you know . . . that way I always know what devilment Rose
is up to." She waited impatiently while Susan Higgins brought
in the tray, and put the teapot at my hand. When the door
closed she took up the tale again.

"So I went around to see Larry, and *he* went around to see
Tom. Tom was drunk—before noon, this was, mind you. He
didn't go to the Stores today. And he won't go after Rose,
Larry says. Nothing will budge him. It's a terrible thing—
Rose is running off there after this Dalkeith, and Tom isn't
lifting a finger to stop her. That's been the trouble all along.
What Rose has needed was a husband to keep her in her place,
and Tom had never seen that. It's what comes of marrying
outside your religion . . ." she finished, illogically.

I felt my hand tremble as I poured the tea. "Are you quite
certain that Dalkeith is at Rosscommon?"

"I am indeed," she answered unhappily. "That was part
of the fight. It was about Dalkeith, of course. The sister-in-
law began about him to Rose, and then the two of them were
away like fire and Tom must needs be dragged in, whether he
wanted it or not. The wee girl heard Rose screaming that she
would go to Langley Downs just to be near him—just to spite
them all. It was all over the house, Emmy, and a great scandal
those idle busybodies of servants will be spreading through the
town this day."

"What can be done?"

"Nothing to stop her, I'm sure of that. Only something to
make it look a little better. If you were to go, Emmy, it would
look better. To have another woman there would make it
seem better. And you two being friends . . ."

"Rose and I are not friends," I said bluntly.

"And well I know it—or do you take me for blind in my
old age? But it is not for Rose you'd be going. It's for the
rest of us. For the wee children, Emmy—for Anne and James.
For Larry's four as well. For Con and Margaret—would you
have Con shamed before his wife's family? Anything you can
do to quiet the scandal will be all for us, Emmy."

"Why do you not go?" I persisted, unwilling to give in even
though I sensed I was already defeated. "Who better than
her mother to be there?"

She set her lips in a firm line, and her face flushed an ugly
red. "I said I would never cross that man's threshold except

for a birth or a death, and I'll keep my word. And that's the last I'll have to say on it."

I sighed, feeling the exasperation and anger rise in me at this family. They were unyielding, implacably stubborn in their ways, each sure that the others were wrong and sure that they would not be the one to give ground. I wondered if I must forever be pulled between them in this fashion, trying to make peace where it was impossible. I thought of Rose and wondered why it must be I, of all people, who had to go to her now, and to Langley Downs, of all places. She had too often mocked me, too often taken me for granted. I would not go back, I thought, to that place where she had almost had her final triumph. There was a limit to what I would stand from Rose, and Kate must know it.

I began to say the words of refusal. "Kate, I can't do it! Please don't ask this much of me! There must be someone else who can go. Some other woman . . ."

"There's no one else in the family who can go."

That was all she said, but it was final. I was of the family, and I knew it. With a few words now I could have shrugged off its burdens, but then I would have been outside of it forever.

I said, "We had better call Larry up. There are things to discuss."

It was Larry's carriage that took me to Langley Downs— Larry's carriage that was barely six months old and had never been intended for the rough usage of those rutted country roads. But he insisted that I take it, and he saw that it was loaded with comforts for the journey. It bothered and vexed me to see Larry so humble. Since I went unwillingly I wanted to make no claims to virtue. And so Eunice's tears when she came to bid me goodbye annoyed me.

"Try to make her see reason," she whispered. "She'll be ruined—and we'll never get over the disgrace. Tell her if she would just come back we would . . ." She looked embarrassed.

"Forgive her? I don't think Rose looks for forgiveness."

At the last moment Tom came to wish me a good journey.

"You should be going," I said, "not I."

"I'll not go. I've stood enough. Tell her, Emmy—oh, tell her nothing! Nothing! Tell her Tom sends her nothing."

He wheeled and strode away rapidly, and Eunice gave a low wail of distress. "I don't understand it," she said. "I don't understand what any of it's about!"

So I went back to Langley Downs after seven years. The house did not seem changed, nor the garden. The rough whitewashed brick, the wide verandas, the heavy, dusty scent of the roses, none of these were changed. But I was. I looked at the house with a shock of recognition, and I knew then how much the dreamy silences of its afternoons had lived in my heart, how the serenity of its gentle pastures had stayed with me through the years. I came back to something I knew that I had missed, deeply and continually. I came back to a sense of love.

The children greeted me, tumbling boisterously off the veranda into the blazing sun as soon as the carriage was sighted. They had not expected me, but they knew Larry's carriage; when I leaned out and waved to them they raced down the steps, and James did not wait for the carriage to stop fully before he had the door open. They crowded in on me, leaving marks over Larry's beautiful new upholstery with their dirty boots. Their embraces were joyful, exuberant; I hardly knew this untidy, rowdy band as the same four children who knocked on my office door in Melbourne.

They did not question the reason for my coming. "Have you come to stay, Miss Emma? How long will you stay?"

"As long as you want me."

As I walked into the house with them and they fought each other over my bags and over the fruit and sweets which Larry had provided, I knew my folly of having refused to come here with them all through these years. No quarrel with Rose should have kept me away from them in this different, freer environment. I had almost missed seeing them here—I who so jealously observed every other aspect of them. I no longer feared Rose when I had them. I felt the strain and the unease drop away from me as I entered the cool deep shadows of the hall.

Mary Anderson had come hurrying from the kitchen regions when my arrival was announced to her.

"Good afternoon, Mrs. Langley. Welcome back to Langley Downs."

And strangely, remembering her old devotion to Rose which had excluded me, I think she meant it. She seemed relieved at my presence; perhaps she was.

Rose was away from Langley Downs.

"She's gone since early this morning, Mrs. Langley," Mary Anderson said. "Riding—by herself." The jerk of her head indicated the paddocks, and it may have been accidental that it also happened to be the direction in which Rosscommon lay.

I spent the afternoon with the children, watching them perform acrobatic stunts on the spiky grass. I did not reprove Anne for her hoydenish behaviour; it was a revelation to me to see her break out of the polite confines of the Melbourne schoolroom. Her stockings were torn, and the backs of her wrists were covered with tiny scratches from the grass. Over her right eye was a rapidly swelling lump where she had banged her head against the stones that edged the flour-beds. She looked and behaved nothing like the child that John Langley's training desired. But she was outrageously happy, competing fiercely with her brothers in everything. But unlike her mother, she did not mind her defeats.

We ended the afternoon by cutting a basketful of roses for my bedroom table.

"Tell us about Grandmother," James said. "Grandfather tells us about her every time we come here."

We sat by that pretty, untragic grave in the corner of the rose garden and I invented tales about a woman I had never known. I had only the slightest knowledge of the woman through the remembered conversations with John Langley. So I told the children stories of the time when she had come here, the time before there had been churches or graveyards. What I told them was mostly the story of the house itself, how it had been built, how the land about it had been cleared, how the prize merinos and the horses had been brought here, how the oak furniture had come from England with their grandfather, and was much older than he, how the garden had been planned and made for their grandmother. They grew quiet as I talked, their exuberance giving place to a dreamy tiredness. When the shadows of the trees lengthened across the paddocks they went back willingly to the house with me, as decorous and docile as on any Melbourne afternoon.

The light was almost gone when Rose returned. From the sitting-room I sat and watched through the open french windows as it drained out from the land, leaving the paddocks in near-darkness, leaving only a flush of colour in the sky above a bar of crimson. The trees at the western edge of the paddocks were black against it. I heard Rose's quick footsteps on the path from the stables, then on the boards of the veranda, and at last she was etched against the lighted door frame as sharply as the trees. As she stared in at me I could not distinguish her features, only the lovely, well-remembered sweep of neck and throat as she turned.

"Well, Emmy!" They told me you had come." She advanced a few paces into the room. "Have you come to be my goaler?—my keeper?"

"No one is your keeper, Rose."

She slapped her crop on to the table, and flung her hat after it. Then she swung furiously to face me. "Or to spy on me? Is that why they sent you?"

"Tom thought you might need . . . someone."

"I have my children. There's no one else I need."

"Is there not? Not anyone?"

"None of that pious lot back there. I've had enough of their sermons. What I do is no more than they would like to do—if they had the courage. They envy me because I'm free."

"No one is free. No one but a fool believes that." I stood up and moved past her, to the door. It was too dark now to see more than her outline, but I did not want to be the one to bring the lamp. "But I'll give you no sermons. I'll give you nothing—nothing more—until you ask for it."

III

The pattern was established and continued for a week. Rose would ride out soon after breakfast, and return about sundown. She refused to have a groom with her, and she never spoke of where she was going, but we knew it was to Rosscommon. We knew it for certain when the gossip came back from the servants at Rosscommon itself. I felt that I had failed Kate and Larry because I made no move to stop her. But this was a season of madness for Rose, and it would have to endure until it was burned out, or until something shocked her out of it. I wished daily for John Langley's return.

Perhaps I was even, in my secret heart, a little glad that she went and left us, for whatever reason. I held the children to me closely, jealously, never having had before the luxury of whole uninterrupted days with them. I gave James and Anne their lessons, and started the younger ones on learning their letters and simple words. In her flight from Melbourne Rose had refused to bring the governess, so I was undisputedly in possession here; I enjoyed my riches extravagantly, feeling that they would not be mine for very long. There was a sense of holiday in everything we did. Lessons took place on the shaded side of the veranda with the view of the wide paddocks before us; I ended them at noon, and on most days we took a picnic lunch down to the creek that flowed by the line of trees at the far boundary of the home paddock. We took off our shoes and stockings and waded in the water, and told each other to watch out for snakes. Sometimes the two little ones slept there in the shade, tired from the heat and the long walk to the creek, and the vigorous splashing. They were drowsy hours in the early afternoon, the air singing with the hum of insects and the heat haze growing thick on the horizon. I felt very far from the office at the Stores and my black silk dresses I wanted this time never to end.

Then in the evening Rose would return, her face tensely exultant. There was little ease in her. Even her movements seemed to lose that smooth sensuous flow that had been their beauty, they came brittle and sharp. Her whole face and body sharpened, as if her senses were keyed to an almost unbearable pitch. She seemed to be living each moment at a heightened intensity, and the empty hours of the evening and the night, the hours without movement, must have been torture for her. We ate our evening meal together—with a pretence of conversation for Mary Anderson's benefit, and then she left me. Late into the night I could hear her pacing on the veranda outside our bedrooms. In the morning at breakfast she wore her riding habit, and she bolted her food with unrepentant haste.

IV

Pat came in much the same way as he had come before to Langley Downs. This time I sat alone in the sitting-room—Rose had left me early, as usual. While I read I listened to the sound of her footsteps above me in the bedroom, but I heard nothing from Pat until he called to me softly from the open french windows.

"Emmy!"

I gasped with the shock of hearing my name, and the book slipped from my hands and fell on the floor. "Don't make a noise!" he cautioned.

As I got up and went to him he had already turned and closed the doors behind him. Then he gently drew the curtains across to screen the windows. With a gesture he motioned me to do the same to the other two windows, and then he laid a finger across his lips to warn me to silence. I did as he wanted and then turned back to him, fearfully.

"Pat—what is it?"

"Who's still up?" he said. "The servants?"

"Gone to bed—I would think. They're at the back of the house. Rose is awake. I'll go and get her. Just wait . . ."

"No, don't!" he said. "She'll only make a fuss. What I've come for concerns you. I've only a minute, Emmy. I've left my horse down by the creek, and I don't think anyone will find him. But I need a good many miles between here and me by daybreak."

"Now I was truly afraid. "Why?" I said. "Who would be looking for you?"

He did not answer me directly. He sat down in the chair I had left, and then I saw how weary he was. His limbs did not relax into the chair, but remained stiff, as if he expected to have to spring up again. He passed his hand for a moment across his eyes. The dust on his face was streaked where the sweat had run.

"I've been to see Matt—I've been riding all afternoon to get there, and it's probably one of the places they'll look for me. And then they may come here looking—because of Rose being here."

I strode over to him, bending down to look at him. "*Who* may come? For God's sake—*Who!*"

"The police." He took a long breath, watching my face. Then he spoke again. "It's happened, Emmy. It's happened just the way everyone said it would—Larry and all the wise ones. I'm in trouble, and I'm running. I have to run because at best I'll go to gaol, and at worst they'll hang me. I'd as soon swing than be shut up, so I have to run."

I sank down on the ground beside the chair; I felt each of his words inside of me separately like blows. The numbness of the shock did not last long enough, and I was left too soon with the horror. I searched his eyes and found in them, beside the weariness, a look of appeal, of dumb groping for reassurance. There was none I could give, because by his own words he was beyond that. He had said he must run. I touched his hand then grasped it until the hold must have been painful to him.

"Tell me," I demanded.

"The bank at Yucamunda," he said. "The manager was shot. If he dies, we'll hang."

"We?" I whispered. I was so cold it felt as if the blood

282

in my veins had stopped flowing. It was an effort to pronounce even that single word.

"The Russells—Joe and Luke. We were mates on a cattle drive once. I knew they turned their hand to it now and again, and I didn't care. This was a big one and they wanted help. They asked me in—and I went. It didn't work out the way we planned. The bank manager shot Luke, and Joe shot him. We managed to get Luke on his horse and we took him away with us, but by that time he and Joe had been recognised. It won't take the police long to put me in with them. People knew we were together a lot . . ."

"The one who was shot?—what happened to him?"

For the first time then he looked away from me. "We tied him to his horse. But after we had ridden for about an hour we found out he was dead. You understand, Emmy—we couldn't stop until then, until we were sure we'd shaken off that mob that were behind us. We couldn't stop or it would have been the end for all of us. You understand that."

Now he looked at me again, his eyes shamed and wretched. I did not release my hold on his hand. I could not. To me he was not the man of this tale, of violence and mindless death. I did not shrink back from him, but I could give him no comfort but this.

"Is the . . . the other one waiting for you?"

He shook his head. "We split up. We have a meeting place. There's a camp in a valley back in the mountains. If we can once get there it'll take more than the police to track us in. Once we get there we're safe."

"Until the next time," I said slowly.

He stood up, looking down at me still kneeling by the chair. "Yes until the next time. It's no use saying there won't be a next time. I'm marked now, Emmy, and there's nothing I can do but go on the same way."

"You will be killed," I said the chilling words and knew their truth. "Someday."

He nodded calmly. "Yes." He was brave enough to look at me when he spoke. Then I saw that I was mistaken. He did not fear the thought of death or lie to himself about its coming. He expected it, and I guessed that he wished it would be soon.

"Is there no way else?" I said.

"No way."

A ship?" I said, hope waking in me again. I called myself a fool for not having thought of it before. "To San Francisco, or to the Indies. If I asked Adam he would take you. After a

283

while, when they have stopped looking for you, you could come to Melbourne quietly. Adam would help you. I'm sure he would help you. He understands . . . a man's trouble."

He shook his head looking down at me as if he pitied my ignorance in thinking that there could be such an easy way for him. "No," he said. "It doesn't matter." And I knew then that he sought the death which seemed to wait so surely for him.

He stretched out his hand and raised me gently from the floor. He spoke quietly and swiftly. "I've stayed too long, Emmy. I came for just one thing, and that must be done before I leave." He fumbled for a moment in the inner pocket of his coat and finally brought out a folded piece of paper.

"It's all here, Emmy. I think it's legal. I don't know if they can confiscate the property of a man who's a criminal, but in any case my name isn't on the deed to Matt's place."

"What have you done."

He put the paper in my hand. "The Sweeney place belongs to me. Matt would have lost it years ago if I hadn't kept it going—my money, and a part of yours, Emmy. Well, I'll never farm it now, so it's yours. It will be yours as soon as the poor old devil dies. I've signed over any claims and shares I have in the place to you . . . what's the word they use?— irrevocably? Yes, I remembered to put that in. It's not witnessed except by Matt, but it's only between you and me, Emmy, so we'll not be needing witnesses. And I made Matt swear that he would sober up enough to get himself to a lawyer and make a proper will. You'll have to pay the interest on mortgage, but the title will be yours, free and clear. I'll get what money I can to old Matt for as long as I can. You'll not forget your promise about looking out for him, Emmy?— you'll not forget?"

I shook my head dumbly, and he folded my stiff fingers about the paper.

"See that you make something of it, mind! See that you do all the things I didn't have time to do in this country."

He turned away from me then, and went back to the windows. I gestured for him to stop as he put his hand on the curtain.

"Wait!" I moved to his side again. "See Rose before you go. See her for just a moment. It will help her . . ."

He shook his head. "She would never stand it," he said. "I could never trust her to take things in the same way as you do. It will be easier for her when they come asking questions if she hasn't seen me. Besides . . . I don't want her to see me

like this. She's already gone far enough to the devil himself."
Now he smiled a wretched crooked smile that seemed to me
sheer pain. "I don't want her to know what the devil looks
like."

He was about to turn again, and I touched him. "Then
wait. Wait just a minute."

I lit a candle from the oil lamp, and softly opened the door
from the sitting-room to the hall. In the dining-room John
Langley kept his wines and spirits, and I used the key that
Mary Anderson had handed over to me. I took a silver hip
flask Langley kept for travelling and filled it with his finest
brandy. Then I took it back to Pat and put it in his hand. It
was a nearly useless gesture when his trouble was so great,
but it was all I could think of to offer.

"Bury it when you reach where you're going. He never
forgets any of his possessions." We both knew I spoke of
John Langley.

Pat kissed me gently, not the hard kiss of our last meetings.
I felt his sadness in that, though he would not speak it. Then
his lips moved on mine for a brief second.

"Something to remember," he said.

Then he vanished into the blackness beyond the veranda.
I thought I would probably never see him again alive. He
would go on, perhaps for years, living in his hidden valleys,
picking his way through the stony places so that he left no
tracks, visiting Matt Sweeney at night, secretly and rarely.
There would be more episodes like the bank at Yucamunda.
He would go on his way until he finally found the bullet he
had seemed to seek since the morning that Sean had taken his
place at the barricades on the Eureka.

I only remembered one other time in my life when I had
sat as I sat after he had gone, stupefied and numb, aware that
time was passing but without feeling for its length. This was
how I sat on the stairs at The Digger's Arms with Will
Gribbon lying dead in the room behind me. It was the same
sensation of pain and fear, of helplessness. But I had been
alone in that action, and it had ended with Gribbon, had not
gone beyond him. I began to think now of the others, of Kate
and Dan, Larry, Con, Rose, the Langleys—all of them would
be involved; whether they had loved Pat or not they would
suffer for this day's work. But because I had had my hour of
sitting dumbly on the stairs of The Digger's Arms I knew
better than any of them what thoughts went with Pat as he
rode. I knew the loneliness, the feeling of being cut off, of
having pushed oneself beyond the limits of all that was

accepted and familiar. I had been brought back from that despair, but Pat must live with his forever.

And then I thought of Rose, lying sleeplessly in her bed, enduring her own kind of torment that came from within her, fed by the same streak of wildness that had destroyed Pat. His loneliness and desperation no one could ease, but I began to think it was possible to stretch out towards Rose and make contact again, remembering that once she had stretched out her hand towards me.

I got up stiffly and went upstairs to her.

V

After I told her about Pat, Rose gave a cry that was half-scream, half wail. It was a savage cry of protest, of unbelief. I think there was no pity for herself in it, only for him. After that one cry she lay inert on the bed and I moved slowly closer to her ; at last the light of the candle fell on her averted face and I saw the tears, silent, unchecked. I laid down the candle and put my hand tentatively on her shoulder.

"Rose . . . don't! Don't weep so. Try to bear it."

"Oh, Emmy. I'll never see him! It's the end, isn't it?"

"It's never the end. No one can say . . ." And I found myself stroking that tumbled hair, trying to soothe her in just the way I had always done in the old days. She turned her face into the pillow and her weeping shook her whole body, an anguished weeping. I sat on the bed and took her in my arms. Her response came like a child's, clinging, pleading to make the world right again. But in the old days Rose would have expected the miracle to happen. Now she expected no such thing, and so her tears were bitter and near to acceptance. Finally, from exhaustion, she slept, and I lay down beside her for the first time since the night she had run away from the Eureka.

It was barely dawn when she wakened me. I heard her voice through my sleep ; she was not beside me on the bed but standing by the open doors to the veranda. She was looking out to where a misty greyness lay on the garden and paddocks and blurred the outlines of the tree-tops. She was speaking aloud, but her talk was for herself.

"The greyness looks so sad. It's better to stay in bed until the sun is bright, and then you don't see the greyness. I wonder where he is . . . I wonder how far he got last night. Did he have any food, I wonder."

Then she must have sensed my movement in the bed, and she glanced back at me. Except for the fullness of her bosom she might have been taken for a child in the half-light, with her hair lying in dark curls on her shoulders, and her bare feet showing at the ruffled edge of her nightgown. She looked hardly older than the last time I had seen her this way, the morning when she had asked Adam to take her away from Langley Downs. The memory stirred, but it did not bring the expected pain.

Now she spoke to me directly; her voice was brooding and withdrawn. "It's all so different from what I expected. Nothing seems to turn out the way it should." She gestured, a vague gesture of helplessness. "I didn't ask for too much, did I? I got most of the things I asked for, but they didn't seem to be the same as what I'd wanted." She did not speak Pat's name, but I knew that this was still her lament for him.

"I wanted to laugh, and be gay," she said. "That was what I wanted most of all. Do you remember Charlie Greenley, Emmy?"

"Yes, I remember him."

"Charlie used to make me laugh, and it was so good. He had only to come into a room and I felt happier because of it. But they took Charlie away from me. They sent him away, and he never came back. They always spoil all the good things."

The childish questioning voice was almost ghostly in the morning stillness. I wanted to give her comfort but there was none that had any truth in it. Once I could have given her love, but that was gone long ago and could not come back as it had been. Now I pitied her.

VI

We stayed at Langley Downs another two weeks, Rose did not go again to Rosscommon and Robert Dalkeith was not invited to Langley Downs. They were days we kept deliberately tranquil because we armed ourselves against the talk and rumours we knew were going on outside. We lived in the children's world for two weeks.

The police came once to Langley Downs, very respectful and polite, and apologized to Rose for troubling her. She simply told them, with truth, that she had not seen her brother, and no more was asked. In these days she still wore the air of childish sweetness and puzzlement which had fallen on her in that early dawn conversation, and I could see that the police-sergeant was hard put to it to believe that this was the woman that the whole district had seen riding daily to Rosscommon. As she romped with her children on the lawns and down at the creek, wading and splashing with them, tumbling just as they did, she seemed to partake of their innocence and dependence. I think her fear for Pat, her grief, had driven her back to the memories of her old childhood. Robert Dalkeith had no place in these memories or this time, and so for the moment he did not exist for her.

Each day she would talk of going back to Melbourne. " I should go back, Emmy. But I don't want to. Not just yet a while. It's so peaceful here, so . . . healing. I should go back and try to comfort Dada. He will be heartbroken about Pat and I should be there to help him. And I should go back and try to make it up to Tom. Poor thing, he means no harm. But there's all the talk, and having to face it, and that great house where no one ever laughs. I'm so afraid I'll grow to be like Elizabeth—not even wanting to laugh. Just imagine how dreadful that would be!

" We'll go back soon, Emmy. But not today. Not just yet."

Chapter Four

We returned to Melbourne and Rose's time of peace was at an end. To my ears the town seemed to vibrate with its gossip about the Maguires and the Langleys. I heard it all about me —at times when I was not intended to hear it, and at times when I was. Among the clerks at the Stores I heard it, and among the customers.

One woman seemed to say it for all of them. I heard her as I passed through the aisles ; she leaned towards the assistant who was unrolling a length of striped calico for her and I saw her fierce old face grimace with a kind of enjoyment.

"It's true what they say about her, isn't it? Well—they're tarred with the same brush, she and that brother."

There was nothing now that John Langley could do, even if he had been in Melbourne, that could have held back the tide of gossip and speculation. Pat Maguire was wanted for robbery and attempted murder, and if he had been obscure

Melbourne would have paid no more attention to him than a dozen others of his kind. But he was Rose Langley's brother and the brother of Larry Maguire whom many thought was already getting above himself. For those who did not like the Langleys it was a time of triumph—to have both Rose and Pat to point fingers at. Now was the time to remember every indiscretion of Rose's and drag it back into the light, to recall every imagined slight and pay it back. Not in a lifetime could Rose have as many lovers as talk gave to her then. There was no mercy and no pity.

Ben looked at me gloomily over his whisky in my office.

" If Dalkeith had any sense he'd go. It would be the kindest thing to do—to leave it to blow itself out."

" It frightens me," I said. " It's as if they've all been waiting —and storing up. I don't think it will ever blow itself out. Or be forgotten."

Ben shook his head. " She's gone too far this time. This town will never forgive her for not caring a snap of her fingers about what they thought of her. She has always had John Langley to protect her. But now there's Pat's trouble, and it's too much of a combination. It's too much to expect of human nature that they wouldn't take this chance and fall on her like a pack.

" Poor foolish woman . . ." He took a long reflective pull at the whisky. " I remember her back at Ballarat . . . there wasn't a female that walked those streets that had half the magic for a man as Rose Maguire. She knew she had it, too, but she never knew how to use it for her own happiness."

He stretched his head back and stared up at the ceiling. " Oh, yes—the town is having a good time, believe me. How the mighty Langleys are fallen! They're busy telling each other over the teacups that this is what comes of taking one of those Irish-Catholics in and trying to pass her off as a lady. Rose Maguire would have had an easier time of it if she hadn't gone so high, and proved to them all that she could twist the old man around her finger."

" What will happen when John Langley comes back?" I said. I could feel the furrow between my brows which seemed to be there almost perpetually these days. " He must have had the news about Pat by this time . . . and the other. News like that always reaches those that it concerns in one way or another."

" He'll bear it," Ben answered. " Like the rest of us must. It's the same sorrow for all of us." His face, as he peered down into his whisky, was a long mask of melancholy.

"Tom takes it badly," I said. "He never seems to be sober, and he hardly bothers to come near the Stores any more."

"As sorry as I am for his trouble, I think the Stores won't suffer for his not being there. They've never needed him, and he knows it, and that's almost as bad as knowing his wife doesn't need him, either."

I had thought Rose could not change, but she did in these weeks. I had done her an injustice in thinking that her concern was only for herself, because she seemed haunted by fear for Pat, compassion for his wretchedness. She talked of him constantly to me, and he seemed never to be out of her thoughts. And in thinking of him she seemed to forget herself, her own reasons for unhappiness.

She took to coming with the children to the Stores almost every day in place of the servant who had always accompanied them. She became part of the tea-time ritual in my office, but strangely for her, she did not dominate it. She sat quietly and observed, and said little. She always asked me to return to the Langley house with her.

She paused once, at the head of the stairs as the children went down before her, her fingers plucking nervously at her glove.

"I'm so alone there, Emmy. Elizabeth doesn't speak to me, and Tom barely makes a pretence of it in front of the children. They don't want me. I know that."

What she did not say but what I knew without her speaking of it that she also could not escape the company of her husband and sister-in-law. Since the gossip spread about her and Dalkeith, and since the wanted notices had gone out for Pat, the invitations had stopped coming to the Langley house. There was nowhere for her to go, except here and to the Maguire pub. She refused to go to Larry's house.

"If it were too good for Pat," she said to me bitterly, "then it's no longer good enough for me. I won't have Eunice drawing back her skirts as I pass, and hoping I won't talk to her precious children for fear I might contaminate them!"

I, and the rest of Melbourne, knew that Dalkeith had remained at Rosscommon. Rose never spoke of him, and I did not know if she wished to see him again. She was quite alone here, except for me and for her father, who was so stunned by the news of Pat that he was able to stir himself only a little to help Rose. Her mother, in some confused and vague way, seemed to hold Rose partly responsible for Pat's tragedy, and each time they met, she would berate her again about Dalkeith. There was no peace for Rose in her mother's house. She sought my office and my company as the only refuge left.

Once, after a long silence as we sat alone in the drawing-room at the Langley house after supper, she leaned towards me and said:

"It's too late now to ask forgiveness, Emmy. They don't believe it—it's too late!"

II

Since Rose's return from Langley Downs Elizabeth had taken her meals alone in her housekeeping room, so that there was only Rose, Tom and myself at the table at supper when John Langley came back. We did not expect him; there had been no advance notice of his coming, no message sent from Hobson's Bay to have his carriage come for him. It was not his habit to travel by hackney cab, and the fact that he broke his rule for the sake of haste was in itself enough to give us a warning. There was something close to fear in Rose's expression as we heard the first rapping at the front door, and then his voice curtly returning the servant's greeting.

"Where are my son and daughter-in-law?"

"The family is still at supper, sir, in the dining-room."

We had no time to collect ourselves before the door opened with unusual force and John Langley stood before us. Tom thrust the decanter away from him and rose to his feet a little unsteadily.

"Welcome home, sir," he said.

The old man said nothing; he looked at us carefully, each in turn, his eyes questioning, severe. He still wore his cape, and one gloved hand rested on the silver-topped cane. He looked worn as he stood there—older, but not weakened or feeble. I felt the chill of his presence in my own heart.

Rose could bear the silence no longer. Her chair scraped noisily as she pushed it back and half ran the length of the room towards John Langley.

"Papa Langley, you should have sent word you were here! We would have come to fetch you in the carriage. I know how you hate those dirty cabs . . ." She stretched on tip-toe to kiss his cheek, but abruptly the action was halted and frozen. His expression had not changed by even the twitching of a muscle, and it was not a face that one would reach up to kiss. She stepped back from him, faltering.

"Sit down—both of you," he said.

Silently she returned to her place, and Tom took his seat again. The old man flicked his cape back off his shoulders and walked down the room to his own seat. As he passed the bell cord he pulled it, and then when he had settled himself he nodded in my direction.

"Good evening, Miss Emma."

I opened my lips dryly, and at first no sound came; I felt myself infected with the fear and apprehension about me. When my voice came finally it was a strange-sounding squawk that responded to his greeting. Then we waited in silence until the manservant came in answer to the bell.

"Bring the port," John Langley said.

Rose interrupted nervously. "Have you eaten, Papa Langley? It will take only a minute to have you served . . ."

"I am well aware, Madam, what orders I may give in my own household." He nodded towards the manservant. "Just bring the port." And again we sat in silence while the decanter was brought, and the glass.

"That will be all, you may leave us now," John Langley said. He even waited until the door had closed behind the man before he picked up the decanter to pour. Then he sipped it, and waited, and sipped again before he spoke.

"I have come, leaving matters unfinished in Hobart, because in my absence you have brought infamy and disgrace to my name." He held up his hand. "No—I will not be interrupted! I have come to find your name, Madam, a subject of common gossip in Melbourne because of your indiscreet dalliance with Robert Dalkeith. I will not call you by the harsher names that gossip gives to you because I make no accusations without proof I have seen with my own eyes. What you are in your heart you yourself know. And you, sir . . ." He nodded grimly towards his son. "*You* have made my name a laughing stock. Whatever this woman is, she is because you have permitted it —even encouraged it with your foolishness. You are beyond pity—beyond contempt. I cannot think——"

He stopped short as I stood up. "You don't need me here, Mr. Langley," I said. "You don't need me to listen to this!" I felt no fear now because the anger was greater. I could not bear to look at Tom's face.

"Sit down again, Miss Emma." He tapped the floor with his stick for emphasis. "I ask you to sit down. The business of this family has been your business for a long time now. You have your place here among us—in good times, and ill." He nodded for me to take my seat again, and I did.

He sipped his port before he went on. "Apart from all this

we are allied with a bank robber and a murderer. How my enemies must laugh! How our good name is dragged down!" His thin fingers trembled on the glass stem, so that I thought the port must spill. But he had always been, and still was, too much in command of himself to permit that. His face showed the effort at control, though; it was pinched and beaky as the candle-light played upon it.

"And if that is not enough, when I landed Lawrence Clay brought me word that the bank at Corandilla has been robbed, and that witnesses have identified Maguire and Russell as the bandits." He was white with fury as he looked at Rose. "If you did not know it, Madam, may I tell you that I am the principal shareholder in the Corandilla bank!"

A low cry broke from Rose's lips. "No—it was not Pat! It could not have been Pat!"

"Positively identified!" John Langley snapped. "A deliberate insult! A deliberate and fiendish insult! He mocks the Langleys, but I swear he will not have the last laugh!"

"What will you do?" The words came as a whisper from Rose.

"He will be hunted as any common criminal must be, but I promise you that Commissioner Braddock will have no rest from me until this man is brought to justice for his crimes. I will show this colony that I believe in justice, no matter who suffers. I will show them that I will not permit this breed to flourish as it pleases. His kind are a blight on this country, and must be wiped out!"

Tom suddenly lurched forward. "You are a monster!"

"And you! What are you? You and your wife have dragged down my name, and dragged down my grandchildren's name. I am too late to prevent what is already done, and I share the blame and disgrace because I have been for too long permitted this. My enemies will say I have grown soft in my old age—that I am a doting and foolish old man! But they are wrong. I have made mistakes, but I will make no more. If I have let you both make us the subject of gossip and disgrace and by that to injure my grandchildren, then I will be doubly careful to protect them in the future. You, sir, and you, Madam——" pointing towards Rose, "will not be allowed to squander their inheritance. As long as I live I will strive to protect their property. I will take out of your hands the means to bring them to financial ruin."

Now Tom reached deliberately for his wine, swallowing it back quickly. When he put it down he said to his father, "What do you mean?"

"I mean that you will be no longer associated with any of the Langley enterprises, and that my grandchildren, not you, will inherit from me." He turned to Rose. "And I assure you, Madam, that you will do well to keep in mind my favour, because it is a simple matter to cut off your credit. I will have no more disgrace brought on this house."

None of us spoke again as he finished his port. I saw the unhappiness cloud Rose's eyes, and I was frightened because for the first time I saw no rebellion there. I waited for a protest from her, or from Tom, but none came. And I, as craven as they were, said nothing. He held us all, that old man, bound by his anger and coldness. I knew that the relaxation of these years of Rose's time here was ended. Now the house would go back to what it had been before she came, and the children would grow up as Tom and Elizabeth had done, shrinking from the sound of John Langley's voice. In them he would search for and try to eradicate every flaw that he believed he saw in Tom and Rose. A darkness seemed to close, not only on us but on them also, as we heard the old man's words.

III

On the previous evenings that I had spent at the Langley house Tom had always called for the carriage when it was time for me to go back to Langley Lane. But tonight, because I seemed to bear the weight of John Langley's disapproval no less than Rose and Tom, I left the house very quietly as soon as John Langley had gone upstairs, telling Tom to get my cape and bonnet so as not to summon a servant. He put his hand on my arm. "I'll walk back with you, Emmy . . ."

I nodded. He got his hat and he walked beside me in the quiet darkness of Collins Street, his hands clasped behind his back and his head bent forward. He hardly seemed aware of me beside him, though his hand came up to my elbow automatically each time we came to a crossing. Once a man whom we passed spoke to Tom, and raised his hat to me, but Tom didn't look up, or return the greeting. He mumbled some indistinguishable words to himself as he walked; but he did not speak to me directly for the whole length of Collins Street, not until I took out the key to unlock my door. He raised his head then to stare at the familiar buildings about us, the stables, the warehouse, the high wall of the Stores towering above the little house. Although the night was warm he seemed to shiver.

"Let me come in, Emmy," he said.

He stood with apparent helplessness while I lit the lamp; as I turned back to him his eyes seemed to beg me for comfort. I nodded quietly towards Adam's chair.

"Sit down . . . stay a while before you go back."

"Have you any whisky?"

I nodded. It would have done no good to refuse him; he would have gone to the nearest tavern for it. He drank the first glass I gave him almost in a gulp and held it out again to be refilled. This one he drank more slowly, and after a time he looked over at me.

"My father has us now, hasn't he? He has us tied so tightly, Rose and I, that we won't be able to move. Now that he has his grandchildren he's just content to have it this way, whatever he says about the disgrace. My father has never trusted what he couldn't control."

"John Langley doesn't own you," I said. "You could go —and take your children with you."

He shook his head, and his twisted smile mocked my words. "Oh, no—it's far too late for that, Emmy. My father bought us in the beginning with money, and he'll hold us that way. He bought each of our children. Did you notice that it never occurred to him to doubt that we'd stay—whatever conditions he chose to impose on us? He knows us well, my father. He knows we have nowhere to go unless there's money. Don't you see, Emmy—without the money we would have only each other, and my father knows that isn't enough. We don't love each other, so we need the money . . ."

"You used to love Rose."

"Perhaps in my trusting moments I still do love her, but those moments are very few now. Not enough to get us through . . ."

"Rose has changed . . ."

He shook his head, and again I saw that unbelieving smile that was part of his hurt. He went to the table and filled his glass again, his movements were all made with that careful precision that characterised him when he was drunk. He did not go back to his seat at once; he leaned against the table as he spoke.

"Rose hasn't changed. She is only afraid. She is afraid of my father—not of me. If she were afraid of me I'd like it. I'd like to see Rose look at me just once and wonder what I would say to her. But she never will—she doesn't even bother to listen any more. She listens to my father. She's afraid that the old man will throw us out. And there we will be, Emmy—just Rose and myself, and no money between us to soften the words. No money for drink or a new gown, or a carriage to get away from me. She likes me to drink because then she doesn't have to bother with me. If I were sober she'd have to put up with me just the way I am. Rose wouldn't like that . . ."

"You have your share of the *Emma Langley*."

He shrugged. "Not enough. Not nearly enough. Sooner or later my father will get that from me, too. He likes to hold the reins short."

"Why do you give in so easily? Isn't there something worth making a fight about? Surely there . . . ?"

He waved the glass at me in dismissal. "Oh, Emmy—don't you have any pity for the ones who are not like yourself? *You* would fight—I can't. Don't make it worse."

I felt ashamed. As gently as I could I motioned him to the chair opposite me again. "I'm sorry, Tom. If I could help . . ."

He sat down again. "Don't bother with me and Rose. Try to help them before the old man makes them afraid. It's not too late to help them."

I nodded. I knew he spoke of the children.

He added shortly, "Yes—help them."

Then he drank for a time in silence, no longer looking at me, his eyes fixed on the floorboards, holding his glass in both hands. His surroundings seemed to have slipped away from him and he made no effort to hold them. His face became relaxed, and I thought I saw on his lips a trace of a smile that had little to do with the bitter mockery of the other ones.

"Tom . . . ?" I said softly.

He looked up suddenly, startled to see me there. "Emmy?" Then the smile came fully. "She was lovely then, wasn't she, Emmy? In the old days . . . you remember her going about Ballarat with her petticoat trailing in the muck and her hair all wild. She was the loveliest thing I ever saw."

I thought I dreamed, that night, a violent and unhappy dream in which I saw Rose beating with her fists on the closed door of the Langley house. The dream changed, so that Rose stood before John Langley and she laughed at him; the beating now had become John Langley's silver-topped cane rapping futilely, angrily, on the floor. Then I half-awakened, but the pounding in my head did not vanish with the dream. Along with the pounding, near and loud, I heard my name being called, and I knew it was no dream.

"Emmy! Emmy! For God's sake—Emmy!"

It was Tom's voice. As I flung aside the bedclothes I struggled to bring myself to full wakefulness, and to call an answer, but I had no voice against the smoke that already filled my throat and lungs. It was dark in the bedroom, but the sitting-room was lit by the red glow that came through the chinks in the curtains. Out here the smoke was dense. I could hear Tom's pounding still at the door, and the new, more menacing sound that was a wind and a roar in the background. Tears streamed from my eyes; the smoke and lack of air made me stupid. I stood transfixed, looking at that red glow. Then suddenly the front door crashed inwards, splintering at the lock. Tom's rush, which had broken the lock, propelled him on. He sprawled at my feet on the floor. For a moment he lay there, winded, and then as he gasped for air, the smoke also reached his lungs. He struggled to rise, and then saw me.

"Get out of here!" he gasped. "Get out! The whole place will go up in a few minutes."

He grasped my arm and thrust me towards the yard.

"Wait—there are some things . . ."

"No time! Get out."

Then I felt the surprising strength of his body as he caught me by the shoulders and pushed me through the doorway. Out here there seemed more air to breathe, but the walls of the house no longer shielded me from the full heat. The Langley stables were on fire, the flames shooting to the sky with the roar that had seemed like the wind to me. In the distance, across the town, I could hear the clanging of the fire bells, but the horror now, close at hand, was not the flames and the searing heat, but the screams of the horses. I could even hear the crash of wood tearing apart as their great hooves smashed into the stalls. The whole of the hay-loft above the stalls was ablaze, and the first tongues of fire had already burned through the roof in one corner. There was only a slight breeze but enough to fan it toward the wall of the warehouse.

Above the roar Tom shouted in my ear. " Don't stand here! Run down the lane. Get help! Where's that fool Watkins . . ." He dashed away from me, across the yard towards the stables.

" Tom—come back. Don't go near that . . ." Even the paving of the stable yard seemed to be burning under my bare feet. I reached Tom as he was wringing out a handkerchief in a water-butt; near the stables the heat was intense. I had to shield my face with my arms. Frantically, I hauled on his arm to make him notice me.

" Come away! The roof will collapse! It's too late to go in!"

" My father's horses . . ." he shouted. " His prize horses!" He knotted the handkerchief over his nose and face, and then freed himself of my clutching arms with one sudden jerk. " Get out, Emmy!" Then he ran for the big stable door, and passed beneath the flaming arch.

I stood helplessly there, holding my hands to screen my face, trying to see his figure against the glare, trying to listen for his voice above the screams of the horses. The roar of the flames seemed all about me. I looked up and saw that the frame of one of the warehouse windows directly above the stable roof had caught. With the heat I was forced backwards from the yard towards the lane. The last thing that I saw in the yard was that the sparks were falling on the roof of my house.

Then I turned and ran up the Lane towards the small group of men who had come out of the doorways along Collins Street, awakened from their sleep by the clanging of the fire engine bells and irresistibly drawn by the flames that now shot higher than the roof of the Langley warehouse. They were the derelicts of the town; I screamed into their stupefied drunken faces.

" Help me! There's a man in there . . ."

They shook their heads.

" It's 'opeless, Miss! 'Opeless!"

The stables burned, and the warehouse burned. Everything that the flames could reach they destroyed. Every fire engine that Melbourne had reached the site eventually, but there was never enough water pressure for the street pumps to let more than two fire companies work at the same time. My house vanished with all the rest; the Stores were saved because of the blank, windowless wall that faced on the yard. The flames from my house did not go high enough to reach the roof of the Stores, and the fire companies, on the orders of John Langley, concentrated on keeping the walls and roof wetted down. The sparks caught the back rear room of the Ladies Department, but the hoses could reach its roof, and so it was saved, while John Langley stood by and watched the whole of his warehouse gutted until only the roofless bluestone walls were left.

We knew, while the warehouse burned and kept the fire companies out of the Lane, that Tom lay in the ruin of the stable. Though they said the next day, when the charred beams had cooled enough to let them search, that he had not died in the fire, but had been trampled by one of the great horses that drew his father's drays.

Time and again, as we watched the fire from across Collins Street, the watchman, Watkins, came to tell his story to John Langley. He repeated it through the crowd to whomever would listen, and I heard snatches of a dozen different versions as I stood there.

"It wasn't my fault, Mr. Langley, sir. I found him there early on. He came in through the side door of the stables. Dead drunk he was—and lookin' for somewhere to lie down and sleep it off. I thought it best to leave him a lamp—him being Mr. Tom, an' I didn't fancy leavin' him to knock about by himself in the dark. But I swear to you, Mr. Langley—I swear to you, sir—that it was hanging on its hook. He had to take it down, Mr. Langley—he had to have lifted it down with his own hands."

He always spoke to John Langley while he said these things, and kept his eyes away from Rose, who watched the blaze with a dumb, petrified face. She screamed once, when the roof of the warehouse fell in, but she had come too late to see the collapse of the stables. People wondered at her, standing there silent and unweeping, but I felt her fingers digging into the flesh of my arm as she held me, tightening cruelly each time a beam crashed down. She remained there unmoving, unspeaking, for the hours that it took for the consummation. She obeyed mechanically when John Langley spoke.

"Come—it is time to go."

He took my arm also. "Come, Miss Emma."

He walked between us, and the crowd parted to let us through. It was a large crowd; the flames had lighted the sky for miles across the city, and the fire bells had made their urgent summons. When the word had gone around that it was the Langley warehouse that was burning, some men had put on their top hats and ordered their carriages and come to the fire in the way they would have come to the funeral of an important citizen. They shook hands formally with John Langley and bowed to Rose. Hats were lifted now as we moved through the crowd, but by this time they knew about Tom.

Kate and Dan were close behind us. They had stood beside Rose through the hours, not speaking to John Langley, almost managing to avoid seeing him. The word had reached Larry at St. Kilda, and he had come and was still working with the volunteer fire brigade. The Langley carriage, sent by Elizabeth to bring her father and Rose home, was waiting at the fringe of the crowd. John Langley handed Rose in.

Kate touched my arm. "Emmy, you'll be coming back to the pub with us?"

John Langley turned around. He removed his hat carefully before he spoke to Kate. "Madam, I thank you. But Miss Emma is a member of my family and her proper place is in my home."

And so I arrived to live at the Langley house in my bare feet and nightgown.

Chapter Five

The day after the fire, in time to ride in Tom's funeral procession, Adam was back.

When news came that the *Emma Langley* had docked at Hobson's Bay I went not there, but to Langley Lane. My sense was not wrong; Adam was there before me, standing in the littered stable yard among the men who still worked to clear up after the fire. He looked in an unbelieving fashion at the place where our house had been, at the tall blackened wall of the Stores rising above it. Even with the work Adam had done on the house, it had been a flimsy structure, lacking the broad posts and beams of the stable. It had been almost entirely consumed. What was left seemed to me a pile of ashes which might blow away with the next good wind.

I raised the black veil that draped my bonnet.

"It's all gone, Adam," I said. "We were able to save nothing."

For an answer he bent and picked up a charred piece of wood. "Look at this," he said. "Look at it—I don't even know what it was. It might have been something I made
300

myself. It could be a shelf, or a piece of a chair, or a floorboard. What is it, Emmy?"

He held it before me. "I don't know," I answered. I felt the loss of what lay in those ashes. All I had of Adam seemed to be here. All that he had fashioned with his own hands in pride, and at times I believe, in love, was here. It had been our anchor and our support, a tangible thing to look at and with which to reckon our years together. Now it was gone, and I could think of nothing to replace it.

He took my arm and turned to go. I lowered the veil over my face again. "We'll go to the Langley house," I said. "John Langley expects it."

"The Langley house?—to stay there?" He dropped my arm.

"Yes—I've been there since yesterday."

I saw the old tightness come on his face, that maddening, baffling look that told me nothing, that would reveal nothing beyond his disturbance.

"Let us not go there. We'll find a hotel."

"A hotel? But they need us there! The children need me!"

He shrugged. "In that case we'll go."

I had made a mistake, and I already knew it.

The cortège was very long—more than a mile—as befitted the funeral of a Langley. The hearse was drawn by six plumed black horses, in itself a thing rare enough in the colony to be remembered. I do not know where John Langley found those horses, but they were there, beautiful, shining in the hot sun, and as black as the wreath on the door of the Langley house. John Langley, Rose and Elizabeth rode in the first carriage. Adam and I rode alone in the second; the fact that we bore the name of Langley sat heavily on us at this time.

After the funeral the callers continued. We all learned the ritual of the five minutes of condolence, the five minutes spent in the drawing-room where the shades were lowered with those who spoke of Tom in mournful, hushed tones. Most of Melbourne came, it seemed to me, some with kindness in their hearts, most with curiosity. John Langley was adamant that the ritual be observed in every degree. Every wreath sent was to be noted and responded to, every letter—and they came from all parts of the country, from every colony, from New South Wales, Van Diemen's Land, from South Australia, even, in time, from the Swan River Settlement—every letter was to be answered. Every caller was received.

Once, as we sat together in the dining-room and the knocker sounded yet again at the front door, I saw Rose's hand cover her eyes in a kind of agony of weariness and rebellion.

"I cannot!—I won't!"

"You must!" John Langley said. "As my son's widow, it is your duty."

II

The darkness of that house in the first week after Tom's funeral was something that seemed to enter the soul. Now we all wore the black dresses that I hated and we all seemed to be imprisoned together behind those drawn shades. There was no escape from that atmosphere or from each other—the silent meals, swiftly served and swiftly over, that left only the long empty gap to the next one, the long evenings with only the crackle of the newspaper in John Langley's hands to divert us. We went to bed early to be away from each other, and then lay awake tossing in the warm summer night. Elizabeth mostly stayed in the housekeeping room, but I seemed constantly to glimpse her stiff, disapproving black-clad back on the stairs and in the halls. I think that she believed that my presence in the house threatened her own position; she was hardly more than civil when she spoke to me at all. She had ceased to wear Rose's opal brooch.

I had my embroidery to occupy my hands, if not my mind, but for Rose there was nothing. Because the house was in mourning she could not play the piano or sing, there were no carriage drives, no callers except those who came to offer condolences. More often than not Rose pleaded indisposition, offered her excuses, and sent me to receive in her place.

"You should not," I said. "You are passing on too much . . . you are giving away too much. You are mistress of this house."

She pretended not to understand me. "This house has no mistress. Only a master."

We fiercely envied Adam, who was free to go each day. He could walk out of that house, clapping his cap on as he stepped into the sunlight, walking down Collins Street to get the train to Hobson's Bay and the *Emma Langley*. The *Emma* would sail again within the week, a long voyage to England with a cargo of wool for the Yorkshire mills. It was loading now, and Adam stayed on board to supervise it. He left early before breakfast, returning just before the dinner hour, and I knew

302

the kind of relief that was in his heart when the door closed behind him each morning. He was free to go to his world of ships that had nothing to do with this world of women, of black dresses and hushed tones. He could escape from the tears of grieving and, yes, from its boredom too.

I saw that Rose waited every night for his return in the way she had once waited for John Langley. Somehow she seemed to sense the time of his coming. She was on the stairs when he rang to be admitted, or she risked John Langley's anger by parting the curtains of the dining-room to watch for him coming along the street. Then she had the door open before he had time to ring. She plied him with talk, with questions; it was the only time during the whole day that the house sounded with voices. This would last until the bell rang for dinner; John Langley would emerge then from his study and the talk was ended. Perhaps they had ten minutes together, always in the drawing-room with the doors open, their talk innocent enough to be heard by anyone who passed. And yet I sensed the intensity of those minutes, a short space of time into which was compressed all of Rose's aching need for companionship and love and admiration. In Adam's voice I heard that special quality which was always there when he spoke to Rose, the words that must always be different from the words that he wanted to say. There was I thought, in those brief meetings a communication between them, a feeling so special and exclusive that never once did I have the courage to enter the drawing-room myself, to interrupt that talk, to make my claim of Adam before her. I hovered on the landing above the drawing-room, and I listened. But I never went down. I prayed silently for the dinner-gong to sound.

Rose complained that her black gowns did not become her, but I thought that she had a regal appearance in them that was mostly missing in anything else she wore. The pallor of her face, above the blackness, was very appealing, very beautiful. This was how I saw her; I had no way of knowing how Adam saw her.

Neither John Langley nor myself went to the Stores for that first week, although the confusion and disturbance caused by the fire had made more work for everyone, and we were needed. Every day Clay brought his books to John Langley's study and they spent many hours together. I was permitted, reluctantly, to join some of their discussions. John Langley still did not openly admit to outsiders how much a part of his business I had become. We still played a pretentious little game in which none of the suggestions or decisions seemed to come from me. I often listened to my own words in his mouth, and nodded agreement as if I had never heard them before.

One decision was made without my knowledge or help. I was summoned from the schoolroom where I was doing lessons with the children, on the fifth day after the fire. In the study John Langley and Clay were waiting for me, the books closed on the desk, as John Langley greeted me I thought I saw a ghost of pleasure and excitement in his wintry eyes, the look that an old face sometimes wears when it has had a swift visitation of youth.

"We have been into the matter thoroughly, Miss Emma, and we find that the insurance was adequate. Our losses in the fire are fully covered, and we have decided that the warehouse will be rebuilt on what remains of the building. The Ladies Department is another matter. It must go. The top floor is badly water-damaged, and Clay says the cost of repairing is uneconomical."

"You are closing . . ?"

He held up his hand for silence. " I propose, when the lease expires next year on the two properties directly opposite the Stores—the baker's shop and the dressmaking establishment— to tear them down and replace them with a four-story blue-stone building. It will be in your charge, Miss Emmy—ladies' wearing apparel, bed linens, drapery—a place to sell children's garments and toys—anything that a lady might buy for her household."

I felt the excitement rise in me, but I kept my voice calm. When I answered, it was in his own manner. " Books," I said. " We should have a section for books."

He frowned. " It has not been my experience that ladies are greatly interested in books. Books would do better on the *other* side of the street . . ." He raised his hands in a rare gesture of enthusiasm. " It will be as fine as anything Sydney has—no, even finer! It is time Melbourne had a store of some dimension."

An hour later we were still talking about it, about the money to be raised, about the methods of merchandising, about the distribution of the departments. We fought over some things. I won children's books from him, and he kept the general provisions and grocery ; the old Stores would continue to sell men's boots along with men's apparel, but I got children's boots on my side of the street. We argued, and for a time he forgot that I was a woman and therefore not worth arguing with. We were talking still when I heard Rose's steps quickly on the stairs, and her glad welcome as she opened the door to Adam. I felt a kind of sickness of dismay in my heart as I listened to their voices, and as Rose's words came clearly to me.

"Emmy?" There was a shrug of dismissal in her tone. "Oh, she's in there talking business."

III

There was one other, more important thing that I won from John Langley which had nothing to do with the Stores. It happened on the morning of the day that the *Emma Langley* was to sail. The ship would sail with the evening tide, and as I mounted the steep stairs that led to the floor where the children's bedrooms and schoolrooms were, I felt a depression that was close to panic come on me. Adam was leaving me again, and it was more than an ordinary leave-taking. He had never been with me in this house—a stranger who listened to my words but did not hear them, whose face was turned elsewhere. I had groped and struggled towards him, but not reached him. We desperately needed time to ourselves, a place to talk, a place, perhaps, to share laughter. We needed the familiarity of things shared in common, as we had had in Langley Lane, to help us towards communication. There had been no communication in this house. The atmosphere here, and Rose's presence, had frozen it. And this evening Adam would leave on a long voyage. I wondered if he imagined me happy here, if he thought I did not know his disquiet. I wondered if he thought that for me the discussions with John Langley were enough, if I wanted nothing beyond the Stores and the ledgers. I felt dumb and helpless, cursing my own inability to break through the wall of diffidence which bound me. Why could I do so many other things, and not this one which was the most important? There was a tightness in my throat and I think I was close to tears when I entered the schoolroom.

The children were finished with their morning lessons. There was a tacit understanding between the governess, Miss Wells, and myself that we did not come into each other's territory. We were rarely together with the children; I think she was often glad to pass them over to me, especially when James grew difficult to handle, as he was that day. I could see the tear-streaks on Anne's face, and William was standing over by the window sniffling. Henry had placed himself in a corner with a book obstinately held in front of him, ignoring James's efforts to distract him. They were a discordant, unhappy group, quarrelsome because they had been too long confined, ready to break out against the unnatural restraints which this house of mourning had imposed on them.

James turned to me expectantly. "I wanted to play at being a bird, Miss Emmy—but no one will play with me."

"That's because you're such a pig!" Anne retorted. "No one will play with a pig!"

"And you're an elephant . . ."

"That's enough," I said. I too was tired of the silence and the gloom; as badly as any of them I wanted to throw off my depression, my foreboding that Adam was leaving this house and would not come back to it. "We'll all play at being a bird."

They looked at me hopefully, their expressions brightening.

"Anne," I said briskly, "bring that old blue cloak of yours. And you, James, bring the two rugs from the night nursery. William—Henry, you put these two rugs here in front of the table . . ."

It was a foolish game I invented, climbing on the big school-room table by means of a chair, walking its length quickly and jumping on to the piled rugs beneath. At first they all waited patiently to have the cloak put on, with the strings of ribbon I sewed on looped over their wrists. This as it fluttered behind them, for Henry and William at least, gave the impression of flight. But the older ones soon became impatient with this formality. They simply climbed on the table, ran along it, and jumped off, sometimes rolling on the floor to make something more of the jump. The four of them followed each other in quick succession, pushing and urging the one in front to hurry. They were noisy and rough, even Anne; I listened to their boisterous, excited shouts and I felt some of my own tension released with theirs. I was glad of the tumult they made in that quiet house.

Anne's cries grew shriller and more high-pitched. She was showing off, dancing on the table. James, impatient for his turn, climbed up and nudged her off the edge. She fell on the rugs in a sprawl that left her momentarily breathless. When she had a breath again she laughed aloud, instead of crying; her cheeks were flushed scarlet with excitement. There was a sudden blooming of Rose's wild spirits in her at that moment.

Then the door opened, and John Langley's voice cut through the cries and the shouts.

"Silence! What is the meaning of this? Anne, get up at once! You are a disgrace, Miss. And you, James—get off the table." He looked at me coldly. "I don't know who is responsible for this, but it is an outrageous display in a house of mourning. Have you children no respect for your father?"

I watched their heads go down, the uneasy shuffling of their feet. Their grandfather's voice seemed to hold them spellbound. The excitement and pleasure died on Anne's face; it grew still and withdrawn. The sight of it affected me strangely. I saw too much of Elizabeth there; too much obedient patience replacing the rush of high spirits.

I said to John Langley, "I must speak to you."

The children watched silently as we left. Outside in the passage I faced him. He seemed very tall above me.

"They are too young to be hushed like this," I said. "Mourning or not, they are children. Would you have them turn into shadows around this house—like Elizabeth?—like Tom?"

"In my own house . . ." he began.

I interrupted. "Your own house? Then do you want to inhabit it alone? Because I, for one, will not stay to see them live here without raising their voices."

"We will discuss this later," he answered, turning away from me. "At a more suitable time."

But we never did discuss it. It was the first of the small battles I won against him; I knew there would have to be many more. I went back to the children; they were subdued and a little wary. We did not return to the game and no one mentioned their grandfather's visit. They waited for me to relay orders from him, to talk of punishment. When none came their confidence grew again.

IV

Rose ordered the carriage sent round that afternoon. It was the first time she had been out since the funeral, and the whole household seemed to be nervously aware of the preparations. "I need some air," she said, "or I won't sleep tonight, either." She did not invite anyone to accompany her.

But less than a minute after the front door had closed behind her, we heard her ringing again for admittance. I came out on to the landing as I heard her angry voice. She half ran up the stairs, the veil thrown back from her bonnet; her body seemed to quiver with anger.

"The curtains were drawn tight," she said as we met. "He had instructions to turn back if I opened the curtains! Turn back—I *sent* him back!" She brushed past me, going into her bedroom, leaving the door open for me to follow. I went as far as the doorway, and paused there, watching her pull off her bonnet, and hurl it towards a chair, which it missed.

"He's trying to stifle me," she said. "He thinks if he wraps me in black long enough I'll suffocate." She paced the length of the room; she seemed like some creature trapped and roped, something that struggled endlessly for freedom.

"I wanted a little air," she went on. "Just an hour to drive out and see people on the streets. To feel the sun . . . But no—to him that's not showing proper respect for the dead. That's not my duty as his son's widow. But when he gives me all these talks about doing my duty he doesn't mean grieving for Tom. He means wearing black and keeping the shades drawn. He'll be satisfied as long as I keep to my room and keep my voice low." She turned back towards me. "but I should have gone, after all. I should have driven round Melbourne with the curtains open and my veil up, bowing to everyone I knew, whether they returned the bows or not! *That* would have given them something to talk about! But I suppose he was afraid of that." She smiled a little, with malice. "He was afraid I might stop at Hanson's to call on Robbie Dalkeith. He's in Melbourne, Emmy. He's back in Melbourne. Perhaps I should have done that—to frighten the old man . . ."

She resumed her pacing, but she paused now before the mirror above the dressing-table, bending towards it to peer at her own reflection. "But Robbie wouldn't want to see me like this—how pale I look! This ugly black! I look as if I'm dying already. Emmy, do you remember what used to happen to the grass at Ballarat when someone put up a tent?—even for a few days? Do you remember how the grass used to turn white before it died? It was white before it turned brown—still living, but white, not green. That is what he wants to do to me. He would like to see me turn white and half-dead, with no will to lift my head."

I could not tell her it was not so. I said, "Try to be patient, Rose. The time will pass. In a year . . ."

"A year! I can't live like this for a year. He knows that. He knows there are ways to wear me down. He means to hound me in just the same way he will hound Pat. Until both of us are done to death . . ."

"No, Rose! He doesn't mean that."

"He means it. He has said he will go after Pat, and he means to. He will keep at the police, he will keep raising the reward money until one day he has the satisfaction of coming and telling me that Pat is dead, or is in prison and will be hung . . . That would pay me back, wouldn't it, Emmy? He would like to see me die a little before his eyes. Death doesn't really matter to him—I think he doesn't care that Tom is dead. He's better out of the way before he causes more trouble—that's what the old man thinks. He's had what he wanted from Tom—and from me, so he doesn't care what happens to me now. There will be no more grandchildren of the Langley name, so he doesn't need me any more. I am of less use to him than Elizabeth. At least she can keep house."

As she spoke she had toyed with the perfume bottles on the toilet table. Now suddenly she snatched up one of them and began to perfume her neck and wrists lavishly, wildly. "If I can't wear my jewels at least I can annoy him by the way I smell. I'll smell like a harlot in a bawdy house at dinner, and that will upset him!"

I came farther into the room, closing the door behind me. "We could go away, Rose," I said. "We could take the children and go to Hope Bay. It would be better for them to be out of this house. Better for all of us. The *Emma* sails this evening—we could go tomorrow."

"Hope Bay?" she echoed. She shook her head. "I've never been there. I don't want to go. Tom never liked Hope Bay. He told me about it—lonely, with the sea sweeping in and the seals barking on the rocks. There's no other house for miles. No . . . I wouldn't like Hope Bay."

"It's somewhere to go," I pointed out. "He couldn't object . . . heaven knows, there's nowhere more out of the world for you to retire to. We can't go to Langley Downs . . ."

She laughed harshly. "No, certainly not to Langley Downs. It's too close to Rosscommon, isn't it? And Robbie Dalkeith might follow me back there from Melbourne, mightn't he? Oh, no, that wouldn't do at all. Not more scandal so soon after Tom's death! Oh, Emmy—Tom knew what he was doing, didn't he? It's better to be dead than buried alive."

"Tom knew . . . ? What are you saying?"

She did not answer immediately. I saw her unlock her jewel case and raise the lid. For a minute or so she seemed to be absorbed in the contents. Even in the dimness I saw the flash of the jewels as she handled them, the diamonds, the sapphires, the pearls, the tributes that John Langley had given to her when each child was born, the symbols of position and wealth which were to mark her apart in Melbourne society. She fingered them thoughtfully, as if she were recalling the time and the way each had come into her possession. With the diamond necklace still in her hand she turned away from the mirror to face me.

"Who knows what really happened that night? Watkins says Tom was so drunk that there was nothing he could do but leave him there to sleep. But the lamp was hung up, he says . . . Was Tom still so drunk when he woke that he didn't know what he was doing with the lamp? Did he take it down off the hook and drop it—or did he throw it down, Emmy?"

Having said that she turned back, holding the diamonds to her throat but still watching me in the mirror.

"You know more than any of us, Emmy. You were the last to see him. He came to get you out of the fire, so you are the only one who could know what was the truth. Did he try to destroy himself or destroy the Langleys with that fire?"

I held my hands together to still their trembling. "It was an accident. I will swear to that. You are never to speak of it that way, Rose. Never! No matter how much it is in your thoughts you are never to speak of it!"

She lowered the necklace; her eyes, as I saw them in the mirror were hard and searching. "It is spoken of," she said. "All through this town people are wondering about that. They are asking those questions, Emmy."

"Let them ask! They don't know the answer. So long as they don't know for sure . . ."

She broke in, gesturing with the diamonds. "The Langley name is safe just so long as they don't know for sure? Is that what you are thinking, Emmy? That there can be no scandal because Tom is dead and no one knows for sure? Then why don't you say it? It would go well in your mouth. Why— you're more Langley than he is! You have the soul of a Langley—if the Langleys have souls. You work hard for this family, and you bring no disgrace to this name, and you wait around until it all falls into your hands."

I backed away slowly until I felt the door hard behind me; unconsciously my fingers sought the knob, sought escape. But I held myself there. "What . . . what are you saying?" I whispered.

Once again she turned from the mirror. Her voice was firm, authoritative.

"You are a taker, Emmy. You with your meek ways and

310

your quietness, you are a taker. Who would ever think that you had such large ambitions? You were quiet, weren't you, on the road that day when we met, when you came running after us. You said nothing, and no man would have looked at you twice, so we all felt safe. But remember what happened?—how it happened? First you began helping Larry, and then he began to depend on you. And next it was Con running to you at every turn. My father ate out of your hand —steady and sensible Emmy, who never did anything wrong! In the end, when he had to run, it was you Pat came to see. I was there—in that very house with you both—but it was only you Pat spoke to. He must have known that it would break my heart, but he came to you . . ." Her head snapped back. "And don't forget Tom! *My* husband, but you were the last person he ever spoke to. I knew he used to go there to your house. I know that he must have said things to you that he never has been able to say to me. 'Emmy understands,' he used to say to me. *Emmy understands*—yes, Emmy understood very well how to get Tom's father, too. The great John Langley needed a woman of sense about him, someone he could talk to, someone he could trust. Well, you made sure he found her, didn't you? You showed him the kind of son and daughter he should have had, because you became both of them to him. And you showed him what a mother should be when you put your hands on my children. Deny it!—You've put your hands on them, and they are more your children than mine. You've won them all! All of them—my brothers, my husband, my father-in-law, my children. And besides that you took the man I love. You took Adam away from me."

Her voice grew louder. "You could have had all of them, and I would have let you—and gladly. But you took Adam, and he was the only man I ever wanted."

"Why——?" I asked. "Why have you waited until now to say this? If this has been in your heart why have you never said it before?"

"I thought I needed you too—the way everyone seems to need you. But I don't. I see that now."

I watched her as she began, one by one, to replace the jewels, laying them carefully back on their velvet pads.

"Well, you're welcome to them all. Take them all, Emma— and much good may they do you! Take the money and the power and the name. If this is what you want, take it! Even my children will come to you in the end because I know very well that if I try to take them he will fight me even to the highest court in England. And he will win them. Are you

311

surprised? Since when has a mother of tarnished reputation ever won out over money and lawyers?"

She pushed the locks back into place on the case and turned the key.

"I don't know why I didn't think of it before," she went on, "but I only knew it for sure when I saw those drawn curtains on the carriage. I won't stay here to die a little every day in this house. I'm done with it. There's just one thing I own which is really mine, apart from these jewels, which none of you have thought about. I know you haven't thought about it yet because none of you have tried to take it away from me. I still own Tom's share of the *Emma Langley*, and I intend to use it. I'm going to sail on the tide with Adam."

v

Rose was gone within the hour, taking with her only the jewel case and one small bag. She had put aside her black gown and veil; when she left she was wearing a blue travelling costume. She did not call for the carriage, but carried her own bag out on to the street and hailed her own cab. She stood there waiting for a cab for perhaps ten minutes, her back turned towards the Langley house as if it did not exist. It was the last gesture of dismissal, the final snap of her fingers at the Langleys. It must have been spoiled somewhat for her by the fact that John Langley himself was not there to see it. There were only the servants' wondering glances—those, and Elizabeth's questions to me, which I did not try to answer. Rose made a brief visit to the schoolroom, but I never learned what she said to the children in those few minutes. What I remembered were the words she used to me as she came down. She said them as she passed me on the stairs, and they were the last words she ever spoke to me.

"They will never need me so long as you are here."

After she had gone I went, not to my own room, but to hers. The first thing I did was to open the curtains and let the afternoon sun flood in. Then I turned and surveyed the disorder of the room, realizing now there were things about its occupant that I had never known, and things about myself that I was learning for the first time.

I found myself seated in Rose's big chair, staring at the clock on the mantel, watching its hands move with great deliberation towards six o'clock, when the *Emma Langley* would sail. I did not stir or think about making some effort to stop Rose, or to plead with Adam, because I knew that I was not just minutes late, or hours, but many years. It was eight years since Rose had run away with Tom rather than witness my marriage to Adam, but after eight years she had won him finally, and I had lost. I had refused to concede until now that he could never be wholly hers, but now I knew that when she presented herself on board the *Emma Langley* that he would be gone from me finally and he would never come back.

I heard again, sitting there, the words she had said. " *You are a taker, Emma.*" It was not the whole truth. The truth lay somewhere in between giving and taking. I had not taken any place in the lives of her family or children that she herself had ever wanted to occupy. But Adam was the one person for whom we both had struggled, and here the truth was harder to find. I had given much to him, but I had not taken enough, I had not demanded from him the tributes of love ; I had left him alone to experience his thoughts and his desires, his love of Rose, his love of ships and the sea. I had not disturbed his life in any way, I had asked no sacrifices of him, had burdened him with no responsibilities. I had failed to give him children, but I had borne the full blame myself, never seeking comfort from him, or solace. I had been too stoic in my hurts, not crying aloud for the things I wanted, never using the tears and the threats and pleas that were the weapons of other women. I had thought so little of myself that I had not believed I was worth loving. I expected little, and I got little in return. I had taken almost nothing from Adam, and this was why I had lost him.

His life with Rose from now on would be a torment. It would be a life of wild confusion, of the chaos he hated. The calm orderly routine that Adam loved would be shattered ; he would never live a day when he knew complete peace and quiet. He would be at her back and call, at the mercy of her whims and tantrums day and night. He would slave to earn the money that he cared to little for so that she might have her comforts, she might have the clothes and servants she demanded. Rose would never scrub a floor or mend a petticoat, and Adam would never expect it of her. It would be a kind of hell for the creature of habit that I thought I knew. But he would be alive and living for every moment of it. She would never let him look at her and not see her. He would feel and experience and know every hour of every day they were together, and when they were apart he would hurt in the absence of the torment. She would be a barb in his flesh, and a goad. She would be a lodestar too.

313

She would stir and move and shake him, and he would wonder why he had ever looked for peace.

I stared at the clock and knew it was too late to beg and too late for tears. The pride and diffidence that had kept me from crying out aloud my love for all these years still stood in my way. I had no words to go and plead, no words to demand. My tongue wasn't used to them, but I would have somehow made myself say them if I had thought they had any power. But the ticking of the clock was against me. " Too late—too late." I could not bear to watch its moving hands any longer approaching the time of the tide. I got up and went into my room and put on a bonnet. Three minutes later I was out on Collins Street, walking among the people on their way home to dinner.

I walked along Collins Street and it suddenly occurred to me how little of this city I knew, how little it knew of me. In all the years I had spent here, there were only four places with which I was intimate, which would receive me and not question my presence. The Maguire pub was one of these, and there I could not go at this moment. I would not be the one to bring them news of Rose. I was leaving the Langley house, which was another. My own house was burned, which left only the stores. How narrow it was, I thought—how tight. Adam must have found it narrow too, and constrained, with my interest focused on so few people and things. I felt ashamed, and I discovered another part of me, then, felling that way. I crossed the road to the Stores quickly, as if I needed to hide myself, and all the things that I had learned so swiftly and hurtfully.

It was closing time, and the customers were gone. There were large FIRE SALE notices tacked above the doorway and on each window. Ben had made an excellent job of stacking the damaged merchandise in an attractive display just inside the door, and I saw that even with marking down, we would still make a profit. The ceiling was water-stained, and all the top shelves had had to be cleared. These things I noted automatically, with the part of me that still functioned as the woman of routine. How would it seem to Ben, I wondered as he hurried down the aisle to greet me, if he could know that I was noticing these things at just about the time when Adam was leaving on the *Emma Langley* with Rose on board?

" Miss Emma! It's good to see you back again."

" How are you, Ben?" Even to me, my voice sounded strange.

"Emmy?—What is the matter?" He took my arm. "Are you ill?"

"Ill? No—not ill. Nothing is the matter. I just came to see how things were getting along. It's been . . . strange . . . I've missed coming here each day, Ben."

He smiled a little. "We've missed you, Miss Emma—but as you see we've kept the doors open. The Old Man hasn't been here. Do you know what his intentions are—will he rebuild? The damage is quite bad upstairs. Clay was here poking about, but I couldn't get a word out of him."

I wanted to tell him the news of the bluestone that would rise on the other side of the street. It would have been good for Ben to know that. But I could not make the effort to tell him then. All that I was really aware of what that it was already past six o'clock.

"There'll be word on that soon," I said. "I think—tomorrow."

"Would you like to see upstairs? It's in a bad way. Some holes in the roof where the firemen chopped out burning tiles. Everything got soaked. The furniture's ruined—but then it was never worth much. Perhaps it's just as well we didn't get that fancy office I was always urging on you."

"The next one will be fancy, Ben. All mahogany. Very rich. I'm going to be a very grand lady, Ben. After all—what do I have to lose now?"

He frowned, touching me again. "Are you sure you're all right, Emmy? You seem . . ." He paused, tugging at his moustache. "Emmy—why are you here ? I thought the *Emma Langley* sailed this evening. I thought you'd surely be at Hobson's Bay."

I half-laughed. "Oh, Adam knows the way out of the Bay by now." Then I pulled away from him. "I'll take a look upstairs. No—don't come. I'd like to go alone. Lock up, will you, Ben—I'll lock the front door when I leave."

"Emmy—wait!"

"Tomorrow, Ben. I'll be able to talk to you tomorrow."

And I walked away from him, down the aisle to the back stairs, knowing that he, and the assistants who should have been tidying the stock and covering it with dust covers, had all stopped to stare after me. I wondered if I looked so strange—if for once what was inside of me had broken through the calm efficient surface that was Emma Langley. And I smiled wryly as I started to mount the broken stairs because if it had happened it had come too late.

In my office the battered desk was in its place, and someone, probably Ben, had made some attempt to put the place in order. But the bookshelves had been swept clean by the firemen to get to the walls as they smouldered, and the floor was littered with papers and books, some smoke-blackened, all of them water-soaked. I was surprised to see how many there were. Who could have imagined that in these few years I had collected so much of the impedimenta of business about me? I bent and turned over the first ledger, and saw that it was marked with the date of the first year we had begun business. I knew that when I had written up most of those pages, I had been filled with a bitter hatred of Rose, smarting under the memory of that morning when she had tried to make Adam take her from Langley Downs. But I had not blamed Adam, and I had not spoken to him about it. That had been my mistake—the stupid blunder of self-effacement that had cost me him in the end. I put the ledger down, and moved on, picking up now a blackened doll that belonged to Anne. The heat had made the wax run. It was distorted, ugly. I dropped it back on the pile. Then I came to the desk, where Ben had replaced my chair as if he had expected me back that first morning. They knew my habits well, these people. I had never surprised anyone.

I sat at the desk and took careful stock of the room, looking at the things that represented me, and the Stores, and the Langley children. Was it for these things that I had lost Adam? It was not enough. Then I did what I had done too seldom in the past. I put my head down on the desk and allowed myself to weep.

The sounds all around me had diminished. Collins Street was quiet now, the shoppers gone, the strollers drawn off towards Bourke Street, and the gayer parts of the town. Beneath me the shop was shuttered and deserted. I gazed about me helplessly wondering where I should go and what I should do. I had never before been at a loss for what to do. So I just stayed there, the weeping finished, but my head still resting in my arms on the desk, and my face still wet with the tears I did not bother to brush away, while the dusk of the summer evening approached. I stayed there, crouching almost, until I heard the sounds beneath me, the footsteps on the boards and then on the stairs, careful footsteps because it was dark there and the debris of the fire lay about.

"Adam?" I whispered. "*Adam!*"

He stood in the doorway in the shadow. "I went to the

Langley house looking for you. They didn't know where you were, so I came here. I thought you would be here."

I half rose, then fell back weakly on the chair. "You were to have sailed on the tide . . ."

"The *Emma* has sailed—late. She almost missed the tide."

"Without you?"

"I got Ralph Nevins to take on command. He's a good man. He'll handle her well."

"But you . . .? Rose . . .? Where is Rose?"

"On board."

"Alone? She went alone?"

He shook his head, and now he stepped away from the shadow of the doorway. He came close to the desk, leaning on it, staring down at me.

"She didn't go alone. Rose could never go alone. Dalkeith was with her. That's why we held the *Emma*—waiting for him."

"*Dalkeith!* But she said . . ." I paused. "Why did you let the *Emma* go without you?"

He shrugged. "I'm not full owner of the *Emma*. Together they own two-thirds. It may be that the *Emma* will never come back to port here. They may sell her in England—or send her somewhere else. I may never see her again."

I stretched out my hands and touched his—no, more than touched them, gripped them strongly and possessively. "Was there a choice, Adam? *Was there?*"

"Yes."

"You could have gone in Dalkeith's place? She offered you that?"

He hesitated only a moment, but he looked straight at me. "Yes."

I let out a long, pent-up breath, and my grip slackened on his hands.

"But you let the *Emma* go . . . Your greatest love—and you let her go."

He leaned closer towards me, bending so that we were near each other. "My greatest love?" he repeated. He spoke slowly. "I think that no man ever knows what that is until it is about to depart from him . . . until he is about to leave it. Then he knows."

"Do you know, Adam?"

"I know—yes, I know."

Perhaps it was not true, but now I was going to believe him. Rose was gone from our lives and we were free. No woman would ever count with Adam against the love of his ship and

317

his calling; but he had given up his greatest love and had come back here to me. His offering was there—calm, seemingly unemotional, as things always would seem with Adam. The will and the intention was there, freely offered, waiting to be accepted. Now it was I who must learn the new ways of love. The man was mine, as much as any woman would ever possess him; now I must begin the fight to win the passion and the heart.

Catherine Gaskin

A Falcon for a Queen

All Else is Folly

Blake's Reach

Corporation Wife

Daughter of the House

Edge of Glass

The File on Devlin

Fiona

I Know My Love

Sara Dane

The Tilsit Inheritance

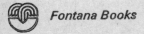 *Fontana Books*

Fontana Books

Fontana is a leading paperback publisher of fiction and non-fiction, with authors ranging from Alistair MacLean, Agatha Christie and Desmond Bagley to Solzhenitsyn and Pasternak, from Gerald Durrell and Joy Adamson to the famous Modern Masters series.

In addition to a wide-ranging collection of internationally popular writers of fiction, Fontana also has an outstanding reputation for history, natural history, military history, psychology, psychiatry, politics, economics, religion and the social sciences.

All Fontana books are available at your bookshop or newsagent; or can be ordered direct. Just fill in the form and list the titles you want.

FONTANA BOOKS, Cash Sales Department, G.P.O. Box 29, Douglas, Isle of Man, British Isles. Please send purchase price, plus 8p per book. Customers outside the U.K. send purchase price, plus 10p per book. Cheque, postal or money order. No currency.

NAME (Block letters)

ADDRESS
